Cover portrait by Gail M. Williams
website: www.williamzworld.co.uk

I am particularly grateful to Mrs. S. Reynolds, portrait copyright holder, for
her kind permission to reproduce the portrait for the sole purpose of
illustrating this book cover.

Foreword

As this book is the fourth in an ongoing series, please allow me to introduce you to the characters central to the story. Of course you may already have met Harriet and Mark Glover in my first novel, 'A Question of Answers' where the scene is set. Harriet and Mark first meet at university, in the supplies store. Behind each other in the queue they discover they share the same surname, 'Glover'. Herein lies the problem. This coincidence serves only to reinforce Mark's need to remain single. Serves only to reinforce Harriet's desire for marriage and one more baby. Frustrated, she finds herself falling for her boss, the head of her school; the charismatic, charming Mr. Sanderson.
And so we have:

Harriet and **Mark** and their two daughters **Rachael** and **Clare**, both in their early twenties and newly married, living down South.

Harriet's mother **Frances**, intent on impressing all her WI friends with her social standing, lives constantly in fear of Harriet dragging herself and her husband **George** down to a level from which they'll never recover. Frances is a snob and can't deal with the changing mores of everyday life. Harriet struggles to please her. After all her brothers have managed marriage. **James** to posh **Geraldine.** They have a married daughter **Clarissa. Paul** married **Susan** whom Harriet envies. She had another baby last summer. And they already have four children!

From the outset Frances has had no time for Mark since he got Harriet pregnant just as she started university but made no attempt to marry her, until two weeks ago that is when he left her standing at the church. Completely surprised when **Joris Sanderson** bailed her out, she continues to be furious with Harriet for reneging on his offer of marriage. Had Harriet gone ahead, the whole family would have enjoyed such an increase in social status as to be almost too good to be true and that's just what she fears as Joris's refusal to inform everyone the wedding is off, deludes her into thinking it will still happen. She's constantly at Harriet to make a new date and threatens to do it herself.

Mark's mum and dad, **Shirley** and **Harold** aren't too sure about Harriet, either. Oh they were delighted when their own daughter frothed her way down the aisle in a cloud of white netting but no, they're more than happy Mark has never made the same commitment to Harriet. They are good, solid down-to-earth people. Not short of money since they've spent a life-time watching it very carefully.

Harriet and Mark had been wanting to move house for a while. Finally a buyer came along and they planned to move from **4 The Willows** to **1 Haystack Close** immediately following their wedding. With contracts exchanged and on the verge of completion Shirley and Harold stepped in, offering to pay Mark's half of the compensation due to Joris Sanderson, who was purchasing the house to add to his business property investment portfolio.

Mark is a scientist working on global warming along with **Geoffrey** and **Melissa**, married only briefly. Melissa is now leaning heavily on Mark as she recovers from a quick divorce. Harriet can't stand Melissa Scott who's telling Mark she's pregnant after a brief affair. Mark relied heavily on Melissa and her parents to get him through his inability to commit to marriage and was very grateful her parents stepped in to buy 1 Haystack Close for Melissa which saved the chain from breaking.

Harriet teaches at Stetmead Street Primary school. This school has many disadvantaged children and Harriet works very hard to redress the balance. The children love her, as do the parents. She's acquired a certain authority; a certain influence over them that **Mr. Sanderson**, the Head and **Mr. Whittle** the Area Chief Inspector of Schools find difficult to deal with. Not to mention **Mr. Brown**, the caretaker. He's convinced Harriet has it 'in' for him and he's constantly threatening her with legal action, always consulting **Mr. Potts** the union man much to Mr. Sanderson's fury.

Of course Harriet's undoing is Mr. Sanderson. No matter how hard she tries she just can't get this tall, good-looking man out of her system and she continues to pay a very high price for compromising her professionalism. On her wedding day, unable to handle rejection and acceptance in the space of half an hour, she needed space to think and so ended up on an escapade in Venice with Tricia. Here they met **Barry Giordano** and his colleague **Andy** which was to prove disastrous for Harriet. Barry, amongst other things is an artist. Divorced, he fell for Harriet in a big way and on learning of her pregnancy and Mr. Sanderson's marriage proposal, he set out to eliminate the competition. Having sketched Harriet, fully clothed, lying on his sofa, and understanding the marriage was to be reinstated, he decided on a wedding present for them both, presenting Mr. Sanderson with a large painting of Harriet lying naked, heavily pregnant, on the sofa. Mission accomplished!

Mr. Sanderson relies heavily on his newly appointed deputy **Lucinda Lawton**, with whom it's rumoured he's been having an affair from the time Harriet reneged on marrying him. His frequent absence from school is due to him attending to various business interests, the main one being Starboard Marine North West, a boat chandlers. A skilled yachtsman he saw the need and opened the business just over a year ago. Never still, last Christmas he installed a coffee shop there after buying out an American coffee franchise company. The place is now well frequented by the parents, as intended; the aim being to lift the life chances of both children and parents alike. Courses of all kinds are run there, including many related to sailing.

A much respected member of the sailing club, Mr. Sanderson has managed to gain cooperation from **Tarquin Bridgewater** the commodore, a cannabis-growing widower whose hobby Harriet inadvertently exposed to the whole of **Stetmead**. He, together with the majority of club members, willingly agreed to give the school children and their parents the opportunity to learn the skill. It's flourishing. It seems the whole of Stetmead is thriving under the direction of the charismatic, wealthy Joris Sanderson.

Not surprisingly, his parents, **Olivia** and **Charles** are very wealthy, too. They have long-standing friends with one daughter, **Belinda Oxfordshire**, who grew up with Joris. She's classically beautiful and completely obsessed with him, as many women are. She's aware of Harriet's feelings for him and stops at nothing to put her down particularly since he broke off their own brief engagement. Seeking consolation she saw fit to lure Tricia's husband Bob away from her and much to Tricia's fury he now uses the family home simply as a place of convenience. Now on the brink of divorce, her passion now is to save Venice.
She works in an administrative capacity at Starboard Marine North West alongside Tricia employed as a personal assistant/cashier.

Harriet and Mark know **Tricia Harrington** and her husband **Bob** through the sailing club. Bob married Tricia knowing she was already pregnant with her son **Adam**. They have their own daughter, **Michelle**.

Harriet and Tricia are long time friends, though initially Harriet saw Tricia as a threat. Her unrelenting flirting with Mark constantly irritated her. However they both do have one thing in common, their attraction to Joris Sanderson. Almost opposite characters, yet this attraction serves to bond them into a friendship which deepens as Harriet comes to understand her better.

Tricia is scatty and alongside Harriet they make a lethal team. Desperate to provide a celebrity to draw the crowds to the school fete they landed on a local rock band "**Rapping Hammer and The Ironing Bards**" which, throughout the series has proved disastrous. They are the crudest, filthiest bunch of drug taking low-life around, causing mayhem and disruption the minute they appear.
Rapping (**Wayne**) **Hammer** has a brother, **Guy Hammer** who works in the local garden centre and has taken a fancy to Harriet.

Harriet first came into contact with **Simon Barnes** the "**INTERNEWS TV**" reporter on her return from Bruges. Because this guy has forged the link with

Harriet and Joris Sanderson with his friends in very high places, he's never far away. Needless to say, Rapping Hammer has done more than his bit to ensure Harriet's and Tricia's appearance on "INTERNEWS TV".

Harriet and Tricia met **Cedric** and **Violet Moss** during their trip to Venice. Violet considers herself to be posh so it's not surprising she was looking to downsize to a nice area and ended up buying the bungalow next door to Harriet's mum and dad. Now able to help their pregnant daughter **Avril** to buy a house, Violet is frustrated and insistent it be Harriet's as it would seem 4 The Willows is the only one Avril really wants.

Harriet met **Molly** and **Percy**, both widowed, on "**The Christiana**" cruise ship. Subsequently married they decided to sell both their properties to buy a house close to Joris Sanderson's in the wealthy location of **Lower Tideside**.

At school **Danny Bustard** is the bane of Harriet's life. His mum Beattie worships Harriet for always taking the parents' side. She's never forgiven her husband **Bert** for his involvement with **Sara Atkins'** mum who, as a result of her sailing lessons moved up a notch to take a shine to Mr. Sanderson; especially after winning a brand new sailing dinghy in the school draw. Danny is most resentful of that and dislikes Sara Atkins intensely.

Finally I turn to Harriet's dearest friend, **Pepper**, her cat. Pepper is central to Harriet's well-being, though she has a mind of her own! This little black cat licks and purrs comfort into Harriet when there's no one else to turn to.

Now, I hope you've learned enough to make you want to read 'A Question of Answers' followed by 'Ne Obliviscaris: Do Not Forget' and 'San Marco the End of the Road', before this one.

The first book spans ten months, from new year to late autumn. The second continues on through Christmas to the following June. The third covers the next three turbulent weeks in Harriet's life whilst this one moves the story along to mid September.

However all the books do stand alone as new strands feed into the ongoing story of Harriet, enabling each book to conclude in its own particular way.

Also by Margaret Henderson Smith

A Question of Answers *arima publishing 2008 (Kindle edition forthcoming)*
Harriet's life is going nowhere! Tired of trying to get her commitophobe partner to marry her, she finds herself falling for her boss, the gorgeous six foot blonde in charge of her school, only to discover she's not the only one! She soon learns he has fingers in other pies and dubious friends in high places.

This is a contemporary novel sparking off the conflicts between the differing worlds of the haves and have nots. Live the highs and lows of Harriet's dilemma as she takes you on a passionate yet humorous journey in pursuit of her dreams.

The Bookbag: review extract
"Margaret Henderson Smith has to perfection Harriet's feeling of being completely enraptured by the man and there were times when my heart ached for her."

"I hope that we'll hear more from Margaret Henderson Smith - and Harriet Glover."
Sue Magee: reviewer

The Writing Pad: review extract
The book is well written and has been well proof read, which makes a pleasant change. It's a promising debut from this new writer and we look forward to seeing more.
David Carter: reviewer

Ne Obliviscaris: Do Not Forget *arima publishing 2009 (Kindle edition forthcoming)*
Harriet. Caught between the steady and the charismatic. Wavering. Two very different men. She's trouble. Can't stay out of it. Still digging away. In serious danger of collapsing the fragile corners of her triangular existence into one big hole.

Can Mark really put his fear of marriage behind him? She's only looking for one answer. Unless of course 'that gorgeous hunk of a blonde' in charge of her school gets there first. Him? Unlikely. Different worlds. Too many questions.
A weft pf answers weave their way through the story. In and out. Criss-crossing the threads of rivalry, jealousy, anger, passion and desire. Ride all Harriet's emotions as she takes you on the rest of her journey. Then ask. 'Was she ever in control of her dreams?'

The Bookbag: review extract
"I enjoyed the story, particularly when we got towards what turned out to be a nail-biting finish."
Sue Magee: reviewer

"The story unfurls with countless twists and turns that will keep you guessing right up to the very last page. Do Not Forget, Ne Obliviscaris, and do not forget to think about acquiring this book when you are next in buying mood.
David Carter: reviewer

A Flight of Fancy!   *arima publishing 2010*
A collection of writings from 'The Big 40 Blog'

San Marco the End of the Road   *arima publishing 2010*
Just now Harriet envies the traffic lights outside Starboard Marine North West. Programmed. Devoid of anxiety, turmoil, indecision. Her life? One big hole! How did she manage to dig three men in so soon? She's fighting to get back to amber. But can she? In the face of serious revelations there's no safe place to be. How did she end up in Venice with Tricia? In serious trouble now. Both of them embroiled. Way out of depth.

This story, spiked with humour and the third in the series, tells the next three weeks in Harriet's life. Passionate, painful, tense and intriguing; go with the trail of devastation and fury only Harriet could leave as she tries in desperation to cling to her dreams.

The Bookbag: review extract
"She's adept at the Wodehousian slapstick scene, the quirky turn of events and the ridiculous consequences made to seem almost logical."
Sue Magee: reviewer

The Writing Pad: review extract
"What on earth is going on? Well, mayhem, conspiracy and fun would just about describe it, but that dear reader is for you to discover.

There are some really funny one liners in this book.....

Harriet Glover is a character we have grown to cringe with, laugh with, sup with, cry with and sympathise with too."
David Carter: reviewer Author of 'The murder Diaries - Seven Times Over' (Kindle)

Contact via websites:
www.margarethendersonsmith.co.uk
www.aquestionofanswers.com
www.quicksandtimerbookreviews.wordpress.com

For you my dear reader,
with thanks

" amor caucus est"

Amber

Margaret Henderson Smith

Published 2011 by arima publishing

www.arimapublishing.com

ISBN 978 1 84549 525 1

Printed and bound in the United Kingdom

Typeset in Garamond 11/14

Swirl is an imprint of arima publishing.

arima publishing
ASK House, Northgate Avenue
Bury St Edmunds, Suffolk IP32 6BB
t: (+44) 01284 700321

www.arimapublishing.com

Chapter 1

Harriet sat with head in hands at the kitchen table trying to make some kind of sense of it all. So much had happened in such a short space of time. After all these years of struggling to get Mark to the altar, she would never have thought he would bug out. It was a despicable thing to do yet she had just done the very same thing herself to Mr. Sanderson, the head of her school. After falling hopelessly in love to the point of being pregnant by him, her courage had failed miserably since accepting his offer of marriage. She'd needed to run and fast. At the time Venice had seemed a good idea but certainly that was not so now, not since she and Tricia had fled back for fear of their lives. She recoiled at her penchant for digging holes faster and deeper than anyone else she knew. Somehow she managed to find trouble big style around every corner turned but last night's disaster topped it all. She could barely bring herself to recall it, for after confidently and finally settling her mind to marriage with Mr. Sanderson, the dream shattered as he accused her of the most reprehensible behaviour he'd ever had inflicted on him. He'd flung the diary to one side, instantly terminating all prospect of marriage, once and for all.

'If we hadn't dashed off to Venice so impulsively, we'd never have met Barry Giordano. He could never have painted that disgusting picture I never even posed for. He could never have given it to us for a wedding present and Mr. Sanderson would never have thrown it all back at me, the way he did last night.'

Harriet's thoughts circled through the chaos of her whole life. Of course she could go back further than that. If she'd acted in a more professional manner and not allowed her feelings for the man to run riot none of this would ever have happened. She thought about Mark, dear Mark, arriving home to pick up the pieces. She couldn't ask for more than that; yet like a butterfly trapped under the lid of a glass jar, still her feelings fluttered and landed, fluttered and landed. 'There's got to be some way to get that man out of my system for good; oh, if only I could stay on amber,' she thought as she stood to answer the ringing phone.

'Oh `arriet, I do hope you don't mind me phonin` so soon after yesterday but I am really worried about you. I've spent the whole of the night wonderin` what's `appened to Mark. I think you might just be needin` `im, with you `avin` a baby and all that and I'm dyin` to know what `appened to make you chase Barry away like that. It must `ave been really awful. That was such a coincidence `im wantin` you to go back to Venice with `im and bookin` you both into the same `otel as I `ad planned for us. What made `im do that?'

'Oh hi Tricia. I was going to phone you, I was wondering if you and Bob were alright. It sounded like he'd gone berserk down the phone last night.'

'I know. I'm sorry I `ad to cut you off like that. `e was explodin` with rage. I've never seen `im like that before. Even when that garage girl gave `im the impression I was pregnant and `e went to see Simon Barnes. You remember `arriet?'

'Not one I'll forget Tricia!'

'No, me neither. Well `e was even worse than that. Anyway I `ad to calm `im down. I was so frightened `e'd `ave a stroke or a heart attack I made `im a cup of tea with plenty of sugar in it. After all I did `it `im over the `ead with all those cake tins at the school fete. Anyway `e went really quiet when `e was drinkin` it and `is eyes were the saddest I've ever seen them so I put my arms round `im and `e buried `is `ead in my boobies. Do you know `e actually apologised for `is behaviour? `e put it all down to `is age, like it was a male menopausal thing and `e told me `e never wants me to leave `im again and all `e wants now is for us to get back together, the way we were.'

'And are you OK with that Tricia?'

'Well I told `im I'd think about it and it depended on `ow well `e behaves from now on. But the only trouble was I felt so sorry for `im all evenin` because a lump `ad come up on the back of `is `ead, `e was `oldin` it all night so I went back to our bed to give `im some sympathy but it ended up makin` matters worse.'

'Worse Tricia? That sounds like a lovely thing to do to me.'

'Well it would `ave been but once I'd got into bed `e underwent a remarkable recovery and suddenly wanted it.'

'Gosh you wouldn't be expecting that so soon.'

'Oh no I wasn't. But `e couldn't do it. When I suggested Rappin` `ammer's therapist might be able to `elp `im `e `it the roof again, so I suggested `e'd worn it out on `er, Belinda Oxfordshire and that's why she finished with `im. So there you are `arriet, I couldn't get to sleep after that and I started wonderin` what had `appened to Mark. Oh I `ave been really worryin` about both of you.'

'That's really kind Tricia but you've got enough to worry about. I'm sure things will sort themselves out with Bob, though. We've got to admit we have given the men in our lives a lot to contend with of late.'

'Well, I suppose we `ave. Just as long as `e doesn't see me topless on television. I'm keepin` my fingers crossed, I'm `opin` the crowds were too thick for Simon Barnes and `is camera to get near enough. Anyway enough about me, `ave you `eard from Mark yet?'

'Oh yes, I can't begin to describe the relief. Last night I'd had enough. I was sobbing to the cat when I heard the key in the lock. I knew which one of them I wanted it to be.'

'`as Mr. Sanderson still got your key then? I would be gettin` it back from `im if I were you. So it wasn't `im. It must `ave been Mark then. I'm very relieved `e's alright. Where `ad `e been, did `e say?'

'He told me this morning he'd stayed over with his mum and dad.'

'And what about the baby `arriet, can `e deal with it? Are you two back together for good now?'

'Hopefully, he seems to be up for taking the baby on, at the moment anyway. We'll just have to see if he can deal with it. I'm not even thinking about that. I'm just so glad to have him back. I was pretty desperate last night.'

'I'm so pleased for you `arriet. I'm sure it will all work out. One thing, `e `as `ad time to weigh it up for `imself and I'm sure `e doesn't want to lose you. Do you think `e'll be marryin` you now?'

'No Tricia. We've both come to terms with that. If he can take on this baby of Mr. Sanderson's then he'll be doing well.'

'Oh yes `arriet, I'm sure it will be a challenge for `im at times but `e will need to know you've finished with our friend Joris once and for all.'

'True, but I also need to know he's finished with Melissa Scott once and for all, wouldn't you say?'

'Oh yes I would. You don't want that froggy-lookin` woman coming between you. I don't know what `e ever saw in `er, `e would `ave been far better off with me. Once you'd got married to Mr. Sanderson, I mean.'

'Well who knows how things would have worked out? There's certainly no chance of that ever.'

'Why `arriet? What's `appened?'

'Barry Giordano, Tricia. Remember the day out we had in the Lake District and we went back to his penthouse?'

'Ooh yes, I do remember that.'

'Well, I can't remember if I told you or not but he sketched me lying across the sofa, *with my clothes on*, I might add. He was keen Tricia. Too keen. You know he asked me to marry him? Well he really meant it. I couldn't take the pressure. I just had to come clean and tell him about the baby. He guessed it was Mr. Sanderson's but it didn't make any difference. He loves kids. His wife never wanted them. I think it made him even keener. He's an artist Tricia. Got that mentality. Doesn't deal in moral absolutes.'

'Moral what's `arriet?'

'No, what I'm trying to say is he's not judgemental. He sees us all as children of the universe, says we own nothing, that kind of thing. Anyway, when I got home from the fete there was a message from Mummy. You wouldn't believe that Belinda Oxfordshire! But I'll tell you about all that in a tick. Anyway Mr. Sanderson picked me up, remember we were going to Molly's for dinner?'

'Oh yes `arriet and you didn't want to go, did you?'

'Not until I'd played Mummy's message, I didn't. We were on our way when he got a call from Molly. Of course Mr. Swift, not realising, had given them some of those plants and they'd had the police round all afternoon investigating. Poor Percy ended up in bed with a migraine, so we couldn't go.'

'Oh dear, just like Bob. I think everyone in Stetmead must `ave been suspected of growin` cannabis. `ow did Mr. Sanderson's gardener get `old of those?'

'Tarquin Bridgewater told me to pass some on to Mr. Sanderson. Don't you remember him loading up his car round here?'

'Oh yes of course I do now. It was funny though you taking the wrong ones from `is greenhouse.'

'I don't think Tarquin Bridgewater will think it very funny when he gets back. He's probably been questioned already by now. He's not going to be very pleased with me.'

'Oh I wouldn't worry about it `arriet. `e shouldn't `ave been growin` them in the first place. Rappin` `ammer will have to find a new supplier now.'

'That's if they haven't all been rounded up.'

'Well they were definitely on their way to Venice yesterday `arriet. I don't expect `e's goin` to be too pleased with me for not turnin` up. I was supposed to be wavin` my "save Venice" tin at the audience seein` as `e was doin` me the favour lettin` me use `is concert to raise money for my good cause.'

'We're in trouble again, aren't we Tricia? We're worse than a couple of school-kids.'

'Well it's not our fault `arriet. We get sucked into things beyond our control and the sooner everyone realises that the better.'

'Too right, we'll just have to keep on defending ourselves.'

'We'll certainly do that `arriet. Now `ow come Barry booked that same `otel in Venice as me? I don't get it.'

'Well, as I was saying, Mr. Sanderson suggested we carry on to his house instead. We were sitting in the lounge chatting. He'd told me at the fete Barry had given him a wedding present for us and didn't he just decide to march out to his car and bring the thing back to open so we could get him thanked in advance.'

'But I thought you didn't want to marry `im any more `arriet? You told me `e was `orrible and it was all finished.'

'Oh I know I did Tricia but that man, that man I can't stand him, but I'm drawn to him like a bee to honey. It was when I played Mummy's message. She said his mother had told her all about Belinda Oxfordshire not being able to have children because of a congenital deformity. He couldn't have aborted her baby Tricia because she was never pregnant! It was lies she told Mark at the wedding reception.'

'Oh I see. I must say I'm very relieved to `ear that. And just between you and me `arriet I'm ashamed to say even that didn't put me off `im. I've still got the very same feelin` for `im, `owever `ard I try it won't go away. I couldn't bear to leave my job at Starboard Marine North West. I know it's the closest I'm ever goin` to get to `im.'

'Oh Tricia, we *are* just like two silly school-girls with crushes, aren't we? You'd think we'd both be able to rationalise it all a bit better than this.'

'No `arriet it's not rational is it? Sometimes it's very `ard to sit on your feelings. They overtake you, no matter `ow `ard you try. Oh I do wish you `adn't just told me all that, now I'm feelin` really jealous.'

'No need Tricia. Barry scuppered every last shred of hope.'

'Why `arriet? What `appened?'

'The painting. Oh Tricia I nearly died. He'd painted me lying naked on the steps of St. Mark's Square heavily pregnant with my legs apart. Mr. Sanderson hit the roof. He read the title "San Marco the End of the Road" and told me it couldn't be more appropriate. He said it was certainly the end of the road as far as he was concerned and took me home straight away. I cried myself to sleep.'

'Oh you poor thing `arriet. Did `e not give you a chance to explain what `ad `appened?'

'No and I couldn't tell him, he'd put all the barriers up. I was in a right state in the car going home. It really hit me how close I'd been to that minder. Everything just crashed in on me. That's why I was hesitating when you phoned to ask me to go back to Venice with you. And then Barry Giordano drives up, expecting me to go away with him, thinking he'd shot Mr. Sanderson well and truly out of the frame. Well he did that alright. It was nothing short of sabotage Tricia. I'm absolutely furious with him and I let him know. I don't think I'll be hearing from him again.'

'Oh I wouldn't be so sure about that `arriet. `e doesn't strike me as the type that's put off very easily.'

'Well I don't ever want to see him again. I can't believe Mr. Sanderson could have thought I'd be capable of posing like that.'

'Well I'd make sure `e knows that. You're goin` to `ave to make sure `e knows the truth.'

'But he's already accused me of telling lies over this pregnancy, and I have, pretending things have returned to normal. I'm sure he knows though. He's probably thinking if I can lie about that, I can lie about anything. Whatever I say he probably won't believe me now.'

'Well Barry's goin` to `ave to do it then. That was a really rotten thing to do. Mr. Sanderson's your boss `arriet. You don't want `im thinkin` that of you.'

'Well it's not just the painting is it? He now knows I've been talking. Gosh Tricia I've never ever seen him so angry. No! It's all over now. I can't even stay on amber. I'm lucky Mark came back. I'll not be rocking any more boats.'

'Oh it's that metathingy again. It always makes me think of `im. `im and `is big yachts. Well after the way `e's treated you, I don't think my `eart will be flutterin` any more over `im. You've got Mark. I've got Bob. I think we're far better stickin` with what we know `arriet. Oh, must go, it's the doorbell. It'll be my mum bringing the kids back. She'd rather look after them `ere when the `olidays are on. I've just seen `er over the hedge pointin` `er finger at our Adam. I wonder what `e's been up to now?'

'Oh OK Tricia, thanks for phoning. I'll see you soon.'

'Adam, you just stop that! Oh sorry `arriet. Ooh `arriet. `e's just driven up. Mr. Sanderson. Oh bloody `ell I'm supposed to be in work. It's Monday. It's because I was goin` to be takin` a couple of days off to go back to Venice. I should `ave gone and got my "save Venice" tin back. It would `ave been better than seein` *im*. Oh I'll `ave to go now `arriet. See you.'

Chapter 2

Harriet started trembling at the prospect of *him* arriving on her doorstep, as was his usual practice once he'd been to Tricia's house.

'Oh Tricia was right Pepper. I should have got that key back long since. It's not his house, *yet*. He's no right to be coming and going as he pleases. Oh get out of it Pepper. No I haven't forgotten to feed you. No, on second thoughts Pepper, he most definitely won't come here, not after Saturday. No, he said it was "the end of the road", he'll keep his distance, I'm sure.'

She tipped the dry pellets of cat food into the bowl and slopped a saucer of water down at its feet. Rushed to the lounge. Tucked herself behind the curtain watching until she was satisfied there was no sign of him then scrambled her way upstairs. She needed to get changed, just in case. He had a habit of throwing a surprise. Now sitting on the edge of the bed, panicking, her old jeans heaped on the floor. Shoving her feet through the legs of her tight, black ones, she knew they looked good with the white skimpy top by her side. Her hair ruffled covering her face as she stretched her old T-shirt over her head to land on the carpet. A car door. She rushed to the window. Him. It was him! Him striding away from his silver Mercedes. Layers of blonde hair shifting in sync with his gait. His face strong. His expression serious. Harriet flustered her fingers through her hair. Struggled to fasten the top button of her jeans as she flew downstairs to answer the ring of the doorbell.

'May I Miss Glover? I promise you this won't take a minute.'

She didn't want to hear that. She wanted it at least to take all day. Silent explanation already falling from her lips. She needed to tell him. Tell him about the painting. Tell him how very mistaken she'd been about him. Tell him how dreadful she felt for believing Belinda Oxfordshire's lies could all be true.

'Coffee Mr. Sanderson? I'm about to have one myself.'

'No, no thank you Miss Glover. Er this damned camping trip next week. See your way to being there will you?'

He reached to the inside pocket of his jacket. Produced a couple of folded sheets of paper.

'You'll find all you need to know in these.'

He passed them over. She caught his glance. Saw no margin of forgiveness in those crystal clear blue eyes. Felt that familiar, uncontrollable flood of desire saturating her body, anguishing into an aching, gathering need, unrelenting, culminating low down, draining, deepening to an unbearable intensity; an anathema to the tight black jeans holding her in.

He cleared his throat. Marched off. Without a word he was gone. It couldn't have been more than two minutes at the most. Feeling uncomfortable she needed to change. With papers in hand she crazed her way upstairs. Rolled on the bed, scolding herself for feeling this way yet again, as she slipped the top button of her jeans from its buttonhole. She wriggled herself free unwittingly bringing her pink and white flowery pants with them. All thrown on the carpet now. She stretched again. Her body still surging. Exhausted, she lay back in just her top. Her hand across her lap. Wondered about her tiny baby. His tiny baby. Wanting like nothing else to have him deep, deep inside her once more. "For old times sake." She'd said that to Mark. This was different. She needed closure. She desperately needed him just one last time.

Pinning the thought down, she relaxed her legs. He'd never seen her like this. Just once they'd made love, barely undressed. Just once on the warm wet sand to the setting sun on that beautiful cove near Falmouth. Her mind going back now, her senses draining from the need for him. Somewhere in the distance the sound of the phone ringing. Instinctively she pulled at the sheet crumpled under the duvet on the unmade bed, covered herself as it finally gave up. She jumped as the bedroom door opened.

'Ah there you are Miss Glover!'

She gasped. Scrambled further down the sheet. Two seconds earlier and he would have seen her like that.

'But I thought you'd left Mr. Sanderson.'

'Hardly Miss Glover.' He glanced down to her clothes piled on the floor. 'I don't recall saying "good day". I was merely going back to the car. That damned painting. It's downstairs. I've left it in the hall.'

Harriet could feel herself going as pink as the flowers on the briefs resting in the jeans at his feet.

'You might have done me the courtesy of waiting Miss Glover, before taking to your bed. I, at least, expected you to follow me to the door.'

'I'm so sorry Mr. Sanderson. I thought you'd gone. I just had to get out of those uncomfortable jeans.'

'Clothes starting to get a little tight now Miss Glover?'

'No, no. Of course not.'

'In line with the painting I've just placed in the hall, perhaps?'

'No, definitely not Mr. Sanderson. See for yourself.'

She lowered the sheet just enough to reveal her bare stomach. The need for him burning away her common sense.

'Well, I'm pleased to observe, certainly *not* like the painting Miss Glover, *yet*. Allow me just one moment will you?'

She lay still as he drew the sheet back just far enough to allow him to press his hand firmly against her abdomen. Just for a second she flinched. Watched him step back to rest his thumb and forefinger against his chin.

'Hmm. Interesting Miss Glover. Any tenderness around there?'

Harriet hesitated.

'Come, come Miss Glover. I am a doctor you do recall.'

'A little when you started to press more firmly.'

'Indeed. You do appreciate I really need to know Miss Glover. Answer me honestly. Pregnant or not?'

'Most definitely NOT Mr. Sanderson!'

'I'm not convinced. I would be most surprised if you weren't.' He stepped back to look at her. 'Regardless of your insistence to the contrary I am quite certain.'

Harriet lay still. His hand had gently pressed against her bare skin. The intimacy she craved had been so near, yet so far. This gorgeous, gorgeous man. With her body throbbing its need for complete exposure she covered herself with the sheet again; her heart pounding, even her fingertips tingling now from such close proximity. He strode to the window and back.

' "Quad erat demonstrandum",' Miss Glover.

'I'm not sure what you mean Mr. Sanderson?'

'It means, "I rest my case", particularly in view of now having made this professional examination. I'm emphasising the word "professional" to make the distinction Miss Glover, as I most certainly have my doubts as to whether it would have been the case during your sitting for Barry Giordano. Indeed I suspect there was nothing professional about it whatsoever.'

'But Mr. Sanderson.....'

Too late, he was gone.

Chapter 3

She waited. Heard the front door bang shut then the car door followed by the sound of the engine. He was away. She lay there dazed, staring at the window in a trance, struggling with the aftermath. Just the cat leaping onto the bed, clambering its tiny paws against her legs, forcing her back to reality.

'Oh Pepper, I've done it again. I've let myself fall all over again for that despicable man. I've lost him forever now. If he'd just let me explain at least I could have stayed on amber. I don't want to feel like this Pepper. That's what Tricia said, you can't just turn off your emotions. I love Mark. You know I love Mark, Pepper, he's the best in all the world so why do I sodding well feel like this? No Pepper you're not going to sleep here. I'm getting up. I've got to find somewhere to hide that revolting painting.'

She shoved the cat off the bed, rescued her pants, then threw on her old jeans and T-shirt. She hardly dared go down to the huge painting he'd left in the hall.

'Oh gosh Pepper, at least he's wrapped it again. I can't have Mark seeing this. It's going to have to be the shed. Oh get from under my feet. Just let me open the back door. Oh sod Pepper, the phone. Let me get to it, will you?'

'`ello `arriet. I did try to ring before. You `aven't got `im there `ave you?'

'Oh hi Tricia. No not now, he's not long gone though. Didn't he just bring this flipping big painting back. I've got to hide it. It'll be curtains if Mark sees it. I'm just hoping it'll go in the shed.'

'Oh that man's such a menace. `e wanted to know why I `aven't turned up for work and I `ad to pretend in front of my mum I wasn't well. What with `er flappin` and `im goin` on about this campin` trip, I'm glad to see the back of them both. At least I managed to persuade `er to take the kids `ome with `er. They weren't `ere two seconds and she `ad them back out again.'

'Oh I'd get her to keep them and take the rest of the week off if I were you, it'll give you chance to recover from all the trauma; especially if he's roped you in for camping as well.'

'Yes, that's a very good idea. `e's organised it for this coming Friday so we've only got three whole days to get ready. I told `im I was `avin` severe stomach cramps and do you know, as soon as my mum left with the kids, `e started asking exactly what my symptoms were. So I said "Well you can examine me any time you like Mr. Sanderson." I thought I'd spotted that look `arriet. You know the one that draws you in but I was very much mistaken, I'm afraid. Then do you know what `e said?'

'No Tricia, go on.'

'Well `e said "That would be highly unethical Mrs. Harrington. I suggest you make an appointment to visit your own GP if the symptoms continue beyond twenty-four hours." '

Harriet knew just how she felt. Still tingling all over she seized the opportunity to return to amber.

'Oh he can be such a toad, that man. We're going to have to make a supreme effort to get over him. We're very lucky to have picked up the threads again given Mark and Bob can't stand him. I'm mostly OK, but it's when I see him…' Thought. '*Especially without my knickers on…*'

'Yes, carry on `arriet.'

'…I just can't help melting, Tricia.'

'No, I know `arriet. The trouble is I want to see `im. I don't want to let go. It's very `ard to know where to start.'

'Yes I know and this camping trip isn't going to help. Do you know who else is going?'

'You don't really want to know that, do you `arriet?'

'Oh no, not Belinda Oxfordshire?'

'Yes, I'm really sorry to be `avin` to tell you that `arriet. That's if she recovers.'

'Recovers?'

'I'll tell you about that in a minute. Now who else `as `e got?'

'Not that gushing deputy of his, Lucinda Lawton?'

'I'm sorry, but yes `e did mention `er as well.'

'I thought as much.'

'Oh and there's a new guy. `e said somethin` about `im startin` in September. Now what was `is name? Er it was posh, very posh. Er, Ross something. Ross Farquerhart. I do remember it now because I repeated it and it came out all the wrong way round. I started gigglin` in silence `arriet. It's very `ard that is. Once your shoulders go the game's up. Anyway `e moved on very quickly.'

'That name rings a bell. I can't think where I've heard it before. But a new teacher Tricia? I didn't know that. I didn't know anyone had left.'

'Well `e didn't go into the ins and outs of it with me but `e said `e'd volunteered to join the trip to give `im chance to get to know the children before `e starts.'

'Oh, he never tells me anything. I'm glad you messed his name up Tricia. Sounds like he could be one his buddies.'

'Well we'll `ave to wait and see. We'll chat `im up `arriet. Get our own back on our friend Joris. `e's not the only fish in the sea.'

'Too right Tricia. Very appropriate metaphor.'

'Oh it certainly is `arriet. I've just remembered `e said somethin` about `im doing `is PhD. Somethin` about the theory of evolution. When I told `im I'd `eard of it but wasn't exactly sure what it meant `e said "to put it simply we all started a bit like fish in the sea and gradually changed, Mrs. Harrington." So I said "some of us `aven't changed very much Mr. Sanderson, some of us are still very cold fish." '

'Gosh Tricia. That's just so funny. No wonder he got a bit shirty with you.'

'Oh I don't care `arriet. He's only `elpin` me to go off `im.'

'I'm well off him just now,' replied Harriet, propping the painting against her leg. 'I don't think we've got room for this thing in the shed, either.'

'Did `e give you chance to explain what Barry did, `arriet?'

'No. Not at all. I tried but he just marched out.'

'`orrible man! There, that's today's good reason to go off `im. I know, we'll write them down and when we weaken we'll read them. I've got a diary `ere I `aven't used yet. What a pity we didn't start in January. Still the end of July's alright. We can always go back to earlier ones when they come to mind.'

'Good thinking Tricia. We'll both make a concerted effort to get that man out of our systems once and for all.'

'Well it might be a bit more difficult for you `arriet. You are `avin` `is baby after all.'

'Yes but would it want a father like that? I think in some ways Barry's right. We are all children of the universe. We've all evolved from the same source.'

'It's that evolution thingy again, isn't it? Yes I can see your baby wouldn't want a cold fish of a father `arriet.'

'That's it Tricia. It's love that counts and I know Mark's got plenty to give.'

'Just like Bob `as for our Adam. `e's always been a good father to `im and Michelle. It's just a pity `e went off the rails with that drip of a woman. I can't stand `er. I'm sure I'll find a much better way to get my own back while we're campin` than `avin` `er slide in `orse manure.'

'You didn't do too badly with that at the school fete, Tricia. She certainly went a cropper.'

'Well I still think there's got to be an even better way to get my own back although there's more to come. I `aven't told you yet `ave I?'

'No Tricia, what?'

'`e's got Iris runnin` Starboard Marine North West at the moment because she's gone down with a tummy bug. `e said she thinks it's due to contamination from `er slippin` in all that stuff.'

'She's not actually blaming you is she Tricia? I'd hate to think of you getting accused of intending to harm her.'

'Oh I think she is and I don't care. It's only what she deserves. Anyway whose side are you on? I don't want to `ear you talkin` like `im `arriet. `e's just told me to watch my step with `er, as well. `e says I'm in danger of takin` this revenge thing too far.'

'Of course I'm not talking like him. Don't forget you are my best friend and I wouldn't like to see you end up in court. I'm sure she's capable of it Tricia.'

'`er? She wouldn't dare. All I've got on `er! In any case I'm only inflictin` what I consider to be minor accidents `arriet.'

'Like bashing her over the head with those cake tins at the school fete you mean?'

'Bob got it as well don't forget and it's only what you did to that `eavy `arriet. Come to think of it you should `ave got recognition for your bravery.'

'I don't think so Tricia but gosh you're right. I didn't think twice either. It never crossed my mind at the time. I could have killed him but we might have all been shot to ribbons if I hadn't knocked him to the ground.'

'You were very brave indeed `arriet and those tins were all you `ad. You `ad to do somethin` being faced with `im like that. `ittin` `im over the `ead with four cake trays wouldn't `ave finished `im off but that's what I'm sayin`. You only stunned `im, like I did `er and Bob.'

'Golly but he did end up flat out on the ground Tricia. I must have given him quite a crack.'

'`e asked for it. You `it `im really `ard because `e was a threat, whereas I was merely deliverin` them both a warnin`.'

'Yes of course Tricia. Sorry, I see where you're coming from now.'

'Well I am glad about that `arriet and that's somethin` else to write in our diary, "`e's always on Belinda Oxfordshire's side and we get blamed for everythin`. Oh and "Failed to give `arriet due recognition for `er bravery." We're not going to `ave very much trouble fillin` these pages in, I don't think.'

'No, you're right, it's all coming to mind. Do you know I think this is going to be a very cathartic exercise.'

'Oh no `arriet, I've `eard of arctic, but who's Cath? `e's not got another cold fish lined up to go with Ross Farquerhart I `ope. Well they can both bugger off to the South Pole together as far as I'm concerned. I'm already feelin` a bit inferior goin` on a school campin` `oliday. I do `ope I'm not goin` to be `avin` to watch my step with `er as well. I'll be very glad when this trip to Dorset's over.'

'I'm not sure how you arrived at that one Tricia, but no, it just means "emotional release". Anyway, so that's where we're going, is it? He never told me that either. He's just making sure I read the leaflets he thrust at me, I suppose.'

'There, I've just written that down. "Doesn't tell `arriet anythin`".'

'That's a really good one Tricia. You know that's one thing about him that really does annoy me. Anyway, Dorset you say?'

'Yes, that's it `arriet. Dorset.'

'Ah and I think I know why. That's what it's all about. It will be the Jurassic coast; fossils, evolution, Ross Farquerhart. Now it all makes sense.'

'However did you remember `is name?'

'It came to mind when you mentioned fish. It must have been by association. Food, hampers, "Exclusively Farquerhart's". Haven't you heard of them Tricia? They advertise in all the posh mags.'

'Oh I don't buy any of those `arriet. I can't afford them.'

'Me neither. Geraldine gives them to Mummy and she passes them on to me. They do nothing below four hundred and seventy-five pounds.'

'Do what `arriet?'

'Very posh hampers Tricia. I wonder if he's got anything to do with them? It's an unusual name. I'll need to practice it just in case he's rich and gorgeous. I wouldn't want to start off on the wrong foot.'

'Oh no I don't think `e'd like me gettin` `is name all mixed up, either. But what's the connection `arriet? Why would `e be comin`?'

'Charles Darwin Tricia. It looks like we're going on an expedition. We're taking the kids fossil hunting. Yes of course, that's where they are. It's protected coastline.'

'That's what `e thinks. I won't be lookin` for any old fossils. The biggest one by the name of Joris Sanderson will already be there.'

'Couldn't agree more but that reminds me, I'll have to go and hide this thing.'

'Why don't you stick it under the bed `arriet? I don't expect Mark will go lookin` under there.'

'No, good point. I'll try and get it upstairs.'

'I'll write that one in. "Left `arriet to struggle upstairs with enormous big paintin` when pregnant".'

'Yes you're right Tricia. He's only thinking about himself. Frightened someone high and mighty will stumble across it during one of his "at home" evenings.'

' "Selfish." There `arriet I've just written that down as well. There's definitely not goin` to be much space left for today at this rate.'

'Keep filling it up Tricia. I've gone right off him already.'

'Will do. See you `arriet. We'll get together before Friday.'

'Too right we will. We might need to plan a survival guide. Anyway must go. I've got to find somewhere to hide this thing safely just in case Mark comes back early. See you soon. Thanks for phoning. Bye Tricia.'

Harriet looked at her watch. She needed to do it now. Tried desperately but couldn't think of anywhere better than under the bed. She struggled to get the painting upstairs then struggled again as she lay flat on the floor, shoving and pushing until it finally disappeared taking Mark's old trainers with it.

'That's all we need Pepper, Mark finding out about that!'

Chapter 4

'Had a good day at work Mark?'

'Not bad, not bad. How about you? Lard ball steering clear, I hope?'

'Oh gosh Mark, no. I've had just about enough of him. He called on Tricia first and then came round here, not for very long though. We've been roped in for camping on Friday for a whole week.'

'You don't have to go. I thought it was supposed to be the summer holidays? When are you going to learn to say "No" to that lump of lard, Harriet?'

'I've still got to work there Mark. This has been on the cards for a while now. It's probably all been sorted with the office long since. At least I'll be getting paid. Anyway I always used to get a kiss as soon as you came in.'

'Sorry Hat. Come here. I'm afraid he's been playing on my mind. When did you say this baby's due?'

Harriet felt her stomach turn over. Wondered if it could ever work out with her and Mark.

'March 12th or thereabouts, I think.'

'You only think Harriet! How far gone are you now?'

'Not quite two months. It's early days, anything could happen.'

'No, don't get me wrong. I'm not going back on my word. The baby's the innocent bystander in all of this. We'll look after it. I've thought about it long and hard. I'll see if I can't make the case for adopting it Harriet. He's not going to be wanting involvement with us lower echelons. He'll obviously have access but he might just see the sense in injecting some stability into the arrangement.'

Harriet swallowed hard. Didn't want Mark to see how quickly her eyes had filled.

'Love you Mark. Love you, love you, love you. If you could choose your parents, I know our new baby would want you. You couldn't be a better father. The girls can vouch for that. His house is big, too big. No, there'll be all the love, warmth and comfort here, any child could need.'

'You're probably right. Love you too, Hat. Any room in there for another one?'

'Well I'm not sure it works like that but we could always try.'

'Mmm Hat. Coming up? I've got to get changed anyway.'

'Oh I wasn't thinking of now Mark. Not just this minute. I've got to see to the meal.'

'Come on Hat. Not for old times sake, this time for our future. Help me get lard ball out of my system once and for all.'

She suddenly thought of the painting. Decided it would be as well to go up, just to make sure he didn't go fishing under the bed.

'OK Mark, coming.'

'Close the curtains Hat.'

'No Mark, don't put your shoes under the bed,' she insisted, thankful she'd followed her instincts.

'Why ever not Hat?'

'No let *me* take them off.'

'Ah I see Hat. Your turn and then mine.'

'You guessed Mark.'

'Now yours Hat.'

'Now mine. Now mine again.'

'You're going out of order Mark. I've hardly got anything left on.'

'Just the way I like it Hat. Just the way I like it.'

Chapter 5

'Off to Mummy's this morning Pepper. I can't say I'm fussy but I promised to do her hair since her hairdresser's away on holiday. Gosh she does rollers Pepper. I don't even know how to put them in. No you stay there. Did you know more car accidents happen on the drive than anywhere else? Mark and I don't want to lose you, you know.'

Harriet, steeped in contentment after losing all shreds of desire for Mr. Sanderson, backed off the drive, vowing not to even glance at Starboard Marine North West when she reached the traffic lights.

'Green, they're on green,' she delighted, pulling the shade down to screen her eyes from the sun.

'I wonder if Tricia's gone in today? Bet she hasn't. Bet Iris is now well roped in. Poor thing, probably worrying herself sick about Tarquin Bridgewater.'

She thought about the fete and the cannabis plants. Felt bad for dropping him in it like that, then decided he shouldn't have been breaking the law in the first place, growing those things.

She looked up. A helicopter overhead. Relief, those heavies both caught now.

'What a time it's been. We could have been kidnapped Tricia and I. No I don't think I want to be going back to Venice again, in a hurry.'

She jumped, from behind a blasting horn refusing to stop.

'OK, OK so I was a bit late indicating. Keep your hair on.'

She looked in her mirror. *Him!* Following her.

'Oh no, he can't be going to Mummy's as well.'

She put her foot down harder now on the open road, then slowed towards the crossroads to turn right. Saw him turn left.

'Oh no, Canterbury Drive. I'm sure that's where Lucinda Lawton lives.'

* * *

'Oh hello Mummy, sorry I'm late. Got caught up in the traffic. Daddy not in?'

'No Harriet he's playing golf with James. I do believe Sir Joris is joining them for a round this morning.'

'Oh, that's nice.' Thought. 'If he's still got the energy after having it off with Lucinda Lawton.'

Harriet could feel the onset of a very bad mood. ' "Impatient on the road, beeped at me without good cause." Another one for Tricia's diary.'

Her mother's impatience impinged on her thinking.

'Do stop daydreaming Harriet. It's never going to dry in time for my WI meeting this afternoon. You do know Violet Moss never has a hair out of place? I've a feeling she rinses it Harriet. She can't be very much younger than me you know, bound to be grey. I've looked but I've never been able to spot the roots. What do you think about me Harriet? Maybe a golden blonde?'

'Oh no Mummy you'd look horrible. You're far too old now to be thinking of dyeing your hair. It's no good coming away with a euphemism like "rinsing" Mummy. It's nothing short of downright dyeing. You'd look like mutton dressed as lamb.'

'No need to go over the top Harriet. It was only a thought. Now we can chat while you're doing my hair. You can wash it over the bath Harriet. The shampoo's there on the side.'

'Oh I don't call that rinsed Harriet. Here pass it over to me. Oh Harriet there's water everywhere. What a scatter-brain you've turned into. I don't suppose you've made a date for your wedding yet either. Sometimes I not sure why Sir Joris Sanderson bothers hanging around. I've told you. You mark my words. If he doesn't go back to Belinda Oxfordshire, he'll find some pretty girl, a lot younger than you Harriet, to marry. He'll be wanting children. He's not going to want to stay single for very much longer.'

'Yes Mummy. Just let me get the stool from the kitchen.'

'No Harriet. I'm coming through. I'm not sitting in here with wet feet. You can do it in there.'

'Ouch Harriet, not quite so hard!'

'Well bend your head a bit more Mummy, I'm struggling to get these bottom rollers in at the back.'

'You know Harriet, Avril was very disappointed your house wasn't for sale after all. What in the name of goodness is going on there? You've no right to have it displayed in Bryce Rae Roberts' window if it's not now on the market.'

'Well I didn't put the photograph in the window, Mummy. It's nothing to do with me. Maybe you should ask Sir Joris.'

'Indeed not Harriet. I wouldn't like him to think I was being nosy. I thought Belinda had bought it for the business to add to his property portfolio?'

'She did but it didn't quite go to plan in the end.'

'Well there you are. Phone them up and tell them to take the board away. Or are you now trying to sell it again? Sometimes I do find it difficult to understand you Harriet. You won't need it once you marry Sir Joris. He's not going to want your little semi while he's got that beautiful mansion overlooking the sea.'

'The river mummy. It overlooks the river.'

'Don't be pedantic Harriet. The river runs into the sea. I'm perfectly sure you can see the sea from his windows. Now hurry up will you. You've still got this side to do. I'll need to be away by half-past one at the latest. We've got a Mr. Hammer from the garden centre coming to give us a talk on colour scheming the garden, including hanging baskets. You'll have noticed when you came in Daddy's taken that one down. Once Violet passed all those dreadful cannabis plants over to the police she got Cedric to take her to the garden centre straight away. You can't miss those trailing petunias hanging next to her front door as you walk down our path. I've been at Daddy to sort ours out. I hope he's not losing interest Harriet. You do seem to put the jinx on our front garden one way or the other.'

'Oh that's not fair Mummy. Look I'll get you some more flowers and sort it out for you myself.'

'When Harriet?'

'Tomorrow morning Mummy.'

'Is that a promise Harriet?'

'Yes Mummy.'

'Ouch. That one's far to tight. Oh come here. Let me put that pin in. My word it has gone black out there. Oh dear, that sounds like Daddy. Oh no he hasn't brought them all back here has he?'

'Quick, go in the bedroom Mummy. I'll pass you the hairdryer.'

Chapter 6

'Oh hello Daddy. Just sorting Mummy out. She's drying her hair.'

'Hello love. You alright? Been through a bit from what I can gather. It should be on the news tonight.'

'Oh they've probably blanked it Daddy. I think Tricia and I stumbled into something a bit undercover. Anyway how did you find out?'

'They miss nothing down there love. I even think old Joris was taken by surprise. He didn't say much only that you and that girl, the one your mother doesn't like, got caught up in it all. Anyway he's in the lounge with James. Any chance of a cup of coffee for us all love? We've been rained off. You wouldn't have thought the weather could have changed like this.'

Harriet turned to see her mother heading for the lounge, patting frantically at her head. She whispered as loud as she'd dare.

'No Mummy, don't go in, they're all in there.'

Too late! She caught a brief glimpse of Mr. Sanderson sitting on the sofa chatting to James as her mother, flummoxing an apology, backed out of the room.

'You forgot my hairnet Harriet. It's on the mantelpiece next to that photograph of you when you were a very sweet little girl. Beautiful blue eyes and lovely blonde hair. You had such a poignant expression for a little girl. Daddy brought it out, wanting to remind me of how sweet you used to be, I expect. He still sees you like that. I don't find it so easy Harriet, especially with what you've just put us all through. Anyway you'd better fetch it. These rollers will have fallen out before I can get the dryer on them. Now the last thing I wanted was for Sir Joris to see me in these. Go and get it Harriet, don't just stand there.'

Harriet took a deep breath. Kept her head down as she rushed to the mantelpiece. In a sideswipe knocked the photograph straight into Mr. Sanderson's hands.

'Oh sorry. Thanks for catching it, not that I think it would bother Mummy if it got broken. Excuse me. Won't be a tick, she just wants this.'

She heard the chuckle from behind as she passed her father in the doorway. Looked back to see Mr. Sanderson studying the framed photograph intently.

'Come and join us love.'

'No. In a hurry. Must go Daddy.'

'Well you can't go before them anyway. Your car's boxed in now.'

Harriet put the kettle on. This she did not need.

'At least Mummy's safely out of the way,' she thought as she spooned the coffee granules into each cup. She jumped.

'One for me as well, Harriet, please.'

'You're drying your hair Mummy. Do you want it in the bedroom?'

'No the lounge, thank you, Harriet. I shouldn't be too long.'

Standing behind the door with five over-filled mugs wobbling on the tray, she nearly dropped the lot as Mr. Sanderson popped his head round to open it.

'Hi Sis. One of these days you'll stay out of trouble!'

'Very funny James and I don't think. You nearly didn't have a sister at all.'

'Oh as bad as that was it?'

'Worse and I don't want to even think about it.'

'Wasn't very nice giving Geraldine's dress to the school fair Sis. She's still got a cob on.' He was laughing.

'It was ancient James,' she returned.

'Geraldine's got a long memory. Mum convinced her you'd like it.'

'Then it was Mummy's fault then, wasn't it James?'

'What am I supposed to have done wrong now?'

'Mummy where have all your curls gone?'

'You wound them far too tight Harriet. I'd have had no hair left if I'd sat like that drying them for half an hour. No. I'll just have to go with it straight. I'll find Mrs. Doubty and sit by her. I've observed she's going a bit bald on top. Others are bound to notice should they walk past. It will distract them from looking at me.'

Harriet turned to see Mr. Sanderson laughing. She'd forgotten how he looked like that. Those elongated dimples. Twinkling, sparkling deep blue eyes. That gorgeous, gorgeous smile. She watched him lift and angle his right leg to rest it on the other. She recalled lying there naked from her waist down. Him, pressing low against her abdomen, intensifying that throbbing, aching need. Just fingertips away from taking her back to that evening in Cornwall when he'd laid her down on the warm amber sand washed by the deepening turquoise sea. Thought.

'Oh NO, NO, NO. Not A-gain! Quick spot something for Tricia's diary. NOW!'

Thought about Lucinda Lawton. 'Those rumours. Could they be true? Mummy might be right. Maybe he has already found somebody younger and much prettier than me.'

The men chatted golf while Harriet tried to fend off her mother's glowering glances.

'Ah that looks like the Stetmead News on its way. Such a dozy boy. I wonder what's woken him up? On time too, for a change. Go and get it will you Harriet before he breaks the letterbox.'

Harriet returned. Passed the folded paper to her mother. Settled back in the chair.

'Good heavens! Now I know! Whatever is this? Well just look at this George. What did I tell you about that common girl? I hope you've learned your lesson now Harriet.'

'Pass it over Dad.'

'No James it's not fit for your eyes. George take that smile off your face. The girl's common and vulgar.'

'Crikey, Simon Barnes again.' It was Mr. Sanderson speaking. 'The PM won't be complaining.'

'Won't be complaining Sir Joris. Whatever do you mean? He doesn't go in for this kind of cheap tittle-tattle does he?'

'Shouldn't think so, but if that's all that's been reported he'll be well satisfied.'

'Oh I see, I do beg your pardon Sir Joris though I'm not exactly sure what it's all about.'

'No one is Mum, just calm down. I think Harriet's been through enough.'

'It's usually of her own making James. Now, oh look at this. Let's move on to better things. Local honours. I don't expect anyone in Stetmead or round about would receive one as high as you. It's such a misfortune your name's appeared alongside this piece of rubbish Sir Joris.'

'Mum just call him Joris, will you? You're embarrassing the poor man.'

Mr. Sanderson turned to James. Laughed. Harriet gasped. That was almost the last thing she wanted her mother to know. She fidgeted in the chair, aware *his* eyes were on her.

'Ah, here's the page. HARRIET! Look here. Your name's under Sir Joris's. A damehood!? *You* Harriet? Whatever for?'

'Well it's not for tripping people up Frances.'

'Oh do be quiet George. They've obviously made a mistake.'

'Oh no they haven't.' Mr. Sanderson was laughing again.

'Oh yes they have.'

'Shut up James. It's not something I wanted spread round the family,' Harriet replied, furiously.

'You mean you didn't even tell your parents Harriet?' Mr. Sanderson asked, turning away from the photograph he'd just placed back on the mantelpiece.

'No Mr. Sanderson and you can see why.'

'That will do Harriet. That's quite enough. I think you should apologise for that.'

'No Mummy. That's not fair. James thinks it's a big joke.'

Mr. Sanderson shifted round to glance again at the photograph. 'No joke indeed, I have to say, seeing as I was the one proposing her.'

'You Sir Joris? The school, is it something to do with the school?'

'Yes, it certainly is. It wouldn't be in Harriet's nature to make a big thing of it but she's raised the standard to such a degree one would hardly recognise the place, Mrs. Glover. This little girl here has certainly proved her worth.' He picked it up. Tapped the edge of the frame gently with his finger.

'Oh do call me Frances, Joris. Yes she was the sweetest of children then. I rue the day we let her go to university. Unfortunately it did her no good whatsoever. I never dreamt she'd get into such undesirable company the minute she got there. Oh yes, she managed to heap disgrace on the whole family.'

Mr. Sanderson cleared his throat.

'That's probably being a bit hard Frances. You have to move with the times you know. Harriet's one of the most caring, genuine people I've ever met. She's certainly done a tremendous amount for our children. There's a lot more to your daughter than you give her credit for.'

'I'm sure there is Sir Joris. You'd hardly be wanting to marry her otherwise.'

Harriet squirmed in her seat. Thought.

'Oh no Mummy please just shut up will you?'

'I think we ought to put all that to rest Frances.' He turned to Harriet. 'Very well done love!'

'Thanks Daddy.'

'Congratulations Sis. So we call you Dame Harriet Glover now, do we? Well done! I couldn't be more pleased for you. That'll put Geraldine's dress in perspective. She'll be falling all over you now.'

'Thanks James.'

'Now don't you be causing any trouble over it James. You know Geraldine's going through a bit of a sensitive phase.'

'You mean she's hit the menopause Mummy?'

'Really Harriet. Not in front of Mr. Sanderson.'

'That's alright Frances. I have heard of it.' He was laughing again.

'Yes of course you would being a doctor. How silly of me.'

'You don't need to go to medical school Mother to have heard of that.'

'That's quite enough James. Oh let me get to my WI meeting. This hasn't been one of my better mornings.' She turned to Mr. Sanderson. 'You so kindly propose my daughter for a damehood Sir Joris and then offer to marry her when that lousy good for nothing hippy of a boyfriend does a runner at the church. You make that most moving, beautiful of speeches and the little madam can't even get her head round making a new wedding date. Just what have I done to deserve all this?'

'Things move along Frances. Life doesn't always pan out the way we'd like it to.'

Harriet's heart sank. He'd just said those beautiful words to her mother, and now he was rubbing them all out saying all of this. He'd stuck up for her and had now just dropped her, like he was tossing her to the waves. She'd never forgive her mother for inviting this. Harriet kept her head down, relieved to hear her turn over the page.

'Oh just look at this. I do hope they'll try to help these poor people struggling to cope. You can't tell me the recession's over. Not when we're in so much debt. You mark my words with this increase in VAT we'll all be feeling the pinch. But these children. My word they look like something out of Dickens. This poor woman's lost her home with four children to look after. Oh lost her job on account of them. Couldn't afford to keep paying for childcare. Oh isn't this your school Harriet, er Sir, er Joris? Oh just look here she's saying "a lot of the parents at Stetmead Street Primary School are in the same boat." '

'It doesn't surprise me at all. The number of children registered for free meals has risen dramatically in the last few months,' Mr. Sanderson informed her.

'Poor mites. I wonder if the PM really knows what's going on at the grass roots, Joris?'

'Oh I'm sure he does Frances. He's under a lot of pressure now. It wouldn't surprise me if there wasn't a snap election.'

'Then I think you should stand for Parliament. You could make a difference for people like this.'

Harriet watched his expression change. He shifted legs, touched his chin. Flicked his fingers through his thick blonde hair.

'Tricky one. Probably easier in feudal times to dispense the political largesse.'

'At least that will shut you up Mummy,' Harriet thought. 'Such a stupid thing to say.' Then she thought again. Her mother had planted the seed. 'There must be *something* I can do to help, though.'

The atmosphere well and truly dampened, Mr. Sanderson stood to go.

'Well, if you'll kindly excuse me, I need to be getting back. Perhaps we'll get a round in once this damned camping trip's out of the way?'

'Don't envy you that one Joris. You have got Sis lined up, I hope?'

' "In omnia paratus" Harriet?'

'If you say so Mr. Sanderson.'

'You can get yourself into trouble like that Sis.'

'Oh she's already in trouble James. The likes of which you'd never believe!'

Chapter 7

'Come on, come on Tricia, answer the phone. I can't say this in a message.'

' `ello, Tricia `ere.'

'Oh, thank goodness you're there Tricia. I was beginning to think you'd gone back to work. Have you had your paper yet?'

'No `arriet, why? You `aven't `ad yours `ave you?'

'Not yet but I tried to get you yesterday afternoon before Mark came in. I was round at Mummy's and she got hers alright.'

'Oh no, I'm not in it am I?'

'All over the front page I'm sorry to say. Of course they weren't going to miss the Rapping Hammer thing but they might have saved you for the inside.'

'Oh `arriet, what does it look like?'

'Well fortunately there's a couple of heads getting in the way so you're not shown as exactly topless, but not far off.'

'Oh, thanks for lettin` me know. Ooh I'm not goin` out today, not until I've got `old of that paper. Bob was in a right mood with `imself last night. I'd `ate for anythin` to make things worse. Thanks for tellin` me `arriet.'

'That's OK Tricia. I'm sorry it's gone a bit downhill for you but it's just the same for me.'

'Ooh what's `appened with Mark then?'

'Oh no, it's nothing to do with him. It's that flipping newspaper amongst other things. I'm furious with Mummy and *him*! Do you know Tricia, I went round to do her hair only to find out Daddy and James were playing golf with *him*. They were rained off and I ended up making coffee for everyone. Of course Mummy was her usual tactless self. Couldn't keep her mouth shut and then James drops me right in it asking *him* if I was going camping. Of course doesn't he just come out with something in Latin to which I said "Anything you say Mr. Sanderson" so then James tells me that's a good way to get myself into trouble. And then, do you know what Tricia?'

'Oh no `arriet, go on tell me.'

'He tells them all I'm already in serious trouble. Oh that's all I needed Tricia in front of Mummy. And then she gets hold of the paper only to discover this flipping damehood. You should have heard the song and dance she made about that. Oh and there's another thing. Of course he was behind me on my way there. Had the flipping cheek to beep at me too. I saw him turning left into Canterbury Drive. Just popping into Lucinda Lawton's, I expect. I think Mrs. Bustard's right. I think it's more than a rumour. I'm sure he'll be marrying her.'

'Now `arriet, I can see you're weakenin`. Just a tick, let me write those `orrible things `e did in my diary. Would you like me to read all them out now, to `elp you to go off `im again?'

'Oh no Tricia, thanks. I couldn't be more off him. Cad! Womaniser! Pompous! Full of himself!'

'`ang on a minute `arriet. I can't keep up with you. I'm trying to write all of these down don't forget.'

'Oh I won't forget Tricia. We'll be spending a whole week with him in Dorset the day after tomorrow. Imagine that! I hope he doesn't pitch his tent next to ours.'

'Oh no `arriet. `aven't you read your leaflet yet? There's goin` to be two dormitory tents one for the girls and one for the boys. Then there's goin` to be one big staff tent pitched between them. There's a rota, too. We're all goin` to `ave to take turns doin` night duty. Two at a time. `e's got the list on the back of the last page. `ere it is, I kept it `andy behind the phone. Friday night Sean Bracken and Enid Frost. Saturday, let's see. Ross Farquerhart and Belinda Oxfordshire. Oh trust `er to get `im `arriet. Let's `ope `e's really `orrible. Sunday, oh yes that's me and I'm with Tarquin Bridgewater.'

'But he won't be long back. I thought he was about to be arrested?'

'Well I don't know do I `arriet? I'm only readin` what's down `ere.'

'Now where was I? Monday, er wouldn't you know it `arriet? Joris Sanderson and Lucinda Lawton.'

'Yes and I know just what they'll be getting up to in that tent, I wouldn't mind betting.'

'Tuesday, Bertrand Bustard and Iris Hall. Wednesday, Algernon Whittle and Samantha Halliday.'

'Oh no Tricia. Surely he hasn't got Mr. Whittle on the trip. He's the Area Chief Inspector, you remember at the fete swinging your "save Venice" tin and clonking him on the backside as he followed Mr. Sanderson in?'

'Ooh yes `arriet. I gave `im a right whack on `is bum. I don't think I'll be goin` near `im if I can `elp it.'

'Where am I then, Tricia? Who am I with?'

'Er, let's just see `arriet. Er Thursday. No, that's Beatrice Bustard with Eric Brown.'

'Oh no Tricia. This is going to be fun. What's he taking the caretaker for?'

'Oh that'll be to `elp put up the tents, I would think. Oh `ere you are `arriet. Oh it looks like `e's doin` two.'

'You're joking Tricia. He hasn't put me with Mr. Brown on Friday night I hope?'

'No not `im `arriet, our friend Joris. `e's doin` two. You're with `im. Oh `arriet you're goin` to `ave to read this diary. I don't want you cavin` in on me, now do I? We'll `ave to take it with us.'

'Oh what a nightmare. And where do we all sleep Tricia?'

'Well accordin` to this. It's like a "T" shape. The dormitories are end on with the staff tent between them, that's all going down. Then either end at the top there's five tents in a row. `e's `avin` the middle one on `is own by the looks of it and the men are `avin` the two to `is right and we're all `avin` the two to `is left. I see `e's seen `imself alright `arriet, as usual.'

'Write it down Tricia. "Grabs one whole tent for himself." Does it say who we're sharing with by any chance?'

'Well you and me are in the one next to 'is with Belinda Oxfordshire and Beatrice Bustard.'

'Oh well at least he's put us together. I suppose he's put Belinda Oxfordshire in to keep an eye on us, next to his tent, I notice.'

'Well I'm just 'opin' they've got separate bedrooms 'arriet. I don't want to be lookin' at 'er all night. I might just be tempted to clout 'er one with the 'urricane lamp. She wore Bobsy fat-face out, she did. I don't know what got into 'im. 'e came 'ome with some lovely flowers last night sayin' some really nice things to me, so, and I should 'ave known better I 'ave to say, but I fell for it. It was terrible 'arriet, nothin' absolutely nothin'. It wouldn't grow and do you know 'arriet 'e blamed it all on me. 'e said no wonder it wouldn't work, I wasn't doin' much to attract 'im lately, so I said "why don't you try puttin' some fertiliser on it, it always works on weeds. You've seen 'ow 'igh they grow." and do you know, 'e told me to "Fuck off" 'arriet. Well I was so disgusted I told 'im "Actions speak louder than words," and I 'ave to say 'ow pleased I was to come up with the right metathingy at just the right time. So 'e said "Belinda knows exactly how to turn a man on." So I said "So 'er microwave works with the door open does it, or did she make you stick it in an 'ot water bottle to get it to sprout? Then I told 'im it wouldn't need to grow anyway for 'er seein' as it must be like stickin' a little wobbly jelly up a snowman's bum. Do you know 'arriet, 'e jumped straight out of bed and went. I don't know where and I can't say as I care . Oh I 'ate 'er 'arriet. Now she's stolen 'im back what's the bettin' she ends up with Ross 'arquerfart as well? She can't resist the challenge. I bet we won't get a look in.'

Chapter 8

'So you're off camping tomorrow morning Hat. All packed and ready to go?'

'Sort of. I do wish I wasn't going Mark. On a coach all that way with the kids. It's not going to be much fun for them fossil hunting.'

'On the contrary, it could be very exciting but in any case I wouldn't think they'd be doing that all the time. There are some smashing places down there. They're bound to be taking the kids out on a few trips.'

'Exciting if they find any, I have my doubts. Anyway lets hope you're right. I'm most certainly not looking forward to being with *him* either.'

'Well that will be your choice Harriet. From what you've said there's plenty of other people going. Just don't go looking for it. He's the head and that's all he is. All you are doing is fulfilling your responsibilities.' Mark twisted his lower lip then scratched his head. 'Oh I wish you weren't at that place. Is there any chance of getting another job instead of going back there after you've taken maternity leave?'

'I shouldn't think so Mark. They're not taking on permanent staff anywhere at the moment. I'm lucky to have a job the way things are going.'

'I know Hat. I'd rather you didn't have to go back to work at all. I'd rather you stayed home to look after the baby.'

'I'd really like that, but do you know what I'd really like us to do?'

'No, go on.'

'I'd like to be able to save enough money to buy 1 Haystack Close. I'd like to live in Millington away from here. I'd love us to be able to make a fresh start, you, me and the baby.'

'Sounds good Hat. Might have a bit of trouble kicking Melissa out, though.'

'Oh why can't she go back to Geoffrey or something? We found that house together. It was never meant for her.'

'Circumstances Harriet. If her parents hadn't stepped in to buy it for her I could never have come back to you.'

'Why not Mark? We were already buying that house. Mr. Sanderson was buying this. Well for his property portfolio he was. Even though you couldn't go through with the wedding, we could still have moved.'

'We'd have done that Harriet, if you'd read my note. If you'd come back to me straight away. Lard ball could have had this and it would all have been over and done with. You accepted his proposal Harriet. No one made you. Once we'd split there was no way the house sale could go through.'

'I know but I thought you'd decided on Melisa Scott, didn't I? Anyway I only discovered I was pregnant that morning. I didn't think you'd still want me once I'd told you that.'

Mark went silent for a moment to skirt round the statement.

'Just think about it Harriet. If her parents hadn't taken over the sale I would have had to buy you out which I could never have afforded. But more to the point lard ball would then have insisted on completing the deal putting the money in just to get me out of the way. Don't forget there was a long chain ahead of us. It would have been highly unethical to let everyone down and I certainly couldn't afford to make compensation payments to anyone. I had no choice but to go along with it. This would have been his house then Harriet, in which case how could I ever have come back here?'

'Oh, don't say that Mark.'

'No, the only way was for me to pull out of the purchase completely and I could only do that because Melissa's parents stepped in to buy Haystack Close. That meant lard ball was the only one let down in the end because you didn't want to sell this one either.'

'Yes Mark, you're right, but I do feel we've still got this compensation thing hanging round our necks. Mr. Sanderson still wants to buy this when we do move. I know your mum and dad kindly offered to help you out by offering to pay him off, but of course when he thought I was going to marry him he decided to drop the whole thing. You were very relieved for your mum and dad at the time.'

'Well of course I was. They were going to be stumping up a lot of money. But we're not off the hook Harriet. You're not getting married to him now. What's the betting if we decide to sell this, he'll be demanding we drop the price to make up for it? No I don't like it. Anyway back to your question. Melissa Scott isn't about to mess it up with her parents. The last thing she's going to do is sell 1 Haystack Close to us, wouldn't you say?'

'Yes, I suppose you're right but as far as Mr. Sanderson's concerned I hate being in his clutches like this.'

'Well it's uncertain which way it'll go. He's had the legal agreement drawn up to say he's foregoing compensation only as long as the house remains on the market and he is given first option to buy. I'm not sure what that's worth. I've always said he's a slick character Harriet and I wasn't wrong. It's just a pity you're going to have to stick it out at that damned school for as long as it takes to give us chance to save our way out of his clutches.'

'I know Mark. I know. I don't believe how much I've managed to mess things up.'

'We both have Harriet. Look I need to tell you something. I didn't want to have to tell you this just now but it's better out I think. There's another reason why we wouldn't be able to get Melissa Scott out of that house in Millington.'

'Why Mark, why?'

'She thinks she might be pregnant, Harriet. She's almost a month overdue.'

'Oh no Mark. NO! NO! NO! She can't be! You said you'd taken care of all that to make sure it wouldn't happen. That would be just too much of a coincidence.'

'I did and I have only got her word to go on.'

'Does she know about me expecting?'

'Yes Hat. I had to tell her I still loved you and I was going back for good. I wanted her to know the whole truth.'

'I just don't believe this Mark. How could that have happened if you'd taken steps to make sure it didn't?'

'Nothing's foolproof Harriet.'

'It would be yours would it? She might have been seeing Geoffrey again unknown to you.'

'Oh no, I don't think so Harriet. From the way they are with each other at work, there's definitely no love lost between those two.'

'Oh Mark I don't know what to say. I don't want her carrying your baby. I wanted yours. Why couldn't you make it work with me? I don't want her having your child.'

'You're having his Harriet. I've had to get my head round that. You smashed my world the day you told me. That's why I walked out and all I could recall of it was you saying to me "It's sometimes the consequence of having affairs Mark. It could just as easily have happened to Melissa." '

'I know. I know. I'm sorry Mark. It's a shock I'll just need a bit of time to get my head round it. It's ironic. We've been trying on and off for years to have another baby and the minute we go off the rails just once. Just the once for both of us, we manage it.'

'Well let's wait and see Hat. She might be wrong, or she might be trying to get her own back. She wasn't exactly pleased when I told her I was going back to you.'

'No, she wouldn't be. Look, we'll work this through between us. We're even now Mark. We'll both deal with it because we love each other. Always have done. Always will. Oh I wish I'd never set eyes on *that man*. I wish I wasn't going away tomorrow, either.'

'I wish you weren't too. Make up for it when you come back?'

'Make up for it Mark.'

He took a deep breath.

'She's not like you Hat. I know you've wanted marriage for years, but you've never pushed it like she has. No you're certainly not like her. She's given me a hell of a time trying to get me to marry her.'

'Oh no, she can't do that. Not if she understands anything about you at all.'

'Oh she can and she has. She set me up she did. I got it from both her and her mother.'

'Oh I'm so sorry Mark, after all you've been through with me. Come here. Love you. No one will ever, ever come between us again, no matter what.'

'No matter what Hat. Love you too.'

Chapter 9

'I'm off now Hat. Hope it all goes well and for goodness sake stay out of trouble.'

'That's the last thing I'm looking for Mark. What will you do next week, oh apart from going to work?'

'Oh I'll be OK. We'll be going through those old dinghies down at the club. See if any can be restored. I think most of them'll be only fit for ditching. I won't bother with meals here, I might just as well eat down there. I'll miss Tricia's cleavage and chips though, she certainly livened the place up. I don't suppose the lads will be too fussy on having mumsy Iris back.'

'That's ageist Mark. You just be nice to her, especially as she'll be feeding you. Oh I don't know, you men are all the same.'

'Kiss Hat. Don't forget to phone. Oh the paper's in the door. Hang on a minute. What's this? Talk of the devil. My word she didn't leave much to the imagination. Pity those big heads got in the way. She'll be for it if Bob gets hold of this.'

'Oh it's come has it? More's the pity. She's terrified of Bob seeing it. Just make sure you don't tell him about it either.'

'Oh come on Hat. What do you take me for?'

'Stop looking at it Mark. Oh give it to me. It'll give me something to read on the coach.'

'Meany Hat. What about me having something to read while you're away?'

'OK then Mark. You have it.'

'If you're going to remove the front page, I won't bother.'

'Good. I'm taking it with me then. It's not funny Mark. Why are you laughing?'

'It's you Hat. It doesn't take much to wind you up. Come here, daft bat Hat. It's you I fancy.'

'Are you sure Mark?'

'Of course I'm sure. Be good and try to enjoy it. I'll miss you Hat.'

'I'll miss you too Mark. Can't wait to get back.'

She waved goodbye. She'd been dreading this. Friday already! She loaded the car wondering just how she'd be able to squeeze in Tricia's luggage as well.

'OK Pepper. OK. Let me get going. And don't disappear on Mark. I'm late, we don't want to be missing the coach. Well we do but I don't think it would go down too well. Oh get out of there you stupid cat. You've already stowed away once. You needn't think you're doing it again. Get out will you, NOW.'

Harriet threw the Stetmead News on top of the luggage and closed the boot.

'See you Pepper. Look after Mark for me. We're back together for good now, you can meow it to all your chums. No more the cat from a broken home for you.'

The cat clawed its way up her leg pushing its head hard into the palm of her hand.

'Ow Pepper! Soft cat. You should have been a dog. Now over you go. Remember what I said about accidents on the drive?'

She watched it, tail in air, walk across the top of the side gate only to jump down again. She backed quickly off the drive for fear of running it over. Looked at her watch. She had exactly two minutes to get to Tricia's.

'I've been lookin` out for you `arriet. I do `ope you've got room in your car for all this.'

'What's that enormous big square thing Tricia? They'll never let you take that on the coach.'

'Well I'm not goin` if I can't take this.'

'What is it?'

'I'm not tellin` you, you'll only laugh.'

'No Tricia. I promise I won't.'

'Oh yes you will. Look you're already grinnin`. Will it go on your back seat?'

'I expect so. Just let me budge all that stuff over.'

'Thanks `arriet. You're a star. Oh I'm not lookin` forward to this one little bit.'

'Did you get your paper Tricia?'

'Oh no, it `asn't come yet. Why, `ave you `ad yours?'

'Yes, it's in the boot. What will you do about Bob seeing it if it comes while you're away?'

'That's what's worryin` me `arriet `e came back this mornin` for `is briefcase and `e certainly `asn't recovered from `is jelly flop. `e's still in `is very bad mood. You'd think `e'd `ave a smile on `is face if `e'd done any better with `er, unless of course `e's already seen the paper. Oh I do `ope not `arriet. When exactly did yours come?'

'It must have been late last night or early this morning because Mark picked it up on his way out.'

'Oh `e didn't see it did `e `arriet?'

'I'm afraid so.'

'Ooh what did `e say?'

'Sorry Tricia. Usual male response.'

'Oh I see. Oh bloody `ell `arriet. Them delivery boys might be on their way now. We couldn't just do the side roads could we? If I could pick one up now, I can tell them not to bother with our `ouse.'

'Well we haven't much time Tricia but we'll see if we can spot them.'

'Ah thanks `arriet. You're a pal.'

'We'll do the roads on the other side first. If I go slowly you can look down them all as we go past. If there's no luck then we'll go round the back of Poplar Drive, just in case.'

'No `arriet. No sign of them down there. They might not `ave got this far down yet. Let's see if they're in the next road.'

'OK, OK go past you twit, can't you see I'm going slow? No need to wake the dead banging your horn like that.'

'Take no notice of 'im 'arriet, another Joris Sanderson 'e is. No, no sign down there either.'

'Not right down the bottom end Tricia? Is there no sign down there?'

'No 'arriet. Oh I think we're goin' to 'ave to be givin' up on this. It's goin' to be makin' us very late.'

'Well just have a quick look down the next one Tricia. If you see them we'll catch them up from the Poplar Drive side.'

'Ooh there they are 'arriet. Two of them with that shoppin' trolley they use. They're just walkin' over that grass, crossing over at the bottom, now.'

'Right Tricia let's see if we can catch them, shall we?'

''ave we got time 'arriet?'

'It won't take a tick. If I can just get back into this stream of traffic, turning left here. Oh sod off. Who was that beeping again?'

'Ooh that guy behind, 'e's shakin' 'is fist at you.'

'That's alright. We've lost him now. Look out for them Trica. About half-way wasn't it?'

'Yes, I think it was Mapleton Avenue.'

'Ah there they are Tricia, just turned the corner. OK we'll catch them along here.'

Harriet pulled up to let Tricia out. She grabbed a handful of tissues from her pocket then blew her nose as she helped herself from the bag sitting in the middle of the shopping trolley. With the tissues still pressed to her face Harriet could see her gesticulating at the lads, pointing her finger towards the main road. Smiling, she rushed back to the car.

'Oh thanks ever so much 'arriet. That's a relief. I tried to cover my face with these, I do 'ope it worked. I told them not to be puttin' one in our 'ouse. I told them the road and the number. I said it's the one at the end with the gate fallin' off and it's just 'ad a brand new gold letter-box that traps your fingers as soon as you touch it. I told them the postman caught 'is yesterday and 'e ended up in 'ospital and I'm still not sure if 'e 'asn't 'ad to 'ave them amputated.' She paused to take a very deep breath. 'Now let's see the worst.'

'Brace yourself Tricia.'

' "'**olly Berry Unveils 'er All to Save Venice**!" Ooh it's a good job those big 'eads are in the way 'arriet. I don't think Bob would be too 'appy seein' this. I'm glad we caught those delivery boys in time. Let's 'ope at least some good will come of it. At least it's given my "save Venice" cause some free publicity. I wonder 'ow Rappin' 'ammer's gettin' on over there? I 'ope 'e's gettin' my tin filled up. I couldn't get 'old of 'im to let 'im know I wouldn't be there 'arriet. I don't think 'e's goin' to be very pleased with me.'

'Well it wasn't your fault Tricia. You could hardly leave Bob in that state.'

'Well no, 'e meant it, and that could 'ave been the last I ever saw of 'im and the kids. No, after 'er finishin' with 'im like that 'e was capable of anythin'. Of course I didn't know she'd be grabbin' 'im back as quick as she did but at the time I didn't want it to be the last straw 'arriet. That's another metathingy well it will be in a minute when I can remember the second `alf of it.'

'I think it's "the last straw that broke the camel's back" Tricia.'

'Well that's another appropriate one. Only Bob's got more than two `umps I can tell you. You wouldn't believe `ow `e started on me again just before `e went back out this mornin`. `e seems to `ave got it in `is `ead that there's somethin` goin` on with me and Rappin` `ammer and `e said I `ad to watch it because if `e decided to divorce me `e'd get custody of the kids because I wasn't a fit mother. I know our Adam's said somethin` to `im since I was in Rappin` `ammer's tent at the school fete. I `eard `im whisperin to `im and I can tell by the way `e's been lookin` at me ever since. `e's not gettin` any more pocket money unless `e comes clean `arriet. Oh I am glad I got `old of this paper first. I wouldn't `ave wanted to send `im completely ballistic again. I don't want to lose the kids. Thanks for doin` the detour `arriet. Oh `ave we come up to Starboard Marine North West already, `ave we? Ooh we must be late. It's all opened up.'

'Gosh Tricia, I'd no idea that was the time. We were supposed to be there at quarter to nine. Look it's twenty past. I'd better get a move on.'

'It's not far from `ere now. `e probably only said that to make sure we all leave at `alf past. We've still got ten minutes so don't worry `arriet.'

'I wouldn't put it past him to go without us Tricia.'

Chapter 10

'Come along. Come along Miss Glover. Mrs. Harrington. You've kept the whole party waiting at least twenty minutes. Mr. Whittle doesn't take kindly to lack of punctuality. Apart from which it's most unfair to keep the children waiting like this. Any later and we'd have been forced to leave without you. Mr. Brown, over here if you will? Luggage. Get this lot onto the coach will you? Good gracious me, you've enough for a whole regiment between the two of you.'

'Sorry Mr. Sanderson. We got held up in traffic.'

'Oh yes we did didn't we `arriet? `arriet got beeped at twice just because she was tryin` to `urry up. Didn't you `arriet? And that's not the first time this week, I might say. I can't be doin` with impatient men myself.'

'Not without good cause Mrs. Harrington.' He shot Harriet a look. 'That's at least the third time this week Miss Glover. It would seem you're either dawdling or speeding. I suggest you take a lot more care whilst driving, in future.'

'All of this in `ere is it Miss Glover?'

'Oh yes thank you Mr. Brown. There's some on the back seat as well.'

'Good heavens! The hold's already full to over-flowing. Did you two not read the instructions? We were all limited to one case and one holdall.'

'I don't remember readin` that Mr. Sanderson. I shoved everythin` in without really thinkin`. I'll be needin` it all, I'm very sorry to `ave to say.'

'Me neither, I can't leave any of it Mr. Sanderson. I honestly couldn't say what was in which.'

Mr. Sanderson turned, his impatience getting the better of him.

'Brown bringing them back. Just as I thought. You'd both better have a quick look in them for any essentials.'

'But they're all essentials Mr. Sanderson. This one's got all my knickers in it.'

'Really Mrs. Harrington. Go back with Mr. Brown and swap it over now, this minute.'

'And you Miss Glover. You do the same. Decide which you are leaving. We'll never get this damned camping trip underway at this rate.'

'I know my things are all mixed up Mr. Sanderson. I did it in a hurry. Wasted too much time putting all those rollers in Mummy's hair only for her to take them out again. I could have spent the time far better packing.'

'I really don't think it's terribly fair to blame your mother Miss Glover. With regard to your private life you seem at the best of times to be frightfully disorganised. I suggest you go with this one and if you're short of anything I'm sure Mrs. Harrington will oblige. Come, come now, I suggest we don't hold the coach up any longer. Get to your seats will you.'

They hurried round the side of the coach then mounted the steps to see forty-seven faces staring at them. Embarrassed, Harriet could feel her cheeks burning as she followed Tricia down the aisle to the last remaining pair of empty seats on the right just before the back row.

'"e's very bossy, isn't 'e arriet?' said Tricia beginning to fidget after just five minutes. 'Just a moment, let me get my bag. I'll write that in the diary.' She bounced from her seat stretching her arms up again to the luggage rack overhead.

'Ooh careful Tricia. Don't bring the lot down. Wait until we've turned this corner.'

'Ouch! My head! What on earth was that?' Belinda Oxfordshire turned sharply.

'Oh I'm terribly sorry Belinda. I was just tryin' to reach my bag. I didn't mean it to 'it you on the bonce like that.'

'Oh no! I might have guessed. I didn't realise I had you two sitting there.'

'Well I don't really think it would take that much to work it out Belinda, seein' as you 'ad the only two vacant seats left on the coach right behind you. I'm ever so sorry but we 'ad no choice but to sit on these, did we 'arriet?'

'I'm afraid not. Still you'll try not to do it again, won't you Tricia?'

'Not only have I got a very delicate stomach since last Saturday, after sliding in that horse manure that wasn't there before you arrived Patricia Harrington; you've just smacked me one right on the lump left by those trays you clonked me with…. JORIS can you come over?'

'What's going on at the back here. Good gracious me we've been on the road less than five minutes and it's started already.'

'She's just dropped that big bag on my head Joris.'

'No I didn't Mr. Sanderson. I was reachin' for it and it fell right out of my 'ands. 'ow did I know it was goin' to land 'er one?'

'Has it opened the wound Joris? This lump here. You can feel it. It will never get better with her around. She's very lucky I didn't take her to court for laying me open to food poisoning. Deliberate contamination and assault that was. Now I'm having to put up with all this.'

'You stole my 'usband don't forget. TWICE! I think you deserved a good clout over the 'ead. It didn't do Fish-feet-four-cheeks Bob any 'arm either, not that 'e'll ever realise what side 'is bread's buttered.'

Harriet looked across, wished Tricia would leave it alone.

'Oh another metathingy 'arriet.' She returned to Belinda Oxfordshire. ''e'll soon be back, 'e 'as been tellin' me 'ow 'e's just got a teeny weeny bit fed up with you moanin' all the time. 'e told me you were as frigid as Cath Artic.'

'And who is she when she's out?'

'Oh you needn't think you've been all 'is Belinda Oxfordshire. 'e knows the rounds only too well. 'e avoids 'er like the plague when 'e wants to get properly warmed up. That's when 'e 'as to of course. 'e never seems satisfied sleepin' with just one when 'e 'asn't got me.'

'That is disgusting, as if I believe you. Anyway it was me who finished with him, if you do recall? Go on tell her Joris. You had that word in my ear, remember? As if she's got any morals. Bob's told me plenty about you!'

'Oh did you 'ear that 'arriet? Fish-feet-four-cheeks' been gobbin' off! Wait 'til I get 'old of 'im!'

'DO YOU BOTH MIND! Will everyone please turn round to the front again. Sit straight in your seats NOW! Including you Belinda. This is hardly the way to make a good impression on our new colleague here. You were given the responsibility of looking after him Miss Oxfordshire. This bag falling. It was an accident. No harm done. I would advise the pair of you to watch your step very carefully from now on. Hardly good role-models for the children. Miss Glover can you see your way to keeping the pair of them apart?'

Mr. Sanderson returned to sit next to Mr. Whittle. Harriet could feel Tricia seething in the seat next to her. Belinda Oxfordshire had been saying anything and everything just to wind her up. She half-turned again.

'Take no notice of her Ross, she's very common. I have the misfortune to work with her at Starboard Marine North West. Well she works for me actually. A right little upstart. I can't think why Joris ever took her on in the first place.'

It was one of Belinda Oxfordshire's deliberate stage whispers. Harriet didn't dare look at Tricia. Didn't have to.

'OH I DO NOT WORK FOR YOU! Actually I work for Mr. Sanderson and just in case you 'aven't noticed I run Starboard Marine North West. Goodness knows what you do in the back all day, apart from paintin' your nails and waitin' for Joris to come in. Now you say you're sorry to Mr. 'arquerfart 'ere for tellin' 'im lies.'

'MRS. HARRINGTON! IF YOU DON'T MIND. EXCHANGE SEATS WITH ME THIS MINUTE!'

Tricia grabbed her bag then jumped up to cross him in the aisle as she found her way to the empty seat next to Mr. Whittle. Harriet fidgeted as Mr. Sanderson made himself comfortable alongside.

'But Joris, I was only making conversation with Ross. It wasn't intended for her ears. I was whispering wasn't I?'

Perplexed and embarrassed Ross shook his head then scratched away at his hair.

'Don't involve me. I'm only here to observe infantile reaction to the discovery of fossils and the extent to which cognitive functioning is enhanced by the affective influence on expectation and the degree to which this can be controlled to enhance learning.'

'Quite Mr. Farquerhart. Well said! Remember that will you Miss Oxfordshire? Mr. Farquerhart is researching towards his forthcoming PhD. Try not to deter him from the task in hand.'

With a final turn of the head she threw Harriet a filthy look then focussed all her attention on the young man at her side.

Harriet felt squashed. She'd hardly noticed Tricia sitting alongside her. Six foot or more of solid masculinity this close was starting to get to her. She could feel a tiny prick in her throat. Coughed. Excused herself. Then couldn't stop.

'Oh dear Miss Glover. Now what do you suppose has brought this on?'

'Don't know Mr. Sanderson.'

'`ere Miss you can `ave one of these.'

'That's very kind of you young man. Shall I pass her the tube?'

Danny was nodding furiously.

'There, one of those gum things. That should help Miss Glover.'

'Not the top one Mr. Sanderson, if you don't mind.'

'Oh yes, I see. Here.'

Harriet watched him slide the first sweet under his thumb and then pop it into his trouser pocket.

'Thank you Mr. Sanderson. Thank you Danny!'

'Arrh, she's taken two Mr. Sandcastles. Me mum said these `ad to last me all the way to Dorset because we `aven't got much money and we `aven't even joined the motorway yet.'

'Oh I'm sure Miss Glover will reimburse you once we stop at the services. That right Miss Glover?'

'Certainly will Danny.'

'Open your mouth Miss.'

Harriet did exactly as she was told.

'Arrh, she's only got one on `er tongue. What `ave you done with the other one Miss?'

Harriet panicked.

'You've given it to Mr. Sandcastles `aven't you?'

'Danny come back `ere and stop pickin` your nose,' Mrs. Bustard called.

'Go on then where did you put the other one Miss?'

Mr. Sanderson not wishing to attract any further attention to this end of the coach fished in his pocket.

'Go on then you can `ave that one seein` as you're takin` us all on `oliday. We're not goin` to Butlins now. Me mum says we `aven't got enough money any more.'

'Well that's most kind of you young man.' He popped it into his mouth.

'Bert will you tell our Danny to get back on `is seat and tell `im to stop pickin` `is nose? `e's been doin` it ever since `e woke up this mornin`.'

'Off you go Danny. Do as your mother says. Thank you indeed for your kindness.'

'Shall we take them out Mr. Sanderson?' Harriet convinced she was sucking on something thick, large and green.

'What and risk offending the lad? He'll be back in two seconds to see if we're still chewing. No Miss Glover, I'm afraid we're both in this together. Like too many other things, unfortunately.'

He'd said enough. Harriet was pleased he'd just made it so much easier not to succumb to this tantalising level of proximity. Staring out of the window she turned her left shoulder away from him. Felt his leg momentarily touch hers as the coach veered right. Her resolution, all gone. In a flash! She turned. Straightened her back against the seat. Tried once again to put him clean out of her mind. Couldn't believe how much concentration it was taking trying not to let this gorgeous, gorgeous man get to her. Desperate, she tried to recall all the entries in Tricia's diary. One last ditch attempt to go right off him.

'Deep in thought Miss Glover?'

'Oh yes, sorry Mr. Sanderson. I was just thinking about something Danny said.'

'Yes, do go on Miss Glover.'

'It's just that his mum told him to make his sweets last. They're obviously struggling. They must have gone through that money intended for Butlins. The cost of living is going up all the time. I know quite a few parents have already been made redundant. It won't get any better, will it? Not while the country's got all this debt to pay off, at least.'

'No Miss Glover, you're absolutely right. Most certainly we're all going to feel the effects of the government's austerity measures. I fear it will be some considerable time before we'll see anything like the start of an economic recovery.'

'Does it really have to hit the poorest people so hard? Surely if they did something about those massive bonuses bankers are still getting, there would be a bit more in the pot for the likes of our parents?'

'Well the Prime Minister's got a bit of a dilemma on his hands Miss Glover. He's having to deal with many bad decisions made by the last government. I fear we're all paying the price for greed and corruption. On the other hand of course, it doesn't matter too much who's in power, it always goes on to a greater or lesser degree. But it would seem that bankers' interests were given priority over common sense. Indeed this latest corruption uncovered has been going on for some time. No, the networking I fear has well permeated both business and politics and it would seem some in high power, especially of late, have been well rewarded for turning a blind eye.'

'And that money was coming from the source we stumbled on in Venice and had been for some time. Is that what you're saying?'

'Well yes Miss Glover. Quite so. I shouldn't imagine for one minute that was the only source but it would seem it certainly played a large part. Anyhow the PM feels support from his own cabinet is ebbing away since the arrests. I wouldn't be surprised if a snap election was called. He doubts he'll get the rest of the measures through. Doesn't feel he's now got the support of the majority.'

'You mean a general election Mr. Sanderson?'

'Could be. Could well be one in the autumn. You see he's an honest man. A good man if you like. He knows these cuts are already hurting but without further measures the country will go under. It grieves him greatly.'

'But he still doesn't seem to be doing anything about the bankers Mr. Sanderson? Even if their bonuses are insignificant in the scheme of things it still looks bad to the likes of our parents.'

'Well I wouldn't disagree with that but it's like all these captains of industry. Their salaries may appear gross but they take high risks. Without such people the economy would soon falter. Incentive would disappear. They'd be leaving the place in droves. But back to your point. Banking is the engine-house of the whole country's economy Miss Glover. The PM is very reluctant to touch it.'

'The other day Mummy suggested you stand as an MP Mr. Sanderson. Have you ever considered it?'

'Strangely enough the PM mentioned it only last week. I'm not so sure Miss Glover. I feel there could well be more constraints than freedoms in such an exercise. There's a lot of run-of-the-mill stuff to it. A lot of time gets given chasing answers usually beneficial only to an individual or very small minority. Of course a cabinet post would be different but as I said, I'm not so sure I'd enjoy the collective necessity to tow the line. I'd probably be better placed as a local councillor. Get in there. Sort out some of the ineptitude blighting Stetmead.'

Harriet caught his smile. The last time they'd had a serious conversation like this they were on his boat in Falmouth discussing the merits of science and religion. She recalled sitting opposite him, scarcely able to believe she was there, actually on his yacht. She recalled how desperate she was for him to make love to her. Suddenly uncomfortable, she tried to push the thought from her mind.

'I believe we'll be hunting for fossils on the Jurassic Coast, Mr. Sanderson.'

'Yes. Yes indeed. I'm hoping it will prove very exciting for the children. It's of specific interest to me, actually. I have a considerable collection in my library. Did you not notice the displays in the glass cabinets on the wall to the left of the French doors?'

'No, I can't say I did but of course we were in a bit of a fluster after watching you wave the PM off. It's not everyday you see a helicopter taking off from someone's garden.'

'No, quite. Quite. I shall be arranging a school visit to the house for say, thirty or so of the most enthusiastic children in a couple of weeks time. Naturally, Ross here will be attending. I would be pleased if you could see your way to joining us Miss Glover.'

'Oh yes, thank you. I'd like that very much indeed. That would be very interesting.'

'I'll keep you posted on that. There will be one or two other members of staff attending, of course.'

Harriet smiled, silently justifying her pleasure. 'It's better to stay on the right side of him for as long as I can, at least until I can't hide the fact I'm pregnant. One of these days I'm going to have to face him with it.' The realisation sent a flood of panging nerves upwards from her stomach. Thought again.

'Not now though. I might just get away with it until half-term.' Then a further comforting thought. 'Unless of course there's a snap election and he leaves to become an MP.'

She glanced across. Decided she didn't want that either. His oatmeal fisherman's rib sweater rolled up at the sleeves. His arms, strong, sunburnt. His hands, capable. Barely still. His legs, long, muscular. The double seams of his denims just taking the strain, as usual leaving him little room for manoeuvre. He stretched, ran his arm along the top of their seats. All the time conscious of it behind her, she looked down. Knew she was blushing.

'Ah the services Miss Glover. Here at last. Hopefully Mrs. Harrington will have calmed down sufficiently to enable her to return to her seat.'

He stood. Stooped his way down the centre aisle of the coach to the driver as he pulled it to a halt. He turned to face them all issuing brief instructions before descending the steps.

'That man. That gorgeous, gorgeous man. Why didn't I just marry him while I had the chance?'

She tried to sink the thought. Desperately brought Mark to mind and kept him there, especially when she saw him stop, laugh, then say something to Lucinda Lawton as she went running towards him.

Chapter 11

'Oh `arriet I'm furious with `im. Fancy makin` me sit all that time next to Mr. Whittle. `e's `orrible too `arriet. `e kept lookin` down `is nose at me and sniffin` all the time. I felt like `askin` `im if `e'd forgotten to bring an `ankie but I thought better of it. `ere there's a table for two in that corner by the window there. Let's grab it shall we?'

'I don't think so Mrs. Harrington. If I might suggest you and Miss Glover assist the children along with the others acting "In loco parentis". Remain with them will you prior to escorting them back to the coach.'

'Oh yes of course Mr. Sanderson. It's probably because I'm not a teacher. I thought I was on `oliday for a minute. I forgot we're only `ere to look after them.'

Harriet steered Tricia towards the rapidly forming queue.

'I bet `e wanted that table for `im and Mr. Whittle. Quick `ave a look behind `arriet.'

'No! He's sat there with Lucinda Lawton. The pair of them laughing. Oh I'm absolutely furious Tricia. I hope I haven't got to put up with that all week.' She felt a tug on her jacket.

'Miss, Miss. You promised Mr. Sandcastles you'd buy me some more sweets when we got `ere.'

'Oh so I did Danny. Look I'm not sure they sell them in this part. Tell you what, we'll all have our drinks and on the way back I'll go over there. Can you see where they're selling those newspapers and magazines? There's bound to be some there.'

'Ah thanks Miss. I told me mum. She said what she always says about you. She said "You're a good'n you." '

'Well that's very nice of her to say that Danny but I'm no different to anyone else. Now you get back to her or you'll miss your place in the queue.'

'You two, stop pokin` your dirty fingers in that almond slice. Just look at them `arriet. No one will want to eat that once you've pinched all the nuts off the top.'

'You're not a teacher. You can't tell us what to do.'

'Well for your information Mr. Sanderson's just told me I'm currently acting "In loco parentis" if you did but know and that certainly gives me the right to tell you off. And we certainly don't want an outbreak of food poisonin` while we're `ere do we `arriet? `ow do you know someone behind you won't buy it? `ere just put it on your own plate!'

'I don't want it on my plate. Ah I'm tellin` Sir of you. `e's on `is way over.'

'Oh give it to me you little bugger. Go on you're `oldin` the queue up.'

'Ah Mrs. Harrington. Will you pop another one of those onto that plate? Save me joining the queue. Self service coffee at the till I understand? Come along Mrs. Harrington, do come along.'

'But there's only one of these left.'

55

'No behind you Mrs. Harrington. There's just one behind you. Put it with the one on the plate. One and one make two. That'll do. Lucinda and I can't be doing with all these other sugary things.'

'Oh `arriet `e's gone off with the one that little bugger's been pokin` `is fingers in. I do `ope `e doesn't get food poisonin`.'

'I know it's not nice to say Tricia, neither do I. I hope *she* does, though.'

'I think Belinda Oxfordshire's already `ad it `arriet. I'm glad she `ad those after-effects after slippin` in that `orse muck. Oh look, there she is sittin` over there with Ross Harquerfart. Look at them over there in that corner. `ow come she was allowed to sit down and `ave `er coffee without seein` to the kids? That's discrimination that is `arriet. We won't `ave any time at all to get ours. Oh bugger `im `arriet. Come on `e can't see us from where `e is. Let's get ours. The kids are all sittin` themselves down. We can join the end of the line on the way back as if we've been lookin` after them. You can see the coach from `ere `arriet. They're not goin` to come to much `arm. It's the only thing parked in the car park anyway.'

'OK Tricia, let's be quick. We'll sit over there where we can see the children though. I'd hate for anything to happen to them.'

'Oh you worry too much `arriet. If `e was that concerned `e'd be keepin` an eye open `imself instead of flirtin` in the corner.'

'Oh I expect he's watching the door. He doesn't miss much.'

'You're tellin` me `arriet. I took the paper out of my bag so I could `ide from Mr. Whittle. Do you know `e'd already taken the front page off. `e must `ave seen it on the back seat of your car when we were unloadin` all the luggage. I didn't notice when I put it in my bag. If it wasn't `im I don't know who else it could `ave been.'

'Strange Tricia. There was only him and Mr. Brown about. Must have been him. Maybe he fancies you Tricia and he's going to pin it up in his tent.'

'Ooh `arriet, now there's a thought. Oh don't make me weaken `arriet. Even when `e tells me off I go funny all over just wantin` `im. I think we'll need to read that diary before we go to sleep tonight, just to make sure neither of us gives way.'

Chapter 12

'Oh I see it's you back again. I'd be obliged if you'd refrain from passing any further comment for the remainder of the journey.' Belinda Oxfordshire half-turned. Looked down her nose.

'Did you `ear that `arriet? I've `ardly `ad chance to sit down and she's started again.'

'Just ignore her Tricia.'

'Well it's not as easy as that `arriet. She's said that to get me goin` again.'

'Ignore her Tricia unless you want to spend the rest of the journey sat next to Mr. Whittle.'

'Oh no `arriet. I don't want that. `ere let me get my paper out. At least it'll `elp me take my mind off `er.'

'`ow long `ave we got to go Miss?'

Harriet turned round.

'Well let's see now Kevin. We'll be stopping for lunch at around half past twelve. Then after that it should only take a couple more hours. We'll probably get there in the middle of the afternoon. About the same time as we would be having playtime in school.'

'Ah Miss that's ages yet. She keeps diggin` `er elbow in my ribs every time she gets `er coloured pencils out.'

'Try to keep your elbows in Susan. I know it's very difficult. There's not much room to move on these seats. Perhaps you could try choosing two or three colours and just leave them on your lap? It would be easier to get at them, then.'

'Not all of them. Miss didn't say all them. You didn't say all of them did you Miss?'

'Stop it Kevin. Now they're all over the floor,' Susan shouted.

'I'll get them.'

'No Kevin leave them where they are for now. Just sit still.'

The last thing Harriet needed was more commotion from the rear end of the coach.

'Eh I've found one. Here Susan. Under here. They've rolled down. Just let me see if I can reach it.'

'Everyone `ave a look under your seats for `er pencils. Throw them back to us.'

In a split second, chaos! Children grateful for something to do, off their seats, scrambling in the aisle. Pencils shooting back and forth across the coach.

'STOP THAT AT ONCE!' Mr. Sanderson now striding down the aisle. Children struggling from the floor to their seats.

'It was Miss's fault Sir. She told Susan to take them things out of the case. She's been diggin` `er elbows in my ribs all the time.'

'He means Harriet Glover Mr. Sanderson. I distinctly heard her giving the child that specific instruction.'

'Oh no she did not Belinda Oxfordshire. I 'eard exactly what 'arriet said.'

'Enough. That's quite enough. You boy, get up from there this minute. Get back in your seat immediately! Enid, would you mind changing places with Belinda? Belinda you go to the front for the rest of the journey. Give Enid Frost the chance to keep her eye on things down here.'

'But I thought I was supposed to be taking care of Ross Mr. Sanderson?' She turned to Tricia. 'I think it would be far better if she went back to sitting by Mr. Whittle.'

'I beg your pardon Miss Oxfordshire. Please do me the courtesy of allowing me to make that decision for myself will you?'

'That jolly well serves you right.' Tricia couldn't help herself.

'Mrs. Harrington resume your place next to Mr. Whittle will you for the rest of the journey. Go! Now! This minute. I'll have no more nonsense from either of you.'

'Thank you Joris. I assume I'm allowed to stay here, now?'

'No, most certainly not Miss Oxfordshire. Can't you see Enid's on her way down?'

Tricia looked at Harriet. Grabbed her bag, squeezed past Enid Frost to return to her seat next to Mr. Whittle. Then a yelp. Belinda Oxfordshire flat on her face, struggling to get up.

'Whatever's going on now? Miss Oxfordshire are you alright?'

'No I am not Joris. I've just tripped over that thing. She did it on purpose!'

'Oh no I didn't Mr. Sanderson. I only put my bag down by my feet. 'ow was I to know 'alf of it was stickin' out?'

'That's quite enough Mrs. Harrington. I'm warning you if you cause any more disruption, I'll have no choice but to send you home.'

Harriet looked at Tricia. Could see the fury painting her face white. Hoped against hope she wasn't going to answer back. Watched Belinda Oxfordshire smirk sideways at her before sitting in Enid Frost's seat.

'Now I'm right glad someone else knows what it feels like. 'ow many times 'as she tripped me up? I wouldn't be able to count.'

Suddenly on his feet. Mr. Brown pointing at Harriet.

'She's the one everyone 'ere needs to be watching. I can 'ardly walk because of 'er.'

Harriet went as scarlet as the one remaining coloured pencil rolling between her feet as everyone turned to look.

'Not now Mr. Brown. This is neither the time or the place.'

'I would disagree with you there Mr. Sanderson. It's a matter of 'ealth and safety. If you're not going to warn everyone then I am.'

'Consider it done Mr. Brown. We'll be running through all safety issues as a matter of course once we've arrived and everyone's settled.'

With Mr. Brown suitably silenced, only the chatter of excited children filled the coach as it travelled mile after mile along the motorway before swerving left to halt for lunch at the services.

'Right `arriet. I've really `ad enough of `im! Come on we can't be expected to `ang round watchin` a queue of kids pokin` their dirty fingers in the mashed potato before we get ours. If ``e says anythin` we'll just `ave to tell `im we're eatin` ours quick so we can see to the children while they `ave theirs. Come on `arriet grab a tray. Anyway once we start eatin` `e's `ardly likely to stop us, is `e?'

'No you're right. Let's sit over there behind that row of plants. With a bit of luck we won't even be noticed.'

'There `arriet. That's better. `ave you got enough room in there?'

'Yes thanks Tricia. I'll manage. Better than being on display.'

'You're tellin` me. `e's very lucky I'm not goin` back `ome. Treatin` me like one of `is school kids. `as `e said anythin` else while `e's been sat down there?'

'Gosh no Tricia. He wouldn't do that. No, I don't think we've said two words. He's leaned forward to speak to Enid Frost from time to time. I couldn't hear what he said and I'm really not that bothered.'

'I'm tellin` you `arriet if I `ave any more from `er I will go `ome. I can't tell you `ow pleased I was when she went flyin` over my bag.'

'Oh I know, I started to shake. He must have noticed. I had to keep blowing my nose.'

'Serves `er right `arriet. Actually I didn't do it on purpose. It was just that I `adn't pulled my bag far enough in.'

'That's just like me Tricia when the PM went tumbling off the stage at the opening of Starboard Marine North West. I couldn't believe it. I don't know what it is about handbags. They seem to have it in for everyone.'

'Your Mr. Brown's not too fussy on them either. Especially yours `arriet. `e `ad to `ave `is little say as well, didn't `e?'

'Oh he can't help himself. Silly man, he'll have more to occupy his mind soon. You'll see him flapping for Britain once we get there, fussing around the tents.'

'`e'll `ave to put them up first, won't `e `arriet?'

'I'm not sure. We might find them already up when we get there, seeing as we're a school party.'

'Oh I do `ope so. I don't fancy `avin` to give an `and with all them. Anyway if I `aven't got my own bedroom away from Belinda Oxfordshire I *will* be going `ome and `e won't be the one sendin` me. There's bound to be a train I can catch from there to Liverpool and then back through the tunnel to `ome.'

'Oh I'm sure you're right Tricia, we can both catch it if it comes to that but let's hope it doesn't. Let's try to enjoy it. At least it won't be like being in Venice. At least we won't have the PM's heavies following us around. We really could do with a break after all that.'

'Yes, I suppose you're right `arriet. I'll feel better once I've written it all in the diary. There'll be enough in there to put us off `im for good now. `e needn't bother pinnin` my front page to `is tent, either.'

'No Tricia. Look, let's just steer clear. We don't have to go looking for him. I wonder how poor old Tarquin's feeling? That must have been a bit of a shock hearing about his cannabis plants getting distributed around the whole of Stetmead and having to come back to face the consequences. I must tell him how it all happened as soon as I can. No we'll be nice to Tarquin instead shall we Tricia? He's going to need it.'

'Yes, that's a very good idea. We'll concentrate on cheerin' `im up. Typical of our friend Joris Sanderson ropin' `im in for this when `e's got all that on `is plate. `ere, let me get that diary out of my bag. "Selfish and thoughtless especially with `is chums". Oh there's the phone `arriet. `ere you write it in while I answer it. `ang on a minute. There you are, my pen's in the bottom.'

'Ah, got it. Thanks Tricia.'

'`ello `ow may I `elp you?' She turned to Harriet. 'Thought I was at work for a minute, then.'

Harriet smiled. Clenched the pen between her teeth while she searched for the right words.

'Oh `ello again. Can you speak up? Only it's very noisy in `ere I'm in a motorway services place.' ……..

'Oh it's you. Wayne `ammer. Are you phonin' from the garden centre?' …

'No, you're not?' …

'Oh Venice!' …

'Oh did you go in place of me then to `elp with my save Venice mission? That was really good of you I'm sure your Rappin` will appreciate that.' …

'You what? You *are* Rappin` `ammer. Oh I'm thinkin` of your Guy. Yes of course. Silly me. I forgot you're really called Wayne. I'm ever so sorry but I `aven't `ad chance to tell you I couldn't make it, yet. We're on a school trip `arriet and I. We got roped in for campin' in Dorset I'm very sorry to say. `ow's it goin` in Venice then?' …

'You what? You're flyin` back. I thought you were over there for longer than that? Trouble? What kind of trouble are you talkin` about now?' …

'The statues.' …

'You measured them and they're thingies are all bigger than yours. Oh no you `aven't been doin` that, `ave you? You must `ave been mashin` the mush over there to `ave done that. `ow much did you take off them?' …

'You what? You made sure they were smaller than yours. Did you not leave them with anythin` then?' …

'Look it's not my fault your therapist spun you one. No, I wasn't lookin` at them when we were over there. Anyway even if I `ad `ow would I `ave known if they were bigger or smaller than yours?' …

'Oh yes I forgot. That was why you needed the therapist in the first place. I do remember now you didn't `ave very much under that nylon scarf.' …

'You what? I `ad no right to pull it off. I think you've forgotten just `ow very rude you were to me and `arriet while you were bein` Father Christmas at Starboard Marine North West, if you care to remember? It's not my fault you went over there and you're `avin` to come back in an `urry. It's a wonder you `aven't been arrested and put into jail.' …

'No of course I won't ell anyone it was you. You'd better get back before someone notices. I don't want any more trouble than I've already `ad.' ...

Tricia listened, took a deep breath then continued.

'Where exactly are we goin`? `ere `ariet pass me that leaflet out of my bag. `ere you are. It's the Cliff over Sea Campin` and Caravan Park, Newsands, Dorset. Why do you want to know that?' ...

'Oh, well that's very kind of you Wayne. Yes we'll be `ere all week.' ...

'It's on your way `ome? But I thought you flew out from Manchester?' ...

'Oh you're comin` back to `eathrow because all the equipment went from there. Oh I see now Wayne.' ...

'No I don't suppose it will be much of a detour. Just give me a call before you come and I'll be very `appy to take back my "save Venice" tin.'

'Oh you've got a stash more as well?' ...

'Yes I understand. You want me to `ave it before it get's pinched. Well I didn't mean to be rude just now Wayne. `ariet and I are a teeny bit tense on this trip. We'll look forward to seein` you very soon Wayne, bye.'

'Gosh Tricia. They're not thinking of joining us at the campsite are they?'

'Oh it's only to deliver my "save Venice" tin `ariet. It looks like they've collected a lot of money.'

'It looks like they're in a load of trouble, too Tricia. Did I hear that right? He hasn't been defacing all the male statues in sight, has he?'

'Oh no `ariet. Not their faces. You know `ariet, their thingies. Oh `ariet `is therapist's got it so wrong. It seems like all theirs were bigger than `is after all. I just don't know `ow `e's goin` to deal with it and there was me startin` to argue with `im. I'll `ave to be nice to `im `ariet if I'm ever goin` to keep `im on board. Oh another metathingy. I'm really good at them now.'

'Gosh Tricia we've just got out of a load of trouble by the skin of our teeth. We don't need to be getting embroiled with him and his band especially while we're camping.'

'Oh don't worry `ariet. We're part of this school trip remember? Mr. Sanderson will soon get rid of them all if they try to cause any bother.'

'Golly Tricia, you'd better be right.'

Chapter 13

Harriet resumed her seat. A cloud of fear spoiling her view from the window as they left the M6 to join the M5 heading towards Bristol.

'Mrs. Harrington so engrossed in conversation as to neglect her duties Miss Glover, not to mention yourself?'

'Oh gosh, I'm terribly sorry Mr. Sanderson we'd decided to have ours first so we'd be free to help out towards the end.'

'At Mrs. Harrington's suggestion, I expect. You know Miss Glover our parents are seldom wrong. It would seem your mother is forever warning you about this particular association. Whilst I admit she has some admirable qualities…'

'What, Mummy? I can't say as I've noticed.'

'No, no Miss Glover, do concentrate and let me finish. I'm speaking of Mrs. Harrington. She's excellent at her job. Being particularly gregarious she's very popular with our customers and parents alike. She has the facility to break the class boundary, for want of a better expression, I might add. You see sometimes parents can be a little in awe of teachers such as yourself. Particularly our parents Miss Glover. Now Mrs. Harrington has performed marvellously well in the coffee shop. Our parents are immediately comfortable with her. I must say she's played no small part in enthusing them to the extent they now feel equally at home with the sailing club. Unfortunately it's these very qualities she often over-stretches to let herself down. Take this instance with that Rapping Hammer boy.'

Harriet's stomach instantly knotted. Thought he'd overheard.

'The concept of saving Venice is undoubtedly admirable. Too much of our past has been allowed to decay. Fall into ruin. Now Venice is an absolute treasure-trove reflecting the best of humanity as you will have observed Miss Glover. If just a fraction of those visiting it were blessed with the same enthusiasm to save it as Mrs. Harrington then indeed the problem would cease to exist. However, there's enthusiasm and enthusiasm. I'm not sure about the morality of using one's body to promote a good cause, though like everything else, it's open to debate. The male is effectively programmed to ensure continuation of the species, as you are very well aware, Miss Glover. If you like they need very little encouragement to approximate their behaviour until the desired response is reached. In that respect the male of the human species is vulnerable Miss Glover. Very vulnerable. Now it didn't go unnoticed the degree to which Mrs. Harrington was exposing her cleavage whilst serving meals at the sailing club. It certainly encouraged generous contributions towards her save Venice mission. And I suppose it's not too far removed from charities recruiting female celebrities to that end and that in itself generally appears to raise no ethical issues. However ending up topless on the front of the local paper, as far as I'm concerned, certainly does. Incidentally I saw fit to dispose of it. She appears to lack the ability to curb her enthusiasm and this I feel is the root of the problem. She simply goes too far. Now Miss Glover I've been somewhat concerned you yourself may have become influenced to some extent by Mrs. Harrington's behaviour, in which case I feel it's my duty to warn you of this, since the assimilation of others' character traits can happen so gradually the recipient is hardly aware of a behaviour pattern change in themselves. It's called 'influence' Miss Glover and your behaviour of late suggests to me you have indeed been well and truly influenced. It's something neither myself or indeed your mother wishes to see.'

Harriet fidgeted in her seat. Knew she'd blushed to excess. Didn't know which way he was taking it.

'The point is Miss Glover whilst there is ostensibly nothing morally wrong in posing nude for the purpose of art, it would seem to me Barry Giordano could well have crossed that fine line between objectivity and meeting the need to satisfy his most basic of instincts You see Miss Glover having just recently professionally examined you, his decision to grossly exaggerate your supposed state of pregnancy in this painting only serves to reinforce my fear. Furthermore, you have indeed raised this pregnancy issue with him which I do not believe would have happened had it not been the case. Now what would your reason have been to tell him that Miss Glover?'

Harriet strained to hear him above the chatter all around, for obvious reasons his words now hardly audible. She wished for all the world she still had Tricia sitting alongside her.

'Come, come Miss Glover. You owe me an answer, surely?'

'He proposed to me Mr. Sanderson. He wanted me to marry him.'

'How much encouragement have you given him Miss Glover?'

'None, absolutely none! I've been trying to fend him off.'

'What by posing for him like that?'

'No Mr. Sanderson. Absolutely not! You didn't give me chance to explain. He sketched me lying on his sofa but I was fully dressed. He wanted me to pose like that but I wouldn't. No one was more surprised than me when you uncovered that painting.'

'Now is this the truth Harriet?'

'Yes, of course it is. I'm furious with him for doing that. I've told him I never want to see him again.'

'And did you tell him you were pregnant by me Harriet in this attempt to fend him off?'

She looked down. There was nothing in her that could take her anywhere near to answering that one.

' "Cum tacent, clamant" Miss Glover.'

For the briefest of moments she felt his hand on top of hers. Caught the intensity in his disbelieving blue eyes.

'Silence is an admission of guilt Miss Glover.'

He stood. She watched him, head lowered, stride down the aisle back to his seat. Felt bad. Didn't expect Tricia to return. Just wanted the rest of the journey to herself. To think.

Chapter 14

'I just 'ad a nice smile and a wink off Tarquin Bridgewater 'arriet. I think 'e must be alright to be able to do that.'

'Let's hope so Tricia. Let's hope he's been let off with a caution. With a bit of luck I cleared all those plants from his greenhouse. It certainly felt like it. If there was no further evidence at his place he might just have got away with it.'

'No wonder 'e always 'as that smile on 'is face. I wouldn't mind tryin' a bit of that stuff myself just at the moment.'

'Oh no Tricia. Don't even talk like that! You know we're so lucky to have got away with all we have. It could have so easily gone horribly wrong. You know it was pretty clear when we were round at Mr. Sanderson's house having dinner with the PM those heavies thought we were colluding with them.'

'What do you mean "colluding with them"? Do you mean with the 'eavies or Joris and the PM?'

'Us colluding with Mr. Sanderson and the Prime Minister, Tricia. They did think we were on their side.'

'Ooh you mean those 'eavies thought that's what we were doin' in Venice, spyin' for Joris and the Prime Minister 'arriet?'

'Yes, of course they would think we were over there gathering evidence. They made a big thing about getting hold of your fake designer dress. They must have thought it was our mission to get hold of one to expose the fraud.'

'Yes you're right 'arriet. I'm sure they did and who's to say they've caught them all? We might still be bein' watched by someone. 'ow do we know we're not?'

'Well didn't Mr. Sanderson seem to think we were more or less in the clear once they'd been caught? He should know, but the last thing we need is to be getting embroiled with Rapping Hammer and his band. We don't want to be involved in anything to do with Venice. We don't want to be drawing attention to ourselves at all.'

'No I see what you mean. I couldn't stop them from comin' over though, could I?'

'No Tricia. I'm not saying that and you need to get your money back. I just hope they don't cause trouble while they're passing it over.'

'Oh 'arriet so do I, especially after 'avin' my picture in the paper. We'll try and slip out shall we? Meet them somewhere. When 'e phone's again I'll tell 'im. 'ang on I think there was a map on the back of that leaflet. Where's my bag? Oh no 'arriet I've gone and left it under that seat next to Mr. Whittle. I shoved it right under so no one else would trip over it. I'm just goin' back to get it. I won't be a tick.'

Harriet watched her bounce up the aisle then drop to her feet. The next thing she saw Mr. Sanderson shooing her out of the way. Standing to let her get in. Then up on her feet again. Mr. Whittle rising to squeeze past her then smartly back in his seat. Now completely disappeared. Suddenly her bottom rising as she backed into the aisle then stretching her legs before wriggling like a worm to get under the pair of seats in front. Harriet wanted to die. Thought.

'Mr. Sanderson's furious with her. Oh no, it looks as if she's tugging at it. It must have got caught on something. Golly Tricia mind how it comes up.'

With a final heave and a swing, Harriet gasped to see it hurtling through the air, the bag thumping Mr. Whittle on the top of his balding head while the strap instantly looped itself round his neck like a hugely fashionable but leather, necklace. As if attacked by the skinned animal itself he shot both arms in the air first wrestling then battling with the thing only to succeed in unleashing it to bounce out of control, catching the side of his spectacles, bringing them, himself and the bag to the floor, trapping Mr. Sanderson now twisted in the limited space between the rows of seats either side of the aisle. Through streaming tears, Harriet saw him push Mr. Whittle's bottom upwards towards the seat managing to land him back whilst jerking the spectacles up his nostrils. Mr. Whittle made to grab them, refusing to relinquish the shoe cemented to his right hand, poised menacingly at Tricia; for all the world looking like he was about to deliver a spanking. Furious Mr. Sanderson struggled to his knees then stood back to allow Tricia to wriggle out from under. Puce and pointing to the seat he insisted Tricia stay there to make her apologies. Harriet feigned a fitting cough trying to control the exploding hysterics as he marched his way back to the empty seat alongside her.

'Can't that damned woman sit still for more that two minutes?' She took a very deep breath. Tried desperately to hold the shrieks of laughter in.

'Oh she only want….. She only wanted to look at the holiday leaflet to ….' Shaking, she wished she hadn't tried to say all that.

'You find it amusing Miss Glover?'

'No! No, no! Not at all. No, it was just to get her bearings she wanted it. The leaflet with the map on the back I mean.'

'Crikey! The damned woman can't even get her bearings on a coach Miss Glover, I shudder to think how she's going to be once we arrive. It was only last Saturday she caught Mr. Whittle rather badly on the rump with that damned "save Venice" tin of hers. Most embarrassing! Next thing the poor man will be empathising with Brown. Oh and perhaps you'd be good enough to refrain from inflicting any further injury on him, either, particularly whilst we are here. It simply confirms my previously expressed observation, you are indeed influencing each other Miss Glover though I have to say it's usually *your* handbag that does the damage. I noticed the PM mentioned it when we were all at dinner. You know he'll never forget crashing from the platform at the opening of Starboard Marine North West. It could have been very nasty indeed.'

'That wasn't my fault Mr. Sanderson,' insisted Harriet, feeling the mirth rapidly drain away. 'All I did was put it down on the edge of the stage. How did I know he was going to come rushing over like that? If he hadn't had his head in the air grinning so much he might have spotted it. Anyway he should have been looking where he was going.'

'That's enough Miss Glover, quite enough. You're very fortunate the Prime Minister is as good natured as he is. You do realise he's made considerable effort on both your behalves to ensure your exoneration from this Venice affair.'

'Yes, sorry,' agreed Harriet. 'That came out all the wrong way. Actually Tricia and I are worried there might be others in the gang watching out for us now those two have been caught. Do you think that might still be a possibility Mr. Sanderson?'

'Well I was intending to remind you both about being on your guard but who can say Miss Glover? It's unlikely, though the possibility had occurred to us given your involvement. Of course the PM and I have no wish to alarm you. I suggest you proceed with caution and do nothing to stir public interest in yourselves. The story will inevitably hit the media. I imagine that Barnes fellow will be rooting around this very minute. It's essential you don't get drawn Miss Glover. That's why I insisted the pair of you joined this trip. I felt it expedient to have you both out of the way.'

'That was very thoughtful Mr. Sanderson, thank you.'

'Oh I do think from time to time Miss Glover. Far more than you give me credit for.'

He stood.

'Right Mrs. Harrington. Return to your seat and try to keep that damned bag to yourself.'

'Oh I `ad to apologise. Do you know `e never said a word. `is face was purple `arriet and `e spent the `ole of the time inspectin` `is glasses. Anyone would think `*e'd* been under the seats. It was `orrible down there. I thought `e was goin` to `it me one with my own shoe the way `e was `oldin` it. `e's only just given it me back.'

'Oh don't Tricia you'll start me off again.'

'`ere now let's get this leaflet out. Let's see `ow much further we've got to go. Where are we `arriet?'

Harriet, glad of the need to concentrate on something, placed her forefinger somewhere between Bristol and Exeter.

'Well that doesn't look very far now, if you'd just keep your finger still `arriet. I wonder if we'll be stoppin` again for afternoon tea?'

'We're about to find out, I think,' Harriet informed her, conscious of her shoulders starting to go again.

'May I have your attention please?'

The coach silenced to Mr. Sanderson's command.

'We'll be stopping shortly. We are about two minutes or so away from the next services. This will be a convenience stop only. If you don't wish to make use of it then please remain seated. Girls line up behind Mrs. Hall if you wish to use the toilets. Boys follow Mr. Bracken. Miss Glover go with Mrs. Hall will you and Mr. Farquerhart will you kindly accompany Mr. Bracken. This will be a ten minutes stop only. We are approximately one hour away from the campsite.'

Harriet left her seat ahead of the scramble of children wanting to leave the coach. She waited for the queue to assemble then walked behind almost alongside Mr. Sanderson desperately trying to think of something sensible to say.

'Do you know what's happening about the tents Mr. Sanderson? Will we all be involved in pitching them?'

'Good gracious me, no Miss Glover, do use your common sense. This particular camp site, although generally available to all, goes that extra mile to cater for school parties. I think we'll find all the tents erected, arranged in the manner indicated on the leaflet. Naturally the children's facilities will be in a separate block from the adults. Mr. Whittle and myself will avail ourselves of the house, of course. The poor man will need it'

Harriet blew her nose. Desperately tried to think of something else to say before she went off again.

'Oh right. Well that's better for the children to be able to see the tents already in place.'

'Quite, if not a little obvious don't you think, Miss Glover? They'll be sleeping on camp beds, linen and such stuff all in situ. Staff and helpers will be accommodated in large four-bed tents.'

'Oh separate bedrooms in each tent, is that?'

'As I understand it. There should be no reason for anyone to experience discomfort during this coming week.'

'Well it actually sounds very nice Mr. Sanderson.'

'Indeed it is. Views of Lyme Bay to the west and Chesil Beach with its Fleet Lagoon to the east. I should try to relax and enjoy it, if I were you. I've been more than a little concerned about your wellbeing of late including your lack of focus. Still you've had one traumatic experience on top of another, albeit largely self-inflicted on each count, I hasten to add. Still on the whole you've come through it all fairly well. Let's keep it that way shall we? However I do think we can do without these uncontrollable bouts of childish laughter particularly on this camping exercise.'

'Yes, I'm really sorry Mr. Sanderson. I think it's nerves. Yes I'm sure a lot of it is due to nerves.'

'Well I suppose trauma does take people in different ways. I'll give you the benefit of the doubt Miss Glover.'

He narrowed his eyes, sweeping her up in a sideways glance. That look again, serious yet gentle but somehow aloof. This intensely virile man searing the whole of her body, yet again, with the uncontrollable desire to lay her aching, hopeless, yearning self naked and open in complete surrender to his every need. Just a hint of a smile. Then his hand across his mouth as if holding the next sentence back. In heaven, she watched him stride forward to join Sean Bracken at the front of the line while gently keeping the boys he'd just left in check. She tried to control the rush of euphoria. Knew this she could not tell Tricia.

Chapter 15

'Oh we're nearly 'ere at last 'arriet. Where did we say we'd meet Rappin'
'ammer when 'e phones me?'

'I think it was Churndale Village. It's right by the campsite, I think we're just
coming into it now. Oh yes this is it. There's not much here. A grocers, jewellers
and a butchers. Oh and a pub there next to that Post Office. Try to catch the
name.'

'The Lantern Box 'otel. There it's on that sign. Ooh that looks very posh to
me. It might be a bit too posh for Rappin' 'ammer,' Tricia decided.

'Well we're not going to get chance to suss anything else out. We don't even
have to go in. Oh look there's the campsite. Look Tricia you can see the sea. Oh
it's a gorgeous place. Lets try to enjoy it after all we've been through.'

'I might stand a chance of enjoyin' it if 'e stops moanin' at me. I can do
without it. I bet 'e's not moanin' at 'er.'

'It certainly doesn't look like it Tricia. Huh, Lucinda Lawton indeed. Just
look at him. He certainly doesn't need to get that close to her to say whatever it
is.'

'Oh you know what 'e's like 'arriet. Likes to 'ave as many of us on the go 'as
'e can.'

'Well that certainly won't be including us Tricia. Look at him now. He's got
his arm right round her.'

'Shush 'arriet you're raisin' your voice.'

'What else do you expect Harriet Glover, didn't you know they're about to
become engaged?' Belinda Oxfordshire turned round to smirk, then whispered
something into Ross Farquerhart's ear.

Harriet furiously dumbfounded, glanced at Tricia for help.

'Oh I wouldn't believe a word she says 'arriet. We know 'ow good she is at
tellin' lies.'

'Well for your information Patricia Harrington, ask him yourself. And you'd
be as well to watch your step if you don't wish me to add slander to common
assault, should I decide to sue.'

'Right I will go and ask 'im right this minute.'

Harriet watched Belinda Oxfordshire's expression quickly change.

'Then again, on second thoughts I wouldn't if I were you. One more strike
and you're out according to him.'

'Oh sod off Belinda. It's got nothin' at all to do with you.'

Desperate to collaborate, Harriet and Tricia hung back to be last off the
coach.

'I can't stand 'er 'arriet. I don't know 'ow I'm goin' to cope with 'er bein' in
our tent.'

'Nor me Tricia. Did you hear that? I wonder if it's true? Surely he wouldn't
be getting engaged to her. Not his deputy. Hardly very professional.'

'Well I 'ope you don't mind me sayin' this but 'e did want to marry you and you're one of `is teachers, so what's the difference?'

'Oh thanks Tricia. Just what I wanted to hear.'

'Sorry `arriet but we're both goin` to `ave to face reality. I know you wanted to stay on amber but that doesn't mean to say `e does. At least you `ad your chance. I never even got that far.'

'Sorry Tricia. Of course you're right. He can absolutely please himself what he does. We're not bothered in the least, are we? We'll just have to zip ourselves into our beds at night and try not to think of what they might be getting up to.'

'Well after we've zipped whining Winnie into `ers so she can't get out. `ow about if we do a little bit of earwiggin` outside their tent. I think Mr. Sanderson's with `er on Monday night and in the meantime we'll watch them very carefully. We'll soon get to know whether whinin` Winnie's tellin` the truth or not.'

'Such good thinking Tricia. It's not that we're at all bothered though. This is more about seeing whether or not Belinda Oxfordshire's telling more lies.'

'Of course it is `arriet Do you know I would `ave gone and congratulated `im but if she is tellin` porkies I couldn't risk gettin` expelled. I want my money off Rappin` `ammer and I'll `ave to be `ere for that.'

'Too right Tricia. We'll soon find out what's going on. Just wait and see.'

'Oh I `ope you're right `arriet. I really do `ope you're right.'

Chapter 16

'Are you OK with that one Mrs. Bustard?'

'Oh yes thanks Miss Glover. I prefer to be in the back corner especially if the wind gets up durin` the night. I was expectin` to be with our Bert as a matter of fact. Who'll be next door to me then?'

Tricia looked across to Harriet then back to Mrs. Bustard.

'We were `opin` you wouldn't mind `avin` `er, whingeing Winnie next door. I don't think I'll be responsible for my actions if I've got `er on the other side of me.'

'Ooh `as that Belinda woman been `avin` a go at you then Tricia?'

'Apart from pinchin` my `usband you mean? `er? She's `ardly ever stopped Beattie. She's been a right cow.'

'You know I've never liked `er. She loves `erself she does. She makes you feel all inferior. She's always lookin` down `er nose at yer.' Mrs. Bustard suddenly stopped.

'Ooh, `ere she comes. Speak of the devil.' Tricia turned with a start.

'Joris Sanderson would like a word with you.'

'What with me? We've only just got `ere. I `aven't done anythin` wrong yet.'

'You must be brain dead Patricia Harrington if you've forgotten the coach journey already. Come along. He wants to talk to both of us and he doesn't like to be kept waiting.'

'Alright, alright I'm comin`. Keep your `air on. `arriet would you mind shovin` those things into my bedroom please?' Tricia was pointing to the inner room compartment near the entrance, diagonally opposite the one they'd just allocated to Belinda Oxfordshire.

'Oh judging by the parked luggage, I see you've already decided where I'm going. Just another complaint for Joris to deal with. It won't matter. I don't expect you'll be allowed to stay very long, anyway. That seems to be the line Joris is taking, as I understand it.'

'Oh is it indeed? Well `e's no right to be discussin` `is intentions with you Belinda Oxfordshire, so you're not the only one who'll be complainin` when we see `im.'

Harriet took a deep breath. Moved to the awning to see her off. She didn't fancy being left without Tricia for the rest of the week. Hoped against hope Tricia wouldn't blow it so soon.

'They don't get on them two. I've seen them down at the coffee shop. You know when we've all been there for them learnin` activities.'

'No you're absolutely right Mrs. Bustard. She does seem intent on winding Tricia up.'

'As she been `avin` if off with `er `usband then?'

'It would seem so Mrs. Bustard. Of course it's not something I'd wish to speculate about. You'd need to be a fly on the wall to be exactly sure but Tricia's had her suspicions.'

'Oh a bit like `im and `er you mean?'

'No Mrs. Bustard, I'm not sure who you are talking about now.'

'You know Miss Glover, `im and `er. Mr. Sanderson and `is deputy. The rumour's still goin` round. `e was supposed to be marryin` er before the summer `olidays. Maybe `e `as for all we know. They might `ave done it on the quiet like. Especially with them both workin` so close together in school.'

Harriet went as flat as the gound sheet under her feet. Then her stomach, curdling with anxiety promptly flooded her mind with regret. She went limp. Couldn't square her residual need for Mark with all this. Hated Mr. Sanderson for removing her option to stay on amber.

'I'll keep my eye on the pair of them. See what's goin` on. I'm not sure it's good for the school if `e `as married `er and them workin` so close together like. Still `e could `ardly not, given she's up the spout, or so they're sayin`. She'll be `avin` to leave anyway before too long,' Mrs. Bustard whispered.

Harriet could hardly believe her ears. Couldn't deal with the thought. What with the possibility of Melissa Scott being pregnant and now Lucinda Lawton. Vowed to herself. 'I'm not going anywhere near that clinic. In fact there's no law says I have to go anywhere. What about surprise pregnancies, especially menopausal ones? You can't go to jail for it.'

She felt the need to change the subject.

'Are you still going down to the group activities at Starboard Marine North West, then Mrs. Bustard?'

'Yes I am Miss Glover. I'd be climbin` the walls if I didn't `ave them to go to.'

'Oh and why's that?'

'Our Bert got made redundant three months ago. It's been on the cards for some time but they've always managed somehow to keep the place goin`.'

'Oh, I'm so sorry to hear that Mrs. Bustard. I know some of our parents have lost their jobs but I didn't realise Mr. Bustard was one of them. Where did he work?'

'Down at the Hop factory, Can't make the blades any more. Costs are too high. The whole lot are going to be done in China and the far east.'

'Oh, you mean H to O Propulsion Ltd? I didn't realise Mr. Bustard worked there. Both my son-in-laws have an interest in that place. Gosh! You mean the company's going to operate from the far east then?'

'Oh no, they're goin` to be makin` the blades out there. It's the factory part that's closed down. It's a wonder you didn't read it in the paper.'

'No I didn't. It doesn't always come Mrs. Bustard.'

'`ave you `ad this week's?' Suddenly Mrs. Bustard was grinning. 'It looked like your friend's on the front page to me. Does she call `erself `olly Berry, sometimes?'

'You'll need to ask her yourself Mrs. Bustard,' said Harriet, struggling to maintain at least a modicum of professional distance.

'Anyway Mrs. Bustard, I'm so very sorry to hear about Mr. Bustard's job going. If there's anything I can do to help?'

'Well that's very kind of you Miss Glover. You already `ave.'

'Really?'

'That lottery ticket you gave me back. You know the one with the three thousand pound winnin` line?'

'Yes I do remember Mrs. Bustard. Don't tell me…'

'Well we `ad to, didn't we? We've been pilin` up the bills. I `ad to borrow money from one of those places so I `ad to cancel that Butlins `oliday to pay the interest on the loans I've been gettin`. We're in a right mess Miss Glover. I've got myself well and truly caught up with this place. It's not long been opened you know. `e's a bad man. A very bad man. `e looks like one of those big bald-`eaded gangsters they `ave in those films. I `ate goin` in the shop. I'm sure `e's got a gun in `is pocket. I daren't tell our Bert. `e thinks we've cancelled the `oliday to leave the money in the bank to give us a bit behind us. We're really strugglin` but we're not the only ones. You should `ear them all talkin` in the playground. We've only been able to come on this because we've been payin` for it in instalments since the beginnin` of the year. That's why I ended up `avin` to go to that place. I wouldn't `ave `ad the money to keep the payments up otherwise but I wanted our Danny to `ave this `oliday at least. I told `im to make the most of this. It'll be the only `oliday `e gets until our Bert gets another job and when that'll be I don't know. We were `opin to get a little boat, too. Nothin` posh, just somethin` big enough to take our Danny out in. No chance of that now. I think that's what's `urt our Bert the most. `e really felt `e was goin` up in the world.'

'Oh this is awful Mrs. Bustard. If only there was something I could do to help?'

'Short of gettin` this gangster arrested or providin` us all with a free supermarket Miss Glover, I don't think there's anythin` anyone can do.'

'We'll see about that Mrs. Bustard. We'll see about that!'

'I've unpacked my stuff, as much as I'm goin` to inside `ere. I'm just off to find our Bert. I'll leave you two to it then.'

'OK Mrs. Bustard. Oh here, give Danny these please, if you don't mind.'

Harriet fished out a couple more tubes of sweets from her bag.

'Well that's very kind of you Miss Glover. I told `im to make `is last. `e'll fill `is gob with the whole lot if `e thinks `e can get away with it.'

'No Mrs. Bustard, it wasn't his fault. I'm afraid Mr. Sanderson and I had a go at them at the back of the coach. It's the least I could do.'

'No one else would `ave bothered Miss Glover. You're a good'n you!'

'How did you get on Tricia?'

'It was worth the tellin` off to see `er get the same. `e told `er as well if she causes any trouble between us we're both goin` `ome. `e said it didn't matter which one of us it was, we would both be on our way. It was simply a matter of two train tickets which he would require reimbursement of. Anyway she's fallin` all over Ross Farquerhart now so she won't be botherin` with me and as far as I'm concerned Joris Sanderson can just get on with it.'

'Oh well, at least he's trying to be fair Tricia. Just make sure you don't say anything she can take exception to. I don't fancy being left here for the rest of the week without you, especially after what Mrs. Bustard's just told me.'

'Ooh what `as she said then `arriet?'

'Just practically confirmed him and Lucinda Lawton are an item. She even suggested they could already be married, seeing as she's pregnant!'

'`ow does she know all that `arriet? Take no notice of `er. She's only gossipin`.'

'I hope you're right Tricia. You wouldn't believe how cheap the thought of that makes me feel.'

'Look `arriet, it's gossip. `e's not goin` to risk gettin` `er pregnant, now is `e? `e's a doctor `arriet. `e knows what `e's doin`. `ow good would it look for `im if everyone found out `e was `avin` two babies by different women? I don't care `ow much money `e's got. In `is circles I'm sure it would ruin `is reputation.'

'I'm not so sure about that. In his circle it probably wouldn't matter one iota.'

'No `arriet. I think you're bein` just a teeny weeny bit too sensitive at the moment. It's probably your `ormones. I bet we don't pick up any sign of anythin` like that from watchin` the pair of them this comin` week.'

'If only, if only. I need to stay on amber Tricia. It's the only place my mind can get any rest. Oh was that his voice then? Yes I'm sure it was, he must be coming over.'

'Mrs. Harrington, Miss Glover, have you not read the timetable? We've assembly in the main hall of the house. Everybody's there bar you two. Bring your holiday information leaflets with you should you want to make notes. It's critical to the smooth-running of the holiday everyone be advised of health and safety issues, time-tabling, things like that.'

They stumbled behind him, through the narrow gap avoiding the tent-pegs sticking up perilously from the ground on either side.

'They've put these a bit close together Mr. Sanderson. I don't know `ow ever you'll get out of yours without trippin` up.'

'More an office Mrs. Harrington. More an office. I think you'll find me suitably alert as to avoid such a catastrophe. I suggest you look to yourselves. Especially you Miss Glover with your inability to stay upright for more than two minutes.'

Just a couple of ill-chosen words sent Harriet fuming. With all concentration gone, her big toe thumped into the next tent peg, sending her off balance and into a sideways roll, the taut canvas springing each peg from the ground in turn to collapse the poles. Somewhere in the middle lay Harriet silent under a mound of canvas.

'Crikey. "Dictum ac factum" Miss Glover!'

'Well I don't see as that's bein` terribly `elpful Mr. Sanderson as `arriet's disappeared in all that tent. Are you alright `arriet? I'm frightened of treadin` on you.'

'Oh do get out of the way Mrs. Harrington. Let me get to her.'

'I was only tryin` to `elp.'

'There, there now Miss Glover. Here let me give you a hand. Are you OK? I'll need to get Brown to sort this lot out. Good gracious we've only been here five minutes and you manage to pull a whole awning down on top of you. Now you can't say I didn't warn you. "Dictum ac factum" indeed! Or to put it another way. "No sooner said than done" Miss Glover!'

'Oh `arriet I do `ope you `aven't `urt yourself?'

'No, I think I'm alright thanks Tricia. Just a bit of a shock, that's all.'

Now feeling his arm around her shoulder. Harriet steeled herself.

'You go on ahead Mrs. Harrington. Ask Miss Lawton to get started will you? We won't be too long. Oh and send Brown over at the same time.'

'Just move along to the end tent here Miss Glover.' Inside, she watched as he unzipped his way into the far compartment to the left.

'Here. Lie down on this for a moment will you? Let's check you out for damage.'

'No, really Mr. Sanderson. I'm quite alright, thank you.'

'Come along Miss Glover. Get on with it. I'd like to take over from Lucinda given half a chance.'

With no choice she lay still. Allowing him to check her out.

'Now any pain at all?'

'Just here.' She rubbed at her shoulder and then her right side.

'Just sit now, if you will?'

Harriet sat, still dazed from the shock.

'Ouch! Golly that hurts.'

'Bound to Miss Glover. I don't think there's too much damage though. The inevitable bruising will occur, of course. Look, I think it would be far better if you transferred to this tent. I was only going to be using it as a bit of an office, more of a base. Shan't be sleeping here. I'll organise a swap. I'll get these things moved to the centre tent. Far better you don't run the risk of tripping over again in your condition.'

Harriet froze. Dreaded what was coming next. Thankful to see Mr. Brown's head poking through the canvas door flaps.

'Ah Mr. Brown. See your way to re-erecting that one will you? And when you've done it be so good as to transfer this lot over and bring Miss Glover's things back here.'

'You been trippin` again Miss Glover? Practicin` on this before `avin` a go at me?' Mr. Brown looked anything but pleased.

Harriet could well have been a beetroot just plucked from the ground. Bursting to be rude, she looked down in sullen silence at her trainers.

'Get on with it Mr. Brown if you don't mind. We need to get over to the hall. Miss Lawton will be damned near finished by now. Oh and show him, Miss Glover, which baggage is yours.'

Glad to get out of the tent, Harriet obliged, then struggled to catch him up, her feet hindered by the grassy clumps overtaking the field.

'Now Miss Glover, where was I? Your condition. Yes your condition. Now what would you like to say about that?'

'Absolutely nothing Mr. Sanderson. I've already told you I haven't got a condition.'

He stopped abruptly.

'Come, come now, Miss Glover. How long are we going to keep up this pretence?'

'But I'm not pretending Mr. Sanderson.'

'Really Harriet? As far as you're concerned it's a case of "Dum spiro, spero" I'm afraid.'

He held one of the old mahogany doors open barely long enough for her to get through; then forward marched leaving her panting behind him through corridor after corridor to the large baronial hall. With all heads turning they parted company as he made his way to the platform. She was hardly aware of Tricia furiously patting the empty wooden chair next to the aisle as she looked for somewhere to sit.

'Ooh you've been ages `arriet. Are you alright?'

'Oh yes thanks Tricia. He's moved me. Oh I'll tell you later.'

The hall hushed as Mr. Sanderson took centre stage. Harriet tried desperately hard to cling to the Latin fast fading from her mind. 'Dumb something. Dumb spirals. No, it couldn't have been that. Dumb spider, spidero. No it's gone. Oh I wish I'd asked him now.' Cross with herself she tried to focus on his announcements, all the time niggling her brain into recall. All the time conscious of his proximity to Lucinda Lawton. A smile. A laugh. Then a pat on her back. Harriet fizzing, decided to let go. Decided he wasn't worth the mental energy. Switched the amber light off. This time for good.

Chapter 18

'So why 'ave you got to move 'arriet?'

'Mind that big clump Tricia or you'll be tripping over too.'

'Ooh thanks 'arriet. This grass is awful to walk on. You'd think they'd try to keep it down, especially with catering for parties of children.'

'I know Tricia. It didn't stop him though, striding back to the house.'

'Oh it wouldn't 'arriet. 'e treads all over everythin' and everyone. Now what's all this about movin'?'

'It looks like he's not using that tent as an office now. He's decided to put me in there. He thinks I'm less likely to trip if I'm on the end.'

'Oh that's such a load of rubbish 'arriet. 'e's usin' that as an excuse to separate us. I think 'e'd be far better puttin' Belinda Oxfordshire in there. Quick 'urry up 'arriet, let's stick 'er stuff in there before they all come out. 'e won't know. 'e'll be sleepin' in the 'ouse anyway.'

'Oh I'm not sure about doing that. Don't forget you've got to stay around to get your money back from Rapping Hammer.'

'Now don't you worry 'arriet. I'll do that even if I 'ave to spend a couple of nights in that Lantern 'otel.'

She took a swift glance behind then struggled to speed up, dragging Harriet behind her.

'OK now 'arriet it's all clear. You get your things back 'ere and I'll bring this lot over. As soon as she comes in we'll tell 'er she's been moved.'

Panting and with only seconds to spare they just about managed it.

'Oh that was close 'arriet. Oh get right in. She's on 'er way now. She's just parted company with 'er new friend Ross. She's not lettin' go of 'im is she? You should 'ave seen 'er all over 'im in the hall just now. She's old enough to be 'is mother 'arriet. 'e doesn't look any more than eighteen. What's that new name they 'ave for cradle snatchin'? I 'eard it on the radio the other day and I said to myself I must remember that. Why is it you always forget what you're tryin' to remember 'arriet?'

'I don't know Tricia. I was trying to remember something he said to me in Latin on the way over, when I sat down by you in the hall, but it just went completely.'

'Bird brains the pair of you!'

'Oh and how long 'ave you been listenin' outside this tent?'

'I've just come in haven't I? I couldn't help but overhear.'

'Well you'll be just goin' out again won't you Belinda? Mr. Sanderson's done a bit of swappin' around and 'e's moved you to the end tent so as you can be on your own.'

'Really, Joris? What's happening to the men then?'

'They're swappin' to the middle one where 'e was goin' to be avin' is office but 'e's not now.'

The joy on her face almost lit the canvas enclosure.

'Oh dear Joris, he's taken note of my complaint. He knows just how ghastly you can be. He's such a sweetie. I expect he also wants the opportunity to have some quality time with me to get him through this frightful expedition. Have my things been moved?'

'Oh yes Belinda, everythings gone. 'e did say not to tell anyone though. You're not even to mention it to 'im because tents 'ave ears and 'e doesn't want anyone thinkin` 'e's favourin` you.'

'Well of course not. Everyone will be far too busy to even notice where I'm sleeping. Oh a whole tent to myself with only Joris allowed to enter. I could never have dreamt your lousy behaviour on the coach could lead to this. I almost feel like thanking you.'

'Oh I wouldn't bother if I were you Belinda. There is just one more thing `e wants you to 'ave though.'

'Oh a gift, too. It will be a special gift. He's left it with you? But yes of course, he would do that. He couldn't be seen to be giving me presents as well. He's certainly vying for my affection. He's probably not at all keen on all this attention Ross has been paying me. Strange! I must have got the wrong vibes over Lucinda Lawton. Yes, I'm sure I did. Highly unlikely he'd squander his reputation on another teacher.' A sense of smug satisfaction pervaded.

Harriet caught her sneer. Never in the whole of her life did she feel more like clocking her one.

'Anyhow no need to be spending any longer in here than necessary. Present please Tricia Harrington if you don't mind.'

Tricia disappeared into her bedroom to struggle out with the large square holdall, it's zip gasping to open.

'There you are Belinda. 'e advises you deposit it in the awning. With 'im sayin` that I think it might be 'elpful if you get taken short in the night.'

'Oh you're just so totally wrong Tricia Harrington. It will be a hamper. Wine and chocolates and goodies. He's such a darling. I don't want to disappoint either of you but don't be too surprised if you hear our engagement's back on. One in the eye for you all including Lucinda Lawton. Such a sponge-head that girl.'

Harriet and Tricia peeped from behind the canvas folds of doorway to watch her totter between the pegs to the end tent; her elbows close to her sides, catching the weight of the holdall.

'What was in it? I thought that was vital luggage of yours? Oh come on Tricia you've got to tell me.'

''as she gone?' Tricia's words exploded from her taut ballooning cheeks as she bent herself in two trying to laugh quietly.

'Yes, she's in there now, present and all. Go on Tricia, tell me. What was in it?'

'I've given 'er my porta-potti 'arriet. Oh I wish I could see 'er face when she opens it.'

With shoulders shaking Harriet made for the bed. Then off it. This was the most excruciatingly painful laughter she could recall. Terrified of being heard they rolled around consuming every corner of space the tent would allow, oblivious to the young man suddenly appearing in the doorway.

'Oh `ello Ross. You'll `ave to forgive me and my friend `arriet. I'm Tricia by the way. We were sittin` behind you on the coach comin` `ere, if you remember?' She just managed to screech the words out before collapsing against the canvas wall, behind.

'Steady Tricia.' He looked across to Harriet. 'You two prepared to share the joke?'

'Oh sorry Ross, you'll `ave to forgive us. It's just that `arriet and I `ave `ad a very funny experience.'

'Go on then, don't keep it all to yourselves.'

He looked across. Smiled at Harriet. Pushed his rimless spectacles further up his nose. 'Hmm! Seriously intellectual, or is it just his glasses?' Harriet thought, watching him scratch momentarily at his curly brown hair.

'Look I'm Ross Farquerhart. PhD gathering, unfortunately. Very pleased to meet you.'

Harriet took his hand.

'Harriet Glover. I'm pleased to meet you, too.'

'Oh no, not *the* Harriet Glover every one talks about. I'd decided it was *her!*'

He pointed a long pale finger at Tricia, then turned back to Harriet. 'You just don't look like you could cause that much trouble. Now if it was her I could understand it.' Harriet sensed him stretching his intellect to the limit.

'Oh yes and what exactly do you mean by that Ross Harquer.., er Ross Farquerhart? And who else `as been sayin` things about `arriet anyway? Apart from that Belinda Oxfordshire. I could `ear `er talkin` on the coach. Well you'll `ave to put up with my behaviour, I'm very sorry to `ave to say. It's my `usband she pinched not `ers. Well `arriet `asn't got an `usband `ave you `arriet, so she could `ardly `ave pinched yours.'

'Oh unmarried. My lucky day!' Ross grinned. Tricia jumped on him.

'`arriet's got enough complications in `er life, `aven't you `arriet, without you startin` to wind up any more. As a matter of fact that's why Mr. Sanderson's moved `er to the end tent along there.' Tricia gesticulated to her right, winking at Harriet as Ross Farquerhart poked his nose out to see just where she meant. Then promptly addressed Harriet.

'I'm good at analysis. Origin of the species and all that. It's probably your genes Harriet. Let's put it down to the rogue gene. A little evolutionary quirk.'

He was looking at her. Gosh it reminded her of Barry. Barry and the way he caught her eye on that first canal trip in Venice. Flattered and flummoxed. She scrambled for words.

'It's probably best not to believe all you hear Ross, especially when it's coming from Belinda Oxfordshire.'

'Point taken. I could have done without it whilst I was trying to come up with my best line.'

'Oh get it written first Ross. Then polish it off if you've got time. What do you propose to do with it anyway? Surely not teaching kids in a primary school?'

'What do I intend to do with it, Harriet? My best line? Well I'd wait and see if I were you. Now what was it that was so funny when I arrived?'

'Oh shall we tell 'im 'arriet?'

Harriet froze. Shook her head at Tricia. Wondered what had got into her.

'Oh I know 'arriet won't mind me tellin' you this Ross, but the first thing we did when we got 'ere was look over the cliff the other side of that fence. Of course we still 'ad our suitcases and 'arriet got just a teeny weeny bit too close to the edge with 'ers and it went over, didn't it 'arriet? The lid flung open and all 'er knickers and bras went flyin'. We couldn't stand up for laughin' could we 'arriet?'

'No Tricia.' The relief accompanying those two words was almost tangible.

'So you might come across them Ross while you're fossil 'untin'.'

'Indeed I might. I'll be sure to return anything I find.'

Harriet wasn't the only one blushing. The poor boy could barely get out of the tent fast enough.

'Oh what was it you came for Ross? I don't think you said.' Tricia called after him.

''e's just said somethin' back 'arriet. I couldn't 'ear what it was though.'

'Just as well Tricia. Gosh I hope we don't get into trouble over all this.'

Chapter 19

'It's very quiet in 'ers. Didn't she come back last night?'

Mrs. Bustard, curious, pointed her finger at the still fully zipped bedroom compartment adjacent to hers.

'Oh we don't know what 'appened to 'er do we 'arriet? Did you 'ave a good sleep Beattie?'

'Oh I did thanks Tricia. Do you know that's the best night's sleep I've 'ad in sixteen years. It's the pickled onions. Our Bert can't stop eatin' them. Well you know that don't you Miss Glover. Remember our Danny pinchin' them bulbs off the lunch trolley in your classroom, and the little bugger already 'ad 'is pockets full from that sack out front. It nearly finished our Bert off that did. Me cookin' them thinkin' they were onions. Still 'e might 'ave to get used to them. I can see me pullin' them up from people's gardens to give us somethin' to eat if things go on like this.'

'Look Mrs. Bustard. You make the most of this break. Get yourself first in the queue for breakfast and make sure you have plenty. I'll keep an eye on Danny too, this week, even when I'm not on duty. It won't do any harm for all of you to strengthen your reserves.'

Harriet swallowed hard on the lump rising in her throat threatening to block her words. Knew her advice was cursory to the point of being useless, serving only to strengthen her own determination to help.

Mrs. Bustard smiled. 'Ah thanks Miss Glover. You're such a good'n you. We'll get by. We'll manage somehow. Anyway 'adn't we better be gettin' to them showers? I think we 'ave to be relievin' the early shift at nine.'

'Oh 'e 'asn't got us all sorted out doin' shifts 'as 'e?' Tricia cut in. 'Where did it say that Beattie?'

''ang on a minute. Look, 'ere it is on this bit of white paper. It was in the middle of that information leaflet 'e gave us. Didn't you get one?'

'It must 'ave fallen out. You didn't 'ave one either did you 'arriet?'

'Gosh, no. Let's have a look. Oh I see. He's done this by tent. We rotate with Enid Frost's lot on early and late shifts. Seeing to the girls we are. Ah right, the men are doing the same with the boys. Then he's gone back to night shift pairs during the day. Oh golly this is complicated. I'm surprised he didn't write it all in Latin to completely confound us.'

'Ah, in here Miss Glover? Fair enough. I trust you slept well enough in the far tent?'

Harriet jumped.

'Oh yes thank you Mr. Sanderson. I'm also being very careful of all these tent pegs.'

'Yes indeed Miss Glover. Just popped in to say, much as I thought, there's a small office over there which I've been very kindly invited to partake of so I shan't be disturbing you. Consider the tent to be your own from now on Miss Glover.'

'Oh thank you, that's very kind of you Mr. Sanderson,' replied Harriet relieved to hear that.

'You're all ready for action, I see?'

'Oh no Mr. Sanderson we `aven't `ad our showers yet. We're just on our way now.'

'Come on get going. We don't want any overlapping of shifts if we can help it. Fifteen minutes and the children will be filing in for breakfast.'

They let him get well away then grabbed their things to head for the shower-block, Mrs. Bustard speeding ahead.

'Oh `arriet, look who it is. She's already `ad `ers.'

'That was a stroke of good fortune Tricia.'

'What was `arriet?'

'The tent, she wasn't anywhere near it just now. He probably had a nose in there first.'

'Well it has just struck me if we `adn't `ad done that we could `ave both shared it. At least we'd `ave `ad a bit more room. We've just `anded it all to `er on a plate. Shall we try to get `er out again?'

'Shush Tricia, she's heading for us.'

'Oh `ello Belinda. `ow did you get on with your `amper then?'

'Just as predicted. Wine, caviar, pate de foie gras, a wealth of cheeses, chocolates. Oh he's such a sweetie. I haven't seen him to thank him yet.'

'Oh `e went back to the `ouse Belinda. I don't think `e'll want you to thank `im `ere, though. Don't forget what `e said about favouritism.'

'Oh well perhaps you're right. I expect he'll pop in to share it with me this evening.'

'Oh but I think you'll find it's your turn for night duty. It's you and Ross Farquerhart tonight if I'm rememberin` correctly. You'll be needin` to get some sleep this afternoon, too. Lookin` at it I think that's `ow Mr. Sanderson worked the rota.'

'Oh well most of it's in the house, refrigerated now, it'll keep for a few days yet.'

She walked off convinced of her words.

'She's good at kiddin` `erself wouldn't you say `arriet? I'd love to `ave seen `er face when she found my porta-potti. I don't see as she'll be goin` out of `er way to be thankin` `im for that.'

'No definitely not.' Harriet looked at her watch. 'Golly Tricia we're going to be really late. OH NO! Look, it's Tarquin Bridgewater waving from over there. He's the last person I want to see at the moment. I haven't worked out what to tell him yet. Come on, quick. We're already late.'

'`e's beetlin` along `arriet. I don't see as `ow as we can `elp but talk to `im.'

'Ah good morning ladies. And Harriet my dear. A bit of a scamp my little Harriet. Got me into a bit of a fix! Still, my fault. My fault! You weren't to know you were distributing my prized cannabis plants around the whole of Stetmead.'

Her cheeks burning red, she looked to the clump of grass caught between her feet.

'I'm just teasing you my dear. Half of them are on it anyway.'

'Jail Mr. Bridgewater, they're not going to put you in jail? Please no. Has Mr. Sanderson bailed you out for this trip? I'm sure you don't feel like being here.'

He placed his large weatherworn hand on her shoulder. Guffawed down her ear.

'Just a caution my dear. You know how it started?'

'No, no Mr. Bridgewater, except that it was me. I really am terribly sorry.'

'No my dear, I mean why I started growing them.'

'Oh sorry, no. Do tell me.' Harriet turned as Tricia offered a quick wave to an already showered Mrs. Bustard rushing past.

'Henrietta. I grew it for Henrietta to ease the pain.'

'Oh I'm so sorry to hear that Mr. Bridgewater.'

'Of course she's been gone a long time now but at the time I needed something to help me come to terms with losing her. I carried on growing it. Of course a loose word. A nod and a wink. Young Guy Hammer at the garden centre soon had me supplying his brother and that rock band of his. Shouldn't have done it really but there you are. Between you and me it's provided a bit of pocket money.'

'Oh I'm really sorry to have dropped you in it. I feel dreadful now. You'll lose all that.'

He touched the side of his nose a couple of times.

'Ways and means my dear. Keep it under your hat though.'

'Oh Mr. Bridgewater please don't grow any more. You don't want to end up in jail.'

'Oh don't you be worrying about me dear. Now when are we supposed to be canoeing in the bay with the kids? That's what I'm here for.'

'Gosh I didn't know we were.'

'Here, let me look at this again. I must admit I haven't taken it out of my pocket since our friend Joris passed it all over. Here it is, inside this lot. The green one as I recall.'

'Oh Mr. Bridgewater would you mind if we borrow it, we'll need to know what's been planned?'

'With pleasure my dear. Oh here it is. Boating tomorrow and Wednesday.'

'Oh thank you Mr. Bridgewater. We'll make sure you get it back.'

Tricia looked at her watch.

'Yes, thanks ever so much Mr. Bridgewater. I'm afraid we're very late and we'll 'ave to go. We're supposed to be 'elpin' with breakfast.'

'Before you go dear I must thank you for standing in for Iris down at the sailing club. You did a good job by all accounts. Oh I heard about that "save Venice" tin of yours too. Sorry I missed the cleavage dear but the local paper's been making up for it.'

A mortified Tricia turned to Harriet as he sauntered off.

'Oh did you 'ear that 'arriet? I'm feelin' really embarrassed. I wish I 'adn't done it now.'

'Can't change it,' Harriet panted as their fast walk turned into a run. 'Wasn't Rapping Hammer supposed to be phoning you?'

'Yes `e was `arriet. I'd forgotten all about it. I do `ope the thing doesn't go off when I'm in the shower.'

Chapter 20

'I see you two have dawdled deliberately. Ross and I have done all the work.'

'As a matter of fact Belinda we got delayed,' insisted Tricia. 'First by Mr. Sanderson and then Mr. Bridgewater. We could `ardly be rude could we `arriet?'

'Ross, they're here now,' she called. 'Let's leave them to it.'

'OK Belinda. I just want a quick word with Harriet,' Ross replied.

They crossed paths as she walked off in a scowl.

'You OK Ross?' Harriet enquired. 'She's not getting to you is she?'

'What, the camp's cougar? I'm made of sterner stuff.'

'Oh that's it `arriet. That was the word I was tryin` to remember.'

For a fleeting second Harriet felt compelled to retrieve yesterday's lost Latin before thinking better of it. He'd blown the fuse on her amber light to take her somewhere dark and empty. She needed to move on now. She just wished she knew how.

'Oh I wish Bob was made of sterner stuff. `e couldn't resist `er charms.'

'I'm not sure I'm aware of any. Now Harriet have you worked out my best line yet?'

'No Ross. Was I supposed to?'

'You were delivered of a clue yesterday.'

'I know, you've found one of `arriet's bra's `angin` off a fossil, `aven't you Ross?'

'Now that would be telling Tricia.' He turned to Harriet.

'No hurry. You've got as long as it takes for me to finish my PhD.'

Off he went with Harriet none the wiser.

'Come along you two, the children have almost finished. Mrs. Harrington start collecting the empty plates will you from the far end of the table.'

'Oh right Mr. Sanderson. I got a fright then. I didn't know you `ad come up behind us like that.'

'Get on with it Mrs. Harrington. Now Miss Glover a word if I may. I need to slip out with Lucinda for a couple of hours. Do you think you could hold the fort along with Mr. Whittle?'

'What exactly are the children supposed to be doing this morning Mr. Sanderson?'

'I assumed you'd be fully au fait with the laid down procedure by now Miss Glover.'

'Well I've only just found out from Mr. Bridgewater there is one, Mr. Sanderson. There wasn't anything included in the information leaflet.'

'Indeed. You do surprise me. Anyhow it won't be difficult. The children are assembling here at ten thirty to hear Ross imparting the whys and wherefores of fossil hunting. We'll be taking them on a short expedition this afternoon but Lucinda and I will be back well before then.'

Harriet knew she had no choice. She took her jealous curiosity out on the dirty plates as she clattered them down one on top of the other along the tabletop meeting Tricia in the middle doing exactly the same. She seized the opportunity to spill it all out.

'I'm not doing it Tricia. I'm going to tell him I've got a migraine or something. I'm not being planted with Mr. Whittle for the next couple of hours while he goes off with her. I can't stand the man.'

'Oh `arriet, `ang on a minute, I think I can `ear my moby ringin`. `ang on just let me get my bag.'

Agitated, Harriet looked round the room wondering whether Mr. Sanderson had already left.

'Oh `arriet, it was Rappin` `ammer. They're on their way. `e's been talkin` to Guy. `e said Belinda Oxfordshire told `im exactly where we were goin`. She'd been to the garden centre lookin` for insect repellent and nobbled `im. `e wants to meet us in Churndale Village in `alf an hour. I told `im we'd meet `im in that Lantern `otel pub place in the doorway.'

'But Tricia, I can't go. I've just told you he's asked me to stay here.'

'Of course you can `arriet. I'm not goin` without you. If we don't go `e'll only end up bringin` `is van down `ere. We don't want them druggies rockin` around the campsite, do we? Look `e's just left the kitchens. `e's on `is way over to `er now. Go and tell `im about your bad `ead.'

Harriet rushed to catch him.

'Look Mr. Sanderson I'm terribly sorry. I woke up with it. I've got a crashing migraine now. I'm going to have to lie down. Will someone else stand in please?'

'Hang on a minute Lucinda. Miss Frost! Miss Frost! A word if you will?'

Harriet covered her forehead with her hand and made to go.

'Miss Glover! Miss Glover! I suggest you take to your tent. Go and lie down at once.'

Harriet grabbed her bag not sure which tent to make for. Couldn't risk the end one. She jumped as Tricia rushed at her from behind the front door.

'Quick `arriet. Let's get goin`.'

'There's only one road out of here Tricia. They'll see us.'

'Oh they won't be walkin` `arriet `e'll get a car from somewhere. We'll `ide behind that lodge by the gates until they've disappeared. Come on `arriet or they'll catch us before we even get there. Jump this wall. They won't see us behind the shrubs.'

Over the wall without a second to spare. A quick peep and Tricia ducked down again.

'They've just gone `arriet. I've just seen `im with `er goin` past in a big posh car. It was beige `arriet, come to think of it I think I saw that parked down that side. I don't like them coloured cars. Anyway by the time we get there, they'll be well on their way to wherever they're goin`, the way `e drives.'

'Yes Tricia and I wonder where that will be?'

'Look `arriet I think you're goin` to `ave to be readin` my diary again. You need to remind yourself of `ow `orrible `e is.'

Harriet took a deep breath. Let it fill her cheeks then blew out long and hard.

'I can't help it Tricia. I can't stand seeing him with her.'

'Well you might `ave to get used to it `arriet. Especially if `e ends up marryin`
`er.'

'Oh thanks Tricia. That's all I need.'

Chapter 21

They'd misjudged the distance. Naturally it had seemed much shorter by coach. It was quite a trek along little more than a country lane before the odd chimney pot appeared over the horizon.

'Oh I do `ope Rappin` `ammer's still there `arriet. I thought it would only be five minutes.'

'Same here Tricia but we're not going to be able to stop long. We'll need to get back, at least before them. I'm supposed to be resting in Belinda Oxfordshire's tent, fending off a migraine.'

'That's alright `arriet. It'll only be a question of `im `andin` the tin over. Oh `ere we are now. Look there's the letterbox and the post office. The pub's a bit more set back as `ow I remember.'

'TRICIA, look over there. Is that *his* car outside the jewellers? Oh no I don't believe it. He's taken her there to buy an engagement ring. Oh we don't want them to see us.'

'That beige one? Yes, yes that's the one `e was drivin`. I'd be more worried about `im seein` us `arriet. Come on let's get into the pub before they come out.'

Singed with jealousy Harriet's sudden spurt left Tricia breathless as they landed on the brown bristly doormat sunk into the carpet on the other side of the door. It reminded her of school. How many times had she hovered on that one, wiping her feet to excess for fear of seeing him.

'I wonder where they are `arriet? No sign of them.'

'Still in that flipping jewellers. His car's still there.' She peered through the lead lights stretching her neck to the limit, just able make it out. She became increasingly irritated by the waves in the tiny square panes of glass, for obscuring the view.

'It's Rappin` `ammer I'm talkin` about `arriet, not `im. It's no good you gettin` all worked up like this, after all you `ave committed yourself to Mark. It won't work if you're feelin` as strongly as this about our friend Joris.'

'I just wanted to stay on amber Tricia. I wasn't bargaining on this.'

'Well I've told you before, `aven't I `arriet?'

'Told me what Tricia?'

'You can't expect everyone else to want to do the same.'

They reached the bar. No sign of anyone. Went through to walk around the open areas either side, then back again along the entrance hall to peer out of the same window by the open front door.

'Oh good, there's someone. Let's ask him,' Harriet suggested, momentarily looking behind her.

'You `aven't seen a short guy with long dark greasy `air `ave you? `e might `ave `ad the rest of the band with `im,' Tricia smiled.

'I'm delighted to say I haven't and should you have the misfortune to locate him, kindly steer him away from here, will you?'

The gentleman in the mid-grey pinstriped suit waved his clipboard towards the door before returning to the bar. Suddenly Harriet jumped and grabbed the door to push it swiftly across the doormat just missing Tricia's toes as it closed. She stepped back in horror.

'Ouch `arriet. What ever are you doin`?'

'Oops, sorry Tricia, they're just on their way.'

'Well never mind closin` it. We'd better shout over `arriet. Let them know we're `ere. We don't want to miss them.'

'No Tricia, Mr. Sanderson and Lucinda Lawton. I've just seen them coming out of the shop. Let's give them a minute. Duck down, get below the glass.'

'Ah, did I hear the door catching your foot? Difficult to attend to down there. Do come through. Have one on the house. I fear my dislike of such people sometimes gets the better of me.'

Always conscious of his reputation and anxious not to offend, the man in the grey pinstriped suit scooped them back along the entrance hall with his clipboard then ushered them forward to the bar. He smiled at Harriet. Placed his hand in hers.

'Clive Engells, delighted to have the pleasure.'

'Oh I'm Harriet Glover and this is Tricia Harrington. We're with the school party camping just down the road.'

'Ah, I see. Lost a few on the way? Secondary school I take it? A dishevelled music teacher and his escapees? A band of rocking students. Heaven help us that they should have arrived here. These days there seems to be no consideration given to the reputation of the school when they make such appointments.'

'Yes, now as *Harriet's* just said I'm Tricia *Harrington*. Very pleased to meet you.'

He shook her hand with less exuberance than Harriet's. She put him in his early fifties, fashion conscious even down to his shiny grey hair, cut in such a way as to be a testimony to the very best in contemporary tonsorial art.

Suddenly he marched to the small table bordering the arch by the far window. The first of many laid for lunch. Pulling the chairs away he nodded them over, looking at his watch.

'Do allow me the honour of offering you both lunch on the house. Now those drinks, what will it be?'

Harriet flashed that devil-may-care look at Tricia. Delighted at the chance to liquefy some of this seething rage.

'G &T please, really that is very kind.'

'Oh and I'll `ave the same thank you. Just a little one though. I think `arriet and I will `ave to be gettin` back.'

Feeling as sour as the lemon sliced to the edge of the rim, Harriet watched the rapidly melting ice cube quickly disperse the fizz popping away at the surface diluting the drink in the glass. Embarrassed she forced a smile as the bottle of Bombay Sapphire crossed her sights, his dazzling white cuffs just below his wrists sporting "CE" gold initial links.

'Of course we get many school parties tripping through Churndale to the campsite down the road. We've provided many a respite for the furtive teacher. It's surprising how easily recognisable they are. It's always in their gaze. Tend to look over your shoulder whilst speaking, as if the enemy were about to land.'

He chortled, then turned, beckoning the waiter. Before they knew it their orders had gone through. They gazed at the gin now considerably depleted in the clear glass bottle he'd placed on the table alongside the untouched bottles of tonic water. Staring at the reason why, both could barely recall any of the earlier need to panic. Harriet laughed as Tricia's exuberance sent her chocolate mousse spinning round the plate pausing it only to lick the back of the spoon before doing it again.

It was great fun until Harriet looked up.

'Keep your head down Tricia. I've just spotted them.'

'Oh no 'arriet I want my "save Venice tin" back. Where are they, I can't see them?'

'*TRICIA! Turn round.*' It was the loudest she dared whisper.

Harriet watched Lucinda Lawton briefly disappear only to catch Mr. Sanderson and Clive Engells up as they launched into conversation like old friends.

'It's Mr. Sanderson Tricia. Look he's talking to Clive Engells. No don't look. Ooooh they're heading this way. Get down now Tricia. Let's get our bags and get out!'

Still as silverfish under threat they watched two pairs of highly polished shoes and one pair of high heels stride past from below the folds of the tablecloth, the accompanying chatter fading as they moved along towards the archway.

''ave they gone 'arriet? I don't think I can 'ear them anymore.'

'Phew, all clear Tricia. Oh no Clive Engells he's on his way back.'

'Good chance to thank 'im 'arriet before we go.'

'Ah ladies. All finished?' He turned to the rumpus, scowling at the thundering noise heading towards the bar. 'The missing musician, no doubt. Hells bells we're serving lunch. We can't be invaded by this bunch of low-life, teacher or not.'

'Oh that's alright Mr. Engells we'll take them outside.'

'Do before they take root.'

'They're fuckin' well sittin' in that bay window. Wouldn't you know it Rux? Iron kecks Mummy-Mamma would 'ave 'er arse planted there.'

Wooziness gave way to fury as Harriet turned to face him. Too late, from behind Mr. Sanderson took the words from her mouth.

'You boy, apologise this minute!'

'Not the music teacher then Joris? But the rest of the lads, I thought yours were primary?' Clive Engells looked as confused as the chocolate mousse semi-disintegrated from being spun too rapidly round the plate.

''is fuckin' music teacher mate? Get real! I'm the world-famous Rapping Hammer just back from Venice. We've pitched our patch down the road.'

'You've done what, young man?' Mr. Sanderson's voice well raised now. He almost forgot where he was.

'It's not just there for your fuckin` lot. We're overnightin` in the field behind the `ouse. Gives me chance to see the ditchwater.' In all her life Harriet had never received a more vile look.

'Lyme Bay you're speaking off?' Clive Engells looked suitably offended.

'Call it what you friggin` like. She nearly `ad the ditchwater banged up.'

'OUT BOY, OUT! NOW!'

'But yours are primary Joris as I've always understood?' Clive Engells queried, registering complete and utter confusion.

'Oh `e thinks I'm bleedin` six. Treats us like we're all `is kids. Just like can-legs over there.' Rapping Hammer smirked at Harriet as her cheeks flushed to the colour of the velvet draping the window. She looked away to see diners shuffling their seats around trying to get a better view of the commotion.

'You'd need a tin-opener on `er.' She caught the lads scissoring their two fingers at her, elbowing each other, falling around spewing out bouts of uncontrollable laughter.

'THAT'S QUITE ENOUGH. OUT BOY, THE LOT OF YOU, THIS MINUTE!'

Such was Mr. Sanderson's rage-laced authority they moved to go.

'World famous, did you say?' With his clipboard Clive Engells suddenly opened his arms like bat's wings, hovered a minute before propelling them towards a closed door to the right of the bar, ushering them into a small room reserved for intimate social gatherings. Then a quick word with the bar tender. Then forward of each other, two bar men, each carrying a tray loaded with drinks disappeared one behind the other as they entered their room.

'Migraine Miss Glover? I hardly think so! Get yourselves back to the campsite this minute. The rota's already in total disarray.'

They watch him stride away to catch up with Lucinda Lawton, long since seated at the table for two, three back from under the arch.

'Well I do `ope we've ruined their little celebration lunch `arriet.'

'I don't think that's all we've ruined today, Tricia. Come on, let's get back.'

Chapter 22

Their legs heavy and uncooperative, their heads thumping, their minds a mix of fury and fear, they made their way through curious faces still lunching and then down the passageway to the bristly brown mat at the foot of the door.

Simultaneously they lifted their eyes. Just brushing the tops of their heads now an arm reaching above them. The gold initials "CE" fastening the spanking white cuff just forward of their noses as he opened the door to first let Harriet and then Tricia out. He smiled.

'They've calmed down. Agreed to a spot of lunch. Of course we're not all au fait with the rock world's rich and famous. I've seen it before. One wrong word tweeted. The likes of them can end up closing a place like this down. But they're hardly *your* aquaintances? You were looking for them, though?' His concern now focussed on Harriet.

'Look if I can be of help I'm only a phone call away.' He slipped her his card. "Clive Engells Solicitor and Commissioner for Oaths".

'But I thought this was your hotel. Can you do both?'

'I can and I do. This is a family concern, one of the few independents left. But the firm runs efficiently enough in my absence, as it should. Sean's somewhere off the Turkish coast leading the flotilla just now. I always stand in. Protecting the investment so to speak.'

'Ah right.' Harriet smiled.

'Joris your head then?'

'Well just now we wish `e wasn't don't we `arriet?' Tricia piped up. 'But `ow come you know `im?'

'Through Sean. He crewed for him in the Fastnet race a couple of years back. He's stayed here on a number of occasions. Yes, I've met a few of his girlfriends, too.'

Harriet didn't need to know this. Her mouth opened like the door just pulled on a tumble dryer, its contents red hot.

'It would seem that's the way he is Mr. Engells.'

'Do call me Clive, Harriet. How fortunate he is to have two such lovely ladies in his domain.' He caught Harriet's eye, so obviously loading the compliment her way. She struggled to say something.

'Fastnet did you say?'

'Yes that's right but they've sailed aplenty round here. Sean's moored in Poole Harbour. I think Joris's is still down in Falmouth since he and Sean brought it back from the Med.'

'So you've met a lot of his girlfriends then?' Harriet couldn't resist.

'I certainly have Harriet. Now who was that very beautiful young lady stayed over just a few weeks back? Couldn't bear to sleep on the yacht so they broke their journey to spend the night here. Oh, it could have been the young lady he's dining with now. What's her name?'

Livid, Harriet instantly became devoid of all speech. Thought. 'And how many others *wanted* to sleep on it, apart from me? He probably sailed each one on to The Bangles to make love on the sand.'

Obligingly Tricia filled the silence.

'Oh I `ave a feelin` that will be Lucinda Lawton, Clive. That's who you were thinkin` of.'

'Ah yes Lucinda. We've all got great hopes there.'

'Well thank you again for lunch Mr. Engells we really need to be getting back.' Harriet could do little to erase the strained tone to her voice. Her legs pressed together she suddenly approved of Rapping Hammer's description. This guy had just pulled the ring on the can and the widget that was Harriet was so frothed in rage she couldn't bare to look at him. She pulled at Tricia's arm. 'We've got to go.'

'Alright `arriet, I'm comin`. Oh and if you want to get on the right side of `im in there, Rappin` `ammer that is, just drop a few `ints that your Sean might take `im on the next Fastnet Race. `e's obsessed with it. Well not as obsessed as `e is with somethin` else but we won't go there just at the moment.'

'Come on Tricia, we'll never get back.'

'Well thanks for the tip Patricia. Such a lovely name. If you don't mind I'd rather not shorten it.'

'Oh not at all Clive. I'm amenable to most things, aren't I `arriet?'

'Sorry Tricia I'm going. We've got to get back.'

'OK `arriet, wait for me, I'm comin`. Bye for now Clive. Thank you ever so much for lunch.'

They turned the corner past the post office and the jewellers on the opposite side.

'Tricia, I'm going in. I'm going in. I've got to find out. I need to know.'

'Goin` in where `arriet?'

'I'm crossing over to the jewellers. Come on, we can pretend we're just looking and we've just decided to drop in.'

'Oh I'm not sure that's such a good idea `arriet. I thought you wanted to get back.'

'Well I do but I need to know Tricia.'

'We'll all know soon enough when she starts flashin` it around.'

'Well I don't intend to be around to find out. I just couldn't stand it. Don't forget I'm expecting his baby.'

'Oh come on then `arriet. We've `ad far too much gin or we wouldn't be doin` this.'

They crossed over trying not to see the beige car still parked outside. Pushing the door open they headed for the display cabinet opposite the counter.

'Ooh that's nice `arriet. I've always wanted a gold bangle like that. It's a bit like yours `arriet. The one `e gave you.'

'No, I don't want to be reminded of that just now, thank you, Tricia.'

'Oh sorry `arriet but I'm just tryin` to remember those lovely words `e `ad engraved for you on the inside. Ooh what were they? In English I mean, not the

Latin.'

'Shush Tricia or she'll come over.'

'Just tell me then. It's startin` to annoy me that I can't remember.'

' "One day this will be pleasing to remember". That was some of it. Oh gosh Tricia. I had him. He was mine for the taking. What did I do?'

'If you'd like to step aside I'll open the cabinet. Was it any particular piece you were interested in?'

They turned to the tall thin lady with dark curly hair and gold rimmed spectacles shaped almost like sideways carrots.

'Oh we're just `avin` a little look, aren't we `arriet? `arriet's gettin` engaged and `er fiancée to be `as asked `er to tell `im which ring she'd like. `asn't `e `arriet?'

'Hmm, perhaps you'd like to come to the counter in that case. The rings are displayed here.'

They followed her over. Harriet wishing for all the world she hadn't started this.

'Now have a look along and anything that catches your eye I'll lift out.' She turned to Tricia.

'And are you to be the bridesmaid?'

'Oh yes most definitely, aren't I `arriet? We went to Venice. Well we `aven't been long back really and `arriet met this gorgeous man. `e `as long dark `air and e's got looks to die for. You fell for Barry as soon as you saw `im didn't you `arriet?'

Harriet pretended not to hear. Moved herself to the far end of the counter, as far away from Tricia as possible.

'Oh lovely. Do you know it's such a coincidence. We had a gentleman in here only today fits that description. Well maybe not that good-looking but then that's always a matter of taste. He was looking at rings too. But then with the hotel and the campsite down the road we do get a lot of young couples buying the ring here. It's such a beauty spot, so romantic. They call that "the honeymoon hotel".' She turned to the window to point across the road.

'Oh do they now!' Harriet fizzed to herself distracted from the task in hand, then she suddenly decided to speak.

'Actually we're working on a surprise engagement present for a couple trying to keep their marriage a secret.' Harriet needn't have bothered. The assistant wasn't listening.

'Does anything there take your fancy?' She continued.

Harriet moved back towards the door. Pointed to a tray of rings groaning with solitaire diamonds. 'Ah there's a gap there, you didn't happen to sell that one this morning to the couple I've just been talking about did you? You see, if you did, we could buy the present from here, now.' The assistant still wasn't listening.

'Ah always a favourite. Now we must remember the three C's, here,' the assistant smiled.

His mother. *His mother* had said that last Christmas day. She'd been wearing Mark's engagement ring. Why wasn't she now? Then she remembered he couldn't commit. She swallowed hard on that lump again, rising in her throat, just as the door started rattling behind her. 'He's good-looking with blue eyes as deep as the sea and a mop of blonde hair. He's got a gorgeous smile with compelling, elongated dimples. You couldn't miss him. It would be so helpful....'

'Now this gentleman,' continued the assistant, deciding to take an interest. 'No, we've just determined, haven't we he's dark, not blonde and he certainly didn't have blue eyes. Do you know I've been racking my brains trying to think of his name. Something very unusual.' She searched Tricia's face for the answer then turned to Harriet. 'This tray is it?'

'No it's that ring there,' said Harriet in despair. 'Top left on the next tray. The amber one shaped like a buttercup.' Tricia stretched over the counter unable to contain herself.

'You're not thinkin` of Barry Giordano are you? That's a very unusual name.'

'Who?' The assistant popped her head up. From her knees placed the tray on the counter. Glanced at the door.

'Barry Giordano,' repeated Tricia loudly, determined to catch the shop assistant's attention. Harriet jumped.

'Yes, I would be inclined to choose that one Miss Glover. Amber! Remind him of just where you like to be!'

'Oh no `arriet doesn't want that one, do you `arriet? She's lookin` for a Bombay sapphire Mr. Sanderson.'

Chapter 23

Harriet tried not to notice Lucinda Lawton darting her eyes around the display in the shop window as they both rushed out.

'Oh 'arriet we'd better 'urry up. We don't want them two passin' us on the way back. I do 'ope I 'aven't made things worse. My 'ead feels very not 'ere with all that gin.'

'No Tricia. It's my fault. It was me that wanted to go in. Stupid. Stupid. Stupid. We've both had too much gin. We'd never have done it otherwise.'

'Keep goin' 'arriet, we don't want them catchin' us up.'

'Gosh my legs feel so wobbly I can hardly move. We're on tea-time duty as well. Oh golly Tricia I'm already in trouble for ducking out this morning.'

'Well it's no better for me 'arriet I wasn't supposed to be 'ere either. And as soon as 'e finds out Rappin' 'ammer's only 'ere because of me and my "save Venice" tin I'm goin' to be in for it anyway. I didn't think 'e would be campin' up 'ere. I do 'ope 'e doesn't cause any more trouble.'

Like startled birds they suddenly flew to the fence, turning to the continuous blast of a horn. Then Rapping Hammer's pantechnicon flattening the long grass almost at their feet as he sped past and away.

'Oooh that was close 'arriet. Talk of the devil. It looks like 'e's drivin' that thing in a very bad mood. I notice 'e wasn't stoppin' to offer us a lift.'

'Thank goodness Tricia. Do you know, this is beginning to feel worse than Venice.'

Still panting, Tricia glanced behind.

'Watch out. Now it's *them* 'arriet. It's 'is 'orrible beige car comin' up.'

Harriet felt sick, with nowhere to hide she hoped against hope he wouldn't stop.

'Oh we're alright 'arriet. 'e's gone ahead. Oh no 'e 'asn't. 'e's stopped. 'e's gettin' out now.'

'Get in, both of you.' Instantly immobilised, Harriet looked at Tricia.

'Come along, come along. Keep moving. Never mind trying to stretch it out to tea-time. We'll all miss this damned expedition at this rate.'

They sank into the rear seats, closing the doors behind them. Already they were speeding down the lane to the camp site with not a word spoken until a barely discernible muttering in the direction of Lucinda Lawton as she moved to get out of the car.

'Mrs. Harrington get back to your duties this minute!'

'Miss Glover. Follow me!'

One step behind him all the way to the small office down the long hall in the big old house. He held the door as she followed him in.

'Take a seat Miss Glover.' The wrong side of the desk.

Then a bang. The wrong side of the door. He disappeared leaving her there without explanation. She looked around. The ceiling disproportionately high for the size of the room. Walls a dingy yellow to the dado rail forming a shelf above the dark wood panelling, the narrow sash window letting in little light. She looked at her watch. Undid, then crossed her legs again. Stranding her hair between her fingers she twisted to look back at the door. Tempted, she moved to open it then convinced herself he'd be back any minute now.

'Flipping heck Mr. Sanderson if you're that keen for me to get back to it what are you playing at?'

The arguments proliferated in her head.

'So you didn't believe me about the painting. Couldn't wait to jump into bed with Lucinda bloody Lawton either and now you're marrying her. Well I hope you'll be very happy! DON'T!' She sniffed on the sneer, threatening to settle on her face when the door flew open.

'I'm afraid Mr. Sanderson's caught up with something else. He says he'll speak to you later.'

'How later Lucinda?'

'Well given his frame of mind it's anyone's guess. I think it's probably better you don't wait here. The children have already gathered for their expedition. I wouldn't advise you be late for that.'

Livid, Harriet grabbed her bag and followed her out of the room. Pleased she'd gone the other way. Thought. 'At least I've been spared that. Huh! He promised *me* that job, then reneged, him and Mr. Whittle between them. Wouldn't think I'd ever got a damehood for all it means.' She fumed her way down the long corridor and out into the early afternoon sunshine to the children clutching at haversacks being bossed into pairs by Enid Frost as she led them towards the gate. Harriet tried to ignore the bright yellow spot in front of her eyes, bouncing from the top of their heads as she walked towards them.

'Oh Enid, can you hang on a minute please? I need to get my stuff. You haven't got them all yet?'

'No, no. That's alright Harriet. I don't know where Sir's got to. We won't be going without him, anyway.'

Harriet rushed off not wishing to know where "Sir" had got to. Her head throbbing now she made towards the tent regretting having ever feigned a migraine. Decided to circumnavigate Mr. Brown, hammer in hand, on his knees, moving his way down the line of tent pegs straight ahead. Decided it was far better to scramble through the fence and walk the short way along the cliff top to enter from the rear.

'Golly Ross, what are you doing sitting here?'

'Admiring the view, hoping your lost bra will breeze into my hands Harriet. Come and join me.' He patted the sandy grass alongside. Glad of the chance to rest she stood gazing out to sea, relieved the yellow spot before her eyes was starting to fade.

'But we're supposed to be taking the children out. They're all lining up by the gate.'

He looked at his watch.

'That's what I'm waiting for. The boss reckons he'll be another half hour.'

'Gosh. Nobody tells you anything round here. Enid Frost doesn't know that.'
Ross shrugged his shoulders. Pushed his spectacles further up his nose.
'Oh sit down a minute. Actually you look a pit pale.'
'A migraine Ross. It'll go off in a minute. Too much Bombay Sapphire.'
'What? At it already?'
He grinned as she sat herself down alongside him.
'Long story. No time. I'm glad of the space though. How did it go with the kids this morning?'
'Oh fine. They're all very keen. Let's hope they find something to take back with them. He's giving the best a prize. A medal or something. Crap hey? It'll only generate unfair competition. I don't know how much he's expecting them to find down there. Well how much they can actually get their hands on, that is. Depends on what the sea's washed up at the time.'
'Oh there'll be plenty. Everything lands at his feet.'
'Like becoming an MP you mean? Did you know he intends to stand for parliament? According to him the PM doesn't think he's going to be able to hold it all together for very much longer. You'll be rid of him then.'
'Rid of him, what on earth do you mean?'
'Well he can hardly do both. He's going to have to let his headship go, at least.'
'No no, I think you're getting confused Ross. He's talking about standing for the council.'
'You hope! Do I note a hint of despair here?'
'Despair? What makes you say that?' She looked out to the horizon. The summer sky hazy against the gentle swell of the sea. The remnants of yellow dancing before her eyes now turning from purple to grey. She breathed a huge sigh. At last it had left her alone.
'That sigh for him? Oh I know, now let me guess? Unrequited love! Is that it? Let me bridge the gap.'
His arm around her shoulder she rested her head against his. An alcoholic wave steeping her in temptation. The sea, Falmouth, The Bangles, that tiny cove. All they'd had together. It was *him* she was desperate for. That gorgeous, gorgeous man with his thick blonde tousled hair. She knew it wasn't fair. Wasn't fair on Ross. Then didn't care. Felt his lips against hers, pressing hard, hard against hers. Lay back, touched the end of his nose as he rolled her away from the cliff edge, removed his spectacles and then rolled her over again. Another kiss, on top of her now. Her mind fuzzy. What would her girls think? About the same age or less. She needed to stop this. 'But *he's* going off to be an MP and marrying *her! Lucinda Bloody Lawton* and I'm carrying *his child.*'
His hand now touching her shoulder.
'Ah I'm disappointed. A bra strap. You've already found it then, or is it another?'
He slipped his hand under to ease it down with her top. Both straps falling towards her elbow. His hand moving down towards her breast. *He* had done this

to her. The field of flowers. *He'd* let the straps go. Slipped *his* hand in her bra to lift the fullness of her breast to *his lips*. Shocked to reality. She pulled away.

'Er no Ross, I don't think so. Look, sorry. You're nice, very nice. You're also old enough to be my mother.' She thought about Guy Hammer. She'd said exactly that to him. Felt the panic rising. This she was definitely not getting into.

He laughed.

'Wrong way round Harriet, as if that makes any difference!'

'Too much gin Ross. Let's just forget it shall we?'

'You like the Bombay Sapphire?'

'How did you know that?'

'You just told me Harriet. Now what about my best line. Surely you read it?'

'No Ross, I don't know what you're talking about.'

'Hells bells it didn't fall off did it?'

'Fall off what?'

'`arriet, `arriet, Mr. Sanderson's lookin` for you. Oh and you as well. What are you both doin` down `ere?'

'Absolutely nothing Tricia, take my word for it.'

She stood up and stepped back. Crunch! Ross Farguerhart's spectacles splinters in the ground.

'Oh fuck I'm as blind as a bat without those. I'm supposed to be looking for fossils.'

He bent down to pick up the frames, now distorted to look like a percentage sign.

'I really am terribly sorry Ross. I'll pay for them. Honestly I will.'

Suddenly he grinned. 'There's only one currency I'm prepared to take.'

'Oh you're far too academical Ross Hargerfart,' declared Tricia, moving them both along. 'Anyone would think we were in Venice. `arriet's `ardly likely to give you anythin` foreign.'

'Oh Harriet's got nothing foreign to me. It's more a question of getting my hands on it all.'

'Of course she `asn't. We put all our change in that box at the airport, didn't we `arriet? I wouldn't worry about that, you're very good at payin` people back, aren't you `arriet? I can't remember now. Did you ever settle... Ooh this is our tent `ere. Did you ever settle with Barry Giordano `arriet?'

'She certainly did Mrs. Harrington. Good style! Now if you three don't mind, you're holding the party up.'

'Ooh you made me jump then Mr. Sanderson.'

Chapter 24

'Well I'm very glad that's over with for today, Tricia.'

'Oh I couldn't agree more. All those steps down to the beach. At least the kids found a few fossils. Talkin` of which, I wonder if Belinda Oxfordshire ever takes them `igh `eels off. Did you see `er clingin` to Ross Farquerhart all the way down?'

'Oh gosh she's very welcome to him Tricia. Let's hope they pair off. In spite of what he said about her being the camp cougar, he's definitely not averse to the older woman.'

'Ooh `arriet. What exactly are you sayin`?'

'Do you know Tricia Mr. Sanderson took me to his flipping office and then left me there. It must have been over twenty minutes. Lucinda Lawton swings the door open to tell me he's otherwise engaged. I was absolutely furious. He hasn't spoken to me yet. I've got it hanging over me now all night until tomorrow. I was so mad, gosh and I'm sorry I did this. I let Ross Farquerhart kiss me.'

'Oh no `arriet. What were you thinkin` of? If you'd already seen `im wearin` Enid Frost's spare pair of pink rimmed glasses you'd never `ave let `im near. `e looked more like `e should `ave been underwater with them on `arriet.'

'Gosh I know Tricia. I didn't dare look at you half the time for fear of laughing. But it's *that man*. That man! I just can't get him out of my system.'

'I don't like to remind you `arriet but `e is well and truly in your system seein` as you're `avin` is baby.'

'Yes and you'd think he'd be a bit more considerate.'

'But `e doesn't know you are still `avin` it does `e `arriet? Or `ave you told `im?'

'No, I certainly have not. Just the opposite but I know he doesn't believe me. And why does he keep appearing like some apparition? He always seems to be jumping out from behind, butting in on our conversations.'

'Well we were both lookin` for you `arriet. `e went one way and I went the other. That's the trouble, we both work for `im. If `e thinks you're expectin` `is baby, `e's never goin` to be too far away is `e?'

'Never going to be too far away trailing Lucinda Lawton behind him you mean? Gosh Tricia I've really had enough. Ross Farquerhart's now telling me he's going to stand for parliament.'

'What experience `as `e `ad `arriet? No one will ever vote for `im especially if `e takes a fancy to those pink glasses.'

'No, not him Tricia, Mr. Sanderson. It's all starting to make sense now. He must have changed his mind about being a councillor. I remember he told Mummy the PM had been encouraging him. Of course he can marry Lucinda Lawton. He'll be leaving anyway.'

'Look `arriet, don't you be gettin` yourself all upset about it. It might be the best thing that could ever `appen. After all you did `ave your chance. I think if you `ad really wanted `im you would `ave gone for it, especially as you are `avin` `is baby.'

'But there was Mark, Tricia. I went back to the house and I just wanted him to be there so much.'

'You thought you'd lost him though `arriet. You didn't know `e wasn't goin` to be marryin` that Melissa woman.'

'No I didn't. I just wanted some space Tricia. That's why we both went to Venice.'

'No `arriet, what you really want is `avin` your cake and eatin` it. Now that's most probably the best metaphor I've ever come out with. Is it one `arriet?'

'Oh I don't know Tricia. I just wanted to stay on amber. How can I now if he's leaving and marrying *her*?'

'Well you can't `arriet and I don't want to `ear any more about it. I think you're bein` really unfair to Mark. You know `ow much `im and Bob can't stand Mr. Sanderson yet your Mark is willin` to bring up `is child. I couldn't see Bob doin` that for me, `e never knew who our Adam's dad was. But the way `e feels about *`im*. I know that's why `e `ad that fling with Belinda Oxfordshire. It was more about gettin` one over on *`im*, our friend Joris Sanderson.'

'Yes, you're right Tricia. You're absolutely right. Neither of them can stand him. It's just a pity we can't get out of his life for good. I've got to stay at that school if we're ever going to get moved.'

'Well if `e's goin` to be leavin` your problem will be solved anyway `arriet. Just look on the bright side.'

'But what about you Tricia? You still fancy him like crazy.'

'There's just a teeny weeny difference `arriet. If `e `as ever fancied me back `e's never asked me to marry `im.'

Wrong words. It felt like Tricia had just poured some kind of growth hormone on her feelings. Now simultaneously swamped in regret and desire all she wanted was to crawl into bed and go fast to sleep.

'It's strange we `aven't `eard any more from Rappin` `ammer `arriet. I do `ope `e's still got my tin. Do you think we should go and `ave a look for `im while it's quiet?'

'NO, NO, NO,' Harriet thought, then relented, recognising the danger of becoming completely absorbed in her own needs.

'OK Tricia. Where did he say they were parking?'

Tricia smiled. Held her clenched hands under her chin.

'I think it was the field on the other side `arriet. If we go round the back `ere no one will see us. Oh look there's Mrs. Bustard on `er way back.'

'Oh hi Mrs. Bustard. Went well this afternoon. Your Danny found a whopper. Could be in for the prize. You never know.'

'Well I don't know about that Miss Glover. `e was hurlin` it around. Got that poor caretaker of yours right on the side of `is `ead. Poor man was only out `ere bangin` the pegs back in. Come to think of it `e mentioned you.'

'Mentioned me? Why what did he say Mrs. Bustard?'

'Something about you puttin' our Danny up to it. I told 'im not to talk such rubbish. You're alright Miss Glover, 'e's a funny one 'im. Take no notice. Oh let me get in and take these off, me bunions are killin' me.'

'Tricia did you hear that? That flipping man. He's gone completely paranoid. Next thing he'll be complaining to Mr. Sanderson and Mr. Whittle about me.'

'Oh I wouldn't let it worry you 'arriet. It's probably somethin' that just fell out of 'is mouth while 'is 'ead was stingin'. Come on let's get over 'ere and round the back to Rappin' 'ammer. Ooh I'm excited to see 'ow much is in that tin. There's a lot of wealth arrives in Venice you know, 'arriet.'

They stumbled over the gate, trekking through the sparse lumpy grass to the next field. Harriet took a last look across the sea to the sun, now a huge burning red ball sinking fast in the evening sky. She brushed her hand against her lips. Then again and again. Couldn't believe she'd allowed Ross Fargerhart to kiss her like that. Indelibly stamped on her mind, no amount of brushing could ever remove it. She hated herself for letting *that man* do this to her.

'Ooh there's quite a few campervans 'ere 'arriet. I was expectin' it to be empty. Ooh there it is. That's a big one. On the end of this row 'ere 'arriet. No sign of them. I'll just give a teeny weeny tap on the window when we reach it.'

'Are you sure this is it Tricia? It doesn't look big enough to me?'

'Oh it is. I remember these three green lines goin' all the way round the middle. 'ere, just let me bang on the window. I do 'ope they 'aven't spent all my money on dope.'

'I'd try the door first, Tricia.'

'No 'arriet they're in there. I think I can 'ear somethin'. Look this end 'ere's rockin' a bit. They're most probably practicin' with the sound turned down. They're getting to be very considerate indeed.'

'Oh go on then Tricia. Get it over with.'

'Oh I just can't reach 'arriet. Will you do it for me? Just a big bang on the window, that'll get them to the door.'

Against her better judgement Harriet landed a cracking thump against the Perspex window.

'Fire! Get out quick,' Tricia suddenly bellowed. The back end of 'ere is covered in thick black smoke!'

The van visibly rocked. The door flew open. His dressing gown hurriedly thrown around him, but not quite well enough. Harriet drawn to the gap opening below his waist sensed this man indeed was not Rapping Hammer. She looked up. His shining silver hair dishevelled. The gap ever widening. A girl's voice from the scramble behind.

'It's a bloody fire *Luc--a* get the hell out of here.'

'Oh we are ever so sorry. I think it's you isn't it Mr. Engells,' Tricia piped up, unable to take her eyes off his assets. 'No, we thought we saw some smoke down there, didn't we 'arriet. But the mist is gatherin' now, it could 'ave been that.'

'Stay put *Luc---a. It's those two.*' His voice tailed off to a whisper.

The door slammed shut. They ran back to the fence at the edge of the cliff hysterical.

'Ooh `ar....'

'Oh don't Tr....'

'Ooh I can `ardly brea.....'

'What the fuck are you two doin` rollin` round down there?'

'Oh Rappin` `ammer, we were lookin` for you, weren't we `arriet? We thought that was your van. That one on the end and we've just `ad a very nasty experience.'

They started again. The tears streaming now. Speech nigh on impossible.

'What you two fuckin` on? `er!' He pointed to Harriet. `er tight-arse Mummy-Mama. We've got a bone to pick with you.'

Like a duster to chalk the mirth disappeared. They watched the rest of the band trailing between the line of vans. Harriet sat on the urge to run.

'We've seen the Ditchwater.'

'Well that's not a very nice thing to call him.' Harriet went back at him.

'We've `ad a word with `im about the mush,' he continued.

'No mush to mash Miss!' It was Rex flinging his arms about. Looking extremely agitated.

'Well it's not your fault is it `arriet? `arriet shouldn't `ave ever been asked to go in `is greenhouse in the first place `im knowing all that was in there. `ow was she to know she'd picked up the wrong plants?'

'School Miss, isn't she? Doesn't she know it all?'

'No I most certainly do not. In fact you could well have been arrested for breaking the law.'

'They found nothin`.'

'Well that's very hard to believe Rapping Hammer. You were all doped to the eyeballs.'

'Oh Chick-Lips Peg-Legs `ere been talkin` `as she?'

'Oh no I `ave not Rappin` `ammer. Don't forget I was outside of that tent fund-raisin` for Venice. And I want my tin back if you don't mind.'

The band huddled then broke apart banging their legs laughing.

'Oh yes and what's so funny now?' Tricia asked.

They pointed at Harriet.

'Eh Wayne, make `er do the splits while she's showin` `er tits before you give it back.' They turned to Tricia. '`ers are much bigger than yours. We've already seen your bits of pimples anyway.'

'OH NO YOU HAVE NOT!' Declared Harriet, furiously.

'Not yours tight-arse, `ers!'

Tricia turned to Rapping Hammer.

'It was for a very good cause if you don't mind. Now go and get my tin before we report you.'

'Report you! `ear that bards?' Then he turned to Harriet. 'The Ditchwater needs a bit of persuadin` to get growin` again. `e's not interested in `er, but a roll round in one of these with you might do it.'

'I beg your pardon, Wayne Hammer. I don't believe I'm hearing this. You are the most perverted boy I've ever had the misfortune to come across.' Harriet's face went as red and as round as the sun, now set.

'That's why `e wants to get `is `and in `er kecks. `e's kinky. `e only wants one night in one of these, but you've gorra bring your cane!'

'Mr. Bridgewater would never, ever say that. He's actually a true gentleman. He would be mortified if he could hear all this disgusting talk.'

'Not when `e's mushin` the mash `e wouldn't. `e's `ad you laid flat many a time.'

'Oh I'm going! I'm not standing around here listening to this filth. Come on Tricia let's get back.'

'I want my tin `arriet.'

'Stop flappin` peg-legs. You'll get it. We'll be clangin` the bangin` round yours later!'

The six of them swaggered off leaving Harriet and Tricia in a state of disbelief, just staring at one another as they walked back.

'Tarquin Bridgewater would never say that Tricia. He just wouldn't.'

'Of course `e wouldn't `arriet. It's them. They're just windin` you up. Stop worryin`.'

'But when are you going to get your money back Tricia? They didn't actually say.'

'Well I got the impression it would be tonight. We'll just `ave to go to bed late and keep an eye open for them. Let's `ope they'll be goin` `ome tomorrow. It's a good job that little lot was out of earshot.'

'Oh I know Tricia. I feel absolutely dreadful. I already felt bad letting Ross Farquerhart kiss me like that but now I feel so awfully cheap.'

'*You* do `arriet! What about me? I really wish I'd never got carried away like that. It was just Venice that did it. All them statues and it bein` so romantic. I felt like I wanted to give my whole self to it. Well to savin` it.'

'I know Tricia and as you said you did it for a good cause. You got plenty of donations don't forget. You don't ever have to do it again if you don't want to.'

'Oh no I don't `arriet. Not tonight, anyway.' Suddenly her shoulders started shaking. Rappin` `ammer would never `ave recovered if `e'd seen `ow big Clive Engells' is.'

Then Harriet's started. 'Gosh Tricia, I couldn't help but notice. His dressing gown splitting like that. No wonder the thing was rocking.'

'We interrupted them `arriet! I thought it was the band practicin` their footwork.'

'But did you hear him Tricia? Did you hear him say Lucinda, in a whisper?'

'Oh yes I did `arriet, `e obviously didn't want us to `ear `er name. I wonder if it is `er? It must be. It would be too much of a coincidence to `ave two of them round `ere'

'Well he did say something about her not liking to sleep on the boat and them breaking their journey to stay at his hotel.'

'Oh yes I know 'arriet. It might be our friend Joris 'as gone to the boat on 'is own sometimes and left 'er there with 'im. They might 'ave got to know each other very well indeed.'

'Gosh Tricia, you might just be right. Someone doing the dirty on *him* for a change.'

Then she felt sorry she'd said it. A pang surged through her. Couldn't stand the thought of anyone treating him like that. Couldn't stand the thought of him not knowing, of being made a fool of. But the possibility threw light on her mind. Enough light to turn it back to amber.

Chapter 25

'We can't be sittin' out 'ere all night 'arriet waitin' for them. Can you 'ear Beattie Bustard snorin' in there? She's been asleep for ages. We're goin' to be like wet rags in the mornin'.'

'What do you want to do then Tricia? I don't fancy going back over there tonight. We could try to catch them early in the morning.'

'I think that's probably the best idea. Ooh look, there's a bit of a light shinin' through Belinda Oxfordshire's awning. I thought she was supposed to be on duty with Ross Farquerhart tonight.'

'Oh she's probably got out of it. Got someone else to stand in just in case Joris decides to pay her a visit. She's welcome. I'm certainly not looking forward to my turn next Friday with him.'

' Ooh I'd much rather be with 'im than Tarquin Bridgewater, even though we're right off 'im 'arriet, especially if there was any truth in what Rappin' 'ammer was sayin' earlier. To be 'onest Mr. Bridgewater as always struck me as bein' a bit like that. No, I can't say as I'm exactly lookin' forward to that tomorrow night.' Suddenly she jumped. 'Ooh 'arriet I'm sure I've just 'eard noises from over there. It sounded like someone scramblin' behind 'er tent just then.'

'Ooh Tricia. Get in quick. *He's* coming over. I've just seen the top of his head through there. I hope he's not coming here, or Belinda Oxfordshire's tent. Oh golly Tricia that's where I'm supposed to be. Come on let's get in.' They held their breath.

'Mrs. Harrington.'

Silence.

'Right Mrs. Harrington you'll find me in Miss Glover's tent on the end. Join me if you will.'

Harriet panicked.

'Oh come on Tricia we'd better get out. We don't want him going to Belinda Oxfordshire's tent. Oh no it sounds like he's already gone. I do wish he'd keep his voice down.'

His face against the canvas. 'Miss Glover. A word if you will?'

They watched him bang his hand on the central pole supporting the centre-front of the tent as they inched their way forward between the two rows of tent pegs. He looked away, then did it again, too hard this time. The entrance flaps now breezing away from the swaying walls.

Suddenly they both jumped. It was Rapping Hammer leaping out from between the two end tents. Harriet startled, decided to stand back in the shadows.

''ere's your tin Chick-Lips. But you're not gettin' it 'till Mummy-Mamma does 'er bit.' Rapping Hammer's voice ringing through the night air, selfishly loud and clear. Then the deafening clank of coins jangling in rhythmical clouts against the rapidly collapsing pole to the side. The whole awning flapping, aping giant bat wings before going down like a torpedoed battleship.

The faint light from within well out now. Just the glimpse of a screaming ball of pink flesh almost rolling out from under. 'Miss Glover. Stop that noise this minute!' Then Rapping Hammer flashing torchlight around.

'Whooooo, she's got 'em down. Mummy-Mamma's showin` 'er bum. Rolled right over, now 'er tum! Well fuck me! Two moons in one night.' Suddenly the other five appeared. Could barely stand for laughing.

'Help Joris, help me! My leg's trapped in something. It's Belinda, Joris, not Harriet Glover.' She could screech no louder.

Mr. Sanderson stumbled over the collapsed porta-potti. 'Alright Belinda don't panic!'

'We might 'ave known it's not 'er,' complained a bitterly disappointed Rapping Hammer. ''er's don't come down or so she thinks we think! Look there she is. There's Mummy-Mamma.' He rattled the "save Venice" tin at her. 'Ger 'em off and do your stuff if you want me to give it 'er back.'

'You boy get from here this minute!'

'Fuck you!'

'I beg your pardon young man. Belinda get that backside covered up this minute.'

'I can't. I've already told you I'm trapped under here.'

'Miss Glover, Mrs. Harrington, take control of yourselves. Give her a hand. This is neither funny nor clever. Get that torchlight away from her this minute, you vile boy. Just what are you doing sneaking around here in the dark anyhow?'

'We could ask the same of you Gov.'

'Impudence. Sheer impudence. And stop shaking that damned thing. You'll wake the whole campsite the way you're going. You two, haven't you done it yet?'

'They can't Joris. You're obviously not listening. I've got my leg trapped under this.'

'Hell's bells what's going on? Is that Belinda screaming? What's happened?'

'Ah Ross, the whole damned campsite will soon be awake with this noise. Has it already woken any of them over there?'

'Not when I left. I was just coming over to see why Belinda hasn't turned up.'

'Get Brown for me will you. Tell him it's urgent.' He turned to Rapping Hammer. 'And you, you rat-tailed boy just GO! Take that hoard of screeching vermin with you. NOW!'

'PULL 'EM OUT BARDS! ONE, TWO THREE!'

Harriet momentarily ceased struggling to release the tent pole determined to keep Belinda Oxfordshire trapped. She looked up to see each one of the band now heaving at the metal structure angled in a stubborn state of semi-collapse. Then in an instant, flying rods, shooting, landing. Bodies and canvas collapsing into a tortuous lasagne, a screaming heap struggling in the black of the night.

'Fuckin` 'ell let's get out of 'ere.'

'If we bleedin' could!'

'Not until you give me my tin back Rappin' ammer.'

'Ow geroff my leg will yer Rux?'

'It's Rex, 'e's got 'is bleedin' arm up my arse. I can't move, I need my fuckin' mush.'

'Well we 'aven't got any thanks to 'er under me. Fuck you Mummy-Mamma.'

'Pulled 'er drawers off yet?'

'Get real Rax, I can't see a fuckin' thing.'

'Oh sod off Rapping Hammer. Just roll over will you. I want to get out from under here.' Harriet was furious.

'Eh I've found somethin' soft and warm down 'ere. 'ang on, it's a bum,' Rix triumphed.

'You fuckin' get that 'and out of my trousers Rix. I'm bleedin' well not 'avin' a rewire fancyin' you under 'ere.'

'That bum yours, not 'ers? Your jeans must 'ave rolled down Rex. 'ang on who's bum is it then?'

'Get your disgusting hand away from me this minute. I'll sue you. Joris. Joris please help, now my pants have got caught in something and there's a hand on my arse.'

'I thought that bird was too posh to 'ave one. Give it a slap Rix, see if it's real.' 'JORIS, JORIS, they're all on top of me now. I'm going to die. JORIS SAVE ME!'

'Alright Belinda. Alright. Just stay still. YOU BOYS STOP THAT THIS MINUTE! Mr. Brown is on his way Belinda.'

'He's pinching me now. There take that you vulgar scarecrow.'

'She's just thumped something into me fuckin' balls. 'ere I'll belt your bum for that.'

'JORIS, he's hitting me now. HELP JORIS, HELP!'

'Ah Mr. Brown. Good man! Untangle them will you? Ross help him.'

'You just get your 'and out of there Rex Bard.'

'Oh come on Chick-Lips. You can see I've got nowhere else to put it.'

'No I can't. It's black in 'ere. Stick it in the air or somethin'. Just get it off my bra!'

'Oh no, you're not stoppin' me feelin' them tits Chick-Lips.'

'Eh well scored Rex. I can only feel a cold 'ard pole.'

'You on top of Mummy-Mamma Rux? Stick it up 'er arse.'

'NO HE IS NOT!' Harriet balled.

'That's me Rux. No luck!'

'Oh just shut up Rapping Hammer, Harriet seethed. 'It's bad enough being this close to your leathers.'

'What's this big 'ard thing I'm touchin'.'

''avin' better luck under 'ere Wayne?'

'It's most probably Belinda's porta-potti you're touchin',' piped up Tricia. 'Serves you right.'

''Are that's disappointin`. Is she not doin` anythin` to `elp your pole Wayne? Try givin` `er a kiss.'

'Don't you dare Rapping Hammer. I mean it. Just wait until we're out of here. I'll clout you with one. Then you'll know all about a cold hard pole.'

'So you're gettin` your cane out after all? Hey Bards. Mummy-Mamma's gonna whack us all. Let's see if I can pull the rings on can-legs. See if they'll open.'

'You boy, just hold your tongue. WILL YOU? Mr. Brown I'd start at the top if I were you.'

'No, it's no good that. It'll send the rest of them down. Don't forget this is the second time I'm `avin` to be puttin` one of these tents back up. No Sir, if you and Ross could take a corner each I'll try and pull it all back from here.'

'I've warned you `aven't I. You little bugger!'

Suddenly Tricia found enough space to jerk her knee upward and forward. His hand shot from her bra whilst his feet found the ground to instant freedom. Nursing all that was most precious to him Rex hobbled away.

'Bloody `ell Rex what you do that for?'

'Chick-Lips nearly cracked me conkers.'

'Fuck you Chick-Lips, it was good in there. We were kinda gettin` used to it weren't we?'

As if never entangled Rapping Hammer slid between the canvas and poles.

'Come on, the game's up Bards. Who got the closest?'

'If I'm hearing what I think I'm hearing I understand you've all been lying on top of these poor girls on purpose. You disgusting boys. I've never heard the like. Common assault. Now clear off the lot of you. Get off this site now before I call the police.'

'Alright, alright we're goin`. We were only tryin` to `elp Gov.'

'Stop rattling that tin immediately. Be gone this instant you gross, indecent boy!'

'Don't give `er that fuckin` tin back Wayne. I `ate `er!'

'She aint gettin` `er fuckin` tin back Rex. Well we'll see `ow she wants to say sorry, shall we?'

With the tent poles collapsed between the folds of canvas, Harriet and Tricia emerged from its origami perimeters to see Belinda Oxfordshire fasten the top button of her jeans, rub her left leg and hobble alongside Mr. Sanderson in the direction of the house.

'We could do with a bit of preferential treatment ourselves, `arriet. It was `orrible under that lot. Serves `er right, though! I never realised `ow my porta-potti would `elp me get my own back.'

'No Tricia. Gosh I thought we were going to die laughing until that lot collapsed in a heap on top of us. What a turn-around. It was anything but funny having Rapping Hammer on top of me. I've never been so furious and scared at the same time. They're so crude. If he'd had touched me anywhere with those filthy hands of his I'd have found a way to batter him under there with that pole.'

'Do you think they collapsed it all on purpose just so they could land on top of us like that?'

'I'm sure that was their intention Tricia. I saw them all pulling the whole lot out.'

'That's terrible 'arriet. There could 'ave been a nasty accident in there. I'm fumin' at 'im for what 'e did. Oh I do wish I 'adn't gone topless. They think I'm easy prey now, I know they do and I still 'aven't got my tin back. Did you 'ear 'is partin' shot? 'ow we're we goin' to say sorry to 'im! 'e's got to be jokin'!'

'So that's all you two have got to worry about, that flamin' tin.' An angry Mr. Brown somehow materialised behind Harriet.

'You again. I expect you're responsible for this little lot. I've a good mind to make you 'elp me put it all back up.'

'No Mr. Brown, I'm very sorry but you definitely can't blame me.'

'You were underneath it all.'

'Along with everyone else. Maybe you should ask Mr. Sanderson how it happened?'

''e's on 'is way back now. I might just be doin' that.'

They turned to see him beckon. Then his voice, clear, distinct in the night air.

'Miss Glover, Mrs. Harrington. Wait there. Stay just where you are.'

'Now's your chance Mr. Brown.'

'Oh later. I'd best be gettin' on with the task in 'and. I'll do it later, mind you.'

'Ross return to your duties immediately. Miss Oxfordshire will be joining you shortly. Wait at the far end of the two sets of tents will you. We'll be using yours for a few minutes. You two, follow me.'

They walked behind him, watching Ross Farquerhart quicken his step. It was very evident Mr. Sanderson was not in the mood for nonsense.

Inside the tent, he parked them on a couple of folding chairs before moving swiftly to the other side of the table, then sat himself down to face them.

Just the oil lamp hanging, lighting the corner to their left. His face shifting, every muscle taught with anger.

'Gosh he's gorgeous.' Harriet hoped it wasn't showing on her face. Still basking in Lucinda Lawton's betrayal of him, she struggled lest the amber light now set in her mind should switch to green. 'No, no, no Harriet, just think about Mark.'

'Right you two!'

The impact of his hand thumping the table reverberated deep inside Harriet's chest. A strange sensation of pain now rising in her throat, like she'd just swallowed a hard-boiled sweet, whole.

'Miss Glover you lied to me this morning. You told me you had a bad migraine and needed to rest. Far from it! I see the both of you dining at Clive Engells' place. Not content with that the whole establishment's treated to a visitation from that obnoxious band boy and the rest of them. I assume you were meeting up with them there? How dare you both turn this exercise into some kind of flippant break. I assume you invited them to park up on the field over there? No don't bother answering any of it! You both have the temerity to disturb Clive Engells by banging on his campervan window, bringing the poor man to the door, waking him from his sleep to frighten the poor man nearly to death. He truly thought the van was on fire.'

Tricia took a deep breath. He stopped her in her tracks.

'No I don't wish to hear anything whatsoever from either of you right at this moment. Now I'm wondering why Belinda Oxfordshire is thanking me profusely for allowing her sole use of the tent. The tent Miss Glover, I instructed you to use. She's apologising to excess for falling from and breaking the seat on that damned porta-potti I'm supposed to have provided her with and that's not all. The blasted woman has received a one-line proposal attached to a hamper she imagines I've sent and I'm up to my fucking eyeballs in it since she's already informed her parents the engagement is back on! You now have chance to explain.'

'Well 'ow many women can you be engaged to at once Mr. Sanderson? 'ow could she 'ave come away with that idea?' He turned to Harriet.

'Miss Glover may I remind you just in case you didn't get the message loud and clear the first time, San Marco was the end of the road for you and me. It's high time you put Mrs. Harrington and anybody else expecting marriage between us, straight.'

The pain in Harriet's throat throbbed like her heart was trying to choke her. Completely unable to reply she swallowed back the water filming across her eyes now finding a fast route out down her nose.

'Well I 'ave to admit to lendin' 'er the porta-potti Mr. Sanderson. I thought I was bein' 'elpful but we 'onestly don't know anythin' about the 'amper, do we 'arriet?'

'Well someone sent the damned thing. Or maybe it was intended for you Miss Glover since you were the one supposed to be in that tent? Who the hell have you been cavorting with now?'

Then it struck her. Ross Farquerhart. That kiss on the cliff edge. Thought. 'Oh no, surely he didn't see us.'

'That damned woman found it amongst the pate de foie gras and the caviar.'

'Found what Mr. Sanderson?' Tricia couldn't refrain.

'A white lace bra. Was it for you Miss Glover? Yes it would be, you are a 36D' He stared straight at her breasts. 'Of course you are Yes all of that and getting larger, I notice. Only someone with such an intimate knowledge of your anatomy could have got it right first time. Who is it Miss Glover? Who have you sucked into your irresponsible existence now?'

Harriet felt the lantern in the corner deliberately flicker large to illuminate her crimson face. Ross Farquerhart had mentioned the one-liner only this afternoon. She couldn't ever have imagined it would be a proposal of marriage.

'Your silence is interesting Miss Glover. Very interesting indeed! Could it be you've abducted our young PhD student? I seem to recall some association with Farquerhart Luxury Hampers. I fear you've both got some apologising to do to Belinda Oxfordshire before you leave in the morning.'

'Leave in the mornin` Mr. Sanderson. Whatever do you mean?'

'Clear enough to me Mrs. Harrington, not helped in your case of course being exposed in that way by the press. No, I'm afraid on top of this Venice fiasco, neither of you has the wit to lie low. I'm just not prepared, on the grounds of health and safety alone, to take any more chances with either of you on this trip. You'll be travelling back with me. I only came along to get the damned thing underway. You're both suspended from duties here. You'll be returning with me sharp at eight tomorrow morning.'

Chapter 26

'Ooh do you think we'll be `avin` to sit by `im all the way back on the train `arriet?'

'Well he hasn't got a car, unless he uses that beige one. I shouldn't think he'll do that though, who ever lent it won't want him taking it all the way back to Lower Tideside.'

'We're in trouble again, aren't we `arriet?'

'I would say so Tricia, good and proper this time.'

'I'm not really sure we've done anythin` wrong though. We've only just come, aven't we?'

'Apart from frightening Clive Engells to death while he was having it off Tricia, oh and fraternising with Rapping Hammer and telling lies and me swapping tents. Apart from that we've done nothing wrong at all. Oh and it looks like he whipped the front page from your paper Tricia. Don't forget about that.'

'As if I could `arriet No I know you're right. What do you think will `appen to us? I've never been suspended before.'

'Well I have and it's not very nice. You stick at home all day wondering whether you're going to lose your job and every time the phone goes you think it's him. You wonder what he's going to declare next.'

'Ooh no `arriet that doesn't sound very good to me. `ow long will we be suspended for?'

'Well, as he hasn't mentioned Mr. Whittle I'm keeping my fingers crossed it isn't a formal suspension. He might just want us out of here. With Belinda Oxfordshire staying for the rest of the week, I can't see him leaving Starboard Marine North West in Iris's hands while you're about.'

'Oh so you think we might just get away with last night's tellin` off then?'

'Let's keep our fingers crossed. We're into the school holidays now and he's well roped me in with regard to all those extra curricular activities. There's no mileage in it for him.'

'Well I `ope so `arriet. Come on we'd better go over to the showers. Beattie Bustard went ages ago. We'd better not be late for `im.'

'No, coming now. At least we're all packed. Oh that reminds me Tricia, I don't suppose you've got a spare pair of pants I could borrow, please? The rest of mine were in the case I had to leave behind.'

'Oh of course I `ave `arriet. `ere, `ave these. I always keep a couple of spare pairs in my bag, just in case.'

'Oh thanks Tricia. They're fine. You've saved my life. Golly we've only got an hour to get sorted and have breakfast.'

'Ooh that's not long `arriet. What do we do if anyone asks about last night?'

'We'll just have to look blank, Tricia. Pretend we don't know what they're talking about. Gosh Mrs. Bustard must go brain dead once she lies down. Fancy her not saying anything when she woke up.'

'Just as well `arriet. Do you know I'll be very glad to get `ome. But we `ave got to explain everythin` to Belinda Oxfordshire first. I nearly forgot, `e told us to do that this mornin`.'

'He did but how can we? We don't know for sure where the hamper came from. It could easily have been delivered to the wrong campsite. There's a few round here, quite close by.'

'But it did `ave a bra in `arriet. I don't suppose many `ampers come with that. I did tell Ross Farquerhart you were still lookin` for yours.'

'Yes well, I'm still not saying anything Tricia. Let him sort it out with her. We're in enough trouble as it is.'

'Ooh you're right `arriet. If `e asks we'll just tell `im we `aven't `ad time.'

With just a few other campers scattered around the dining hall they finished breakfast grateful for their anonymity.

'Ah you two. Bags packed I hope? Meet me at the gate in fifteen minutes time. Oh and don't forget to sort it with Belinda Oxfordshire.'

Mr. Sanderson marched on leaving them hurrying back to their tent, hoping against hope they wouldn't spot her.

'Oh you're not leavin` me `ere all by myself Miss Glover?' Mrs. Bustard then turned to Tricia. 'You goin` as well? It's only Sunday. I do `ope I `aven't been keepin` you both awake. Bert's always tellin` me I'm snorin` but `ow would `e know? I never even get to sleep when I'm next to `im for the row `e makes.'

'No Mrs. Bustard, please don't worry. It's Mr. Sanderson, he's going back and he wants us to go with him. There's the school summer club to get under way and this year he's working between the school and Starboard Marine North West, oh and the sailing club of course. I think he wants it to be all finalised for next week.'

'Oh I see, `e probably wanted you `ere just for the first couple of days to make sure the children were settled then?'

'Something like that Mrs. Bustard. We'll see you around. I expect you'll want Danny to be joining in the summer activities.'

'Yes, you can say that again Miss Glover, not `alf. Oh that's someone's phone goin`. I'm just off to the launderette anyway. Both of you `ave a good trip back.'

'Ah thanks Mrs. Bustard and don't you forget what I said about all of you making the most of being here.'

'I won't Miss Glover. `adn't somebody better answer that!'

'Hello, hello.' Harriet wandered outside. 'Oh it's not *you* Barry Giordano I don't believe it! Didn't I tell you I never wanted to see you again after that painting?'

….. 'Where is it? You might well ask. But if you must know it's under the bed gathering dust until I can think of a better way to dispose of it.'

….. 'Oh I've already told him it was you and your warped imagination.'

….. 'No, of course he doesn't believe me. I think the least you can do is set the record straight.'

..... 'Be on our guard. What do you mean? You're making it sound serious. Mr. Sanderson hasn't emphasized it like that.'

..... 'No Barry Giordano. If I wasn't prepared to go to Venice with you, you can hardly expect me to agree to a trip to Peru. Are you off your head or something? After what you did to me!'

..... 'No I've given *him* the boot too.'

..... 'Yes, yes, I forgot, the other way round thanks for reminding me.'

..... 'No there certainly is no chance of us getting back together. Toad of a man. Just like you. You're all the same.'

..... 'If you must. No I'm not there.'

..... 'Dorset. A camping trip with the school.'

..... 'Fossil hunting if you must know.'

..... 'No, it's been curtailed.'

..... 'You don't actually need to know that.'

..... 'Yes, we're going now. I'll phone you tonight against my better judgement. I want to know just what you're talking about, "Be on your guard" indeed. That's what I should have done the first time I set eyes on you!'

..... 'GOOD BYE!'

'Come on let's get clear before we see Belinda Oxfordshire. That wasn't Barry on the phone was it? I couldn't `elp `earin` just a little bit `arriet.'

'Oh no, that's OK Tricia, don't worry. It certainly was, flipping cheek! He said something about being on our guard though Tricia. He might just know something we don't.'

'Ooh you'll `ave to find out `arriet. I was `opin` that Venice affair was all over and done with.'

'Oh gosh yes. We certainly don't need to be looking over our shoulders again. I've told him I'll call him when I get back. I'll let you know exactly what it's all about as soon as I know.'

'Ah thanks `arriet. Come on let's get goin`. Ooh, is that Clive Engells walkin` up there?'

'It looks like it Tricia. Come on let's go round the other way.'

Bags in hand they turned left to follow the hedge leading to the gate.

'I don't seem to `ave `alf as much as I came with. `ere `arriet let me carry that for you. You're strugglin` a bit there.'

'Oh thanks Tricia. To be honest I'm feeling a bit sick for some reason.'

'You could be startin` with mornin` sickness. `ow long is it now?'

'Oh let's see. What's two weeks before June 26th?'

'Well it's the last day of July today `arriet if that's any `elp.'

'Oh I can't think!'

'Two weeks and another one and four weeks in this month. I would say about seven `arriet. Just about right I would say for mornin` sickness to get goin`.'

'Well let's hope I can make the journey Tricia. I don't want to have *him* on my back after all this lot.'

'You can 'ave one of my boiled sweets 'arriet. It used to do the trick for me. I've never stopped eatin' them since.'

'Lucky you Tricia. If that's the case nothing will make you put on weight. I'm dreading this. Especially now at this age.'

'Look 'arriet, I 'ate to say it but I think after what Barry's just said we'll both be burnin' off all our excess calories in nervous energy.'

'You're right Tricia. This is probably a reaction.'

'LOOK 'arriet. No don't look now. LOOK NOW over there by the car park. Clive Engells and 'im 'ave just got into that beige car. Oh they're sittin' there, talkin' 'arriet. I do 'ope 'e's not comin' with us.'

'It must be Clive Engells' car. Golly, I hope *he's* not driving us all Tricia, not after last night. Don't forget Mr. Sanderson hasn't got his own car.'

To their relief they saw them both get out. Mr. Sanderson was getting back in now, taking the wheel. A quick wave to Clive Engells then away. Mr. Sanderson stopping at the gates.

'Right. Luggage in here.' He snapped the boot open. The engine humming on the Bentley, its flashy presence somehow in keeping with its owner.

'Oh I wish it wasn't beige 'arriet. I do really 'ate beige cars. I'm sure 'e could 'ave found a nicer colour.'

'Come on, come on. Thank your lucky stars you're not having to struggle on the train with all this. Far more than you deserve!'

Mr. Sanderson, anxious to get away, ushered them into the back. Speeding along, already they'd passed the Lantern Box Hotel. Well away from Churndale Village now, burning up the country lanes. A couple of hours devoid of all conversation. Heading for the motorway now Harriet jumped as he saw fit to break the silence.

'We'll stop at the first services we come to. Get a sandwich or some such like. I need to be back before two.'

'Oh that's alright with me Mr. Sanderson. 'ow about you 'arriet?'

'Absolutely fine with me.'

'Yes, of course it will be won't it 'arriet, with you 'avin' to make that phone call to Barry Giordano. We need to know what that's all about. We don't want any more trouble.'

Harriet nudged her. Too late. She found herself being spoken to.

'More trouble, Miss Glover? I wouldn't have considered it possible. Clive Engells is furious with both of you and I'm not sure you've heard the last of it. He's a solicitor you know. Not the best of people to agitate. He'll be up collecting this shortly. See your way to apologising, will you? Both of you.'

'But you must 'ave noticed the mist gatherin' last night Mr. Sanderson. It was swirlin' under 'is campervan and we really thought it was smoke, didn't we 'arriet?'

'Come, come Mrs. Harrington, the night air would have been filled with the smell of it. Anyhow at that proximity you would surely have noticed the difference.'

Harriet caught his expression as he glanced into the rear mirror waiting for an answer. That sea-green shirt again. His thick blonde hair newly settled into the layers his hand had just made, the blonde curls just resting along the fold of his open collar. This gorgeous, gorgeous hunk of a man. Hated herself for letting her nerves ruin her life. Thought about Mark. Lovely, good, kind Mark. Wished she'd never, ever set eyes on Mr. Sanderson. Wished she'd never dallied. Flirted. Such a safe game to start with. Of course there wasn't a female in the school that didn't find him attractive. Up for the competition, she never missed an opportunity to gain ground. 'He doesn't want you Harriet. Not any more he doesn't. Get that through your very thick head once and for all will you? He's TOLD you he doesn't want you, you STUPID girl. Last night he switched you to red. Just flipping well stay there!'

'Miss Glover.'

Shaken from her thoughts she looked up to see the approaching slip road to the services.

'Miss Glover. What's all this about Barry Giordano? As I told you, I'm not entirely satisfied there won't be further repercussions following this Venice affair.'

'I never had an affair with him Mr. Sanderson. I wouldn't have needed to anyway seeing as he asked me to marry him at the outset.'

'Quite, quite, Miss Glover. We're talking at cross purposes here.'

She watched the steering wheel slip through his hands as they turned left into the car park. Thought about the field of flowers. That magical journey home. Thought about Falmouth and The Bangles. The tiny sun-lit cove where he'd made love to her on the warm sand close to the lapping tide. Thought about his baby. At least she had this part of him. They'd always have this together, no matter how much he didn't wish to marry her.

Gliding into the nearest space, he parked. Got out to hold the door open for her.

'Silence yet again Miss Glover. Barry Giordano will naturally be clued in far better than me. I'll need to know exactly what's going on. I suggest we make that phone call at the same time as dropping you off.'

'Oh right Mr. Sanderson. Yes. I suppose it could be serious.'

'Suppose, Miss Glover? Well yes, on second thoughts it could just be an excuse for communicating with you. We'll see. No doubt we'll see.'

He glanced at Tricia.

'Do stop struggling with it Mrs. Harrington. You'll end up breaking the damned thing. Here, just wait. I'll let you out.'

Harriet skirted the rear of the car to hang back for Tricia. Wished he hadn't just said that. Just wanted to get back to Mark now. Feeling sickly, the reality of pregnancy fast homing in.

'Just a coffee Miss Glover? I'd rather hoped we'd all take a bite to eat here, save any further prolonged stops. Actually you're not looking too good at all. Are you alright?'

'Yes thank you. It's probably the same bug Belinda Oxfordshire had.'

'Vitamin B6 Miss Glover, shown to help with pregnancy induced nausea. Just a 50mg capsule per day should do it. Oh and try ginger. Sweets preferably if you can get hold of them. Pop back to the counter will you Mrs. Harrington. Sometimes they have ginger biscuits in those small packs. I noticed them alongside the till.'

'Now Miss Glover, you're not going to continue to deny this pregnancy are you? Ah yes, a very pretty shade of pink. I've got my answer.'

Harriet looked down. His hand firmly placed on the blue and grey mottled melamine-topped table.

'What exactly is it Harriet? Sometimes you behave as if you're almost frightened of me? Anyhow we're looking at March 12th, or thereabouts, would you say? Ah Mrs. Harrington. It looks like she's managed it.'

It felt like forever. Harriet was glad to be back on the road again. Relieved Tricia had inadvertently curtailed that particular line of enquiry. All quiet in the back. Just the engine humming to the gear changes as he pulled out and away to the outer lane of the motorway. His foot hard down. Harriet sat behind him. It felt like miles away as if the distance he'd put between them had somehow elongated the car. Somehow she felt she didn't deserve to be any closer to him than that.

'I take it neither of you saw fit to enlighten Belinda Oxfordshire judging by this morning's greeting?'

'Oh we 'aven't seen 'er 'ave we 'arriet? But in any case Mr. Sanderson that 'amper was nothin' to do with us. 'ow was we to know that was goin' to arrive in 'er tent with a proposal of marriage stuck to it?'

'Are you quite sure both of you didn't put Ross Farquerhart up to it? I understand his father's line of business is exactly that.'

'No of course we didn't, did we 'arriet? Why would we want to do that?'

'Well Mrs. Harrington you do still seem intent on settling this score with her.'

'And not without good reason Mr. Sanderson, 'er pinchin' my 'usband back again like that. It's not somethin' that's very easy to forget in a hurry. You agree don't you 'arriet?'

'Oh don't go asking Miss Glover. She's not in any kind of position to make a moral judgement.'

Fuming, Harriet looked down for fear of catching his eye in the mirror. Tricia continued.

'In any case Mr. Sanderson, as you mention it, that thin streak of misery is 'ardly a 36D. If it was anythin' to do with us puttin' Ross Farquerhart up to it, he'd 'ave got that right, I would say.'

'Which brings it back to you Miss Glover. My first instincts are usually correct.'

'Well I honestly wouldn't know Mr. Sanderson as it wasn't addressed to anyone. Ross Farquerhart's said nothing to me whatsoever. Yes, I've got to admit it was my idea to let Belinda Oxfordshire use that tent and I didn't think you'd mind for one minute. I could hardly let her think that though. There didn't seem any harm in telling her it was your suggestion.'

'And that damned porta-potti Mrs. Harrington. How likely was it I'd have brought that along, never mind as a means of addressing Belinda Oxfordshire's creature comforts?'

'I was only tryin` to make `er feel at `ome Mr. Sanderson. Only tryin` to cheer `er up.'

'Oh you've certainly managed that Mrs. Harrington. Both of you have placed me in a very embarrassing position.'

Her heart racing, Harriet could scarcely contain her anger. This one she just had to say.

'With respect Mr. Sanderson, that's something sometimes people do without intention. *I know* I've caught Belinda Oxfordshire's tummy bug but you've been trying to put a very different construction on it which *I* find very embarrassing.'

'Ah, I see. Then you must accept my apologies Miss Glover.'

Tricia nudged her. Harriet looked across to catch her grin. Suddenly she felt better. She couldn't ever remember daring to put this man in his place, before. Then a nervous pang, conscious of reality in misalignment with her words. She knew she couldn't hide it forever.

Chapter 27

'That's about it with regard to your luggage Mrs. Harrington, save that damned porta-potti. Goodness knows what Brown did with it.'

'Oh that's alright thank you Mr. Sanderson. I won't be wantin' that back now it's broken. 'e can ditch it if 'e likes. Oh by the way it's Monday tomorrow, I take it you won't be wantin' me down at Starboard Marine North West seein' as 'ow you've suspended me?'

'Merely an informal suspension Mrs. Harrington relating to the camping holiday. As you well know Belinda Oxfordshire's away for the rest of the week and it's certainly not fair to take any further advantage of Iris's good nature. Report for duty as normal if you will.'

'Oh that's alright then. I take it you won't be suspendin' 'arriet either?'

'Not your business Mrs. Harrington. Now if you would kindly remove that piece of hand luggage from the boot, I need to be getting back. Miss Glover was it absolutely necessary for you to get out of the car, too?'

'Just making sure our luggage didn't get mixed up Mr. Sanderson. Actually you can drop me off here. Save holding you up.'

'Yes 'arriet come and 'ave a cup of tea with me. We're parched after that long journey.'

'I think not Miss Glover. You're forgetting your car is still at school We've urgent business to attend to once I get you home.'

Harriet shrugged her shoulders at Tricia.

'I'll call you later.'

'It's OK 'arriet I've just spotted Bob's car on the drive, you wouldn't want to be seein' 'im. I'll go in quietly and see if I can't frighten the life out of 'im. It makes a change for me to be the one gone missin'.'

Harriet turned round to see Mr. Sanderson holding the front passenger door open for her. Wasn't sure she wanted to be sitting alongside him. Wasn't sure whether she was suspended or not. Felt intimidated. Her former courage long since evaporated.

'If you don't mind Miss Glover I'll get this back and garaged. Good of Clive to do the honours but I'd rather it was off the road. I'm sure Mrs. Harris will brew us a pot of tea whilst you're making this phone call. I'll pop you back in the Mercedes. I'll need to unlock the school gates for you, anyhow.'

Harriet suddenly thought of Mark. Decided it would be better this way. She wasn't up for a scene should he suddenly burst in on them. Mr. Sanderson was never going to let her make that call on her own.

'No that's fine Mr. Sanderson. I left a message for Mark last night to say I'd be back sometime today. It's probably better all round to get this call out of the way before I go home.'

'Quite. Quite. So Mark's been temporarily reinstated has he Miss Glover? Or maybe he hasn't? Possibly this is a very short arrangement of convenience to you both, given you appear to have other plans now.'

Harriet shifted in her seat as he eased the car into a three-point turn before scorching away from Tricia's road.

'You see Miss Glover, I'm asking because, as I've already mentioned, it's highly likely I'll be wishing to resume the purchase of your house.'

'But I thought you wanted to be given the first option if we decided to sell Mr. Sanderson? I thought from what Mark said, you had drawn all this up with your solicitor. Mark said you were dropping the compensation claim for being let down after exchange as long as you had first option if we decided to move.'

She watched him turn right into the main road, lifting his hand from the gear lever to his chin to take a deep breath before placing it back on the steering wheel.

'You are surely aware Miss Glover, Bryce Rae Roberts still have your property on the market, albeit covertly? I'm afraid with regard to this breach of contract Mark has misunderstood the terms of the agreement in his hurry to let his parents off the hook. I understand they were the ones paying his half of it. Of course at the time your half wasn't going to be a problem since you'd agreed to our marriage. Circumstances are of course very different now, should you be thinking of breaking the agreement I will naturally be looking for the full percentage.'

Harriet couldn't believe he'd just said that. Oh how much now she just wanted to go home. Well past the end of her road now. The way he was driving they'd be at the traffic lights outside Starboard Marine North West and heading for the country lanes to Lower Tideside, in no time. She had no choice but to stick with it.

'But what exactly was the agreement Mr. Sanderson? I'm not surprised Mark's got himself thoroughly confused, not the state he was in at the time.'

'Exactly Miss Glover and I don't hold him in very high regard for allowing you and your guests to get to the church before he informed you it was all off.'

'But he'd been away Mr. Sanderson. He'd only just got back. He didn't know his fear was going to be so crippling as to make him pull out.'

'Not good enough Miss Glover. Phobics know their limitations only too well. This woman, this woman and her parents he left the church with. What was going on there?'

'Melissa Scott you mean? He works with her that's all.'

Moving away from the main road now, well past Starboard Marine North West. Soon they'd be turning left into the country lanes to the rising land and the hills on the far side skirting the river.

'Hmm the name's familiar. But in any case how do you know "that's all" Miss Glover? She could have been instrumental in his decision not to marry you.'

'No, if you remember he gave me a note Mr. Sanderson. A note asking me to forgive him and take him back. I didn't read it for ages, though.'

'Hmm, interesting. Of course that was then. Things move on. Most interesting though. You see I do a little private work from home when I can manage it during the holidays, always have done. I like to keep my hand in as it were. Where does this woman live now, if I might ask?'

'She's in the house we were going to buy in Millington, Mr. Sanderson. 1 Haystack Close.'

'Crikey, I thought it rang a bell! The woman has quite an unruly thatch, couldn't help linking it to her address.'

Harriet panicked, previously intent on looking out for Molly and Percy's house they drove past it unnoticed. Her thoughts whirring, she desperately needed to know why he'd just said that. Mark's words flooding in. Her stomach churning now. This was somewhere she just couldn't go.

'Right here we are Miss Glover.'

He drew the Bentley to a halt on the gravel. Opened the door for her.

'Are you feeling alright Miss Glover? You've gone very pale. A couple of ginger biscuits en route, that's not enough to keep body and soul together. I'll get Mrs. Harris to rustle up a snack.'

She followed behind. The beautiful big old house making little impression on her now. Her head full of Melissa Scott's pregnancy. She needed to know. Knew he'd never betray a patient's confidentiality. Even the thought of selling the house had fast lost its impact.

'Now is it Conny or Onny?' Mrs. Harris twinkled a mischievous smile at Harriet.

'This is Harriet, as you'll recall Mrs. Harris, though I've no doubt she'd prefer a change of identity.'

'Of course it is dear. I'm only teasing. Now what a do that was! If I'd have known I was dealing with criminals that evening, I'd have been away like a shot. I'm so pleased they caught them.' Mrs. Harris tossed her head towards Mr. Sanderson.

'Sometimes having friends in high places isn't all it's cracked up to be.'

Harriet watched him grin. His strong, even white teeth, just the slight imperfection holding her gaze. The dimpling in his cheeks elongating now to lines drawn from the laughter sparkling from his clear blue eyes. The deep pile rug under her feet. She could scarcely believe only a couple of short weeks ago she'd lay there almost naked just wanting him to take her.

' "Any way you like." ' Her words swimming round her head, powerful recall, momentarily sinking almost to her subconscious any thought of Melissa Scott. Then the reality of him and Lucinda Lawton. In the jewellers, buying that ring. Thought. 'Of course he was. What else would he have been doing in there with her?'

'Er Mrs. Harris, we'll be in my study. Could you see your way to rustle up some scrambled eggs on toast for us both if you would be so kind?'

'Certainly Mr. Sanderson. Where would you like it?'

'The dining room if you would please, Mrs. Harris. Oh and follow it with tea and that delicious ginger cake you made yesterday.'

Mrs. Harris nodded and beamed. 'Ah you remembered?'

'It wouldn't be Sunday without it.' He smiled. A little praise took her far.

Harriet followed him through.

'Take a seat Miss Glover. Here, by the window, we'll each take an armchair. I must say one does get used to one's own car. He couldn't budge that damned seat. It's good to be able to stretch one's legs.'

He sat opposite. She looked around the room. Paintings and glass all against white, every shade of the sea.

'Now Miss Glover, this is all very familiar to you. Must be the third or fourth time you've been in here.'

'Yes Mr. Sanderson. Sorry, it's just that it gives me such pleasure to look around, to be here.'

'Really? You do surprise me! Now, where were we? Ah yes, this woman from Millington.'

Harriet took a deep breath. Thought. 'Surely he's not going to break patient confidentiality after all?' Panicked. Couldn't bear the truth.

'It's starting to ring loud and clear neither you or Mark will be requiring 4 The Willows now in any case, Miss Glover. Therefore it presents a very appropriate opportunity for me to acquire it at this time.'

'But I'm not sure what you mean Mr. Sanderson. Are you suggesting Melissa Scott is pregnant so Mark will be rushing back to her?'

'Indeed I am not suggesting anything of the sort Miss Glover. I'm not in the business of betraying patient confidentiality as well you know.'

'Well what did you mean then Mr. Sanderson? Why should Mark and I be looking to sell just now?'

'Circumstances Miss Glover. Self-evident or so it would appear. It shouldn't be necessary to detail you.'

Harriet fumed. Her house for Lucinda Lawton? No way!

'That suggests you know something we don't Mr. Sanderson because I can't think of one single reason why we would be wanting to sell just now.'

'Really Miss Glover. Now that does surprise me. You paint an interesting picture indeed. Now, let's move on shall we?'

He turned to the knock on the door.

'Yes, yes, come in. Do come in Mrs. Harris.'

'Oh only to say if you'd like to take your seats in the dining room your meal is almost ready.'

'Ah thanks Mrs. Harris, we'll follow through now.'

He stood a few seconds ahead of Harriet. She felt his arm brush around her shoulders as he ushered her forward while holding the door open.

'Just through there Miss Glover. But of course you know. I'm forgetting it was only a short while ago we were dining in here with the PM.'

Harriet had far from forgotten. She tried to squash the nervous pang spreading in every direction from the depths of her stomach.

'Now Miss Glover, it's probably better we eat before making that call. You certainly need the sustenance by the look of you.'

He lifted the chair away from the solid oak table to allow her to sit down. Just two glasses and a jug of iced water. Tried to forget the bottle of red tantalisingly close sitting next to the table lamp to her right at the end of the sideboard.

'Ah Mrs. Harris. Splendid! Thank you.'

'I'll leave you two to it then.'

Harriet smiled and thanked her. Looked down to the hot buttered toast almost lost under the neatly spooned heaps of yellow fluffy egg. Just a sprinkling of fresh green herbs towards the centre.

'Now Miss Glover, I want to see a clean plate, please.'

He smiled her that smile as he pushed his chair backwards to rise to his feet. Started muttering.

'Come, come Mrs. Harris. One of these won't do us any harm. At all!'

Harriet jumped. Turned. He smiled again. Bottle in hand two wine glasses in the other.

'We've had a long journey. I think this might help it down.'

She smiled. Watched his hand on the bottle as he popped the cork. Listened as the symphony of glugs played before her. He took his seat, raised his glass.

'To whom or what are we toasting?'

'For you it had better be the purchase of 4 The Willows Mr. Sanderson, I can't think of anything else.'

From above the rim of his glass, his eyes penetrating blue, cutting straight into hers. One eyebrow not quite catching the other in a frown. His eyes narrowing now. His chest expanding to make his breath heard. Still his eyes holding hers, she had to look away.

'I need to know Miss Glover. For goodness sake can't you see I need to know?'

Instinctively her arm crossed her waist. Suddenly desperate for this gorgeous, georgous man to know. Then the thought of Lucinda Lawton instantly killed it dead.

'But I can't give you an answer until I've spoken to Mark Mr. Sanderson. It's his house as well.'

'You're purposely deviating Miss Glover. This is not something you're going to be able to hide for too much longer. Now I suggest we eat.'

He cleared his throat then raised his drink.

'To you Miss Glover. Whilst the light's still on amber.'

She blushed almost to the colour of the Chateaux Neuf du Pape trembling in her glass wondering just how he knew.

'No to you Mr. Sanderson. It's better to toast to green.'

'Green Miss Glover? I'm afraid I don't quite follow.'

'But you're always on green Mr. Sanderson. You're always up for everything.'

'Ah, I see. In that case let's make a toast to red, "respice adspice prospice". We'll toast to that shall we Miss Glover?'

'No I can't possibly. Not until I know exactly what it means.'

'Just a little advice to stop and take stock Miss Glover. Just think about the past, the present - where you are at now and the implications for the future. Here's to common sense prevailing Miss Glover.'

She lifted her glass to his, was beginning to think the opportunity to take her first sip would never arise. Allowing her taste buds to fully indulge the spiced warmth of fruit, almost melting in relief she stretched her legs forward then suddenly made a grab for the cream linen napkin sliding from her lap to the floor.

'What ever are you doing Miss Glover? Here let me give you a hand. Good heavens don't choke down there.'

Clutching her napkin to her face, eyes streaming, trying to cough and coax the raw burning away from the edges of her throat she felt his hand patting her back.

'Here, take a sip of this.'

Over her shoulder he stretched forward, she could feel his arm against her right cheek.Trapped, cradled to his chest as he passed her the glass he'd just filled with water.

'Take it steady Miss Glover.'

'Oh I'm terribly sorry Mr. Sanderson. I didn't spill any did I?'

'Just down there I'm afraid Miss Glover.'

She turned to look down. Feeling his fingertips barely touch between the top of her breasts she braced herself against the instant surge of helpless desire running through her body settling into that familiar aching need.

'Just a little, I can't tell if it's gone any further down.' He reached for his napkin. 'May I?'

Harriet nodded to the quick dab. In a tick he was back in his seat.

'Sorry about that, but thank you for that. For sorting me out, I mean. I do apologise though. At least let me take the napkins home to wash.' The words were all wrong. Like the whole thing. Uncomfortably Ross Farquerhart came to mind. Wished she'd never stopped to chat. 'I'll take them home...,' she continued.

'No, certainly not. No harm done!'

She barely heard his words or the wine leaving the bottle as he topped up her glass.

'Now let's eat this shall we before it gets cold?'

Flushed, she fell into a dazed silence as the scrambled egg refused to hold to her fork.

'Now, forgive the connection Miss Glover but how do you suppose that bra ended up in Ross Farquerhart's hamper?'

'Oh I really wouldn't know Mr. Sanderson. I don't even know whose hamper it was to start with.'

'Come, come Miss Glover, I have it on good authority you were actually spotted on the cliff top with him.'

'No Mr. Sanderson, that's not fair! Anyway who told you that? Oh no don't tell me. It was Belinda Oxfordshire I bet, going out of her way to cause trouble again.'

'It may or may not have been Miss Glover. You and Mrs. Harrington certainly appear to have gone out of your way to make life difficult for her, not to mention me. It was enough to convince her that damned engagement's back on. Someone's got some explaining to do and it's certainly not up to me. Now this bra?'

'Well surely it's up to whoever sent the hamper Mr. Sanderson? It's up to them to explain.'

'It's inevitable you're referring to Ross Farquerhart. The boy's got his damned wires crossed. His parents are in the business. It couldn't be anyone else.'

'Just because we sat chatting a little while on the cliff top hardly means he's going to propose to me.'

'From all accounts it was a little more than that Miss Glover. Another damned man wanting to marry you. No, I stand corrected. A boy, what? Can't be any more than twenty-two years old. You can give him twenty years or more any day Miss Glover!'

'No, not more, less actually and in any case it was Belinda Oxfordshire making the beeline for him, not me. He called her the camp cougar and wanted her off his back.'

'Precisely Miss Glover, you've rather hit on the truth. You were supposed to be in that tent. Ross Farquerhart would never have had that delivered to her. Mrs. Harrington indeed, informing her I'd arranged for a hamper to be delivered. No wonder the bloody woman thinks it's all back on! Nothing could be further from the truth. Anyhow as you are aware I've suspended you Miss Glover until such time as I find out exactly what's going on. This is another reason for bringing you back here. You were on contractual duty this week and it appears your behaviour has been highly inappropriate. I need to know what this business is all about. If you are not already aware, Ross Farquerhart has taken a gap year to research his PhD and I'm closely involved in this. I'm not putting my reputation on the line as to be party to any affair you may or may not have embarked on.'

'Well I haven't embarked on anything Mr. Sanderson.'

'You were seen Miss Glover. It's in your interest to tell me the truth now.'

'That is the truth! Yes we were sat together on the cliff top and before I knew it he rolled over to kiss me. Then he tried to lower my straps and I called a halt. And that's the truth. What do you take me for?'

'After that painting, I'm not too sure Miss Glover.'

'But I've already told you when we were on the coach, Barry Giordano made it up. You can ask him if you like, I'll be phoning him soon.'

'Yes indeed! I might just do that. Now back to Ross Farquerhart. The bra size. Bang on! It hardly bears your story out.'

'How do you know it was bang on. How do you know I'm a 36D? I don't recall ever showing you any labels.'

'Ah you seem to forget Miss Glover. Your bra, my bow tie, I took them both if you recall from your tumble dryer, last year. Indeed I checked the size. Not something I'd forget in a hurry. Come, come Miss Glover, he must have known. Not something that can be so accurately assessed.'

Suddenly enraged Harriet placed her knife and fork down.

'I'm NOT a 36D. Look at the label in this if you like.'

They both pushed their empty plates to one side. She felt him lift her top from behind.

'No, I'm afraid I can't see the damned thing from here.'

'Well the size is there on the label. Oh come here.' Furious she dropped the straps. Reached around her back to unclasp it, then pulled the whole thing through the armholes of her top.

'There Mr. Sanderson. As you won't be convinced otherwise, take a look for yourself. I think you'll find it says 36DD.'

'Indeed it does. You've gone to great pains Harriet to try prove your innocence.'

'When I didn't have to, actually. If Belinda Oxfordshire had stayed a bit longer wherever she was snooping from, she would have seen us both sit up. You would. Anyone would because that's what happened. Absolutely nothing!'

'Yes, please do accept my apologies Harriet. I'm having the greatest of difficulties coming to terms with the events of the last couple of weeks. I probably need to get away for a while. You're a total paradox Harriet and in a strange way I've been both drawn and repelled by those very personality traits that frequently give way to mayhem. I'm perfectly satisfied now. As with Mrs. Harrington this will go no further than an informal suspension. If you could see your way to giving her a hand at Starboard Marine North West this coming week the status quo will be maintained. I've managed to talk Clive Engells round though goodness knows why. As far as he's concerned he's dropped the idea of making a case of your behaviour but he remains furious with the pair of you. Indeed it appears he owes me one. Unfortunately it would seem he's roped me in for taking that damned Rapping Hammer boy on the next Fastnet race. There's always a payback for a favour Miss Glover, though somewhat pre-empted. Now I think I've got Mrs. Harrington to thank for that. What the hell was she doing getting embroiled with him to the point he parks that hideous van of his on the campsite? Did she invite him? Really between the two of you, I've been well and truly landed. Right in it I'm afraid.'

Instantly she felt for him. Could feel herself drowning in a tsunami of regret. Instinctively wanted to take him in her arms.

'Oh I'm so very sorry Mr. Sanderson, you don't deserve any of it.' She twisted the bra in her hands.

'Well that's a first Harriet!' His smile spreading. Drawn like a bee to pollen she wondered yet again just why she'd turned this most gorgeous of men down.

'Now, I'll just pop out whilst you put that back on. You must try Mrs.

Harris's ginger cake. I'll get her to serve it in the lounge.'

He smiled. That smile again. Flicked his thick blonde hair through his fingers. Raised his eyebrows, turning his head to one side.

'Or perhaps I can give you a hand with that?'

The throbbing back in an instant. In her mind. 'Yes, yes, yes! His baby in here. Inside me. Now. Let him Harriet. Let him! Let him!'

His hands on her shoulders. From behind slipping both the straps of her top away, gently easing it down to her waist. She turned to face him conscious of her naked breasts, full and heavy. He stood back to look. His face serious now. Moved closer to brush his fingertips briefly, gently against her nipples; erect, sending waves of erotic desire through her trembling, throbbing body. His hands firm, simultaneously raising both breasts, for a few seconds supporting the fullness.

'Beautiful Harriet. You are magnificently beautiful but they're fuller and heavier than I recall. Forgive me Harriet if I'm wearing my doctor's hat but I don't think I'm wrong in saying these breasts are beginning to show signs of pregnancy. The reason for the "DD" perhaps?'

A quick knock came from behind.

'Yes, yes Mrs. Harris. I'm just coming.'

Her head popped round. Harriet nearly died. She'd never witnessed a door close so quickly in all her life.

'Let's get you dressed now Harriet. I apologise for that. Most unusual for Mrs. Harris. Of course she wouldn't be expecting it knowing I wasn't in consultation.'

'In consultation?' Harriet queried, blushing profusely, as she scrambled back into her bra and top.

'Yes, I think I've already explained to you, in addition to locum work, I do have a small register of private patients. Mrs. Harris is aware of that.'

'Just a minute, you didn't bring me here to turn me into another one of those, I hope?'

'No of course not Harriet. Look we made love on the sand. I asked you to marry me. We've been as close and as intimate as two people in love can be. You told me you were pregnant and now you're telling me you're not. You don't seem to be able to appreciate the position you're putting me in. You want to stay on amber as you call it. But things move on Harriet. You can't bury your head in the sand forever. Come through to the lounge. Just let me have a quick word with my long-suffering housekeeper.'

He turned in the direction of the kitchen pointing Harriet towards the lounge door. Instantly she bumped into Mrs. Harris, tray clasped to her matronly bosom.

' "A change of identity" I think he said. I reckon he could do with one himself. Oh don't worry too much about it Harriet, it's happened before. Well just once, when I didn't realise he still had a patient in there.'

Harried breathed a huge sigh of relief. Then she didn't.

'Oh apart from one night last week,' she lowered her voice. 'Brought a young lady back here. Can't think of her name, Belinda, Cassandra, Lucinda, Andrea? Oh I can't remember which one it was. He thought I'd gone and I thought they'd both gone. My word I'm getting good practice at closing these old doors quickly.'

'Ah Mrs. Harris. A word in the kitchen if you will?'

Harriet sat herself down. Swallowed hard. Tried to rationalise the incident.

'He's a full-blooded hunk of a man. Why should he live like a monk just because I wanted to stay on amber?' Then she corrected herself. 'Not wanted. No that's not right. Want. No it's definitely "want" now. Well it certainly wouldn't have been Belinda. No. Yes it was Lucinda. And didn't I just know it! No it's definitely not "want to stay on amber" any more. I'm on green. Absolutely on green from now on. Why should he be the only one on green? Just wait until I make that phone call to Barry Giordano. Oh I wish I just hadn't let him do that to me.'

'Ah Harriet. All sorted with Mrs. Harris now. You can be assured of her complete confidentiality.'

'And I don't think,' Harriet thought. She stopped herself from blurting it out.

'Ah jolly good, we have the ginger cake at last. Come along Harriet, do try it and don't forget to take my advice. The sooner the better if you're not to be plagued with morning sickness for the next couple of months.'

'Not morning sickness Mr. Sanderson. It was a bit of a tummy bug. I think I've told you that already. Actually I'm feeling very much better now.'

'Good. I'm most relieved to hear it. Another four weeks will see you at the end of this first trimester Harriet. We do indeed have much to discuss, not least of which yours and Mark's intentions particularly in relation to the sale of the house.'

Harriet felt the bit of cake in her mouth turn to a dry hard pumice stone. She swallowed hard. Thought. 'For Lucinda Lawton? No, no, he's absolutely not getting away with that one.'

She gulped her tea then reached for the mobile phone in her bag.

'I'd better phone Barry now.'

'Do use the landline Harriet. Here let me bring the table over to you.'

She fished for her address book. Watched the two pressed buttercups fall from the back inside cover to the dark polished rosewood table-top now placed in front of her.

'Do find out exactly what's going on, if you will Harriet?' He smiled her that smile. She carefully stored it to the back of her mind.

'Oh hi Barry, Harriet here. I promised to call you back.'

......'Oh fine thanks. No I wouldn't count on that. Not yet anyway.'

......'No I'm with Mr. Sanderson at the moment Barry.'

......'But what's it all about anyway?'

......'A backlash? Oh gosh. But we thought it was all over and done with.'

......'No, surely not?'

...... 'Oh here, Mr. Sanderson wants a word about the painting.'

...... 'Sanderson here. This damned thing not sorted yet?'

...... 'Oh I see. Right thanks for that.'

...... 'The painting?'

...... 'Oh, I'm afraid I'm not of a mind to discuss it.'

...... 'No it's your affair. Totally your own affair.'

...... 'Yes I'll get on to the PM right away. The warning's appreciated. I'll pass you back.'

...... 'Hi Barry.'

...... 'No don't worry, we'll be very careful. Oh just before you go I've seen a perfect ring. Amber stones set in the shape of a buttercup.'

...... 'Peru Barry? Yes I'll certainly give it some thought. Must go now Barry. Don't be getting embroiled in any of this yourself. Take care.'

With an enormous sense of satisfaction Harriet replaced the receiver. Watched Mr. Sanderson lift the table away with one hand, steadying the phone with the other. Now at her feet. His palm uplifted.

'I take it you won't be wanting to keep these any more Harriet?'

The two pressed buttercups. She shook her head whilst screaming in silence, begging him not to throw them away. He strode out. Her satisfaction gone. What had she just done to her precious buttercups? Her precious moments with this gorgeous, gorgeous man in the field of flowers. What had she just done to get her own back? And on top of all that the last thing she wanted was to wind Barry Giordano up again. She fidgeted in her seat, waiting for his return.

'So it would seem there's a straggle of them to watch out for Harriet. Naturally enough I suppose they've not taken to having their cover blown. Of course Giordano couldn't say too much but whilst they expect the focus to be on London, there's an outside chance of a reprisal up here. I think we just need to be cautious for a while. Certainly their operation has been well blown but as the PM said Interpol will remain vigilant.'

'Oh no, I thought all that was well and truly done with. Well let's just hope there'll be no one up here trying to kidnap Tricia or me. Or both! Double ransom!'

'What! Would anyone be foolish enough to pay to bring either of you back?'

She watched his face serious, now breaking into that most mischievous of grins.

'I'd pay them to take the pair of you away, no bother!'

'Well that's not a very nice thing to say Mr. Sanderson, is it? Given what we've just been through.'

'Self inflicted Harriet. All self inflicted. You could have been safely installed here, making me ginger cake, but you didn't want that either.'

'Look Mr. Sanderson I've seen that Aga sitting in your kitchen. You'd have had me shovelling coal into that thing trying to get a bit of a ginger cake to rise. I'd have been terrible. Certainly no match for Mrs. Harris. I'm much better off as I am.'

His shoulders moving now to his laughter. Harriet watching the blonde curls at his collar. She'd just said all the wrong things again. Thought. 'How can I possibly stay on green with this gorgeous hunk of a man around?'

'Oh come on Harriet, let's get you back to your car so you can get home. It's been a long, long day.'

Chapter 28

'Hi Hat, I got your message to say you were coming back early. You just forgot to say when. I was going to phone you tonight to find out what was going on. Had a good trip?'

'Hi Mark. Yes thanks, it wasn't bad. You had a good day? What have you got your suit on for? You haven't been to work, have you?'

'I had to go in Hat. My share of weekend entertaining. We've got the Swedes over.'

'Oh right. Had a good lunch then?'

'Not bad, not bad. When did you get back?'

'I've been in about an hour. Gosh it's good to be home. Missed me?'

'Come here Hat, of course I've missed you. What brought you back so soon? You haven't been causing mayhem in Dorset, you and Tricia, have you?'

'Oh something like that Mark. We seem to attract it. Mr. Sanderson insisted we come back with him.'

'So lard ball's had enough too?'

'Oh he was only going to get the thing off the ground. He wanted to get back to make sure the summer activities are all in place. They start next week. Of course he's roped me in.'

'Yes he'll probably dump the lot on you Hat. Looks like he's got bigger fish to fry.'

'Bigger fish Mark, what do you mean? Could his fish possibly get any bigger? Oh hang on you don't mean him standing for parliament do you?'

'That's exactly it. It's all over the sailing club. Let's hope he gets elected. Gets out of that school for good.'

'We'll need a general election for that Mark. They seem to be clinging on. Anyway I can't see him risking his job for that. Suppose he didn't win? What would he do then?'

'Oh come on Harriet. With his string of directorships? And don't forget he's still got Starboard Marine North West and that coffee franchising business. He's hardly going to be twiddling his thumbs all day. That headship's neither here nor there to him. Gives him the chance to swan around, gets him the holidays, I suppose. Let's keep our fingers crossed Hat. The way things are going I don't see this government making it to Christmas never mind next May.'

Harriet went quiet. Instantly switched from green to amber. Even if he left to become an MP, even if he married Lucinda Lawton she still needed to see him. Needed him to be at the school. Then realisation! 'My baby! He'll always be a part of me no matter what. Whatever happens my baby will keep me on amber.'

'He did mention something about becoming a councillor though.'

'Not his scene I would think. Oh no, you mark my words if he's going to do anything he'll do it big.'

'No Mark he's wanting to do something for the people such as our parents who are really feeling the pinch. People like Mrs. Bustard. You know her Bert's been made redundant and they are just so hard up. She's become embroiled with a pawnbroker, a money lending place, now. Oh I feel so sorry for her. That's why I know they'll be over the moon to get this boat. You are good Mark. Really, really good.'

'Yes Harriet I'm just too good to be true. Coming up while I get changed?'

'Now that depends what for Mark. I've had enough for today.'

'Oh I see. You've had enough for today then? I won't ask who with.'

'Oh Mark just shut up. Stop grinning like that. It's not funny. I've travelled all the way back from Dorset don't forget.'

'Hardly the South Pole Hat. Which reminds me we'll be off again soon.'

'Oh no, not so soon Mark, surely? How long for this time?'

'We haven't had the details yet but this one sounds good. At some point there'll be a trip to the Galapagos Islands to link climate change data.'

'What and then flying back to the South Pole? Oh no that sounds like a very long trip to me.'

'Well it's one of those. They seem to make it up as they go along. It might not be me that gets to go there but however long, it's going to be too long Hat. You're going to need me to look after you both soon.'

Melissa Scott immediately flashed through her mind.

'Us both? Exactly which both do you mean? Flipping heck Mark how can you say it so calmly?'

'Oh I've well come to terms with it Harriet. I thought you had, too?'

'Well I've only been away a few days, I've hardly had time to get my head round it.'

'Come up Hat. We can talk up there. I want to get back to the boat. I want to get it finished before I go away.'

'Oh down Pepper, down. No you just stay down here a minute.'

She shoved the cat into the kitchen with her foot and closed the door quickly to catch Mark striding up the stairs two at a time.

'What boat is it exactly you're working on Mark?'

'I found an old Mirror dinghy down there in not bad condition at all. It should suit the three of them just fine.'

'Oh Mark, that's absolutely wonderful. Come here, let's give you a kiss.'

'Oh is that all I'm getting Harriet? I'll need a bit more than that if I'm going to get it finished in time.'

'Mark what are you looking under there for? You know your loafers are in the bottom of the wardrobe. No Mark don't put them there. Shoes don't go under the bed because they get kicked far too far back and the cat sits in them, remember?' She panicked, wondered if she'd pushed that painting far enough under.

'Stop trying to change the subject Hat. Wrong! I've just put my hands on them. Best place under the bed.'

Sure she'd put them in the wardrobe she panicked at the thought of him finding the painting, sensed Mark was about to ask a question.

'Now I think I want to know. Who have you had enough with Harriet?' She breathed a sigh of relief.

'I've just told you, it's not anybody, it's the long journey, that's all.'

'Then let me refresh you Hat. Are you really pleased with what I'm doing?'

'Oh Mark of course I thank you from the bottom of my heart.'

'Only the bottom of your heart Hat? Oh I think you can do a bit better than that.'

'No I can't. It's exactly how I feel. I can't tell you what it will mean for Danny and his mum and dad right now. I can't tell you how thrilled I am.'

'Of course you can't Hat. Words are totally inadequate. But you can show me how you feel. I worked and worked. I've got no strength left in my hands. You'll need to undress me Hat. I can't go down there in my work suit.'

'Oh Mark stop being so silly. Here let me take that tie off.'

'But the sun's shining straight in Hat. Everyone can see us. Close the curtains first.'

'Oh Mark I'm not your nursemaid. Anyway, it seems you're all set to look after the two of us. You'll need a bit more energy than that, hopping from one to the other. Night feeds, nappies. I honestly don't see it working.'

'Come here Hat. What are you talking about?'

'Melissa Scott, pregnant. You're certainly going to have your work cut out. I don't believe it's happened. It's just too much of a coincidence to be real. I don't want you to be looking after us both Mark. You'd be far better going to live with her in Millington. Less complicated. At least it will be your child. I don't really see you being here, taking on all that work for *his baby*.'

He pulled her down to the bed.

'Look Harriet, let's get this straight. This one's going to be mine as well. For all intents and purposes I'll be its father. If he'll agree I'll adopt it. If not I'll be here with you anyway. I'll be seeing far more of it than he will. Looking after the two of you is the two of you lying right next to me here. That's all I'm wanting to do. As far as Melissa Scott's concerned I don't even know whether she *is* pregnant. She took responsibility for that herself, or so she assured me, but I didn't take any chances either. I honestly think it's most unlikely but even if she is, it's all over between us. I wouldn't have called it an affair exactly, anyway.'

'But what about financial support Mark, won't you have to pay towards it? We can't afford that. Mr. Sanderson's still going on about buying this again and he's talking about his compensation.'

'You know why, don't you Harriet?'

'No I do not. Go on tell me.'

'Not unless you let me take your top off Hat.'

'Oh Mark I've already had it off today.' She rolled towards him, buried her face in his neck for fear he'd notice her blushing.

'Ah so you *have* had enough for today. Who was it with Harriet?'

'No Mark you're getting the wrong end of the stick. I put it on inside out to start with. Had the label on the outside.'

'Oh I see, well let me show you just where the label goes Hat. ......There, that's better. Now just a minute. Is this on inside out too?'

'Oh Mark, you know quite well it wouldn't fasten if it was inside out.'

'Come here Hat. Roll that way. The label's certainly showing 36DD. My word you're getting to be a handful. Or two, even.'

'Mark. You don't need to undo it.'

'Oh yes I do Hat. This label needs to be straightened. Look it's got itself all creased up the wrong way. You can't possibly wear it like this.'

'Are you going to tell me now Mark?'

'Not until you've wriggled yourself out of these.'

'But Mark you've undone it. I thought you were in a hurry to get to the boat.'

'Oh I am Hat. That's why I need your full cooperation.'

'Look Mark I really want to know.'

'There, just slip the other strap off. Now that's better. That's so much better. You're beautiful Hat. Do you know that?'

'No Mark, I don't know that at all. Now why is Mr. Sanderson wanting to open up this compensation thing and get us out of here as well?'

'Not while I'm this close to you Hat. Mmm I've missed you. What about everything else? These jeans. The label in good order is it? Roll over again Hat. No just let me undo the button and unzip this. Come on Hat slide them off. .....There that's better. Much better. You know you've got the most gorgeous legs? Now these. What about the label in these? It's most important I check it out Hat.'

'These are staying on Mark.'

'But Hat you always make me do that. We get this far and you won't take them off. Now why's that Hat? Roll over again. I need to check the label. Oh I can't see it. Let's just slide them down a bit.'

'No Mark these are staying on.'

'But you know there's no room for me in there as well Hat. Remember the struggle we had last time? It never used to be like that.'

'And you never used to be like this.'

'But you just get more and more gorgeous. You can't blame me. It was so, so good last time. You can't have forgotten already?'

'No Mark I haven't forgotten. It was so good we did it again and again.'

'And again Hat. And the next morning. "For old times sake" I seem to remember. Mmm Harriet. Is my luck in? These aren't the stretchy ones by any chance, are they?'

'Afraid not Mark.'

'Mmm there's a label somewhere in here Hat. Would it be down this side?'

'Just don't go any further with those Mark, back to where they were please.'

'Oh Hat I haven't got to start stretching again, have I? One of these days I'll lose it completely faffing about like this and then where will you be?'

'I'll just have to find someone else better at stretching then, won't I?'

'Let's try round the back Hat. Oh that's much better. No one could stretch these like this. Could it just be I'm that man after all?'

'No Mark no, this is just so unromantic.'

'Let's take them off then Hat. Let's do romance my way, shall we?'

'No Mark, no, I've just told you, these won't go that far.'

'They did last time Hat.'

'But these are different ones. These aren't mine at all.'

'What do you mean Hat? Do you mean I'm playing with someone else's knickers?'

'Well yes, if you must know.'

'Oh I must know Hat. Whose are they then?'

'Not now Mark. Not when we're as close as this.'

'Spoilsport Hat. Did you lose your own?'

'No Mark absolutely not.'

'How come then Harriet?'

'It's a long story Mark. I'll tell you when you get back.'

'Mmm Hat. When I get back? Back from where?'

'The Galapagos Islands Mark, when you get back from there.'

'But I might not be chosen and if I am you mean I've got to wait until then?'

'You've got to wait until then Mark.'

'Oooh there's more give in this than I thought. No one could ever stretch elastic as well as me and still be ready for action. Lesser men would have wilted by all this delay. I'm surely that man Hat. No one could perform to this standard. I've really got the hang of it now. Mmmm Hat, I'm just about there.'

'OUCH! Mark you flipping well twanged that right against my back.'

'The bloody phone Harriet. Who the hell's that? Oh someone's prattling now. Might have guessed it sounds just like your mother. Can't you hear her demolishing the answer machine? Frightened the life out of me it did.'

'Serves you right for showing off. Thanks a bunch Mark! I'm back to *green* now if you did but know it. I'll find me a man that can hang on to the elastic even in the face of adversity.'

'Then you'd better just do that Harriet. Did *he* manage it any better then?'

'Out of order Mark. Completely out of order! And what about Melissa green?'

'Oh that's what you meant. She's just turned into a colour has she?'

'Yes, froggy green if you must know with a haystack head. I suppose she wears paper ones. Saves the environment. You'd only have needed to manage a tear.'

'Very funny Harriet and I don't think. If you were normal we wouldn't be having this row. How many men have to cope with stretching elastic, I ask you?'

She thought of the small patch of blue lace resting on the warm damp sand. Felt guilty at never even asking *him* to try.

Chapter 29

'Right I'm off then Harriet.'

'But aren't you going to have something to eat first? Look Mark I'm sorry. I didn't mean it. Go and get a takeway for us both and a couple of bottles of wine. We've had a busy day. Leave the boat for tonight. We really do need to talk.'

'OK Hat. Look I'm sorry too. I can't help fancying you like crazy. You know that don't you? I shouldn't have gone there just now but you're radiant Harriet. You're absolutely radiant. It's ridiculous, after all these years together, I can't get enough of you.'

'No it's not ridiculous Mark. I love you too, don't forget. We've both been through a lot. We've put each other through it. It's going to take time to come to terms with it all, we're both going to have to realise that. We need to get things sorted out, like the house and what's happening with Melissa Scott. That's something we could both have done without. Tell me Mark why *are* you being so good about this baby? Why should you want to take all this on? It was all of my own doing going with *him*, I just wish I hadn't. I've been desperate for another baby so many times. Maybe it was disappointment or maybe Mummy was right. It could be something to do with my age and hormones making me go off the rails like that.'

'It's more to do with the fact I haven't been able to commit Harriet. I know you've always wanted another baby but you wanted marriage for it, too. I couldn't give you either. Though it will be damned perverse if I've managed to make Melissa Scott pregnant, rather than you. I don't think I'll ever be able to fathom it out, if she is.'

'There's not much we can do about it if that's the case Mark but let's hope not. We've enough to deal with.'

'I know Hat, I know. You could have married him Harriet. He wanted you, he probably still does, but you chose to come back to me even though you're having his baby. He gave you both of the things you wanted, both of the things I couldn't but you chose to come back to me. We're not married. You're not legally bound to anyone. You've stayed loyal to me year on year and like I said, deep down I feared this very scenario but I kidded myself it wouldn't happen. You're beautiful Harriet, men find you attractive, desirable. I know. I see the way they look at you. I've always known Sanderson for what he is. You're not the first. You won't be the last. But this baby is not all his you know. It will very much be a part of you, the you I love. I can do it Harriet. I really can do it. Don't ever question it again. Promise?'

'I promise Mark. It's lovely to hear you say all that. I know I don't deserve you.'

'We deserve each other Hat, the way I see it we're now absolute quits. In a strange way you've made me feel so much better about myself. I've always had you on a pedestal. It's good to know we've both got faults and failings.'

'Yes you're so right and it's good we both recognise it. Look, you go and get the meals and I'll set the table and warm the plates. Let's just enjoy a night in together for a change, shall we? I'll play Mummy's message while you're gone.'

'Oh drat Harriet, I've just remembered you're away. Still I might just as well continue now I've started. You know Mrs. Moss was telling me she's been to your estate agent herself wanting to know exactly what's what with your house. Apparently Avril's fallen in love with it. Short-sighted girl. That good-for-nothing hippy you insist on staying with has let it go to seed. Anyway you told me you weren't doing viewings Harriet. Don't you remember leaving the poor girl standing there on the doorstep with her mother for hours that Saturday morning? Well I told Violet surely she could do better than that. It does need a lot doing to it, that loafing partner of yours hasn't done much to improve it over the years. I couldn't help but notice the morning of the wedding. Well, shall we say the supposed wedding, letting you down like that. I'll never forgive him Harriet. Good heavens haven't you got any sense whatsoever? There's Sir Joris just waiting for you to come up with a wedding date and all you can do is stall him. Such a handsome, charming man Harriet. So very well connected and such a joy to listen to. Very well spoken. So very knowledgeable, too. Oh such an intelligent man. A gentleman so refined, truly fit for royalty. He'd be snapped up if there were any of them at the Palace needing a husband, I'm quite sure but it seems he's not good enough for you. Harriet will you please come to your senses for all our sakes? Daddy and I want to see you settled. We want to see you do well for yourself like James and Geraldine have. You're not as young as you used to be you know Harriet. I've told you before there are plenty of younger and prettier girls than you around. Now where was I? Ah yes, Avril. You know the poor girl's pregnant Harriet. Violet's at her wits end with her. Another stubborn little madam if ever there was one. Violet doesn't want them piling in with her and Cedric because they've nowhere decent to live when the baby comes. The lease on that poky little place they're renting is coming to an end you know. Violet and Cedric have got the money to help them out but it's not much use if she only wants your house, Harriet. Violet's been told it's still on the market but it's "resting", whatever that means. The agent is supposed to be getting in touch with you to find out what's going on. I want to know if you've sorted it out with them yet? Violet is getting very impatient with it all and I do wish I could be of help but of course you're away. I'll just have to tell her that. You either sell it or you don't Harriet. You don't leave it hanging in the air. And that reminds me you promised to sort my hanging basket out the day you did my hair, but no, nothing. But then that's how you are yourself Harriet, just hanging in the air like a bat. And as blind as one as far as your future's concerned. Do phone the minute you get back and I want to know the date. If you don't get on with it I'll be fixing it myself. I will not see you throw away this chance for bettering yourself. After all Harriet you are a dame now. That's why he did it you stupid girl. He's levelled you up to sit better with his circle of friends. He couldn't have done any more to help you Harriet and you have no sense of appreciation whatsoever. Just listen to me will you for once!'

'Golly Pepper, Mark was right. It's a wonder this thing hasn't sparked into flames and burnt itself out. She's so heated. She doesn't believe in mincing her words either. I think we'll delete it Pepper, right now. We don't want Mark hearing any of that. Come on Pepper let's lay the table, he'll be back before we know it.'

* * *

'What did she have to say then Hat?'

'Oh just the usual. Apparently Violet Moss's daughter still wants this. I got the impression she's been shown around as she seems to have fallen in love with it. You haven't had them round by any chance, have you Mark?'

'I haven't Hat. Well not me. I gave the agent the key and told them to get on with it.'

'But you didn't say anything before when I told you Mr. Sanderson wanted to buy it back.'

'Too much else on my mind.'

'But why did you do that Mark? You know we're legally contracted to sell to him.'

'Oh I've lost track of the whole thing, it's easier to do as I'm told.'

'Well the flipping estate agent should have checked it out when Mrs. Moss went in pestering. I don't know what's with that girl. There's plenty of other houses up for sale round here. Why can't she just buy one of those?'

'Don't ask me Harriet! Anyway Bryce Rae Roberts will have been on to lard ball, surely? Maybe he wants to do a double deal or something.'

'What, without consulting us?'

'Well it sounds like he's already raised the question with you Hat.'

'To be honest I don't know where he's coming from. All of a sudden he's talking about buying this and claiming compensation. It's not as if he needs the money.'

'These'll go cold Hat. Come on we can talk while we're eating.'

'Wow you've pushed the boat out. "Chateaux Neuf du Pape" and two bottles. Oh well done. Just let me get a couple of glasses. Gosh we both need it.'

'Cheers Hat. Here's to us and our new little one.'

'Cheers Mark. Here's to us all. Not forgetting Rachael and Clare and our new sons-in-law. Oh gosh Mark, what on earth are they going to say about all this?'

'Our lives Hat. At least we're together. You never know they might produce a few of their own. Wasn't there some talk about them coming to live up here, all of them?'

'Well if there was it can't be imminent. The pair of them are looking at houses down there, next door to each other if they can manage it. That's the impression I got, at least.'

'I wonder where I got that from then Hat? We'll just have to see how things pan out. Ironic isn't it? Them both getting married on the same day and on the same day as we both didn't. It's bad Hat I don't think I'll ever forgive myself for letting you down like that.'

'But don't forget how much I was letting *you* down Mark. I can't ever imagine you'd have been able to take the shock of it all and then go on to get married. A quick chat in the vestry while all the guests were waiting in the church. It was never going to happen. I was about to let you down in just the same way.'

'I'm glad it happened the way it did. Looking after you now and taking on the new baby helps make it so much easier to live with myself. I love you. You'll never know just how much I hated the thought of you marrying him. That toad! Him stepping in like that. He couldn't wait for me to bow out from under.'

'If he'd been that keen Mark he could have asked me to marry him at any time, not waited until I got ditched at the church.'

'So he could Harriet. In it for the glory. That's what that was all about. Here let's top you up.'

'Oh thanks Mark, I don't ever think I've been in need of this as much as I am now.'

'Me too Hat. Oh by the way did I tell you it's been brought forward. We're off on Sunday?'

'Sunday? This Sunday? No you didn't tell me it would be as soon as that. How long for this time?'

'It depends how it goes. Obviously we've got to wait for the Galapagos Islands' results to come through so all this climate change data can be linked. We've got a heavy run of ice core sampling ahead before we can do the comparisons. It will all take time, unfortunately.'

'Oh that's not what I wanted to hear Mark. Is Melissa Scott going to be there by any chance?'

'Afraid so. Geoffrey's going too. That should be fun!'

'So she's putting up with him because you'll be there?'

'Look Hat I've told you I'm not interested in her. It's my job. It's her job. That's what we get paid to do.'

'Oh yes and how's she going to manage being pregnant if it's an open-ended exercise?'

'It's not that open-ended. These trips never last longer than three months at best. Anyway we don't know she is pregnant for sure, do we?'

'I wouldn't mind betting. It's all so perverse Mark. It's like something you read in a book. A bad book at that. It's just too much of a coincidence.'

'Let's hope Hat. Let's hope!'

'Mark I don't want you to go away so soon. I need you to be here.'

'No choice Harriet but this could well be the last trip for me.'

'Why Mark, what do you mean?'

'It's all the cut-backs. I think this is as far as they're prepared to take this line of research for the time being; well as far as we're concerned anyway. They're talking about collaborating with all the major research centres. Rationalising task distribution to reduce the need for unnecessary travel. It makes sense. They've got one in New Zealand and another in Tierra del Fuego, both much closer to the action. Of course it would mean some key staff moving to wherever.'

'It wouldn't mean you, would it?'

'*Some* key staff Hat, don't forget the place is top heavy with scientists, for most of us it's more like redundancies will be the order of the day.'

'Oh no Mark, not you, surely?'

'Who can tell? There's a lot of speculation at the moment and we're not being told the whole story by any means.'

'Gosh Mark and *he's* wanting to buy this! There's no way we can go along with that in these circumstances.'

'Let's wait and see, shall we? This is why I haven't mentioned it before. It's all speculation at the moment. It could turn out we'll be damned glad of a buyer, even *him*!' There's plenty of people needing to downsize in the current economic climate. If it comes to it we won't be the first.'

Harriet looked around. Didn't want that. Didn't like this dollop of uncertainty suddenly thrown at her. Didn't want Mark to go away either, especially in the face of Barry Giordano's phone call. Didn't like the thought of "stragglers", more of those heavies on the look out for her and Tricia. Didn't want to tell Mark all that just now.

'No, he's got more than enough on his plate,' she thought.

She twisted one hand into the other then rested them both across her lap. 'More than enough.'

Chapter 30

Monday morning. Harriet decided to bypass the shower in favour of stretching out in the bath. It had been a long journey. She'd been hot and tired and desperate for bed last night. With the water running fast and the bubbles gathering, she sat mesmerised by the creamy swirls of liquid soap oozing from the bottle in her hand, tipping it until every last drop was gone. Sloshing it around she watched the bubbles grow, rapidly laying a soft quilt over her, leaving only her breasts partly exposed. She thought about *him*. Hoped he'd forgotten about her relapse. She'd allowed him to take both her breasts in his hands. Could still feel the brush of his fingertips gently against her nipples. Just the thought sending wave upon wave of intense yearning through her body. She lay back, closed her eyes to let him make love to her one last time.

Completely transported. She didn't know for how long. The bath water began cooling around her. More hot water, each time. She didn't know how many times he'd made love to her while she'd been lying there. The front door banging closed suddenly brought her to. Then she hated herself. It must have been Mark going out. He'd probably called whilst the tap had been running. She'd never heard him. She sat up, washed and dried quickly gearing herself for the day at Starboard Marine North West. Nervous, she wondered if she'd see *him*. He'd been reasonably amiable when they'd parted. She hoped it was nothing to do with all that, especially knowing his commitment to Lucinda Lawton. She cringed at the thought of having stood in front of him, naked to the waist. She cringed and hated herself for allowing her passion for him to outstrip her reason.

She went downstairs, vowing with each step she took, to turn the amber light out once and for all.

'I'm so glad Tricia's going in Pepper. I'd better get ready. Oh get down from my leg, will you? OK, OK I'll feed you first. Ah the phone. That's probably her now. Hang on a minute Pepper'

'Barry! What on earth are you calling me at this time for? I've got to get ready for work.'

….. 'Oh yes I know I said I'd love to go to Peru with you but that was yesterday Barry. I'm not so sure I'm free to do that kind of thing any more.'

….. 'No Barry it's not back on. With *him*? You've got to be joking! He gave us a lift back that's all. You achieved what you wanted with that painting. He won't believe me to the point where he wouldn't even discuss it with you on the phone yesterday. You've well and truly scuppered that one. Not that I'm bothered.'

….. 'No actually I'm *not* bothered Barry Giordano. What does bother me is how I'm going to dispose of the flipping thing. It's under the bed at the moment. You wouldn't care take it back would you?'

….. 'You will? Well that's something anyway.'

….. 'Well if it's got to be today I can probably get back here for four o'clock.

Will that be OK?'

….. 'Right Barry I'll see you later then.'

'Oh come on Pepper, come and get this. Oh no not again. This phone never stops. Oh they can just wait or leave a message or something. There you go Pepper. I'm going up to get dressed now, or I'll never get there. Oh not again!'

'Hello!'

'There's no need to be so abrupt Harriet. Daddy heard on the grapevine you're back. I left a message yesterday but I suppose you haven't had much chance to call me yet.'

'No Mummy, I'm sorry. Look I've got to get ready for work, can I phone you back later?'

'Work Harriet? It's the summer holidays. Unless of course you're popping along to school to help our dear friend Sir Joris out. He'll be a little bit more than a friend soon Harriet. I do hope you've got that wedding date sorted by now.'

'No Mummy I haven't. Things are not quite as straightforward as you seem to think.'

'Oh they never are with you Harriet. It's not that lazy hippy of a would-be scientist you're so intent on clinging to is it? Heaven help us if the planet's in his hands.'

'Who are you talking about now Mummy?'

'You know only too well Harriet. How dare he leave you standing at the church like that! I'll never forgive him. I think you've taken leave of your senses. I know you've gone back to him. I asked Violet to have a good look round when she viewed with Avril the other day and as far as she can make out there's definitely a man living there. Unless you've got someone else Harriet like a toy boy and you're not telling me. Oh I don't think my reputation at the WI can stand too much more of this. I'm already getting funny looks from Mrs. Winterbotham. Of course her daughter Isabella is chair of the committee. She's been making good use of her spare time for years Harriet. Supporting the community. Happily married with two dear children. Puts me in mind of Geraldine. Oh I do wish you hadn't thrown our family into moral turmoil. You have no idea of the effect this is having on Daddy and I.'

'Look Mummy, I've got to go to work. I'm not even dressed yet.'

'Well before you go Harriet I just wanted to tell you not to bother getting me any more plants for the hanging basket. That dozy young man, what's his name? Guy something? Guy Hamper is it? From the garden centre Harriet, you know? Well you should know seeing as he got caught up in that cannabis trap you laid for us all. He mentioned it you know.'

'I beg your pardon Mummy, what on earth are you talking about now?'

'Guy Hamper Harriet. All of us from the WI went to a talk about colour scheming the garden. Well he looked straight at us trying to make it into a bit of a joke at the end. Went a bit flat on him though. Violet and I were terrified we were going to be identified. Anyway the nice boy gave us six trays each of his demonstration plants for nothing Harriet. Daddy's already filled the basket. Of course Violet wasn't waiting for anyone. Cedric did hers the same day as those awful cannabis things were taken away. We had a bit of a chat. I told him it was all your fault Harriet and that it was nothing to do with us. Do you know he brought out this scribbled-on bit of paper and told me to pass it to you. That's why I'm phoning Harriet. Not even an envelope! Would you like me to read it out?'

Harriet dithered before realising without doubt her mother would already be well familiar with the content.

I'm going to anyway Harriet and I hope you're ready for it.

"I'm warning you our Wayne's gunning for you and her, your friend. Tell her to forget her "save Venice" tin if she wants to stay out of trouble. They're watching him so he can't get the mush and it's driving him up the wall. He's blaming you now he's run out of the stuff. He says it's up to you to find Him some more and he won't listen to reason. I've tried. I don't think His visit to the campsite helped matters either. Yours forever (just say the word) Guy Hammer." Oh it's Hammer Harriet, not Hamper.'

'Gosh such a load of rubbish, when did you get it Mummy? When was your meeting?'

'Yesterday afternoon. We all met at the garden centre. I must say Harriet I felt really furtive taking it from him. Oh and there's this on the back. A "PS".'

She paused to take a deep breath.

' "You're as sweet as a lilly
would your knicks be so frilly?
Just like a rose,
down to your toes.
You're flowers grown from seeds
without any weeds.
There's water in my can,
so think of this man.
My love's blossomed and grown
Like a lawn to be mown
Just say the word
My sweetest love bird." .'

Harriet nearly died. Thought she'd sorted him out once and for all last year.

'Oh there's something else here on the bottom Harriet.

"PS. Room for a bed in that very big shed? Has that lazy bugger of yours done anything with it yet? I'll come and do it any time. I'll put the shed up for you too." .'

'Oh Mummy take absolutely no notice of that stupid thing. How dare he write like that to me.'

'You must have encouraged him Harriet. I don't know what it is with you. There's Sir Joris waiting, wanting a date. He's waiting for you to make your mind up Harriet, wanting to know exactly when you'll condescend to marry him and all you can do is flirt around with a bit of a kid. My word Harriet I do feel the menopause is taking you very strangely indeed. Perhaps you should have a word with Dr. Holden, I'm sure he'd be able to give you something.'

'No thank you Mummy. I've absolutely no interest whatsoever in Guy Hammer. He's sent 'so called' poems before and unfortunately he must be thick, so thick he doesn't seem to have got the message.'

'Not as thick as all that Harriet. He's certainly got that good for nothing partner of yours weighed up. I don't know why he bought another shed for it still to be sitting there propped up against the garage wall. He needs to see Dr. Holden too. Perhaps you could go together. I'm sure he'd be able to refer you both to someone who can sort the pair of you out.'

'No thank you Mummy. Now I've GOT to get ready for work. Gosh is that the time? Tricia'll think I'm never coming.'

'Take her along too. You might just as well all get seen together.'

'Going Mummy. 'Bye. I'll be calling in to see you and Daddy soon.'

'Gosh Pepper it's nearly nine o'clock. Mummy does go on. Oh no that's not a silver car just pulled up, is it? Oh no Pepper it's *him*. Gosh he's hot on it. Let's get to the door before he opens it himself. Oh no, I'm still in my dressing gown. Actually we want that key back. He's no right. I'm going to tell him. Oh Pepper get out of the way if you don't want to get tripped over.'

In a panic she smoothed her hair, stretched the sides of her dressing gown across and tied the belt tightly into one big knot. Just made it. With no sound of the key in the lock, she opened the door.

'Oh golly, Mr. Sanderson, thought you'd get there first. Actually I'm just on my way. On my way upstairs to get ready. Sorry! I got waylaid by the phone.'

She backed her way along the hall. Backed away from the sheer proximity of him. The blonde curl at his collar shifting slightly to break from the row at his neck. He tossed his head sideways to make fresh layers in his thick blonde hair.

'It's really grown,' she thought. 'Gosh it suits him.' She looked down. Didn't want to be having these thoughts.

'No I appear to have mislaid the damned thing.'

'The key Mr. Sanderson? But that's not good. Anyone could ….'

'Quite Miss Glover. That's why I'm here. I didn't give it back by any chance, did I?'

'No most definitely not Mr. Sanderson. In fact I was going to ask you for it. We need them both really. It means I can't lock the side gate.'

'Yes. Quite Miss Glover. Thoughtless of me. I really should have returned it to the estate agents'. Of course with a view to proceeding with the purchase anyhow, it slipped my mind. So it's not anywhere here then?'

'No, I certainly would have noticed if it had been Mr. Sanderson. Can you remember when you last had it?'

'Ah, yes of course. All the keys were on my desk in that office I was using at the campsite. I emptied my pockets looking for some damned thing or another when that persistent woman burst in believing the engagement to be back on.

Of course she wasn't having any of it. It's a hell of a mess and I want it sorted with her today.'

'Why, is she back Mr. Sanderson? I thought she was staying the week.'

'Refused Miss Glover on the pretext of some damned condition or other. Forgot her medication apparently. More to it than that. Had to taxi her back with Tarquin Bridgewater she was in such a state. You and Mrs. Harrington have got some explaining to do and I've every intention of being there to make sure she gets the message. Anyhow where was I? That damned key. Oh yes, mercifully Clive Engells arrived. We all left the room together. At least I'm assuming she followed. I deliberately didn't look behind. Picked up the keys when I got back but I don't recall checking them. It was only last night I noticed it missing.'

'Oh gosh that would have had our address on it. The estate agents' label them, don't they?'

'Naturally so Miss Glover. Look I'll give Clive a call, not that I think it will do much good. In the meantime I'll contact the locksmith's get these locks changed.'

'That would be good Mr. Sanderson. I don't like the idea of a missing key especially after Barry Giordano's warning.'

'Quite. Quite, Miss Glover. You'd have been far better in Dorset this week as planned. Far better out of the way. It's a question of catastrophe, either way you manage to create one, you and Mrs. Harrington between you. Bad combination on a campsite where children are concerned. No. Just not prepared to take that risk. Of course one wouldn't have expected that obscene Rapping Hammer boy to show up. A catalyst if ever there was one. But I can see this damned key thing's given you a fright Miss Glover. Look you get ready and I'll pop the kettle on shall I? A coffee wouldn't go amiss for either of us.'

Upstairs. Her brain disconnected. Opened the wardrobe door to close it again. Then each drawer in turn. Grabbed the brush wondering what on earth he'd been thinking of letting Belinda Oxfordshire distract him like that. In the mirror watched her hair flying away from the static she'd just generated. Powdered her nose. A smear of lipstick. Shoes? Under the bed. Put her hand on them. No not them. Mark's! Felt sick. The picture. Lay on the floor stretching her arm forward. Patted the carpet. Couldn't feel anything. Gone. That nightmare of a painting. Gone! Then from behind. *Him.*

'Crikey Harriet, what on earth are you doing down there?'

Wriggled her way out.

'Just looking for my shoes Mr. Sanderson.'

'Are you looking for these? Look, here, under the dressing table.'

'Oh yes of course. Thank you.'

'You've gone very pale Harriet. I know you've just had a shock but that's not to be confused with morning sickness is it?'

'Er no, not at all. No I'm not feeling sick just now, thank you. No I've lost something that's all. No I'm looking for my knitting. I was going to do some when Mark goes away but it's rolled under there somewhere. Can't find it though. I thought my shoes were there but not. I forgot they were there. No I'm alright quite alright. Really I am.'

He raised his eyebrows. She wriggled out. Scrambled to her feet holding the sides of her dressing gown together. Her thoughts whirling. Couldn't believe the painting had disappeared. 'Mark, it could only have been Mark. I told him not to put his shoes there but he did. He would have said though. Surely he would have said if he'd discovered that?'

'You look dreadful Harriet. Are you sure you're feeling alright? Come. Come. I've made the coffee.'

'Oh sorry, I can't drink it just now Mr. Sanderson.'

'You're feeling sick Harriet?'

'Yes, no. No of course not. No, I think I'm still half asleep from the camping trip. No. No a coffee will wake me up.'

She caught his expression. Concerned. Puzzled. This gorgeous, gorgeous man. 'Don't do this too me.' Another pang mixing with the anxiety, stirring it all up as she followed him downstairs.

'Lounge Harriet?'

'Yes. Yes that's fine, thank you.'

'Ah and what's this bag here in the corner? Needles poking out. Looks like knitting to me. Hardly under the bed Miss Glover, would you say?'

'Er yes. Er no. Er I'm am supposed to be at Starboard Marine North West this week, aren't I?'

'That's the plan Harriet. We need to make use of the time now available between you and Mrs. Harrington. Far better to have prepped as much as we can of the agreed summer club activities. Success is in the planning especially as we'll be working from the three sites.'

'Yes, of course. I'll be based at school, won't I?'

'Yes that's right. Lucinda will keep her eye on Starboard Marine North West and I'll be down at the sailing club.'

'Ah yes so Tricia will get on with her normal work at Starboard Marine North West then?'

'Yes, for the most part. Of course the coffee club will still be operating as usual together with the courses and activities. Must keep our parents on board. Great success. Indeed that's one thing I can be grateful to Belinda for. She's certainly put her mind to getting the whole thing up and running. Mrs. Harrington has, as I've said already, been invaluable in drawing them in but Belinda's got the business head. Made all the contacts. Got the experts to give of their free time. It's virtually a voluntary set up thanks to her.'

Harriet opened her mouth, then closed it again. Had he forgotten so soon it was she who'd instigated it all? Fuming she sat on it. The last thing she felt like doing now was to simper apologies at her for colluding with Tricia to get her to swap tents. She placed her mug on the small table alongside the arm of the sofa. Put her fingers to her mouth. Looked across to the other sofa. At him, sat in his usual place by the door. His right leg propped on his left knee. Right-angled out as he tapped at the seam on his soft leather shoes. She thought of Clive Engells. Wondered if Mr. Sanderson knew of Lucinda Lawton's double dealings? Wondered if they were getting engaged? Wondered if that's why he wanted to buy their house now? 'Somewhere small and cosy for them both whilst she gets used to the idea of living in that huge old house in Lower Tideside looking out over the river running into the sea.' Harriet swallowed hard on the snake of envy curling at her throat, then sank the thought.

'So you're definitely not pregnant Harriet? You've had one normal period and now moving towards another?'

This was out of the blue. She felt a shot of hot beetroot juice had just sprayed her cheeks. Flushed she stumbled for an answer.

'That's the way it is Mr. Sanderson.'

' "Nullaregula sine exceptione" Miss Glover if it is indeed the case but I have no choice other than to take your word for it.'

Instinctively she placed her arm across her waist. 'This is what he wants to know,' she thought, 'to clear the way for marriage. Marriage to Lucinda Lawton.' She looked across. His eyes sharp. In a glance penetrating hers. For the briefest of moments as if piercing her virginity to the core of her soul. His baby inside her. In this very second, tiny cells multiplying. A compound multiplication of living cells that is their baby. She knew he knew. Knew whenever she saw him he'd settle his eyes across the curve rising steadily between her hips. She knew he'd watch her grow but somehow there was no place in her mind to forge the link to the future. She watched his eyes narrowing to the deep breath expanding his chest. She looked down to hear him sigh it away.

' "Amor caecus est" Harriet." '

'I'm not really understanding all this Latin. Translation please Mr. Sanderson." He carried on.

' "Amo te nunc et semper" but we must each go our own way.'

'That's exactly what I thought it meant Mr. Sanderson. Now it's probably time I got myself to Starboard Marine North West. I'd like to get this confession over and done with.'

Chapter 31

Harriet half expected to see his car already there as she turned in. Her head filled with Latin. Not that it mattered now. That was enough. He'd said enough to make his position clear. ' "But we must each go our own way." OK so that's the way he wants it. That's fine by me. Mark and I know just where we're going.' Then the thought collapsed. 'Unless of course Mark's got something to do with the painting vanishing. In which case, in which case it's probably all over between us.' She took a deep breath. Felt like the ball of wool on the end of the half-finished knitting. Knotted and tangled. Couldn't comprehend how she'd managed to ravel herself up like this. 'Why can't I let go of that man? Of course you can't let go, stupid Harriet. His baby's right inside here.'

She flattened her hand against her stomach. Someone beeped her out of her thoughts. She looked behind. *Him* wanting to get in. Didn't realise she'd gone into a trance at the entrance, unable to decide just where to park. He pulled up alongside her. Waited for her to get out.

'Crikey Miss Glover. I've been home and back since I left you. Haven't been finishing that jumper have you, or whatever it was in that elusive bag of knitting? Thought this damned exercise would have been all over and done with by now.'

'Sorry Mr. Sanderson but I was about to get ready when you arrived. You did hold me up a bit. Oh and I had to go back to put the bin out. Anyway it doesn't look like Belinda Oxfordshire's even here yet. I can't see her car,' Harriet returned.

'Ah that's her now. It would seem she's late too. Isn't that Mrs. Harrington's husband she's with, Miss Glover?'

'Oh yes, it looks like Bob's given her a lift.'

'Good heavens judging by that scowl she already knows. Come, come, Miss Glover, let's get inside before the eruption!'

'Oh `ello `arriet. Good mornin` Mr. Sanderson. You `aven't seen Bob on your travels `ave you?'

'He's out there with Belinda Oxfordshire, Tricia. Just driven in,' Harriet replied.

'I'll be in the office. Sort it with her right now, both of you. Get this damned mess cleared up once and for all.'

Mr. Sanderson banged the door shut behind him.

'What's happened Tricia? Don't tell me those lads delivered the paper after all. Don't tell me Bob got hold of the front page.'

'Oh no, I don't think so `arriet. Good lads those. There's no sign of it around anyway. That's the first thing I did when I got in. Checked to see if it was there. We've `ardly seen each other after the row we `ad when I got back. Oh `e's been comin` and goin` but `e wasn't even in bed when I woke up this mornin`.'

'Oh gosh Tricia, you must be wondering what's going on.'

'I think I'm beginning to get the picture alright `arriet. I thought *she* was still in Dorset, campin`. What's she doin` back `ere? And what's `e doin` givin` `er a lift? That's supposed to be all over with accordin` to `im, not that I believed `im of course, I've known all along. Anyway `e's supposed to be at work. Just wait until I get my `ands on `im!'

'Hang on Tricia. She's coming across. I think Bob's just driven off.'

'Oh bloody `ell `arriet, I've really `ad enough of `im. Well she's now goin` to get what's comin` to `er.'

'Good mornin` Belinda. Well I think that's very rude `arriet, don't you? That she's not answerin`. And NO don't go in there because I think you'll find Mr. Sanderson doesn't want to be disturbed. Not just yet anyway because `e wants us to `ave a word with you Belinda Oxfordshire.'

'Oh *he* wants *you* to have a word with me, indeed. Not before I've had a word with him first, I can assure you.'

'No Belinda it's not his responsibility. There's been a terrible misunderstanding and it really is up to us to put you straight on this.' Harriet needed to get it right.

'Oh don't you be doing the school teacher bit on me Harriet Glover. Miss Prim and Proper and I don't think. I know exactly what you got up to with Ross Farquerhart on the cliff edge behind the tents. Absolutely disgusting, especially at your age.'

'I beg your pardon Belinda Oxfordshire. How dare you make any such suggestions.'

'As it happened I saw you with my own eyes. I saw him slip away your shoulder straps. It doesn't take much to imagine what happened next. No you're a cheap little tart Harriet Glover. You lead people on. Wind them up and let them down. You ruin people's lives and I suppose you thought it would be really good fun to play that trick on me.'

'Now what trick are you referin` to Belinda? No don't bother tellin` us. I'd rather `ear about the trick you've just played on me, now. What are you doin` tryin` to steal my `usband back again for the third time?'

'Bob's choice Patricia Harrington. You're nothing more than a cheap little tart either.'

'Oh did you `ear that `arriet? Did you just `ear `er? She's takin` it out on us because she can't get the man she really wants.'

'That's just where you're wrong Mrs. Harrington. If you're referring to Joris Sanderson I lost interest in him years ago. Trying to keep the family happy, that's what that was all about, not that it's any of your business.'

'Look Belinda we're terribly sorry but I think we got you a bit confused when we told you the end tent was for you...'

'Don't go any further Harriet Glover. Give me some credit for rumbling the pair of you. I'm going in to speak to Joris, this minute, if you'll excuse me.'

Guarding the door Harriet and Tricia all but fell backwards as she squeezed in behind them to swing it open.

'Right, all sorted is it? I want no more of this ridiculous behaviour.' *His* voice booming from behind.

He strode out. His face stern. His manner determined. The door slamming behind him as he marched straight out. Stunned, they watched him get into his car, reverse then speed away.

'Oh so we all know where `e stands now, don't we?'

'Oh do we indeed?' Belinda Oxfordshire reached for her mobile. 'Did you manage to change that tyre? I'm in rather a hurry. Yes I got a lift in. Do you think you could bring it round here? Starboard Marine North West, yes, that's the place. Yes you can charge it to the company. I'll drop you back.'

'You goin` somewhere Belinda?'

'Too right I am just as soon as I get my car back. If he thinks I'm spending the day here with you two he's got another think coming.'

She disappeared back into the office, the door frame rattling as she whammed it closed.

Harriet reached for the file in her bag, suddenly turning to the door chime, a draught of cool morning air hitting her legs.

'Oh good mornin` Mr. Bridgewater and what can we be doin` for you today? We're sorry you `ad the campin` trip cut short.'

'Not to worry, but Tricia, Harriet, my dears, I don't suppose old Joris is here by any chance?'

'Sorry I'm afraid `e left just a few minutes ago,' Tricia declared.

Harriet jumped up. Her mother's voice suddenly in her mind reading out Guy Hammer's warning. Instantly she felt sick at the thought of Tarquin Bridgewater fancying her, let alone trading her body with him for cannabis. 'No this is something he can jolly well sort out with Rapping Hammer himself.' The thought spurred her on.

'Oh Mr. Bridgewater I wanted a quick word with you. Just need your advice if that's OK.'

'Marry him my dear. It's obviously not going anywhere with Belinda now is it?'

The door shot open.

'And might I ask exactly what's not going anywhere with me Mr. Bridgewater?'

He jumped. 'Oh goodness me my dear where did you spring from? Are you feeling better now Belinda?'

'Not particularly, no. Now just *what* were you saying to *her* about me?' Mr. Bridgewater's face became peculiarly distorted in a simultaneous expression of both surprise and irritation.

'Marriage Belinda. Let's not beat about the bush. I had great hopes for you two. Oh I know it's all been a bit on and off lately but after this business with Harriet here…'

He turned back to Harriet.

'Terrible thing to happen to such a pretty young lady. Ditched at the church. I can't think what Mark was thinking of my dear. I didn't quite see why Joris should have been so keen to bail him out myself, but that's Joris. He's bred to do the right thing.'

Harriet could feel the first flush of anger burning away at her cheeks.

'Yes, that was just about it. You've got it right Tarquin. He thought he was doing the right thing by her, seeing as she's done nothing but throw herself at him for goodness knows how long now,' Belinda Oxfordshire stormed.

'`ow dare you talk about my friend like that. `ow do you know what Joris was feelin` for `arriet? It's `arriet that decided she didn't want to marry `im after all. Wasn't it `arriet? She'd `ave grabbed `im and not let go if she'd been that keen on `im.'

'Oh I'm not so sure of that. She gets her kicks from dangling people. Guy Hammer for instance. Oh yes I've heard all about the way you've led him on Harriet Glover, old enough to be his mother, too. Now Ross Farquerhart. Well you needn't think I'm keeping that all to myself, as soon as my car arrives I'm off to find Joris and he's going to get the lot. He needs to know exactly what kind of a floozy you are. Cavorting with a young student assigned to the school, indeed. You might find you won't be on the payroll of that place much longer.'

'Oh dear whatever have I started? Must be going girls. Forgive me. I'm meeting Iris at the sailing club. Just wanted to clear a few things with regard to the accounts first with Joris. I'll try his mobile.'

'Both you two consider yourselves told. I have no wish to associate with either of you, you're both cheap little tarts.' Tarquin Bridgewater turned to look back as she clapped her hands loudly in triumph.

'Oh jolly good show! Perfect timing. I'm out of here. That's the tyre chappy driving in. I've got my car back. I'm off to see Joris!' She snatched her bag then grabbed the open door before it closed in front of her. Harriet and Tricia watched her change places with the garage mechanic as Tarquin Bridgewater drove out of the car park.

'Ooh `arriet you weren't goin` to ask `im for advice were you?'

'Not about marriage to Mr. Sanderson Tricia. I've had Mummy on the phone. That silly Guy Hammer goes and gives her an open note for me. Poems and everything!'

'A bit embarrassing that could be, I would say.'

'Certainly was, but this was the worst bit. Rapping Hammer definitely won't give you your "save Venice" tin back unless…, and we both know what he means by that.'

'Well `e made it clear enough `arriet.'

'He certainly did Tricia, but not only that, it seems he's going round the bend without his "mush". Says I've got to find him some more. Well he needn't think I'm sleeping with Tarquin Bridgewater either. Golly Tricia what are we going to do?'

'Oh I see `arriet, so `e's determined to keep this up. Well `e needn't think `e's keepin` all that money and as far `is `abit's concerned, let `im go and find `is own. `e probably `as by now. I wouldn't be worryin` about Tarquin Bridgewater either. They all grow it together most probably. No `arriet I think Rappin `ammer's just tryin` to frighten us. Now `ow am I goin` to get that tin back? It's stealin` that is. I registered my charity and I think there's an `elpline to phone.'

'Gosh Tricia, I didn't realise you'd got it quite so organised.'

'Oh yes you `ave to when you're collectin` other people's money. I'll get on to them. `e needn't think `e's gettin` away with that. I'll be with you in a tick. You get back to your file. We've got quite a bit of organisin` to do, `aven't we? Just let me find the number. It's `ere somewhere.'

Harriet sat down. Leafed through the variety of activities suggested at the last staff meeting. She needed to get them timetabled. Needed to phone around to see if the volunteers were still on board.

'Oh I can't be doin` with it `arriet. If you want this press three. Now listen to the options. Press one for this. Two for that. To speak to an advisor `old. I've been `oldin` for ages now and nothin`'s `appenin` apart from gettin` pins and needles in my arm. Talk about gettin` `elp to get my money back. I need `elp to get past this lot. `ang on isn't our friend Clive Engells a solicitor? Isn't `e comin` up `ere to collect `is car? I think I'll `ave a word with `im. I seem to remember `im offerin` `is `elp. After all `arriet it was `is fault we got sent `ome.'

'You can't do that Tricia. He's hardly going to be in a cooperative frame of mind.'

'Well I'm sure Joris Sanderson will be bringin` `im down `ere wantin` to show off this place. You know what `e's like. I might just get the opportunity.'

'Rather you than me Tricia especially after that fiasco. You know it had to be Lucinda Lawton in there. Too much of a coincidence otherwise, it's not really a common name.'

'Oh `e won't even `ave realised we cottoned on to it `arriet. I think `e'd be just a teeny weeny bit too concerned about tryin` to keep those edges of `is dressing gown together, don't you? Did our friend Joris say when `e's expectin` `im to pick up `is car?'

'Not that I can recall. He had a bit more on his mind than that. He is concerned for us Tricia. I haven't had chance to tell you yet but Barry Giordano's saying there could well be repercussions from the Venice affair. He's telling us to be vigilant.'

'Really `arriet, did `e say anythin` else?'

'Well it was just a quick call I made from Mr. Sanderson's. Actually I might find out more later on. He's agreed to take that painting back. He's calling in as soon as I get back from here.'

'Well that will be a good thing out of the way but you've got to find out more of what's going on `arriet. I don't think I could stand the thought of bein` kidnapped like we thought was goin` to `appen in Venice.'

'No me neither. Look why don't you come back to ours on the way home? Let's both see him together. I'd feel better going in with you. I just don't know what's going on. Remember I told you I'd put the painting under the bed? Well it's not there now. I just don't know what's happened to it. I don't know if Mark's got hold of it or what? Honestly Tricia there's something fishy going on.'

'When did you discover it wasn't there?'

'Only this morning. Of course Mr. Sanderson called in to tell me he's lost our house key. Oh no, someone could have got hold of it and walked straight in to take it. I've only just thought of that.'

'Oh dear `arriet, it's not lookin` very good, is it?'

'No it isn't, but I'm just so puzzled. I could only manage a quick look around once he'd left before coming here. It could be Mark's found it but he'd have soon let me know.'

'Oh yes `arriet I'm sure `e would. Anyway we'll `ave a look together, it's got to be somewhere. Don't worry, I'll `elp you find it.'

Chapter 32

On their knees under either side of the bed Harriet and Tricia stared at each other for one last time.

'We keep lookin` `ere `arriet and we know it's not `ere. I think we've looked in so many places we've become transfixed.'

'You're absolutely right. Gosh I need to know where it's gone, I don't want that thing getting out.'

'Was that your doorbell `arriet?'

'Oh no. Oh no it's not *him*, I hope. I've had enough of him for today.'

'Well you'll `ave to answer it `arriet. Are you expectin` anyone else?'

'Anyone else? I'm not expecting anyone, am I?'

'Only Barry Giordano `arriet. I thought that's why I was `ere.'

'Oh no Tricia. How could have I forgotten that? My brain's going. What with Mark going away and this painting gone missing and Mr. Sanderson putting the boot in. Oh it's no wonder. Come on Tricia, we'd better let him in.'

Harriet stepped back in surprise as she pulled the door open to see a burly chap, head shaven, thrusting a leaflet at her.

'We're `ere to help you out. Anything of value you want to deposit or trade? We lend against all sorts. Times are getting a lot `arder for folks. We've not long opened. We're just round the corner from the school. You know the side street just before you get to that old red brick school on the corner?'

Harriet glanced at the leaflet, felt a rush of nerves to her stomach. His tone was menacing.

'There you are. It tells you there. `ave you anything of value you want to bring us to secure a loan? We take gold, silver, jewellery, electrical goods, mobies as long as they're internet ready, paintings, glass, brass. You name it we'll take it. Of course if you `aven't got anything we do unsecured loans. We're catching a lot of mothers on their way to school. We're all feeling the pinch and we're `ere to `elp everybody out.'

Harriet shook her head.

'Nothing today then? Don't worry love we'll be back'

He put one foot in the hall stretching across Harriet to push a leaflet at Tricia, then backed out kicking the cat away with his foot. Harriet closed the door quickly just missing its tail as it leapt out from behind.

'Gosh Tricia, he must have taken one of those little shops round the corner from the school. That must be the place where Mrs. Bustard goes. Remember her telling us about being in debt and being frightened of him? Well I'm not surprised.'

'Oh `arriet do you know who `e reminded me of?'

'I know. He's the spitting image of that heavy, the biggest one of the two they've just caught. Oh no, don't tell me he's escaped, or he's got a twin brother, or they all look the same in that mob. Oh Tricia don't tell me they're back looking for us. Is that what Barry Giordano meant?'

'Let's 'ope 'e turns up soon 'arriet so we can ask 'im. The same thought crossed my mind. Oh I don't think I could go through all that again. We 'aven't even 'ad chance to recover from Venice yet and bein' followed and all that 'orrible experience you've just 'ad at the summer fete 'arriet. Don't tell me it's startin' all over again?'

'Well we might just be panicking for nothing yet, it could be totally unrelated. Those kind of places do spring up in hard times and our parents are certainly struggling at the moment. Gosh we've got to warn them though. There must be something we can do to stop them getting any deeper into his debt. Poor Mrs. Bustard. I'm on a mission now Tricia. I'm going to see what I can come up with.'

'Oh let me 'elp you 'arriet. We'll feel better if we find out we're wrong. I do 'ope you're right. I do 'ope we're over-reactin'. I didn't like the look of 'im at all.'

'Look we're bound to be a bit edgy. When you think about it there's loads of people look like that. Most of our dads at school, come to think of it. No Tricia, it's probably because we're expecting to be wound up by Barry Giordano. We're bound to be back on high alert. Did you notice if he went next door?'

'Oh no I didn't, I wasn't lookin' out of this window. I was too busy worryin' if you were goin' to get 'im out without catchin' the cat's tail.'

'I know. It put me in mind of Simon Barnes. Remember when the cat went for him?'

'Could I forget 'arriet. It was on INTERNEWS TV!'

'I know and Mr. Sanderson seems very apprehensive about Simon Barnes breaking cover on this Venice affair. Of course that's it. That's got to be it! MI6 put a blackout on the news. Mr. Sanderson's not telling me the ins and outs but they must still be working on the case and they don't want us blowing it. They must be terrified of us walking straight into something going on round and about. We are going to have to be very careful Tricia, even the slightest suspicion of anything untoward will have us back in the news. It wouldn't surprise me if Simon Barnes wasn't having us followed.'

'Oh don't say that 'arriet. Look, just look out there. The cat's stalkin' the wall and 'er fur's all standin' on end, unless she's seein' somethin' she doesn't like.'

'She just has Tricia. She was like that for ages after she flew at Simon Barnes that time. I think she senses a threat. No I'm not happy at all now, I'm sure I'm right. I think we're going to have to avoid that pawnbroker's like the plague.'

'One minute you're calmin' me down and the next you're windin' me up 'arriet. That's what I thought in the first place. I do think there's somethin' very fishy about 'im and I 'ope 'e 'asn't come 'ere to suss out where you live, either.'

'Oh gosh Tricia, the sooner we talk to Barry the better. Any sign of him yet?'

'Not that I can see 'arriet. Oh just a minute, someone's just stopped over your 'edge. It's a black car. Oh it's 'im 'arriet. Quick, open the door. Let's 'ope that 'eavy's not lyin' in wait for 'im.'

'Come in Barry. Quick get in quick.'

'OK Tricia, what's the panic? Shall I start again? Hi Harriet, Tricia. I haven't got long. A quick brew wouldn't go amiss though. Where is it? Let's get this masterpiece out of the way first.'

'Masterpiece of rubbish I'd say Barry Giordano.'

'She doesn't change, does she?'

Harriet followed his glance to Tricia. She cleared her throat.

'Of course I'm not sayin` that your work isn't good Barry, it's just that you `ave caused `arriet a lot of trouble doin` that, especially now it's gone missin`.'

'Gone missing? What do you mean?'

'Just let me put the kettle on Barry. Come into the kitchen both of you and sit down. Have you come from Manchester?'

'No, the great Metropolis. I'm on my way home but we're due to board the plane at 22: 10 hours tonight.'

'What you and Andy? Where would that be to then?' Tricia couldn't help herself.

He thumbed his nose. Harriet kept quiet.

'Now what's happened to this work of mine?'

Harriet squashed the tea-bag hard against the side of the mug before dropping it on the pile.

'Milk Barry, or not?'

'Not thanks Harriet. What did Sanderson do with it, did you say?'

'Gave it me back. I pushed it right under the bed and this morning it wasn't there.'

'Are you sure you've looked everywhere Harriet?'

'Oh we `ave Barry. We've been in the shed, looked under all the beds, anywhere it might fit really, aven't we `arriet? That's why I'm `ere, to `elp `er look.'

'Ah, I see.'

'And who's been in the house since you put it under the bed?'

'Just Mark, me and the cat. Oh and Mr. Sanderson but it wasn't him. He's lost the key anyway. In any case that's the last thing he'd want back.'

'Any chance Mark's got hold of it and for whatever reason isn't cracking on?'

'No Barry, Mark's not capable of not cracking on. If he'd seen that I would certainly have known about it. That would have been another relationship down the drain.'

'All that effort could be working well for me Harriet but either way, it looks like I've done you a favour. I'm quick to pick up positives even quicker with the less than subtle.'

The last phone call. She'd lead him on. Harriet immediately stuck her face in the fridge. Eyed the punnet of gleaming red strawberries. Wished she could join them since she felt like one but settled on the bottle of milk in the hope the draught of cool air would reduce the flush of colour rushing to her cheeks. 'Oh the amber buttercup ring. Stupid girl saying that. Won't you ever learn?' She closed the door on the thought realising her folly in playing games over the phone.

'Oh `arriet you've gone bright red. I don't think you'll be needin` a cup of tea to make you `otter, I'd just `ave the milk if I were you.'

'Of course I get your concern over such an intimate painting Harriet especially as it's accuracy will increase by the day. It needs to be found but I can't do much on that count just now. Keep all senses on high alert. You never know what turns up. Yep, we've got to find it or we won't be able to share the joke when we're old and grey.'

'Oh thanks a bunch Barry. I hope you can be of more help with this. On the phone you told us to be vigilant in case those heavies come back.'

'Not them, they've been remanded in custody. No, it'll be their partners in crime. It may not happen. It's just a question of being vigilant that's all.'

'Oh come on Barry, there's got to be more to it than that. You wouldn't have made such urgent contact if there wasn't more to go on.'

'Possibly but that's the measure of it as far as you two are concerned, just now.'

'I don't think you'll be sayin` that when you `ear this Barry Giordano. `arriet and I `ave just `ad a very funny experience, `aven't we `arriet?'

'Yes, a frightening sense of déjà vu Barry.' Harriet caught his attention. 'Just before you arrived actually. We opened the door to this guy. He could for all the world have been one of those heavies. The same look, mannerisms. Sounded the same. He pushed a leaflet at us. He's opened a pawnbroker's round the corner from the school. One of my parents is well in his clutches. She's terrified. It sounds like they're all going there in droves, they're so broke.'

'Well there's a procedure for dealing with it. Send her to the Citizens' Advice Bureau. There's no need for anyone to live in fear when ready help's available.'

'Oh but it's not as easy as all that, I would say, Barry. She's still got to go in `is shop to pay `im every week. `e was `orrible. The cat didn't like `im either, did she `arriet?'

'Oh no. You should have seen her fur stand on end. Exactly the same when she went for Simon Barnes and his Internews TV crew. She flew at him. Soon got him off the doorstep.'

'Another tale to tell me Harriet. I didn't hear that one. So you've got a psychic cat then?'

'Oh don't be so sceptical Barry. If we come to grief it'll be your fault. Just make sure you come and rescue us if we get kidnapped.'

Barry laughed. Tossed his long dark hair away from his shoulders as he stood to go.

'If you've got concerns keep well away. No doubt the local fuzz will be keeping an eye on it.'

'What's fuzz `arriet? I `aven't `eard that one before.' He turned to Tricia.

'Boys in blue. Even you should have enough on top to work that one out!'

He passed Harriet the cup. 'Must be off. It might be as well to get the locks changed. Keep me posted about the painting. Some sneak thief from the art world hanging on to it in order to make millions, do you think?'

'I think not Barry,' Harriet returned. 'It's alright for you, you only painted it. It flipping well looks like me. I certainly don't want Simon Barnes getting hold of that. Can you imagine Mr. Sanderson's reaction? Oh you certainly know how to dig me into even deeper holes than I manage for myself. And no, it's certainly not funny Barry!'

'See you Tricia,' he called as Harriet followed him through to the front door.

'When are we going to collect this ring then? Amber petals. A buttercup. I like the sound of that. How about Peru for our honeymoon?'

'I won't be around Barry. I'll more than likely be kidnapped.'

Chapter 33

'Had a good day Harriet?' Mark landed his briefcase at the bottom of the stairs.

'Any news about work? About redundancies? Anything like that?' Harriet replied sensing his less than positive mood. In any case the day wasn't something she wanted to discuss.

'Oh we think there's something afoot. Geoffrey's been on the internet. They've been having unofficial meetings by the look of it. No minutes. He's contacted the union guy to see what he can find out.'

'Any chance of Melissa Scott getting made redundant? I don't get her. How can she still work there with Geoffrey around after such an acrimonious divorce?'

'It's a question of needs must, Harriet. She's moved herself to the other side of the office but when she does need to communicate it's usually via me.'

'What, even now she knows you're sticking with me? Or does she know that Mark?'

'Oh I'm getting more than a little bit tired of all this Harriet, you seem to be getting more and more irrational. I'm here aren't I? She couldn't have better proof than that.'

'But if she is pregnant I just can't see her letting you get away with that so easily.'

'We'll wait and see. If there are changes afoot and I have to relocate to the Galapagos Islands or Tierra del Fuego I won't be complaining.'

'Well I might. I don't want to go and live all the way out there.'

'You can't have it all ways Harriet. We don't know where I'll end up anyway if we're forced to sell this. Everything's up in the air at the moment. I know one thing for sure I can't afford to give up my job.'

'Neither can I Mark as you well know.'

'You're not in the first flush of youth and you're having a baby Harriet. You just don't know how well you're going to cope with all that. If you can't be responsible at least be realistic for goodness sake.'

'Well thanks Mark, that's all I needed today. Plenty of women have babies in their forties as you well know. In any case I'll be taking maternity leave after Christmas. Plenty of people do and go back again.'

'They're the young ones Harriet. We can't be sure. We've got to factor all these possibilities into our thinking.'

'Well you factor away Mark,' replied Harriet conscious of him putting distance between them. 'You have a real talent for saying the wrong thing at the worst time. Oh I'm going to start the meal.'

'Not for me Harriet. I'm off to the sailing club, I'll grab something down there. I want to get this sodding boat finished before I go on Sunday.'

'Well that's not a nice thing to say. You just don't know how much that's going to mean to Danny and his mum, especially at the moment when she's up to her eyes in it.'

'In what?'

'I've already told you Mark, in debt to the horrible looking heavy who's opened a pawnbroker's by the school.'

'Oh there we go Harriet. Try to stay out of this one will you? We haven't had chance to recover from your stupid escapade in Venice yet without you and Tricia going looking for more. I'm telling you as far as Bob's concerned Tricia's on her last warning.'

'Last warning? More like the other way round. Oh so what was Bob doing dropping Belinda Oxfordshire off at Starboard Marine North West this morning? Tricia doesn't know where she is with him. It certainly looks like he's got himself back with *her* again.'

'How would I know Harriet? Anyway she asked for it making a show of herself with Rapping Hammer at the school fete like that. She might have known Simon Barnes would have been around with that all singing all dancing camera of his.'

'How did you know about that?'

'Someone's pinned the front page of the local paper up at the sailing club. You can't blame Bob for walking out. For goodness sake Harriet she's supposed to be his wife. If it wasn't for the heads that got in the way of the shot there'd have been nothing left to the imagination.'

'She did it for her "save Venice" cause. She's sorry now.'

'Sorry's getting to be a very cheap word Harriet for both of you. It wouldn't surprise me if you hadn't been doing the same.'

'Oh thanks a bunch Mark. Thank you very much indeed. So that's all you think of me!'

'It's about time the pair of you grew up Harriet, you're as bad as each other.'

Harriet didn't bother waving him goodbye. She knew he was right but couldn't believe he'd let Tricia's topless photograph influence his attitude to *her*. They'd spent so much time talking things through. He'd just about convinced her of his willingness to take responsibility for her and the baby, now this. She felt her eyes fill with tears, then sniffed them away determined not to let this setback spoil their plans. She knew it wouldn't be easy, there would be many difficult days ahead. Summoning every fibre of her being she tried to put it from her mind. She thought about Mrs. Bustard, her situation was much worse. She let the compelling need to help take over her mind.

'Right, once I've got this house sale sorted out with the estate agent I'm going to get moving on that.' She picked up the phone. Put it down again to work out just what to say. She stood for a while feeling the soft brush of the cat's tail twisting at her legs then jumped as the phone finally got its way.

'Ah good afternoon to you...'

'I've been meaning to phone you. Do you not realise that Sir Joris Sanderson has a first option to purchase 4 The Willows, Stetmead? Although it's still on your books, at his request, I might say, it is not actually on the open market. So please don't send any more viewers round. You've absolutely managed to wind Avril Moss and her mother right up. It's the only house the stupid girl really wants and I'm getting the flak for it.'

'Really Miss Glover?'

Harriet nearly died. She'd done this before. Over the phone you could hardly put a pin between them, Mr. Roberts and Joris Sanderson.

'Oh sorry Mr. Sanderson but I can't help it if you both sound the same. Anyway it's absolutely true. It would be so helpful if you could just tie this thing off, one way or the other.'

'In my own time Miss Glover, in my own good time. Now I trust you are well advanced with the preparation of the holiday additionals. We need to be getting this thing off the ground as soon as possible. I don't want the kids on the streets any more than they have to be since the trip has had to be cut short.'

'Cut short? But why's that Mr. Sanderson?'

'Washed out, the whole damned place, according to Lucinda. Looks like the monsoons hit them last night and it's still going. Tents and everything else completely awash. They're on their way back now. Left a good few hours ago. We had no choice but to cut the damned thing short. Anyhow at least it means Clive Engells can collect his car without too much inconvenience.'

'Why, is he coming back on the coach?'

'That's about it Miss Glover. Now how soon can we offer these activities?'

'Well I phoned round this morning and all our volunteers are on board, so I'll go back and check with them to see if anyone can start this week. The place is open anyway so we can coast it with art and craft if necessary.'

'Oh jolly good show Miss Glover. Well done! Now, I've arranged with Mrs. Harris to receive the children on Friday afternoon. She'll prepare high tea for them to take during the interval. I'm splitting the session with Lucinda. She'll talk the children through the history of the tunnel linking the house to the island and then walk them through a short way whilst Ross Farquerhart and myself will be showing the fossil collection before he takes questions. I'd like you to accompany Lucinda if you would. You can gen up on the internet. Just bring up Lower Tideside, local history. Perhaps you'd care to break it down and do a print run for the children. Thirty or so should do it.'

'Right, yes, that's fine. I'll do that tomorrow morning at Starboard Marine North West. You have got a printer there, haven't you?'

'Obvious question Miss Glover. Now I'm hearing Brown's steeped in yet another bout of paranoia. The man's convinced you put that Bast, er, Bustard boy up to hurling that fossil at him. Though I must say it must have been a bit of a whack as it was haemorrhaging rather badly. He ended up having to have the wound sutured.'

'Oh I wasn't aware it was that bad.'

'Second shot Miss Glover. That's what he's going on about. Apparently this Bustard boy had another go, said you'd put him up to it.'

'Oh no. I don't believe that. I just don't believe it. Mr. Brown's got to be making it up.'

'Quite, Miss Glover. Quite. It's fortunate Clive's staying over a few days. No doubt we'll hear from that Potts fellow. Damned unions! Him and Brown will be chasing it for all it's worth. It wants nipping in the bud and Clive's the one to do it.'

'Oh golly, thank you Mr. Sanderson. I can't be doing with false accusations just now. Well not at all but we don't really know what's brewing after those heavies were captured. Barry Giordano called in earlier. I'm sure there's more he's not telling us.'

'I'm sure you're right Miss Glover like I'm sure there's more you're not telling me. Anyhow he'll want to talk this through with you. Friday morning Miss Glover. Ten o'clock on the button, my place. I'm sure Clive won't mind.'

'But I haven't done anything. This isn't fair.'

'It's a lawyer you need to be saying this to Miss Glover. As I say ten o'clock Friday. Good evening to you.'

Harriet scratched her head, dazed. Wondered how much more she could take. Pulled the door hard on the freezer to look for an instant meal. No luck. She reached for the keys spread-eagled on the windowsill. It was going to have to be a takeaway.

'Good,' she thought as she pushed the door open. 'At least that's something in my favour, no queue.'

She swung a high glance at the menu then looked down to see a fish, golden and glowing hot, sat on the shelving above the fryer. Decided to go for it. Nodded towards it as she gave her order to the amiable young man behind the counter.

'Twenty minutes, if you'd like to take a seat.'

She sat to the door opening; a coarse looking woman jangling an excess of jewellery sat herself down a couple of chairs away. They both watched the young man shovel chips into a carton before placing the golden fried fish on top.

'All ready now. Salt and vinegar?'

'Yes please,' Harriet smiled, watching the salt storm disappear into the vinegar as it landed.

'Was that you or her that said that?' The young man behind the counter suddenly said, a look of confusion crossing his face.

Her voice rough, the woman stood to speak.

'No I don't want salt and vinegar. You're not serving her before me are you? I've been hanging round next door waiting for the last twenty minutes. I said I'd be back.'

The young man looked suitably embarrassed as she lunged at the counter banging her hand hard on the glass.

'My Laurie's been good to this place. You wouldn't be standing here messing up if it weren't for us. You wouldn't even have a job.' She turned to Harriet. 'This place is going bankrupt you know. Here's us lending them the money to tide them over, whatever that means, and he can't even get my sodding order right.'

Harriet felt dreadful. The door swung open again. She turned to see the big shaven headed guy who'd landed on her doorstep only a couple of hours ago.

'Come on Carol what the fuck you playing at?'

'Don't ask me, ask him. It looks like she's pinched my fish and had it splattered with salt and vinegar. You know I can't bear the stuff.'

Instantly Harriet felt his hand on her shoulder.

'She right? Haven't I seen you somewhere before? Now where was it? Let me think.'

'Never mind where you've seen her before. We're paying good money out to this rabble and what kind of a service do we get? Call it in Laurie. Let them go down.'

'Look I'm frying up another one. Nine minutes at the most.' The young man plunged his long handled scoop into the bubbling hot fat.

'Stick it. We'll go elsewhere. You'll be hearing from us.'

'What about this egg foo yong under here? You ordered it didn't you?'

'Oh stuff that!'

Harriet, trembling from recognition, breathed a huge sigh of relief as she heard the door close behind them.

'Terribly sorry,' she said to the young man now handing her a white paper parcel.

'Oh it's one of those. Easily done! I don't know why the old man deals with them. I've told him so many times. Too easy I suppose. You wouldn't believe the interest they charge. Of course the daft bastard screwed it up with the banks. I don't know why he just doesn't sell the place before it goes down the pan for good. No one round here's got the money for takeaways any more.'

'Oh you're not talking about the new money-lending place that's opened round the corner to the school, are you? I'm sure that man came to our house trying to drum up trade,' said Harriet flabbergasted.

'He doesn't need to do that. I think he's just about caught most of us round here. The minute they opened my dad was there pawning the family silver. Now he's on straight loans. He won't bloody listen. It'll see my mum off, that's why I stick around. Not that Avril and I could go far. Not with a mother like that. She's expecting is Avril and her fucking mother won't keep her nose out. Got this tatty old semi lined up for us. The silly arse won't believe the estate agent that it's not on the open market. No she just keeps going and going. Of course it's her dosh, she's downsized to get us the deposit. Thinks Avril's getting tied into a wealthy business family and wants to keep her end up, she's out to prove a point. The old bat couldn't be more wrong. That'll have her swallowing the plum in her gob when she finds out she couldn't be more wrong.'

Harriet stepped back to scramble in her purse. Had no idea he was Avril's partner.

'And this tatty old semi she wants you to buy, whereabouts would that be then?'

'Oh what's the name of that road. The old bat seems to think it's a bit above the rest. Might have been fifty years ago. Not any more. That's it, the one with just a few houses in. The Willows that's it. Not a bloody tree in sight!'

Harriet took a very deep breath along with her change.

'Maybe Avril likes it even if you don't.'

'Oh she does but then she would, wouldn't she with a mother like that? Too scared to say any different.'

'Oh I see. Must go. I do hope things work out for you all.'

Glad to be in the car Harriet didn't know which revelation to deal with first. She decided on the insult. That was her home he was referring to and in spite of what her mother thought, she and Mark had done a great deal to improve it.

'Bloody cheek!' She gave way to swearing, vowing they'd never get it. Then the fear kicked in. The lad had just said that pawnbroker's had no need to be drumming up trade. Now she was convinced he'd singled out her house to track her down. All the way home the thought wouldn't go away. She battled to ease the chips away from the paper, remembering Mark's warning not to get involved. She felt very uneasy. Decided to phone Tricia. This thing needed sorting.

'Oh `arriet, I was just about to phone you. Bob's been back and gone again. `e's fumin`. Of course `e wasn't tellin` me exactly why. It's not goin` anywhere this, we don't seem to be able to get out of this spiral `arriet. Of course it would `elp if Belinda Oxfordshire would keep `er nose out. I was wonderin` if Mark's down at the club tonight `e might be able to throw some light on it for me. `e's bound to be talkin` to Bob at some stage.'

Harriet swallowed hard. Decided to stay quiet.

'I'm afraid he's already gone Tricia but listen to this. I think we've got to be very careful indeed.'

'Oh why `arriet? What's `appened now?'

'I've just come back from the chip shop and accidentally commandeered someone else's fish and chips.'

'Whose were they `arriet?'

'That heavy's wife. He came in whilst she was cursing at the lad behind the counter. threatening to pull the plug on their loans because he'd already put salt and vinegar on them. I told him to. I didn't know they were meant for her. The lad seemed to be looking across at me when he asked.'

'Oh `arriet, slow down a bit. You're sounding as scatty as me. What's goin` on as far as we're concerned?'

'Well he recognised me Tricia. I think he's on to me. His wife was so nasty about the lad making that mistake. It seems they're borrowing heavily from them to keep the shop open. He said his dad wouldn't listen to him. That woman, Carol her name is, wants to get them closed down. The lad was telling me that just about everyone round here are caught up with them. I'm just so worried Tricia that he's targeting me. It doesn't sound like he needs to be drumming up trade.'

'But `e `ad an `andful of leaflets `arriet. I'm sure `e would `ave been goin` to all the `ouses round and about. That lad's got it wrong. The place `asn't been opened that long. They're goin` to `ave to let people know they're there.'

'Well yes, I suppose so if he's not a fly-by-night, but it was the way he looked at me when he spoke. He said he recognised me Tricia. If he's part of that gang of criminals he's bound to have got hold of both our photographs. I've got a horrible feeling he's been knocking on doors to find us both.'

'Oh gosh `arriet. I don't like the sound of that. Oh I do wish we `adn't gone to Venice in the first place and I've not got my "save Venice" tin back yet, either. `ave you `eard from our friend at all? `ave you any idea when `is mate Clive is comin` up? I think I'm definitely goin` to be needin` `is `elp with this one.'

'Oh yes that was something else I wanted to tell you. Mr. Sanderson phoned to tell me they've been rained off. The whole place has flooded. They're probably all back by now.'

'Oh so we `aven't missed anythin` then? Was Clive Engells goin` to be comin` back with them to pick up `is car?'

'Yes, that's what he said. I've got an appointment to see him on Friday morning. Mr. Sanderson wants to nail Mr. Brown and Mr. Potts, the union guy. Mr. Brown's accusing me of persuading Danny to hurl fossils at him. As if! Apparently Danny gave him a real humdinger of a head second time round. I expect I'll be sitting opposite them both again like a naughty kid. The man's totally paranoid. He won't be satisfied until he's had me kicked out.'

'Oh I am sorry to `ear that. Maybe I should come along too as a witness. I'll be able to give evidence. After all I was there too. It would give me a chance to mention my "save Venice" tin, as well.'

'That's a brilliant idea Tricia. If we both turn up together he can hardly turn you away. Look I'll pick you up on Friday. He said ten o'clock so be ready for half past nine.'

'Oh I will `arriet, thanks so much for that. At least I've got time now to work out the best way to get Clive Engells to `elp me. You never know what I might come up with!'

'You never know Tricia. Rather you than me.'

Harriet put the phone down, wondering if she had just done the right thing.

Chapter 34

'You wouldn't believe it `arriet. Our friend Joris phoned last night. I didn't bother phonin` you back because I knew I'd be seein` you today.'

'Oh did he Tricia? Hang on a minute I don't think that door's been properly closed. Just give it a good wham.'

'I think that's done it now. Yes I was sayin`, `e said `e thought I'd better be there this mornin` as a witness to this fossil throwin` thing. Just like we said `arriet. Oh and `e wants me to `elp Mrs. `arris with the `igh tea she's doin` for the children so I'm `avin` to go back again this afternoon.'

'Oh brilliant Tricia. You might get your chance with Clive Engells, too. Oh I feel so much better about it all now.'

'Me too `arriet. I should `ave phoned you really but my mum brought the kids back. She wouldn't go. I ended up `avin` to give `er a lift `ome because fat-face-four-cheeks never came back to do it. I've really `ad enough of `im `arriet. We can't go on like this much longer. Ooh watch `im. `e's just pulled out without so much as a signal. Beep at `im `arriet. Blow your `orn `ard.'

'There, that'll teach him, pratt! We might just as well come back to mine for lunch.'

'Oh thanks `arriet. At least we won't be at Starboard Marine North West today. I was thinkin` about that pawnbroker `eavy last night and I'm feelin` very uneasy. I kept visualisin` `im comin` through the door.'

'Yes, I know what you mean . We've been through enough. Mark warned me to keep clear but I can't stand by and let the likes of him sink Mrs. Bustard and so many of our parents. I've got to do something to help but I don't know where to start.'

'That's a good question `arriet. Now where would you start without gettin` involved? Unless of course you mention it to Joris Sanderson. `e's got to be concerned about his parents `asn't `e? Sorry `arriet, just look over there. Starboard Marine North West `asn't even opened yet and it's nearly a quarter to ten.'

Harriet turned right at the lights then looked across to her left.

'No sign of Belinda Oxfordshire's car either Oh no, let's hope he hasn't closed it for the day and we've got to put up with her.'

'Oh I `ope not `arriet. I won't be responsible for my actions if I come across `er at Lower Tideside. `er pinchin` my `usband back again, the cheek of it! Not that I want `im back now. I'd far rather by savin` Venice if I can get my `ands on the tin.'

'Well it's stealing if Rapping Hammer doesn't hand it over. Perhaps you could get Clive Engells to write a formal letter to him when he gets back. That's probably the best way to take it.'

'Yes, I think you're right. It won't take too much of `is time. `e's probably already got one on `is computer. The only thing is `e mightn't be feelin` very cooperative after us burstin` in on `is camper.'

'Well I shouldn't think he'd want to bring that up again, especially with Lucinda Lawton there. I don't get it Tricia, surely she wouldn't be playing about with him if she's all lined up with Mr. Sanderson?'

'Of course it was 'er 'arriet. No mistake about it. I definitely 'eard 'im call Lucinda.'

'Yes and he's been taking her down to Falmouth. He's obviously seriously involved with her.'

'And 'ow long 'as she been at your school 'arriet? Not that long if I remember right. You don't know 'ow long she's been carryin' on with Clive Engells before she started, do you?'

'Oh no Tricia, that's a point. She used to do supply work before she got that deputy post. I know she doesn't come from round here. Maybe Clive Engells had a word in Mr. Sanderson's ear and that's why she got the job over me. Yes I bet she's got them both on a string and that's why he didn't propose in Falmouth. He wouldn't would he? Not if he had her in tow as well. He only proposed to me because he felt sorry for me at the church. I knew it! I knew it! That speech was all about finding out I was having his baby. Ugh! What kind of a marriage would that have been with her in the background? Oh I really can't stand her Tricia. I feel like shopping her.'

''ow about we both get our own back on the pair of them, 'er and Belinda Oxfordshire? I'm sure we could think of somethin' before the day ends.'

Harriet laughed then dismissed the thought. It wasn't in her nature to plan such things.

'No time Tricia. Look we're just coming past Molly's house. I really must give her a call. I wonder if Percy's got over his run-in with the law? My fault that. I don't know how I could have been so stupid as to get those plants mixed up. I think I'm going to need a word with Clive Engells, too. I don't like the way Guy Hammer's passing along threatening messages. Gosh Tricia, it never seems to end. How do we manage to end up in so much trouble?'

'Don't ask me! Oh look this is 'is big 'ouse now. Oh 'e's got the gates open. You can drive straight in 'arriet.'

Harriet crunched through the golden gravel to halt in front of the Georgian bow window through which she could just make out movement, her stomach churning with fury.

'Ah there you are Miss Glover, Mrs. Harrington. First to arrive. If you'd like to go through to the study you'll find Clive Engells ready and waiting.'

Tricia nudged Harriet.

'Ah Mrs. Harris, show them in, if you would be so kind.'

'Not more trouble?' Mrs. Harris queried as she ushered them both through the doorway.

'Hopefully not,' Harriet declared, determined to assert herself.

'False accusations, that's what it's all about Mrs. 'arris. I'm 'ere as a witness but this afternoon I believe I'll be 'elpin' you out with the 'igh tea.'

'Good gracious me no. Did Joris ask you to do that? Absolutely no need.

Everything's perfectly under control. Now if you'd like to go through.'

She knocked then pushed the door ajar.

'Mr. Engells you have already met these young ladies, I assume?'

Clive Engells nodded, gestured for them both to sit down. They watched Mrs. Harris leave, closing the door quietly behind her.

'I believe the campsite was a washout,' Harriet remarked.

'Indeed yes. In fact the whole village has been flooded. Mercifully only a couple of buildings affected. We had a lucky escape. You may remember the shops over the road? The river runs that side, burst its banks just catching the jewellers opposite. Very lucky we were. Very lucky indeed.'

'Oh we are sorry to 'ear that Mr. Engells, aren't we 'arriet? Especially as 'arriet 'ad spotted a beautiful amber ring in there. I do 'ope it 'asn't been washed away not that it matters now. It was going to be for 'arriet's engagement you see.'

Clive Engells cleared his throat, rubbed his hands together.

'Ah and the young man, was he in the vicinity too?'

Harriet nudged Tricia. Knew what was coming. Tricia wouldn't be able to resist the opportunity to link it with Rapping Hammer.

'Oh I'm very sorry to say but 'arriet's been very badly let down. You'll remember Rappin' 'ammer and 'is band in your 'otel? They dined in your 'otel while we were there.'

'Yes, yes. He's the young man is he? Let you down did he petal?'

Instantly Harriet felt his arm around her.

'Oh yes 'e did and not only that 'e's stolen a whole tin full of money. My "save Venice" tin. 'e won't give it back unless, well I can't tell you what 'e's threatenin' but then 'e is 'avin' withdrawal from cannabis and 'e's blamin' 'arriet and 'e's not cooperatin' in any way unless we perform these sexual acts not only to please 'im but 'e's wantin' 'arriet 'ere to sleep with Tarquin Bridgewater to persuade 'im to start growin' cannabis again. It wouldn't be so bad if 'e was gorgeous like the American president, but 'e's 'orrible and old enough to be 'er grandad.'

It wasn't the first time Harriet had blushed to excess in this room. Finally he removed his arm.

'I'm not surprised you broke it off with him petal, though I can't quite understand your involvement in the first place. Still I feel this young man should be taken in hand. Let's put the frighteners up him shall we? Address? Website? Fan club? I'll contact the office, see if we can't get a standard letter out to him. It usually does the trick. I'll have a word with Joris unless you'd like to give me your details now.'

Simultaneously they reached for their bags. Scribbled furiously on whatever would come to hand then passed him their contact details. Harriet needed the help. There was no way she could go against Tricia now.

'Ah voices at last,' Clive Engells uttered, waving his hand towards the door. 'The sooner we get this exercise out of the way the better.'

Harriet's eyes darted from the wall to the ceiling, following the sunlight dancing off the large clear stone set thick in the gold ring on his finger.

'Right Mrs. Bustard, Danny. Through here if you will. Mrs. Harris catch that boy before he sends my prized globe spinning into the chandelier.'

'Danny get yer `ands off it will yer?'

'Mr. Brown LOOK OUT! Oh no, Mr. Potts are you alright?' Mr. Sanderson rushed to his side as Danny caught the globe bouncing off his nose.

'Oh bloody `ell not again. What did I tell you? What she `asn't put that boy up to isn't worth knowin`.'

'I beg your pardon Mr. Brown. I didn't even know Danny and his mother were coming here this morning,' Harriet protested.

'No you didn't, did you `arriet? There you go Mr. Engells, they're `ardly through the door and they're making false accusations.'

'That's enough Mrs. Harrington. Now I trust you are not injured Mr. Potts? Here boy, give me that globe back this minute and take a seat over there along with your mother.' Danny instantly shielding it with his whole body, pouted at Mr. Sanderson. Harriet stood to help, doing an inadvertent dance with Mrs. Bustard, before scrambling to her seat.

'Don't worry,' she whispered. 'We're all a bit scared by this place. It'll soon be sorted.'

Mrs. Bustard caught her hand, shuffled on the chair, nervously clasping at the buttons on her purple cardigan.

'Mr Swift find you alright?'

'Oh yes thank you very much Mr. Sanderson. I was just comin` out of the shop by the school. I knew your car so I flagged `im down. No sense `im `avin` to start lookin` for a parkin` spot round there.'

'I'm not aware of any shops Mrs. Bustard.'

'Well you wouldn't be aware of that shop Mr. Sanderson. Not livin` `ere you wouldn't. It's only the likes of us that `as to go to those kind of places.'

'I `ate going in there. That man's nasty to my mum. `e keeps sayin` if we don't pay we'll be going to jail but `e's the one who should go there. `e's a bad man and she won't let me tell my dad.'

'That's enough Danny. `ere now you just give that globe back to Mr. Sanderson before you get a good hidin`.'

'No I want to hold it. It's boring in `ere, why do I `ave to be `ere anyway?'

'Oh let the boy hold on to it for the moment. He's got a fair point.' Mr. Sanderson tossed his hair back as he rearranged a couple more chairs to allow Mr. Brown and Mr. Potts to sit down.

'If I `ad a big fossil, as big as `er…' Harriet flushed as he pointed his finger straight at her. '… I'd throw it at that bad man and send him crashing to the middle of the earth to burn in the fire.'

'There you go Mr. Potts. Did you `ear the lad? He's threatening someone else now. He's in `er class you know. It's `er doing. She's using `er pupils to get back at me. No, no I'm not taking much more of this, it's obvious she's influencing the boy.'

'OH NO I AM NOT!' Harriet declared. 'I think you should be vary careful what you say in front of Mr. Engells. He's a lawyer and is now witnessing slander!'

Clive Engells cleared his throat to beam at Harriet.

'Where's Joris gone now? The sooner we get started the better. Ah there you are Joris. Shall we get the show on the road?'

Harriet watched him swing the black leather chair away from his desk to sit alongside Clive Engells. His usual position. His right leg angled outwards to rest his foot on his left knee. The blonde curl at his neck leading the row falling towards his collar.

'Gosh his hair needs cutting, on second thoughts *not*. It's gorgeous. He's marrying Lucinda Lawton and his hair looks gorgeous. Oh sod, why did I let him go? Because you knew in your heart he could have asked you sooner and now you know why he didn't. He's been playing with you Harriet. Lucinda Lawton won the race!'

The ring of his mobile phone splintered away her thoughts. They'd all been speaking. She hadn't heard a thing until now.

'Not to worry Lucinda.' He was smiling that smile into the phone. Harriet seethed.

'Look Lucinda we'll clear that one later. No after it's all finished I mean.'

He smiled at the phone again before popping it back to the inside pocket of his jacket.

'Now where were we? Miss Glover I've asked you twice now. What exactly is your response to Mr. Engells' last comment?'

Harriet blanked.

'Oh she totally agrees with `im don't you `arriet?' Tricia piped up. Harriet felt a nudge at her waist.

'Ah she `asn't been listenin. I saw `er lookin` at `er feet. Why `ave we come `ere when Miss `asn't been listenin`?'

'Be quiet Danny and listen to what Mr. Sanderson and Mr. Engells have got to say,' instructed Harriet, trying to retrieve the situation.

'No, *I'm* not listenin` if *you* don't `ave to. Anyway you gave me mum the money to go to Butlins and now we're not goin`. You tell lies Miss. You shouldn't be teachin` us because you tell lies!'

Harriet, mortified, looked straight at Mr. Sanderson. No response. She hadn't meant to do that.

'There you go Mr. Potts. What further evidence do we need? The boy's telling us she's a liar. Now come on boy tell us all how she got you to throw fossils at me. Just like you told me at the campsite, remember?'

All eyes on Danny. Head down, he swirled the globe spinning it on its axis.

'You tell the truth now Danny or I'll tell your dad. What did you say to Mr. Brown?' said Mrs. Bustard fidgeting on her seat.

'Go on young man tell them what you told me,' encouraged Mr. Brown.

'She told me to do it,' he sulked out his reply, pointing at Harriet.

'Evidence Mr. Engells. You are a witness to the truth.' Mr. Brown then turned towards Mr. Potts. 'This is serious now. The boy's admitted it.' Then back to Mr. Sanderson. 'Suspend 'er again Mr. Sanderson only this time don't bother with the hearing. Just sack 'er now. The woman's a menace!'

'Just hold your horses Mr. Brown. I think we should let the lawyer deal with this.'

Mr. Sanderson turned to Clive Engells. He looked at Harriet then Danny.

'Now Danny you do understand there are very serious consequences for your teacher, Miss Glover if you are telling the truth?'

'Oh 'e's tellin' the truth alright. She's stamped on my foot, shot a lunch trolley at me, landed a hanging basket on my head, pushed me off my ladder. She's done so much she can't think of any more so now she's settin' the kids on me. She's guilty alright. Just look at 'er face.'

'Well I am a very close friend of 'arriet's and I am a witness to the fact that she 'ad nothin' to do with that fossil bein' thrown at you Mr. Brown. 'ow do you know Danny 'ere wasn't tellin' you lies?'

'Just the point I was about to get to Mrs. Harrington.' Clive Engells turned to Danny.

'Now young man stop swirling that thing around and listen very carefully because you yourself will be in very serious trouble if you don't tell the truth and by serious trouble it could mean you being removed from your school away from all your friends and going somewhere quite different and not as pleasant I can assure you.'

Harriet watched Danny's face pale as he removed his hand from the spinning globe.

'Now young man, you knew it was wrong to throw stones at Mr. Brown didn't you?'

'They weren't stones they were fossils. You're tellin' lies now.'

'Danny don't you be so cheeky or I'll box your ears. You tell Mr. Engells the truth or you'll end up in a special school for bad boys.'

'Will there be a bad man like the one in the shop lookin' after us all?'

'Yes Danny, a very bad man just like the one in the shop and you wouldn't like that.'

'Come come Mrs. Bustard, I don't see the need to terrify the boy into a confession.'

'I 'appen to know 'im a lot better than you Mr. Sanderson. I know 'ow best to get the truth out of 'im.'

Mr. Sanderson cleared his throat.

'Look Danny, all we're asking is that you tell us exactly what you said to Mr. Brown.'

'I already said she told me to do it.'

'See 'e's said it again. Why are we goin' round in circles? See Mr. Potts how they're going round in circles?' said Mr. Brown, becoming increasingly annoyed.

'Now Danny is that the truth? Did you tell Mr. Brown that Miss Glover told you to do it?'

'Yes I did.'

'Now Danny why did you say that to Mr. Brown?'

Danny, head down, spun the globe rapidly to look up with crossed eyes.

Mr. Sanderson tried again.

'Why did you say to Mr. Brown that Miss Glover had told you to do it?'

'Because, because I didn't want to get into trouble and she's stopped me from goin` to Butlins. I didn't want to go lookin` for stupid fossils I wanted to go to Butlins.'

Harriet jumped up like an uncoiled spring offering her hand to Clive Engells.

'Oh thank you, thank you so much for getting to the bottom of this. It's such a relief.'

He pointed sideways to Mr. Sanderson.

'He's the one to thank, not me.'

'Not necessary Miss Glover. Now Mr. Brown, Mr. Potts. It's unfortunate your time has been taken in this way, especially yours Mr. Potts. Mr. Brown, as far as you are concerned you took the boy at his word and quite frankly with Miss Glover's track record, it's not that difficult to see where you were coming from, though I think we all hold Miss Glover in far higher regard than to suppose she would stoop as low as that. No face lost Mr. Brown and I see your wound is healing nicely. Now I think Mrs. Harris will have made coffee for us. If you'd all like to go through and I'd just like a word with you, young man. If you would kindly stop spinning that thing now.'

Harriet watched Danny bat it for all he was worth, just pipping his mother in the race to take it from him. Instantly grabbing it back, the thing shot from Harriet's hands at great speed just as Clive Engells looked up from gathering his notes, to hit him straight in the eye.

'Good heavens Miss Glover, whatever have you done now?' Mr. Sanderson exclaimed.

Harriet gasped as Clive Engells slapped his hand over his eye, to struggle in his trouser pocket for his handkerchief. Shaking in unison with Tricia, she could feel her mouth stiffening in the strangest contortions as she tried to hold back the screeches. Danny spotted them both, ran towards the door then collapsed laughing, rolling around the floor just as Mrs. Harris entered with the tray.

'Oooh, oooh I thought I'd just bring these…..oooooh….in!' She was down along with the clattering cups and saucers. Broken china, bits flying everywhere. The coffee pot emptying itself all over the highly polished woodblock floor.

'Good gracious me Mrs. Harris are you alright? I assumed we'd be in the drawing room. Danny, you boy get up this minute. No Mrs. Bustard stop just where you are. Hang on a minute Clive. Miss Glover what on earth were you trying to do?'

'Let's get out of `ere Mr. Potts before she lands us both one.'

'Mrs. Harris. Here let me help you up. Oh no, this damned phone again.

"Yes, hello Sanderson speaking. Ah Lucinda, it's you again Lucinda. I'm afraid…….".' Knocked straight from his hand it fell to the floor with the globe bouncing behind.

'Danny you stop chuckin` that fuckin` thing around will you?'

'I'm only doin` what Miss did.'

'I do apologise Clive, I really am shocked by all of this. Miss Glover, Mrs. Harrington, when you've seen fit to stop laughing get hold of Swift will you? Get him to clear this lot up.'

'Ah Swift, good man, a hand needed here if you will. I've just sent them off to find you.'

'Didn't see anyone Mr. Sanderson. Just heard the noise. Oh come here Mrs. Harris, I do hope that's not going to turn into a black eye.'

'Like this you mean?'

All eyes turned to Clive Engells.

'I don't know where he is Tricia. Oh come on let's go home. They won't even notice.'

'Ooh `arriet we might get into trouble.'

'Into trouble Tricia? I've just said they won't even notice. It'll give us some breathing space. We'll be back again this afternoon in any case.'

'Ooh I do `ope you're right `arriet.'

Chapter 35

'Miss Glover, Mrs. Harrington. Just a moment, if you don't mind. What on earth do you think you are doing?'

They jumped in unison.

'Oh just moving the car Mr. Sanderson. Felt it was in an awkward place, right opposite the door.'

'It doesn't take two of you Miss Glover. Now if the pair of you would kindly return to the library, Mrs. Harris is serving coffee there. It's all calmed down, probably due to your disappearance Miss Glover. It never ceases to amaze me the frequency and variety of your repertoire. Now, try to make that Bast... er Bustard woman feel at home will you? She's sat there like a fish out of water clutching that lad of hers for all she's worth.'

'Right Mr. Sanderson. Oh look she's behind you. She's coming out with Mr. Brown and Mr. Potts.'

'We'll be on our way now Mr. Sanderson if you don't mind. Mr. Brown `as kindly offered to take us back so it will save bothering Mr. Swift. Best be getting our Danny back `ome and out of `ere. I think we've caused enough trouble as it is.'

'Ah I see. You'll not stay for coffee then?'

'Er no thank you Mr. Sanderson. I'd better get back to Bert, `e likes me around the `ouse since `e's been made redundant.'

'Ah I see. Right you are then and don't you forget what I've just said to you young man. We can't always have what we want just when we want it...' He looked sharply across to Harriet then continued. '...and we certainly don't go blaming people or trying to get them into trouble.'

Harriet caught his glance. Thought about Lucinda Lawton and felt an overwhelming desire to drop her right in it. Knew Mr. Sanderson would never want to marry her if he was made aware she'd been cavorting with Clive Engells. She watched Danny trailing behind as they walked towards Mr. Brown's car. Saw him grab a handful of golden gravel just before Mrs. Bustard pushed him into the back seat of the car. They were away.

'Ah we'll take the opportunity to run through this afternoon's procedure, I think. Clive's staying over a few days. It wouldn't be appropriate for him to return with a black eye.' Harriet caught his glance. 'We're very fortunate he understood. Anyhow he's more than happy to get involved. Oh that's handy Belinda's arrived! Go through, go through to the library Belinda, we'll be joining you in a tick.'

'She's taken `er time asn't she? Seein` `as `er car wasn't there at Starboard Marine North West when we went past.'

'I'm glad she has Tricia. I didn't fancy her being another witness. Let's just hope she's not out to cause more trouble today.'

'Oh she'll be `ere to go through the arrangements `arriet. I don't know why `e bothered askin` `er to join in.'

'Go on Tricia, keep going. The library's down the very end and to the left facing the hellipad, remember?'

'I might 'ave if this place didn't 'ave so many rooms. We still don't really know 'ow 'e got all 'is money to buy this great big 'ouse.'

'From banking Tricia. I told you his mother explained it all.'

'Well I still don't believe 'er 'arriet. I bet they're all drug barons. That's why 'e lives 'ere 'arriet with the island so close and the 'ellipad to 'and.'

'Oops I can hear them, don't let him catch you saying that again. You managed to get away with it last time.'

'Oh I'm not scared of 'im 'arriet. 'e's just one big womaniser. Serves 'im right if 'e 'as been double-crossed by that silly shrieky deputy of 'is. I can't stand 'er 'arriet. 'ow about if we drop 'er right in it by accident?'

'Shh Tricia, come on let's get this coffee. Let's just see if an opportunity arises. You never know!'

'Right, everybody here? Ah Clive, sorry for the interruption. Nevertheless, satisfactory outcome. I am sure you are very grateful Miss Glover.'

'I certainly am.' Instant fury. Thought. 'I've just flipping well thanked him. I'll show him.'

Before she could stop herself she was off her seat lightly kissing Clive Engells' cheek. 'And I am really sorry about the accident, it wouldn't have happened if Danny hadn't tried to grab it back.'

'Think nothing of it my petal, these things happen and neither of you need worry any more. I'll soon have this Hammer lad off your backs.'

Harriet smiled, resuming her seat to sense the irritation radiating from Mr. Sanderson.

'Ah thank you ever so much Mr. Engells,' Tricia piped up. ''ere let me give you one on the other side.'

'Not another one of these I hope,' he chortled, pointing at his bad eye.

'No just a kiss Mr. Engells for all you're doin' for 'arriet and I.'

'Enough, quite enough you two. We'll have no more from either of you to embarrass Mr. Engells. If he's very kindly offered to help you out of yet another disaster then a quiet verbal appreciation is all that's required. Now down to business. Oh Mrs. Harris would you be so kind as to bring along another cup and saucer for Belinda?' Mr. Sanderson gestured with his hand towards Belinda Oxfordshire as she sat down, then went across to the French doors to pull them closed.

'Oh not there Belinda,' Tricia suddenly shouted. Belinda shot up to look behind her.

'You'll squash the cat.'

'So you think that's funny Patricia Harrington? I happen to know Joris hasn't got a cat. You haven't got a cat have you Joris? She glanced at Harriet. 'You can't stand the things.' She promptly sat down to a piercing yowl, instantly leaping up again, nursing her backside.

'Bloody thing's scratched me.'

'Oh not on your bum again Belinda? Your bum's not `avin` much luck lately is it? I did try to warn you.'

'What's all this going on now? What's that damned thing doing in here again?'

'Isn't that Molly's cat Mr. Sanderson? I seem to remember the blob of white at the tip of its tail.'

'Could well be Miss Glover. The damned thing only appeared after they moved in. Mrs. Harris you haven't been feeding this thing have you?'

'No Mr. Sanderson, not to speak of anyway.' She looked out of it, as if still a little dazed from her fall.

'Well I'd be grateful if you don't encourage it. It needs to get used to its own surroundings. Miss Glover, remind me to give Molly a call before you leave this afternoon. Mrs. Harris get Mr. Swift to put it in the shed will you? Molly will want it back. We can't have her thinking she's lost it. Now to business. Er are you alright Mrs. Harris, you're a little pale? Er you too Belinda. Are you alright Belinda?'

Mrs. Harris nodded, smiling weakly. Belinda Oxfordshire was not about to miss the opportunity.

'It's stinging Joris, it's stinging.'

'I think you might need to rub some antiseptic on `er bum Mr. Sanderson. Cat's claws get into everythin`.'

'Go to the bathroom Belinda. In the cabinet. We won't start until you come down. Now Mrs. Harrington you seem to be intent on embarrassing people this morning. Do you think you could exercise a little decorum? Had you warned Belinda in advance or shooed the cat from the cushion it would have been far more constructive.'

'But I was only jokin` Mr. Sanderson. No one was more surprised than me to see a cat shoot off.'

'Really Mrs. Harrington. Is it necessary to continue to torment Belinda in this manner? One feels you haven't yet grasped the seriousness of your atrocious behaviour towards her whilst camping. You would be well advised to keep your head down.'

'Well that's just a teeny weeny bit difficult Mr. Sanderson seein` as she's managed to get my Bob back off me again. She's done somethin` to make `im fall all over `er again and I've `ad just about enough!'

'Oh dear Patricia are you having marital difficulties as well?'

'Yes, as a matter of fact Mr. Engells I am and it's only since she came on the scene.'

'Then maybe I could be of assistance? We deal with all manner of matrimonial problems leading to divorce and settlements. I'll have a word with you later.'

Mr. Sanderson flicked his hair through his fingers then looking towards the door drummed his nails on the top of the dark wood cabinet housing his expensive collection of very rare fossils.

'Joris, I can't find any.' The call was loud and clear.

'Just a minute Belinda, I'm coming. Just finish your coffee, we'll be down in a minute.'

Clive Engells made for the kitchen with empty cup in hand. Tricia, furious, whispered to Harriet.

'I bet she's got 'im dabbing it on her bum. I bet she's got 'er knickers down right now.'

'Shh Tricia. He *is* a doctor. You never know with cats.'

''ow did I manage to conjure one up out of thin air? I was only jokin' 'arriet. Do you know I think there's somethin' spooky about this place.'

'Oh gosh Tricia, don't say that. I've got to take the kids through that tunnel this afternoon, the one the monks used centuries ago to get to and from the monastery on the island. I don't want any spooky experiences in there.'

'Don't worry 'arriet. I'll come with you. Mrs. 'arris 'as already said she doesn't want any 'elp with the 'igh tea so I won't be missed.'

'Ah thanks Tricia. I'll be glad to get this thing all over and done with.'

'Me too 'arriet. 'ow about we try to lose fancy pants and Lucinda Lawton in there?'

'Shush Tricia, they're coming down.'

'Right, now where were we? Ah yes, this afternoon's arrangements. The children will be coached in following lunch, at two o'clock. Ross Farquerhart should arrive half an hour before that to set the display up. On arrival, once the children have placed their own fossils on the display table, he'll give a short history of the place which will give some perspective to the geological time scale relating to the creation of fossils. However the main point will be to capture the childrens' imagination and prepare them for this tunnel exercise. Now Lucinda and I will be splitting the afternoon. We'll all be in here for the first thirty minutes following which Lucinda and you Miss Glover will escort the children through the tunnel, obviously answering any questions they may have. Then we'll change about. Belinda we'll then do the same while Lucinda's group return here to ask further questions of historical interest which will be addressed to Ross Farquerhart. My party will then return here to join them before high tea, which will be your domain Mrs. Harrington.'

Harriet felt a nudge. Mrs. Harris had disappeared with the tray of cups. It was evident Tricia was leaving it right there as far as Mr. Sanderson was concerned.

He continued. 'Following high tea the most exciting fossil award will be made by myself and Ross Farquerhart, whereupon, hopefully, the coach will have returned to take the children home. Any questions? Oh and if you could oversee the whole exercise Clive I'd be most grateful.'

Clive Engells stood to nod his head in agreement.

'Right that's it then. Everyone back here at ten minutes to two, prompt.'

'Ooh I'm so glad to be out of there 'arriet. 'im and 'is old fossils. 'e's turnin' into one 'imself. 'e's so bossy. Remind me to write that in my diary 'arriet. "Bossy and unable to keep is 'ands off Belinda Oxfordshire's bum." Maybe I'll just drop that one in to Lucinda Lawton this afternoon. That should please `er!'

Chapter 36

' 'ere we are back again. Ooh they're all 'ere already. Thanks for lunch 'arriet, I 'ad an 'orrible feelin' Mrs. 'arris was goin' to bring us all sandwiches. The thought of stayin' there all day really did my 'ead in.'

'It's a pleasure Tricia and mine too. One good thing though we certainly seem to have managed to get Clive Engells on board.'

'Yes and I 'ope 'is letter does the trick. I want that tin back. Ooh I wouldn't park it there again 'arriet or 'e might not believe what you said about movin' it this mornin'.'

'Good thinking Tricia. Now just let me get my notes. There was quite a bit of stuff online about the house and its links to the monastery on the island. Anyway I daresay Ross Farquerhart will have genned up on it all.'

'He's such a swat isn't 'e? I 'ope we don't 'ave any fun and games over that 'amper again. I think it would 'ave been much better if our friend Joris adn't asked Belinda Oxfordshire to this. I wonder who's lookin' after Starboard Marine Northwest?'

'Probably Iris and Tarquin Bridgewater. Don't mention him either! Yes the sooner Clive Engells gets that letter off to Rapping Hammer, the better.'

'Come along, do come along. The coach will arrive in five minutes. We're all in the drawing room.' From the doorway Mr. Sanderson beckoned briefly to disappear into the house. They hurried towards the open door.

'OK, OK we're comin' you bossy old fossil, keep your 'air on.'

Suddenly his face popped out from behind the door sending Harriet's heart thumping, her preoccupation with *that* luxurious rug resting at the fireplace instantly gone.

'Not the best of starts Mrs. Harrington. I demand an apology this instant.'

'Oh I didn't realise you were 'oldin' the door open for us Mr. Sanderson. 'arriet just told me to 'urry up after you said it and I was talkin' to 'er. I was talkin' to you wasn't I 'arriet?'

'Miss Glover appears to be totally mesmerised by the rug on the floor Mrs. Harrington. She doesn't appear to be aware of such a communication having taken place.'

Harriet looked up, could feel herself going bright red.

'Memories taken over Miss Glover?'

She looked down. Thought about her baby, instinctively placed her hand across her stomach.

'Indeed, yes indeed Miss Glover. Deception seems to be par for the course with you two. Now in without any further nonsense. You'll find the staff assembled in the library.'

Ross Farquerhart looked up from under Enid Frost's pink rimmed glasses, rubbed his nose then grinned. Harriet flushed, this was the first time she'd seen him since the hamper revelation. She'd pushed it to the back of her mind. Couldn't quite understand what it was about these bits of kids that seem to be so easily attracted to her. She thought of the kiss, then him touching at the straps on her shoulder. She cringed as she caught Belinda Oxfordshire's glare, then scolded herself for winding him up. Chatter all around, busy, intent, all geared to who's doing what and where, while Ross Farquerhart continued to set out the fossils.

'All sorted? The coach has just arrived. Miss Glover make sure you keep an eye on that Bast... er Bustard boy will you? I don't want a repeat performance of this morning.'

'Oh right Mr. Sanderson. After what he did I wouldn't have expected he'd be allowed back.'

'Politics Miss Glover. Politics. Besides the lad's got to learn there's more to fossils than hurling them around.'

'Oh yes, yes of course. I'll see to him.' She wished she hadn't just said that.

'The children will be lining up outside. Miss Lawton, bring them through will you?'

Ross Farquerhart pushed his overly large glasses up his nose at the gradual invasion of excited chatter.

'Er no, don't start putting them down yet. Come and sit over here on the carpet. We want to name them.'

'They `aven't got names like dinosaurs `ave Mister, even we know that. `e's trying to be a teacher and `e doesn't know anythin`.'

Kids' laughter permeated their excitement.

' `as your banana got a name Danny?'

'Yes it's "banana" you dip-`ead.'

'Shut it you two!' Ross Farquerhart suddenly lost his cool. 'The rest of you come and sit down. No get it off that table. You'll scratch the bloody thing!'

'Ah `e swore. `e just swore Miss.'

Harriet pretended she hadn't heard.

'Over here, this minute. Sit down quietly and wait for Mr. Farquerhart to call your name so he can write it on a label. If you don't put your name on we won't be able to tell who's won.'

All eyes on her now. She'd brought them under control just as Mr. Sanderson and Clive Engells marched in only to about turn and disappear. Harriet continued.

'Now we're all very lucky to have Mr. Farquerhart with us. He knows all about fossils and...'

'Does that mean `e knows all about you Miss?'

'Yes, some would say that,' Belinda Oxfordshire said sufficiently loudly to turn Harriet a deep shade of beetroot.

'That's quite enough Danny and stop shining that torch in my face. All of you switch those torches off.'

'No it's "not quite enough". I've just `eard `er.' Danny pointed to Belinda Oxfordshire. 'She's just said "Yes". Well you did, I `eard. You've just called `er an old fossil. She's an old fossil, she's an old fossil.'

It caught on like a bush fire.

'Stop this nonsense this minute all of you and turn those torches off.'

The room immediately silenced to Mr. Sanderson's command. 'Miss Glover remove that boy immediately.'

Harriet marched him out, stood him in the hall demanding an apology.

'Well it's your fault we're not goin' to Butlins. I didn't like that stupid campin' holiday. I wanted to go to Butlins.'

'Look Danny,' Harriet began. 'No one can afford to go on holidays at the moment. It's not just you, I bet all the children in there are only going to do the camping trip this year and that's because Mr. Sanderson paid towards it. It's a shame about the weather and everyone having to come home early, but look, the sun's shining and he wants you all to have a good time this afternoon. Do you know there's going to be a tea party afterwards?'

Danny pressed the end of his nose down towards his top lip to accentuate his pout.

'I don't like Mr. Farmercart.'

'Well you don't have to like him. He's writing a very important story, a real story about how fossils were made millions of years ago. Now if we go back in I'm sure we'll be in time to see his very special clock.'

'Will it make the time go quick so we can all go 'ome?'

'Well no this is a clock that goes back millions of years to when the earth was first made. It will show us when fossils were formed and then how living things evolved, that means changed. Living things kept growing and changing over millions of years to make it easier for them to live in their surroundings which often changed because of the weather. When things were happy they stopped changing and so we still have all the different forms of living things today. Eventually we came along or so the theory goes but he'll explain it much better than me.'

'So we're all made out of old fossils then. See I was right.'

'Well no, not really, not exactly anyway. Things changed to survive but we have extra, very special things that we don't actually need to keep us alive. Things like music and singing. Beautiful things that can make us feel very happy. Things that all other creatures and animal don't have. Mr. Farquerhart's going to write a good story about it all and I'm sure he'll tell us that some very clever people think God has given us those extra special things.'

'So we're not all made out of fossils then? That's why I didn't see any skeletons in the rocks.'

'Oh you wouldn't have seen any human skeletons Danny, you'll see on Mr. Farquerhart's clock how very much later we came along. When those very early creatures in the sea died, their skeletons became compressed or squashed in the sand and over millions of years, the crust of the earth kept shifting to trap them in layers. The massive movements of the earth made huge steps in the land which we call cliffs and so we can see all these very old creatures in the rock strata, or layers. A bit like a cake.'

'Will we be `avin` cakes at our party Miss?'

'Oh yes, I'm sure we will.' Now this house is very old but not as old as the fossils on the table. You'll see how old it is on Mr. Farquerhart's special clock. He's going to tell you all about the island and how hundreds of years ago a monastery was built there and how the monks built a tunnel under the sea to this house.'

'Oh can we go in it Miss?'

'Yes, we'll be going in there very soon.'

'Will we be able to take our cake with us?'

'Oh I'm not so sure about that Danny. Maybe it would be better to save it for when we come out.'

'Ah that's not fair Miss. I want my cake inside the tunnel not outside of it. You always spoil everything you do.'

'Now young man, we'll have less of that! You may return providing you behave yourself.'

'I am being have myself Mr. Sandcastles. I don't like `er she spoils everything and I don't like that Mr. Farmercart either. I want my fossils back too. They're millions of years old them and they came from the bottom of the sea before the earth moved up to make that cliff by the water. Mine were the biggest of everyone's. I `aven't got one for the table.'

'You're surprisingly knowledgeable young man but perhaps you should have considered that before throwing them at Mr. Brown.'

'She made me do it. She told me to.'

'Now no more lies. That's just why we were here this morning to establish that fact. If you can't behave yourself I shall have you taken home straight away.'

'I don't want to go `ome. My mum's got that `orrible man comin` round now and she `asn't got any money to give `im. She said `e'd be gone when I get back. No, no Mr. Sandcastles I don't want to see `im again.'

'Alright young man, alright. You may stay here just as long as you do as you are told. Now say you're sorry to Miss Glover.'

'Sorry Miss. You won't send me `ome to that `orrible man will you?'

'Of course not Danny. Oh look what Mr. Sanderson's just found.'

'That's one of me fossils that is. It's the biggest one. I want to put my name on that. I want to win the prize.'

'Brown obviously left it in the porch. Take him through Miss Glover.'

'Thank you Mr. Sanderson. Come on Danny let's get your name on that one.'

They returned to the library to see the green felt protecting the table dotted with named rocks of all shapes and sizes.

'There Danny, look Mr. Farquerhart's got a label for you. Quickly now go and tell him your name.'

'Er Miss Glover, a word if I may. Now what's the boy talking about with regard to this man and his mother?'

'It's the pawn shop I thought I'd told you about. The one recently opened round the corner from the school Mr. Sanderson. It seems like most of the parents are in this guy's clutches. He's not nice. I accidently took his wife's fish and chips the other night and his reaction was frightening. He's threatening to pull the plug on the place. Actually as it happens the lad that works there is Avril's boyfriend. You know the couple that want to buy the house. Not that he likes it, he made that quite plain.........'

'Miss Glover do stop babbling. That's another thing that needs sorting, I must get back to it. Now the whole country's in a deep recession. It's not just our parents you know. They are adults and must take responsibility for their own actions. Whilst I have every sympathy for them and we are trying our best for the kids, unfortunately we are not able to go bailing them out of debt. I advise you to stay well out of this one Miss Glover. I think you've probably taken as much stress as you can handle in your condition.'

Harriet looked down, felt him lifting her chin.

'Look at me Miss Glover. You are not fooling anyone you know, least of all me.'

'What do you mean Mr. Sanderson?'

'You know only too well what I mean Miss Glover. You'll have missed two periods by now I should think?'

She stepped back, turned to gaze at the flokati rug resting at the foot of the beautiful old fireplace gracing the central hall. Felt the brush of his hand against the side of her face.

'Again I'm asking you to look at me Miss Glover. Ah the usual flush of colour. Yet again, "Cum tacent, clamant", I fear.'

He turned swiftly on his heel. Went to march off, then stopped to walk back, his eyes settling briefly on her breasts. Oh how she wished she hadn't stood naked to the waist, allowing him to feel their fullness; she knew there was no deceiving him now.

' "Silence is an admission of guilt" Miss Glover, should your lack of recall mean you'll be requiring a translation.'

'But Mr. Sanderson, that man. He looks like one of those heavies. Barry Giordano warned us. He could be one of them.'

'All the more reason to keep away Miss Glover.'

She held back. Her mind spinning, turning the amber light to green. She waited for him to go. She needed to compose herself. He'd just brushed her cheek with his hand. He'd just been expressing concern. He'd as good as undressed her to the waist with those expressive, compelling blue eyes. Oh how much she wanted this gorgeous, gorgeous man to hold all of her before making love just one more time, as they did on the sand. Then she'd tell him she was pregnant.

'Miss Glover, do come along. Lucinda's waiting for you.'

Instantly he blasted it all away. She couldn't deal with the thought of him marrying Lucinda bloody Lawton.

'Come on 'arriet. It's time for us to take the kids in the tunnel. What 'ave you been doin` all this time?'

'Just got involved with Danny again. He's being a little so and so today.'

'A little bugger you mean `arriet. `e came back ages ago. Maybe we could lose `im in the tunnel.'

'What a brilliant idea! Have you had a chance to have a word with Clive Engells yet?'

'Ooh yes I `ave `arriet. `e actually came over to me wantin` some more details about rappin` `ammer and `is licentious suggestions. `is word not mine.'

'Oh right. How's he going to tackle that side of it Tricia?'

'Well `e said `e'd very carefully construct a warning letter and send a copy to `is agent. `e sounds pretty confident `e'll be able to put a stop to it all and get my money back.'

'Oh that's a relief Tricia. Any signs of him flirting with Lucinda Lawton?'

'As a matter of fact I've been watchin` arriet and I don't think `e's given `er so much as a glance.'

'Well he is a lawyer isn't he? He'd be the last one to compromise himself if he thinks she's all lined up to marry Mr. Sanderson.'

'She's welcome to `im. I've just `ad a barney with `im over `elpin` Mrs. `arris out. It was only when she came out and said everythin` was under control and it would be better if I went in the tunnel as it could be dangerous in there, that `e backed off.'

' "No danger Mrs. Harris, as long as the children keep to the left, avoiding the well at the central expansion and stay this side of the door." That's what `e said `arriet. I think I'd rather be `elpin` with the tea.'

'Oh you'll be alright Tricia. I'm glad you're coming. I've looked it all up on the internet. Apparently this place used to be a sanctuary for the monks, well the oldest bit at the back did. It's been rebuilt a couple of times. The well goes up to the garden not far from the helipad. The monks used to hide in the tunnel if they were under threat and they used to keep supplies in the central part by the well. Apparently there's interesting remnants left in the stonework.'

'Oh I see.'

'But that's not all Tricia. It's been used for smuggling too. From the island ships used to be guided straight onto the rocks, then pillaged and all the contraband brought through the tunnel to here.'

'Well there you go `arriet. What did I say when we were `avin` dinner with the PM? That *is* where `e gets all `is money from but of course it will be drugs nowadays. We'll keep an eye open `arriet while we're in there. It sounds like the perfect place for Rappin` `ammer.'

Harriet laughed. 'Along with the rest of them. I wouldn't mind seeing them all locked in.'

* * *

'Now Danny keep your torch on and hold my hand all the time.'

'Eighteen,' triumphed Lucinda Lawton as she put her pointing finger away.

'Make sure we come out with eighteen, you two.'

Harriet looked at Tricia. Didn't quite catch what she'd just mumbled but guessed by her expression she was equally annoyed.

Now Mr. Sanderson's turn. 'Watch the steps as you go down. Five in all. The tunnel slopes towards the centre which is the deepest part, then uphill all the way back I'm afraid. Keep to the same side both ways. That's the left on the way out, right on the way back,' he boomed into the tunnel.

Last in the line, Harriet heard him close the door behind her.

'Keep to this side everyone and try to hold your torches still, in front of you. We're going downhill so be careful, don't rush. It's quite a long walk but we're only going half way. When we get there you can shine your torches on the walls. I know there are some drawings to see but there might even be some fossils in the rocks as well.'

From the rear, Harriet could just about hear Lucinda Lawton's irritating voice issuing instructions.

'Now you've `eard what Miss in front `as just said. Stop pokin` that torch up `er bum will you, try to `old it still,' demanded Tricia.

'It was an accident Miss, he's just tripped me up from behind.'

Harriet could hear Tricia from somewhere in the middle. Glad to be stifling the giggles she needed this distraction. The place was much too dark, damp and spooky for her liking.

'She's just trod on my heel. Now my shoe's come off.'

'I'm afraid you'll `ave to be stoppin` Lucinda while `e puts `is shoe back on. No you can't do it up like that. Stop pokin` `er with that blinkin` thing. `ere give it to me.'

'I can't see where to fasten it without my torch Miss.'

'No all of you, come away from that side of the tunnel now. He doesn't need all those torches to shine on his shoelace. Mrs. Harrington can you send them back to Miss Glover at the end. Oh no, not like that, just one at a time. Really you'd have been far better sticking with the cakes.'

'No I bleedin` wouldn't. You need at least three of us in `ere and if it comes to that you would `ave been better stickin` to the man you're supposed to be marryin`,' answered Tricia, unable to contain her fury.

'Meaning?'

'Never you mind but I wouldn't exactly say you were behavin` in a very professional way on that campsite, all things considered.'

'And you two were? You've got to be joking. At least I didn't make a show of myself at Clive Engells' place. What is it with you two and that filthy rock band? The campsite was in uproar that night. Now this, it's turning into a right shambles thanks to you Patricia Harrington. Oh and kindly address me by my surname in front of these.'

'Sorry Miss, I'm sure,' returned Tricia, fuming.

'Just do as you're told. Can't you see if we don't keep to this side we could easily have an accident? Haven't you noticed the chunks of sandstone loose on the ground? That's what Mr. Sanderson meant,' Lucinda Lawton continued.

'And 'aven't you noticed we *are* all on the right side now,' Tricia finished.

'She's really stupid. She's really stupid. She doesn't know 'er right from 'er left. We're on the left side. We're on the left side.'

'And you can pipe down too, tryin' to be clever. Too clever for your boots I would say, just shut up and watch where you're goin'.'

'She's really stupid. She's really stupid. She doesn't know 'er shoes from 'er boots. I've got my shoes on. I've got my shoes on.'

'You 'ad one of them off just now and don't tell me it was 'im behind you. I saw you messin' about with your feet tryin' to trip up the whole line, you little bugger. Come to think of it you were the one pickin' all them almonds off that slice at the services, the one Mr. Sanderson bought for 'er, Miss Lawton. If you don't behave I'll tell 'er just what she's been eatin'.'

'All of you stop that chanting at once.' Lucinda Lawton turned back to Tricia. 'Mrs. Harrington keep focussed will you? Get them to shine their torches straight ahead so we can all see where we're going.'

''ow much longer 'ave we got to go Miss?'

'Oh not too much further, I shouldn't think Danny. In a minute the tunnel will widen out and we'll all see the well.' Harriet hoped she'd sounded convincing, hoped Tricia would pull herself together so they could all speed the thing up.

'Oh I know let's all sing a song to 'elp us on our way. That one where we all clap our 'ands if we're 'appy,' Tricia suddenly shouted.

By the end of the first verse, with the exception of three dithering torch beams, the place suddenly plunged into darkness as the remaining torches clattered to the ground.

'Ooh I forgot about them clappin' their 'ands and 'oldin' those,' she suddenly declared.

'Pick them up everyone, try turnin' them on to see if they're still workin'. Come on keep singin' but don't bother clappin' your 'ands. That's better, we can still see where we're goin',' Tricia finished, just as Lucinda Lawton blew her whistle.

'I'd hardly say that Mrs. Harrington. Right everybody, this is it. We've reached the middle. Mrs. Harrington, Miss Glover, please make sure the children stay this side of the well.'

Excited, eager little feet hurried forward, torchlight flashing in every direction then gasps as all beams focussed on the far side of the well. They silenced, to watch the wall glisten, throwing sparks of coloured light into the darkness; beautiful shining gemstones, flashing like a million fireworks, implanted from top to bottom in the dark red sandstone, forming a picture of the Madonna and her Child.

'They're the best fossils in the world,' Danny piped up. 'Why has she got a banana round 'er 'ead Miss?'

'No Danny, that's not a banana, that's a halo of pure golden light, because she's very, very special. She's Jesus's mummy and she's holding baby Jesus in her arms. The monks must have done this all those years ago.'

'Gosh `arriet it's beautiful isn't it? Wow it must be worth a fortune. Do you think `e comes down `ere to pull a few off when `e get's a bit short of cash?'

'Shush Tricia. Don't let these hear you say that. Don't you think it's just the most beautiful thing you've ever seen?'

'Oh it is `arriet but I still think there's somethin` very fishy about `im.'

'Right everybody. Try to remember the picture and the colours of the stones because when we get back you're all going to draw it and there will be a prize for the best one.'

'Look Miss there's some pictures on the wall over here, too. I think that one's a bit like a sheep.'

'Yes Danny, you're absolutely right,' Harriet said. 'All of you just turn your lights onto this wall behind you. It looks like the monks have been doing some drawings down here as well.'

Harriet turned back to the bejewelled picture behind her. Touched at the charms resting on her necklace. Caught the tiny little cross between her thumb and forefinger as she thought of her own baby. Spoke silent words, 'Please, please let this all work out.'

'Come on `arriet, she doesn't know I've left the line to get you. They're on their way back. Probably `alf way through the tunnel by now. I know it's very beautiful but you don't want to be trapped in `ere all on your own.'

'Gosh no, thanks Tricia. I'm just mesmerised by it. You know there was no mention of this on the internet at all.'

'Well there wouldn't be would there `arriet? I don't suppose `e wants anyone pinchin` that little lot.'

'I'm amazed he's allowed us all in here. The children will tell everyone.'

'Well I expect `e would `ave assessed the risk `arriet. `e obviously wanted to show them somethin` very special.'

'Well I think a lot of him for that Tricia. It's an amazing experience.'

'You'll be `avin` another one if you don't `urry up `arriet. I'm glad we're not `avin` to go through the rest of it. Wow, just look at the thickness of this door. Just look `ow old it is `arriet. Look at this `andle. Let's just see if `e's got `is sacks of drugs behind `ere. Oooh it's openin` `arriet.'

'Tricia leave it, leave it. Come on let's go. We'll be getting caught up with the next party.'

'`ARRIET LOOK! LOOK `ERE!! JUST LOOK AT THIS LOT!'

'No, surely not drugs?'

'Quick `ave a look.'

'Oh no Tricia. They look like paintings.'

'Of course they are `arriet. Look at them lined up along the wall. Look they go all the way down.'

'Hang on Tricia. Oh bloody hell. I don't believe it. Oh no, that one on the other side behind the door. It's me! Bloody hell Tricia that's the painting Barry did of me. How on earth did it get here?'

'Ooh 'arriet 'e didn't leave much to the imagination did 'e? No wonder Mr. Sanderson gave you the push. I don't think anyone would want to marry you 'arriet if they saw you so pregnant like this. Er I mean Mr. Sanderson being the father wouldn't like to think you'd posed like this for someone else, would 'e? But what are these all doin' 'ere? Do you think 'e's dealin' in stolen paintings and that's where 'e gets all 'is dosh?'

'Oh I don't know Tricia. I just don't know. Why on earth would he have this one when he gave it me back?'

'Well you did say it 'ad disappeared. Maybe 'e 'ad a change of mind because 'e didn't know what would 'appen to it, didn't know who would see it, once 'e'd given it to you.'

'Oh gosh Tricia. You're right. You've got to be right. He's got a key. It must have been him who took it. No it couldn't be him. He said he'd lost it.'

''e most probably told you that 'arriet to put you off the scent.'

'Oh don't say that. I think I'm going into shock Tricia. I feel all wobbly. Come on let's get out of here while we still can.'

Chapter 37

'Miss Glover, Mrs. Harrington, I consider it totally irresponsible to leave Lucinda on her own to bring all the children back like that. Do you realise you've held up the rest of the party? What on earth have you been doing down there all this time?'

'Oh we're very sorry Mr. Sanderson, aren't we `arriet? It's just that when I looked back to the end of the queue I couldn't see `arriet so I made my way back and found `er on the floor. She'd fainted, adn't you `arriet? I struggled to get `er up and as she was comin` round I made `er sit on the edge of the well with `er `ead down between `er knees. Good job you `ad a cover on it Mr. Sanderson I wouldn't `ave wanted `er to fall in. Anyway we `ad to come back slowly because `arriet couldn't `urry.'

'Oh I see. Er yes, yes indeed I see. Explain that to Clive Engells will you. Ask him if he would be so kind as to take my place. Ahh the doorbell. Answer that first, will you Mrs. Harrington?'

'Oh `ello.... , `ARRIET, I think it's your friend Molly,' Tricia called. 'Shall I ask `er in Mr. Sanderson?'

'Of course Mrs. Harrington, don't leave her out there!'

'Ah Molly, good to see you. Has Percy recovered from his interrogation yet? Hardly surprising it gave the poor man such a severe migraine. Er Mrs. Harrington take Miss Glover upstairs to one of the bedrooms. I insist you lie down for a while... No Molly don't leave. I think you'll find Mrs. Harris has your cat somewhere.'

'Now that's just why I've come Joris. I'm so relieved. She's here is she? I didn't dare hope. She's been missing for a few days now and I've been getting increasingly worried. But I can see you're very busy Joris. Look I'll come back later.'

'No, no. No indeed. You must stay and join us for high tea, Molly. We've a school visit going on and I'm sure Mrs. Harris would welcome a hand. Just let me go up to Miss Glover.' He turned to see Tricia reappear.

'Ah there you are Mrs. Harrington, take Molly through will you and look after her for a while. Oh and if you could stand in for Miss Glover whilst she's recuperating that would be splendid. Yes, keep your eye on the children in her absence will you and in particular that Bast... er Bustard boy. Yes it would be most helpful.'

'Certainly Mr. Sanderson. `arriet's lying down. She does look a bit pale but I'm sure she'll be fine after a cup of sweet tea.'

'Of course, of course. Pop along to Mrs. Harris, tell her Molly's here and get her to make some tea for Miss Glover at the same time.'

Harriet lay on the bed, grateful to be off her feet. She felt peculiarly sick. Didn't think he'd sink so low as to rummage around her house to take the painting back. How she wished she'd demanded that key back. All those paintings. 'Surely he's not into art theft but what on earth would they be doing there? Tricia's right, it's all very, very suspicious indeed,' she thought.

'Ah Harriet, you must forgive me for being so abrupt before. I'm sorry you've had the misfortune to faint like that. Of course I should have known better than to send you down there in your condition. How are you feeling now?'

'Just a bit shaken thank you Mr. Sanderson but I'll be alright in a minute.'

She moved her legs to one side as he sat down on the window side of the bed. Watched him brush his hand through his hair leaving those thick dishevelled blonde layers to settle all the way down to the row of curls at his neck. For a few seconds he said nothing, just staring at the window then suddenly he jumped up to look out. He turned sharply, both hands in pockets, to face her. The light behind him now, but still Harriet looked up to catch the determination in his face. Couldn't believe she'd let this tall, solid, gorgeous hunk of man slip through her fingers. His expression serious. His eyes narrowing now, looking straight into hers.

'You know Harriet you've tested my patience for long enough. It's only a matter of time before I'm inevitably going to discover it for myself. You are contractually obliged. It's not a question of just being able to disappear from the scene the minute this baby starts to show. Think about it Harriet. Just think about all this game playing very carefully. I need to know. I really need to know for my future plans. It's pretty certain you were pregnant, that type of indicator is renowned for its accuracy, so have you miscarried Harriet? I demand to know. Indeed as the father I have a right to know. I'm sure you wouldn't want me to have to spell all this out to Clive Engells to make you aware of the legal position.'

He sat down again, feeling both perplexed and frustrated. She turned to one side, flopped her arm across her face. Didn't know whether to tell him or not. Thought about the painting. Hated him, hated him for doing that. Thought about Lucinda Lawton. Knew from Clive Engells she'd always been in the background. Determined now, she made a vow to herself. 'No, no, no. He'll never know. I'm buying myself out of giving notice. I'm going to Tierra Del Fuego with Mark.'

'Silence isn't helping Miss Glover.' He lifted her arm away, turning her face towards him.

'How can this gorgeous, gorgeous man do the things he does?' Her mind whirling, hurling relentless anger into the silence. Conscious of his deepening breaths she watched his nostrils flare. His hand rubbing impatiently at the side of his face.

'Harriet, it's not too late. In spite of your atrocious, irresponsible behaviour we can still get married you know.'

'I think not Mr. Sanderson.'

'It's my fucking baby you're carrying Miss Glover and I'm not about to make it easy for you.'

'Oh I do hope I'm not interrupting anything Mr. Sanderson. Tea for Harriet,

I believe.'

'Just leaving Mrs. Harris. Just leaving.'

'Are you feeling better dear? He wasn't shouting at you was he?'

Harriet placed her hand across her mouth, felt the tears well in her eyes. Tried desperately hard to swallow them back.

'Th..., thank you for the tea.'

'There, there Harriet. It's none of my business you know but just let me show you this.'

Mrs. Harris went to the wardrobe, brought out a painting, held it up for Harriet to see.

'Oh she's beautiful. She's such a beautiful little girl. Those eyes, there's something so soul-searching about those eyes. Just look at their colour.'

'Yes same as Mr. Sanderson's,' Mrs. Harris replied.

'Look at her gorgeous blonde hair too. Oh her face is so sweet. It's divine. I've never ever seen a painting of a little girl like that before. She's just stunning!'

'Do you know Harriet when he first showed me I told him it put me in mind of you. I think you probably looked just like that when you were a little girl.'

'Really? Gosh! Oh come to think of it Mummy's got a photograph of me when I was that age on her sideboard. I'm not as petty as that, but I've got exactly the same blue eyes and blonde hair. It's amazing how similar it is.'

'Oh but you are as pretty as that Harriet. If you want my opinion I think Mr. Sanderson has a very soft spot for you.'

'But who is she and why does he keep it in there?' Harriet asked.

'I've tried but he won't tell me. It's something of a mystery to me. I wanted you to see it because once or twice he's left it on the bed here, when he's been upset and angry. I just wanted you to understand there may well be something else going on with him.'

Harriet listened intently, rubbing her hand against her nose sniffing back a persistent tear.

'So don't let his shouting upset you. As I say he does fly off like that very occasionally. I expect he's got a little impatient with you and your friend coming back a bit late from the tunnel. Did you enjoy it?'

Harriet nodded. Wanted to ask her about the paintings in the tunnel. Wondered if this was another one of them. Didn't dare.

'I've never seen anything as beautiful as the Madonna and Child set in the wall.'

'Well he has told me all about it but to be honest I've never had the courage to go down there. Is it really that beautiful?'

'Yes Mrs. Harris, it's like nothing else in the whole world. The history to this place is just amazing. It's not scary, really it isn't once you get used to it. The children slowed us down. If you went through with him you'd only take a few minutes.'

'Oh I don't know about that Harriet. Perhaps one day you'll take me through? I think I could manage it with you.'

She squeezed Harriet's hand. 'Molly wants to come up and see you. Would that be alright?'

'Yes thank you Mrs. Harris. Oh and thank you for being so kind.'

Harriet turned to sit on the edge of the bed, wondering about the picture as she drank her tea. He'd just asked her to marry him again. She'd just refused. She loved him. She hated him. She wanted him. She needed him. Then she didn't. Suddenly she felt she didn't know him at all. She scolded herself for being so foolish as to get so far out of her depth. Knew from the bottom of her heart Mark had been right.

'Alright if I come in Harriet? Only Mrs. Harris said you wouldn't mind. How are you feeling now?'

'Of course Molly do come in and I'm feeling much better, thank you. It's lovely to see you again. I can't believe we've hardly seen you since you moved in. How's it going? How's Percy? Has he recovered from the cannabis inquisition? I'm just so sorry about that. Do you know Molly I can't believe the size of the holes I keep digging, not only for myself but for everyone else.'

'Now don't you be worrying, Percy and I are just fine Harriet. Ah I see you're wearing your faith, hope and charity necklace we gave you. Oh I'm so pleased dear, you were such a beautiful bridesmaid. Now where was I? Oh yes, now don't you be worrying about that cannabis thing, it was a mistake anybody could have made. The silly man shouldn't have been growing them in the first place. There's no harm done. Did he get prosecuted Harriet?'

'Oh no Molly, I think he got off with a warning.'

'Anything to do with our friend in high places?'

'Oh I'm not sure really. There's been that much going on I really can't fathom what's what with him at all.'

'Oh yes Harriet. He's a bit of a mystery man for sure but he's very well thought of round here. It's a bit like he's lord of the manor, everyone in the village has tremendous respect for him.'

'They wouldn't if they knew what was going on.' Harriet thought. Molly continued,

'Well they would of course, especially now he's been knighted and you too, getting a damehood. Percy and I didn't know we were going to be hobnobbing with the crème de la crème when we all met on that cruise. Have you fixed up a date for the wedding yet Harriet? I can't wait for you to be living here. We'll be neighbours and I couldn't want for a better one.'

'You're lovely Molly. Did you find the cat?'

'Oh yes, she's asleep in a basket in Mrs. Hall's broom cupboard. Joris says he'll get Mr. Swift to bring it back.'

'Oh that's good Molly. It must be a bit strange for it at the moment. It will soon settle down.'

'Yes I'm sure, now how's that cat of yours Harriet? Not been getting into any more mischief I hope? You'll be bringing it here when you get married, I'm sure. Good, it will be a friend for Sammy. I haven't noticed any other cats around here yet.'

Harriet didn't know whether to come clean and get it over and done with. Decided against it. Thought. 'Better not drop Molly into anything. No more holes for other people. He can jolly well tell her himself it's well and truly finished.'

'Anyway Harriet I won't tire you. I've had a nice cup of tea and a cake with Mrs. Harris in the kitchen. She did such a nice spread for the children. She's a good woman that. She's asked me if I'd like to go to the WI with her on her Wednesday afternoons off. I said yes, Harriet. Sometimes I feel just a little bit isolated here when Percy goes off to play golf but it is beautiful. I can't get over the views. We can see the river and the mountains from the back garden you know. I'm always hanging my washing out to give me an excuse to see the view. Of course he'll get a view of the island from here, won't he? Now that must be very special. Still it's only because Percy and I both had something to sell we've managed to come here at all. Lower Tideside indeed, who'd have believed it? Anyway Harriet I must be getting back to Percy. Have a think about when you'd like to come round for dinner. I'll mention it to Joris on the way out. You haven't even seen our house yet! Oh you've finished your tea. Shall I take the cup down Harriet?'

Harriet lay back on the bed trying to collect her thoughts. She felt calmer now. She always found Molly's presence comforting. She looked across to the wardrobe desperately wanting to take another look at the painting. Wondered why it was in there and not stacked with the rest in the tunnel. Wondered what the significance of it was for him. She wanted one more look. Suddenly became desperate for one more look. Was it really like the photograph of her when she was little? She tried to hold both images in her mind then decided to get up. Decided to just take a little peep before going downstairs.

'Ah Miss Glover, are you feeling any better?'

About to open the wardrobe door, she jumped, swivelling the centre seam of her skirt round to the front, instead.

'Yes thank you Mr. Sanderson.' Her voice as stiff as she could make it.

'Look Miss Glover I've come to apologise. I had no right whatsoever to reel off at you like that. I am sorry. Please do accept my apology. You can rest assured that I will never broach the subject of pregnancy or marriage to you again. Now are you on your way to join the party?'

'Yes. Oh just let me straighten the bed cover.'

'No need Miss Glover, Mrs. Harris will see to it. If you'd like to catch up with your children now, Mrs. Harrington can be relieved.'

'Yes, thank you Mr. Sanderson.'

'Oh 'ellow 'arriet, I think I did you a bit of a favour there. It's really 'ard work lookin` after all those kids. I don't know 'ow you do it. 'e was a little bugger that one in the tunnel and 'er, I don't know whether you could 'ear 'er 'arriet but she was so rude to me. They make a good pair 'im and 'er, well suited I'd say. Anyway where was I? Oh yes they've drawn some good pictures though.

Come and see which one you think's best.'

'Thanks for taking them Tricia. They've finished their tea by the looks of it. Have they all had a good time?'

'Oh I think so. I 'aven't though 'arriet. I got so fed up with Lucinda bloody Lawton lookin' over my shoulder after all I've 'ad to put up with, I told 'er to "fuck off." I didn't know 'e was standin' right behind me and 'e took me in the kitchen and gave me a right goin' over. 'e seemed to already be in a bad mood. What did you do to 'im up there, 'arriet?'

'More like what he did to me, you mean. I'll tell you later. Let's have a look at these pictures.'

'Oh that's a good one. Let's see who did that? Oh Sara Atkins. She's in my class. Has this been picked out then?'

'No it hasn't Harriet Glover as you'd know if you hadn't been lying on one of Joris's beds all afternoon. I don't believe you fainted at all. None of the children can recall you falling down.'

'Oh so you've been askin' them 'ave you Belinda? I don't see as it's got anythin' at all to do with you seein' as you weren't even in the tunnel at the time. Now where 'ave you been 'idin' my 'usband? If you can call 'im that. You were supposed to 'ave finished with 'im weeks ago.'

'As it happens I don't see as it's any of your business Patricia Harrington. He's grown up enough to decide for himself who he does and who he doesn't want to see. And just now he doesn't want to see you.'

'You 'aven't tied 'im up and got 'im as an 'ostage 'ave you? Because from the things 'e's told me about you, you're not much good at anythin' only fryin' eggs and bacon. 'e said you're rubbish in bed and by the time you've made 'im wash 'is little bit of a thing before you do anythin' he's almost gone off the idea. 'e said it was a bit like makin' love to a freezer with a door that would 'ardly open.'

Harriet watched Belinda Oxfordshire first go pale and then purple.

'Well at least I don't go parading my bits of tits around on the front page of the local paper. He's always telling me you've got nothing to get hold of.'

'Oh did you 'ear that 'arriet? Did you just 'ear that? And 'ow did 'e know about that Belinda Oxfordshire? We didn't get a paper......Oh I see...you showed it 'im.'

'Not especially. If you must know I pinned it up on the sailing club notice board seeing as you were teasing all the men with your low-cut tops trying to get that stupid "save Venice" tin filled. That was never *your* cleavage. You don't have enough for one. All pushed up with foam pads I expect. At least what I've got's my own.'

'Patricia Harrington keep your voice down. It's just as well everyone's gone to the drawing room. You three are supposed to be in there.'

'Oh and you can just pipe down again Lucinda Lawton. I'll 'ave you know Mr. Sanderson's 'ad 'er knickers down this afternoon, rubbin' cream into 'er bum, or so we think. We don't know what else 'e's been gettin' up to do we?

You needn't be thinkin` you're the only one who can play away.'

'What are you talking about now Patricia Harrington? Ah, I see, so that's where you were leading in the tunnel before.'

'Oh come off it Lucinda Lawton, we know what you were getting up to in that camper van on the campsite. You `aven't looked at Clive Engells all afternoon.'

'Did I hear my name mentioned girls?'

Lucinda Lawton shot past him.

'To the drawing room everyone. The coach has arrived to take the children home. It's time to give out the prizes.'

Clive Engells moved towards Tricia, placed his arm around her waist. 'I'll be returning home tomorrow, a little sooner than planned as something's cropped up down there. I'll get that letter off as soon as I get back.' He moved towards Lucinda Lawton.

'Look at `er face standin` next to `im. She's been rumbled and it's written all over it. I can't stand `er `arriet. I can't stand *im* either but I `ope `e doesn't marry `er.'

'Me too Tricia, but what's Belinda Oxfordshire doing standing right behind Ross Farquerhart? She's got nothing to do with giving out the awards.'

'Right everybody assembled? Now have you all had a good time?' Mr. Sanderson addressed the children.

Loud chorus. 'Yes Mr. Sanderson.'

'Good, I'm very pleased about that. Now whilst we were on our camping holiday Miss Lawton and I drove to the little village nearby to go to the jeweller's shop.'

'Bloody `ell `arriet `e's about to announce `is engagement. Not to the kids, surely?' Tricia whispered.

Harriet felt sick to the core. It was just too much to deal with all this in one afternoon.

'And we went there to buy something very special, didn't we Miss Lawton? Well two things actually,' he continued. 'Miss Lawton would you like to lift the carrier bag and open the boxes?'

'Oh no Tricia. Surely he's not going to place the ring on her finger now?' Harriet whispered.

'There now, thank you Miss Lawton. We have two silver cups. One for the winner of the best fossil competition and the other for the best drawing of the Madonna and Child.'

'Oooooooh,' the children enthused in unison.

'We shall of course have the winning child's name inscribed on each. Now these are solid silver. They are very special and something for the winners to keep for always. Right may we have the winning picture? Thank you. Ah I see it's Sara Atkins. Well done Sara, come and get your prize.'

In an instant, the children clapping and cheering.

'Ah that's not fair. It was `er mum that won the boat. My mum wants a boat and there isn't one for `er to win. She shouldn't `ave the silver cup and the boat.'

'Shhh Danny,' whispered Harriet. 'Let's see who's won the best fossil prize.'

'Now the best fossil was found by…' He stopped abruptly to Mr. Sanderson's interruption.

'Mr. Farquerhart, may you hold it up please and read the name out loud and clear…'

Ross Farquerhart cleared his throat. 'Er I believe this one says Danny Bustard.'

'Well done Danny. Go on, go up and get your prize.' Harriet watched his grin spread wide. He shook hands with Mr. Sanderson then trotted back to her clutching his silver cup hard against his striped T-shirt.

'There Danny. Won't your mum and dad be pleased?' Harriet whispered through the applause.

'No Miss they won't like this. They want a boat like `er mum got.'

It was on the tip of Harriet's tongue then she held back. The boat Mark had done up was to be a surprise for the three of them.

The children's chatter filled the room for a minute or so. Harriet could see Ross Farquerhart edging towards her. She wondered at Belinda Oxfordshire trailing behind. He pushed his glasses up his nose then cleared his throat, waiting for Clive Engells to steer the last child from the room.

'I want an answer. You disappeared without giving me an answer. You left the hamper basket empty in the tent with the card still on it but you didn't give me an answer.' Harriet flushed bright red. Tricia nudged her. Belinda Oxfordshire stepped forward.

'The answer's "Yes" Ross Farquerhart seeing as you sent the hamper to me. I had no idea you felt like that.' She placed a triumphant pair of hands on her hips.

'Let's get the fuck out of here!' Ross Farquerhart grabbed his file and briefcase, faster than a bullet from a gun, shooting past Mr. Sanderson stood in the doorway.

'Er Mr. Farquerhart, a word if you don't mind. Where's the damned man off to in such a hurry? Miss Glover, wasn't he just speaking with you? Whatever have you done now?'

'Oh it wasn't `arriet Mr. Sanderson. Belinda Oxfordshire `ere `as just accepted `is marriage proposal, you know the one that came on the `amper, the one that she thought `ad come from you? It looks like Ross Harquerfart's not very fussy on the idea Mr. Sanderson. Most probably `erd she'd make a better fridge for the `amper than a wife. It's really sad that no one will `ave `er Mr. Sanderson. I'm sure Lucinda Lawton `ere wouldn't mind swappin` you for Clive Engells though as she seems very attached to `is van late at night with the back end bumpin` up and down. They don't do that on their own now do they? So it's funny `ow everythin` goes round in circles don't you think? You see that leaves you free for `er, fridge bum `ere. There, everyone's sorted. I think we can go `ome now `arriet.'

Chapter 38

'Gosh Tricia what on earth made you say all that?'

'Oh I don't know. I think I've just 'ad enough of the lot of them today. Put your foot down 'arriet the sooner we get away from 'ere the better.'

'I'm doing my best Tricia.'

'You know 'arriet the whole lot of them get on my nerves. Now I know why Bob's gone off. It was 'er pinnin' the front page of that newspaper with the picture of me, to the sailing club board, the cow! She must 'ave got 'old of it somehow when we were campin'. Remember 'ow it went missin'?'

'Yes I do Tricia but she must have got hold of mine. Mr. Sanderson told me he'd taken yours. I'm just hoping you don't finally lose your job over all of this. You saw him Tricia, he was absolutely livid. I think he was so enraged he couldn't speak.'

'Well that's 'ow I feel about 'er the cheap toffee nosed stuck-up little snob. She's no more than that 'arriet. She really isn't.'

'Oh gosh, I didn't think you'd drop one on Lucinda Lawton like that, either. At least they didn't buy a ring in the jewellers.'

'We don't know that, do we 'arriet? They could well 'ave got a ring. 'e wasn't really goin' to be givin' it to 'er there. We would 'ave known that if we'd been thinkin' straight.'

'No you're right. Well let's hope he's fully in the picture.. If he tells Clive Engells though, that might be your letter down the drain.'

'Well the mood I'm in I don't care. Don't you worry 'arriet I'll get my "save Venice" tin back come 'ell or 'igh water. Is that a metathingy or not 'arriet? Anyway I don't care. You don't 'appen to 'ave any of that wine left in your shed 'ave you 'arriet? I don't feel like goin' 'ome yet. We'll pretend we're not back. Let's get plastered!'

'I can't Tricia. I'm taking you home don't forget.'

'Oh I forgot about that 'arriet. Still I think there's a drop of somethin' in the cupboard we can 'ave in our tea.'

'Just a drop then Tricia, we certainly need something after what's gone on today.'

* * *

'In we come, just let me phone my mum and tell 'er to keep the kids tonight. Oh I can't be doin' with them arguin' and fightin' and not knowin' whether 'e's comin' 'ome or not. I think I'm goin' to be askin' Clive Engells 'ow you go about gettin' a divorce 'arriet. I don't think I can take much more of this.'

'Oh poor you Tricia. We'll both feel better after a cup of tea.'

'Well I can only find whisky 'arriet. Medicinal that is. We need somethin' strong to numb our brains after all we've been through. It never ends does it? We've 'ardly 'ad chance to get over Venice and those 'eavies when we get dragged off campin`.'

'He wanted us out of the way though Tricia. Oh hang on, steady on that's too much!'

'Oh get it down you. I've got a pizza in the fridge. I'll put a bit more cheese on the top to soak it all up. Now what were you sayin`?'

'I told him about Mrs. Bustard being so frightened and he told me to keep clear. He thought there could well be some aftermath following the arrests. I think he was banking on a week away for us to put some space between it all.'

'Well `e didn't think of that when `e sent us `ome, did `e? No `e says things but `e doesn't really mean them. `ang on a minute, let me write that in my diary. "Not true to `is word, oh there's an 'h' on that isn't there? `ere `arriet let me top that up now you've drunk a bit of tea. You can feel it doin` you good.'

'Go on then. I shouldn't really. Thanks Tricia. But what do you make of that painting sitting the other side of the door in the tunnel? I can't really see him coming back to our house for it, can you? Perhaps it was Belinda Oxfordshire. I know when we were camping she picked up his keys from that room he had as an office. You don't know what she's been up to, particularly as it was labelled. Or it could have been that pawnbroker thug. Maybe he broke in and sold it back to Mr. Sanderson, or something like that.'

'Ooh I don't think so `arriet. `ow would `e know you `ad it in the first place never mind where it `ad come from? None of them I would say.'

'Well how on earth did it get there Tricia? It's obviously got to be someone who knows about the tunnel. Someone who's got access.'

'Well there's just a teeny weeny chance it could `ave been Barry Giordano `arriet. `e's an artist isn't `e? I wouldn't put it past `im to know every tunnel in Britain used for storing paintings given the line of work `e's in. I wouldn't put it past `im to `ave found out who `ad it, either. `e would `ave `ad ways and means of gettin` it back. `e doesn't tell us anythin`.'

'But what about the rest of the paintings Tricia? Are they his as well? And why would he want to be storing them there, even if he could get through from the island?'

'Well I don't exactly know `arriet. Unless `e's on another fraud case. We don't know what `e's up to exactly, do we? `ow about if they're all stolen paintings or fakes? `e might just `ave rumbled our friend Joris. With a bit of luck `e'll be doin` time `arriet. That would keep `im out of `arms way. `e'd `ave no one to chat up then, would `e?'

'Oh he'd manage it. He'd find someone in there to fancy him with his good looks and charm. But you might just have a point about Barry. Not in relation to Mr. Sanderson though, I'm sure his fortune has been acquired by legal means. His mother wouldn't have given us their family history if it wasn't true. Barry could well have ways and means of getting hold of it. There's no way he's going to be telling us what's been going on. I do definitely think you're right about that heavy, it couldn't possibly be him.'

'Oh I don't know `arriet, the more you think about it the more complicated it gets. Barry came to pick it up, `e thought it was at your `ouse `arriet. Unless `e's found it somewhere else and put it there. If it's nothin` to do with Mr. Sanderson, then `e can't `ave any idea either of what's on the other side of `is door. `e probably thinks it's all locked up and no one's been through that `alf of the tunnel since the days of the monks.'

'Probably Tricia. It's certainly a mystery, but while I was in that bedroom Mrs. Harris went to the wardrobe to bring out a painting of a little girl. She wanted to show me because it reminded her of me. It's strange Tricia, why would he be keeping that in the wardrobe? I was wondering if it was one of his collection stored in the tunnel. I just don't know what's going on. Do you know what Tricia he actually asked me to marry him again up there.'

'No, you've got to be jokin` me `arriet. I take it you refused `im or you'd `ave been so thrilled you wouldn't `ave been able to tell me quick enough.'

'Too right I did Tricia. He was going on and on about this pregnancy. I know I can't hold out much longer but I've still a few weeks before it'll show through my clothes. I need the space Tricia, I really do. I just can't get my head round him knowing that for sure, not with him about to marry her and Mark still trying to come to terms with it all.'

'Ooh do you think `e'll `ave problems taking it on `arriet? Bob's always stood by me. Well until that cow came along.'

'I know and I really feel for you Tricia.'

'No, sorry `arriet we weren't talkin` about me, you were tellin` me what Mark thinks.'

'Well he's saying all the right things but I think he's putting a very brave face on it. Why should he want to take on someone else's child, especially *his*. He can't stand him!'

'So you can't really see it workin` out then `arriet. Maybe it would `ave been better if you'd accepted `is offer of marriage. I don't like to think of you strugglin` all on your own.'

'You must be joking Tricia, you wouldn't be saying that if you'd heard the way he asked. Anyway I'm not saying Mark would walk out but I think his commitment phobia might surface again and I think he'd struggle. Don't forget Melissa Scott's still making out she's pregnant. If it's true he'll be getting it from both sides.'

'Ooh I see `arriet.'

'Besides we're not sure what's happening with his job. He may be permanently relocated to somewhere nearer the Antarctic.'

'Oh `arriet I'd miss you so much. I know you'd `ave to go with `im but `ow would I manage without my very best friend. `ere let me top our tea up, I don't think I can `andle the thought of that just now.'

'Oh sorry Tricia, don't worry. It's all very much up in the air at the moment. As I say I don't think he'd walk out but if his job gave him the excuse to bug out of it all I wouldn't put it past him.'

'Oh you poor thing `arriet. It makes my problems with Bob look so insignificant. I don't know `ow you're stayin` sane with all that must be goin` on in your `ead.'

'It's having a friend like you Tricia. We've been through quite a bit together. I don't think I'll be letting our friendship go just like that…. Oh no thanks Tricia, I daren't. Don't forget I've got to drive home.'

'Oh `ave it `arriet. You need it. `ang on just let me put that pizza in the oven. The extra cheese I'm puttin` on the top will soon absorb all the alcohol.'

'Oh I do hope you're right Tricia, I do hope you're right!'

Chapter 39

Flagged down, Harriet steered towards the row of orange cones on the side, trembling.

'It's the road works, oh no it's the pavement they're doing,' she panicked to herself. 'I haven't been speeding. Oh gosh I hope he's not about to breathalyse me.'

The uniformed man strode off the pavement, his foot catching the end of a broom handle left carelessly against the kerb. He kicked it to one side as she jolted to a halt, not realising her nearside front tyre had just jumped on it, sending the bristles high in the air. Stunned, he glowered at her. With the bristly whack still smarting his dust-laden face, he rubbed at his watering eyes. She jammed the brakes on hard. Wound the window down, grey with fright.

'Oh I'm sorry. Terribly sorr…..'

'Bugger off,' came the coarse reply. You're a bloody menace!'

She didn't need telling twice. On through the cones and away, driving full pelt on adrenaline all the way to her front door.

'Oh gosh Pepper. I've just driven over a stick handle and whacked some kind of officer in the face. I didn't see it. Gosh Pepper that was a narrow escape. There's no one following me is there?'

'Only me Miss Glover.'

'Oh Mr. Sanderson how could I not have seen that?' Thought. 'Tricia's fault. Too much whisky.'

'It appears there's a lot you don't see Miss Glover, including broom handles. Now may I come in for a moment? I shan't keep you.'

She fumbled for her key, caught the cat's tail as she tried to close the door.

'Not your day one way or another Miss Glover. Now shall we go in here. Take a seat, do take a seat.'

He sat down in his usual place. Swung his right leg wide to rest his foot on his left knee. Tapped impatiently at the shiny black heel of his shoe.

'Oh before I mention this, has Mrs. Harrington finally lost her marbles?'

'I'm not sure what you mean Mr. Sanderson.'

'That outburst prior to you both dashing off like that. Something about a hamper in a fridge and Belinda Oxfordshire accepting a marriage proposal from young Ross and the innuendo regarding Clive Engells and Lucinda Lawton. I never heard the like. Fortunately he'd taken the children to the coach so wasn't party to it. You are both most fortunate he was so willing to forgive you for that intrusion on his privacy.'

Harriet, in an alcoholic daze and still wobbling looked down.

'Ah silence again Miss Glover. Still. To be expected. You might like to suggest she pays her doctor a visit. Could be she's finally flipped. Is she back with her husband now?'

'She's very unsettled Mr. Sanderson. It's more a question of whether he's back with her. They were trying to patch things up but it looks like Belinda

Oxfordshire's put paid to that again.'

'Ah, I see. Things are becoming a little clearer now. This incident she's referring to in the campervan. Most unseemly. Suggestive even. You might like to inform her that the time Mr. Engells chooses to spend with Lucrezia and how he chooses to spend it is no concern whatsoever of hers, or yours for that matter.'

'Lucrezia, Mr. Sanderson?'

'Yes I said Lucrezia, not Lucinda. Lucrezia's his long term partner. Be good enough to pass that along will you?'

Harriet froze. They must have misheard. They thought he'd said "Lucinda". 'Oh so she's not even being unfaithful to him now,' she thought in disgust. 'That man never gets his just deserts.'

'Now to the point Miss Glover. It's become necessary for me to leave the country very shortly. Unfortunately I was expecting this to happen rather later but there has been an unforeseeable change of plan. Therefore I'm asking you to deputise again for me during my period of absence.'

'Deputise, but what about Lucinda Lawton?'

'She'll be accompanying me Miss Glover.'

'Are you talking about September Mr. Sanderson?'

'Could be, could be. The office will be arranging replacements during our period of absence should it run into the new term. But basically I'm talking about now. Enid Frost has very kindly agreed to stand in for Lucinda so she'll be looking after activities based in the school. Belinda will be taking a far more active role at Starboard Marine North West which leaves you to oversee the three sites. You will of course be suitably remunerated for all this work.'

'But what about the sailing club, who'll be taking your place down there?'

'Tarquin Bridgewater, Miss Glover. The sailing activities will run exactly as they do now so my absence shouldn't present a problem.'

'Oh right. Golly I didn't expect this. How long might it run into the new term?'

'Do you anticipate any problems Miss Glover, should it go as far as Christmas?' Mr. Sanderson shifted his foot to stretch his leg briefly, immediately resuming his former position.

Harriet thought of her pregnancy. Nearly died. Decided to go along with it for the time being. That was the last thing she wanted to admit to right now, especially after the lies she'd been telling him all day. Thought. 'No, definitely not now since he's as good as said he's going off with Lucinda Lawton to get married followed by at least a leg of a world cruise; a honeymoon of undetermined length.'

'Er no Mr. Sanderson I enjoyed it last time you gave me the same responsibility. Just leave it with me. When are you expecting to go?'

'We fly out early Saturday so it will give you the weekend clear to sort yourself out.'

'Right, right no problem at all. How likely is it I'll be required for

September?'

'I'm afraid I can't say at this juncture Miss Glover. Let's just say it depends how it goes.'

'Right, right. Yes that's alright. I'll need to get myself sorted out for all this.'

'Well it would seem you've got the holiday activities well sewn up Miss Glover as Lucinda has. It will simply mean Belinda taking over from you and Enid Frost following Lucinda's work schedule. I've explained the position to Tarquin Bridgewater and he's perfectly happy, so there shouldn't be a great deal to do. If you can oversee everything satisfactorily that will be sufficient.'

'Who'll be standing in as my deputy if it runs to September Mr. Sanderson?'

'Good question. Good question. I've recommended Enid Frost and she's agreed in principle but it hasn't been cleared by the office yet. I'd be grateful if you don't discuss this with her. September's a bit of an unknown quantity as yet.'

'Right, no I won't. No I most definitely won't Mr. Sanderson. Just leave it all with me. You didn't recommend me for that damehood for nothing. I promise I won't let you down.'

'Splendid Miss Glover. Splendid! Now if you'll excuse me I have important matters to attend to.'

No sooner out of the door and Harriet lifted the receiver to call Tricia.

'Oh `ello `arriet. Did you get back alright? Only I was a bit bothered about you drivin` after all that whisky.'

'Oh yes thanks Tricia. Oh apart from getting flagged down at the road works.'

'Oh you mean where they've been doin` the pavements `arriet? Did you `ave to fill the whole survey in?'

'Oh that's what it was. Well what a stupid place to pull people into. I went over a brush handle and the bristles came up to hit the guy in the face.'

'Ooh that's ever so funny `arriet. I don't expect `e was too pleased.'

'No! Choice language. He told me to bugger off and you bet I did. But you'll never guess who followed me down our road.'

'Ooh who would that `ave been then `arriet? It wasn't the man you `it with the brush was it?'

'No it was *him* Tricia, he's been round.'

'Ooh did `e say anythin` about my little outburst?'

'He did but not for long. He was too keen on wanting to tell me Clive Engells' long term partner is called Lucrezia, *not* Lucinda and he could please himself as to when and how he spends his time with her. He was so smug about it all. He told me to pass the message on to you.'

'Well she might be `is long term partner but she's definitely `is short term one `arriet, even if it was a-one-night stand, and I don't think! So `e needn't `ave bothered tellin` you to pass the message on because `e never did call out "Lucrezia". I `eard `im with my own `ears. He yelled "Lucinda" I might be a bit daft but I'm not deaf.'

'Well I didn't see fit to argue it out, in fact I said as little as I could get away with. No he's going away, with her of course but we knew that already,' Harriet suddenly felt strangely sober. 'Well I hope they'll be very happy together.'

'You don't mean that do you `arriet?'

'No, no, no, no! I can't stand her!'

'When are they goin` then?'

'They're off early on Saturday morning. Mark's got to go on Sunday as well. Everyone's off Tricia, except us.'

'Ooh `arriet where shall we go?'

'You're joking Tricia. He's put me back in charge. If I disappear it'll be curtains for sure. I've got to oversee all these extra-curricular activities and there's a chance it could run into September, he just didn't know.'

'Well that's not very considerate of `im, is it `arriet? Given `e's supposed to be so concerned about our safety. Just a minute, I've got my pen `ere. Somethin` else to write in my diary. It's very therapeutic `arriet gettin` it all off my chest. Oh I wish I `adn't just said that metathingy. I'm fumin` with Belinda Oxfordshire. I don't know `ow she could `ave done that to me. The nerve of `er when she's just pinched my `usband back. I definitely `aven't finished gettin` my own back on `er.'

'No and I don't blame you but wasn't it funny the way Ross Farquerhart shot out of the room when she accepted his proposal?'

'Ooh it was `arriet. No chance of fat-face-four-cheeks doin` that. Now `ow am I goin` to get Clive Engells to `elp me through this divorce? Oh `ang on a minute `arriet. Oh `arriet talk of the devil. `e's just got out of `is car. Ooh `e must be comin` to see me `. Oh I do `ope I'm not in for a roastin` over `is Lucrezia. Look `arriet I'll phone you back when `e's gone. Bye.'

Harriet replaced the receiver only to pick it up again.

'Oh hello Barry. Thought it was going to be mummy. I wasn't expecting you. Is everything alright? Where are you?'

'Peru, Harriet. Now have you found the painting yet?'

'Peru, Barry? What on earth are you doing there? No don't bother. Silly question. You're certainly not going to tell me.'

'The painting Harriet. Any sign of it anywhere?'

'Oh you won't believe this Barry. You'll never believe this.'

'Come on Harriet get it out. I haven't got much time.'

'Oh no sorry! It's sitting behind a door half-way through a tunnel leading from Mr. Sanderson's house to the island.'

'Hells bells! You sure?'

'Of course I'm sure. I'm not going to be making that up.'

'No, no of course. Is it on its own?'

'No, as far as we could see there were loads of them all stacked along the wall.'

'How come you were down there then? He's been showing you his treasures, has he? The swine!'

'Of course not Barry. We were taking the children through to show them this exquisite wall art all jewelled of the Madonna and Child.'

'Oh yes, I've heard about that. Where were these paintings then?'

'Well that was the centre of the tunnel where the well is. There's a very old, heavy wooden door which Tricia managed to open. Gosh we were surprised. But Barry why would he give it me back to take it away again? What's he doing with all those paintings down there anyway?'

'Humm, interesting. It's his tunnel. He can put his art collection in there if he wants. A bit of a weirdo I think. Apologies if you're on the verge of marrying him.'

'What *are* you talking about Barry Giordano?'

'I take it from that you've just turned him down?'

'How did you know he'd even asked me again? Are you psychic or something?'

'No but I don't need to be. The swine beat me to it.'

'Beat you to what Barry? What are you talking about?'

'The ring. The amber ring. I tried to buy it over the phone and got "Oh a tall blonde gentleman bought it for a young lady I believe. Yes, they came in together at first anyway. Oh I can't remember now. He might have popped back for it but I do know they were from the school camp down the road." '

'Gosh Barry talk about remembering everything verbatim! It wasn't for me, it was for *her*. For Lucinda Lawton. He's marrying *her*. They're flying off somewhere on Saturday to get married and then they'll join the cruise ship for a world cruise. It's got nothing to do with me that ring.'

'But you've just told me you turned him down.'

'He only asked me out of desperation as a means of finding out if I'm still pregnant. I could see through that. I wasn't falling for that one. There's no one around here who doesn't know he's going to marry Lucinda Lawton.'

'Oh I see. Right. Why don't you come out here? Come and join me. No strings, promise!'

'Aren't you supposed to be working?'

'Yes, I am right now at least.'

'There's your answer then Barry. Actually we're both working. I've got loads to do. He's made sure of that.'

'What do you mean "He's made sure of that". It's supposed to be your summer holidays isn't it?'

'Isn't it just. It doesn't stop him though. He's getting his, with *her*.'

'You did turn me down for a return trip to Venice Harriet. I handed you a holiday on a plate and you didn't turn it down very graciously, either.'

'What, after that painting Barry Giordano? How do I know Mark hasn't seen it and moved it? How do I know Mark didn't deliver it back to Mr. Sanderson, either? It's just the sort of thing he'd do without saying a word. He's off on Sunday down that way. How do I know he'll come back? He probably won't, at least not to me, if he's had anything to do with its disappearance. You've caused havoc with that thing. Let's just hope it stays in that tunnel out of harm's reach. Look I've got to go. Mark will be in any minute now.'

Chapter 40

'It looks like Melissa's sodding pregnant, after all.'

'Well that's a fine thing to be telling me the night before you go away Mark. I really needed to hear that and I don't think.'

'Like I needed to hear you're pregnant you mean Harriet? Everybody's bloody pregnant and I've had enough of it.'

'Smacks of commitment Mark and that's something you don't take to very well, is it?'

'Below the belt that one Harriet, I've already told you I'm prepared to take this one on.'

'And what about your own Mark? Melissa's not going to let you get away with that if she can help it.'

'Look Harriet I've just about had enough of the pair of you. Give it a rest, will you?'

'Well you'll be able to escape tomorrow, or is she still going with you?'

'No, that's how I know. She's withdrawn on medical grounds. Oh sod, sod. If you hadn't taken a shine to that lump of lard none of us would be in this mess Harriet.'

'Oh don't give me that Mark. The number of times I've answered the phone and it's been her on the end. She phones for nothing. And don't think I haven't noticed the two ring tones on a Friday night. "The caller withheld their number." Of course she bloody did.'

'Actually Harriet I have no idea what you are talking about. Are you sure it wasn't one of yours? You manage to stack them up and you don't care how young they are either.'

'Oh no I do not Mark Glover. I don't know where you've been getting all this from. No hang on, I probably do. Belinda Oxfordshire, no doubt. Haven't you learnt yet how spiteful she can be. Flipping dangerous in fact.'

'Well think on Harriet. Don't you forget what she told me about lard ball. Don't forget just how badly he treated her, forcing her to have an abortion as a condition of him staying with her and performing it himself. Scum! That's him, scum! It's the reason I've been able to get my head round taking on his baby. He's scum Harriet and you've ruined both our lives for that scummy lard ball.'

'Well I've got news for you Mark. Mummy told me some time ago that Olivia had told her Belinda Oxfordshire had some congenital deformity whereby she had to have a hysterectomy which means of course she's unable to have children. Now Mr. Sanderson's mother is not going to make that up, is she? Why should she? She's not been party to Belinda Oxfordshire's outburst. It was just you and her outside the dining room in the hotel. She wasn't going to be telling that one to anyone else.'

'Right Harriet and it's taken you this long to tell me. Talk about keeping me onboard under false pretences.'

'What do you mean "false pretences"? We never talk about him Mark. You can't stand talking about him. After all we've been through why on earth would I want to be dragging all that up?'

'Because it suited you better to keep it to yourself Harriet. You have your reasons.'

'Oh don't go off like this Mark. This is exactly what happened last time.'

'It's all of your making Harriet. Your sodding making. I'm afraid we've got a lot of talking to do when I get back. When will you stop digging bloody big holes Harriet? You never ever let go.'

'Look Mark, I'm sorry. I don't think I can take any more of this. Look he's out of our lives now. He's going to marry Lucinda Lawton.'

'Lucinda Lawton did you say? The one with the boat. Well that figures. He's all over her whenever I see them together at the sailing club.'

'So now you know. Can we just put him out of our lives forever?'

'The only way that's going to happen is if I get posted somewhere south of the equator. *Well* south of it. Just now it's exactly where I want to be Harriet. Away from the both of you. Well out of the fucking way!'

'Oh I'm going to start the meal Mark. How can it be my fault Melissa Scott's pregnant? It's not fair to take it out on me.'

'Not fair Harriet. What's fair? Just tell me what's fair in this life?'

'There's people worse off than us Mark, much worse off. We've managed to score even in all of this. We're as much to blame as each other. No, at least we've got food on the table and money to do things with. Not like a lot of people. Just look at our school parents. Mrs. Bustard doesn't know where the next penny's coming from. She's struggling to put food on the table. That's not fair. Why is it the most disadvantaged always have to suffer for the greed of the likes of bankers and politicians and all those at the top with vested interest in making sure the bulk of the wealth stays just where it is?'

'Survival of the fittest Harriet. We might be top of the evolutionary chain but our instinct for survival is as strong and as powerful as ever. Hence your deception.'

Harriet pretended not to hear.

'Survival at the top you mean, with all the trappings that go with it while some people are just struggling to simply stay alive,' Harriet replied.

'Evolution just got sophisticated, that's all. Lard ball a prime example.'

'Well I for one have had enough of evolution. Any chance of finishing that boat before you go? At least that would be something to help take the edge of Mrs. Bustard's miserable existence.'

'Right now. I'm off right now. Don't bother with anything for me, I'll get something to eat down there.'

'Suit yourself Mark, as you usually do.'

Harriet waited for the front door to close, reluctantly waved him off, then went upstairs to the computer. Impatient for it to fire up she sat with her head in her hands hoping Mark would recover from having to readjust his thinking on Mr. Sanderson, at least on that count. She hadn't realised Belinda Oxfordshire's character assassination had swung it for Mark with regard to him taking her baby on. She wished she hadn't just gone there. Tried to put it from her mind. Thought about Mrs. Bustard then sat wondering just how she could make a difference to the lives of her parents. Suddenly a brainwave! Quickly she searched for all the local supermarkets. Emailed them, explaining the plight of the families. Asking, no begging them to allow her to take all their "on" or "just past" sell by date food. She offered to collect it daily. Then realised there might be some legal redress. Decided to inform them her lawyer Mr. Engells had cleared it, as long as she wasn't asking for "use by" stuff. At least she knew that much, she'd heard it on the radio. Excited she decided she wouldn't even need to consult with Mr. Sanderson. She was asking for Monday for all this to start, he'd be well away by then. She looked at her watch wondering when the first reply would ping its way through. Then almost instantaneously, it arrived. She hardly dared open it for fear of rejection.

' "We are interested in your proposal and suggest you engage your solicitor to assist you in becoming registered as a charitable organisation to enable us to deal with your request." Oh, oh, well at least they're interested. Golly, I haven't got to go phoning Clive Engells, have I? I wonder if they are all going to come back with that?'

Harriet, glued to the screen jumped to the ping of the next email. Took a deep breath as she came to the full realisation of what she was letting herself in for.

'At least that's two supermarkets in Stetmead that are not already donating their food,' she thought. 'I'm going for it. Yes I'm going for it!'

She scrolled and searched, making notes, printing stuff off, until she had enough information at her fingertips to formulate her plan. As long as she adhered to all the rules there was absolutely nothing stopping her from getting on with this, especially as she'd now be acting head. Excited she decided to phone Tricia. She'd not long set up her "save Venice" charity. She'd have some idea about the ins and outs of registering it all.

'Oh `ello `arriet. I was going to phone you.'

'Well it's just a quick call Tricia. I was wondering how you got on with Clive Engells. Any comeback?'

'No, nothin` at all. In fact `e was very `elpful, `e's offered to oversee my charity for nothin`. I couldn't believe I was `earin` it.'

'Wow that's good Tricia, they do advise getting a solicitor on board when you register.'

'Oh no I'm not registered, exactly.'

'Oh but I thought you'd told me you'd registered it Tricia?'

'Well it is in a way `arriet because my "save Venice" fund is regulated by the Charity Commission but I'm not expectin` to be raisin` more than five thousand pounds in a year, so I thought I'd save myself a lot of `assle. Of course I don't know `ow much is in the tin now `e's still got it, or `ow much Rappin` `ammer's pinched for `imself. Actually I found Clive Engells very `elpful indeed.'

'Good, that's very good, now wait until I tell you this. I've decided to set one up myself, a food distribution charity to help the parents. Surprisingly there doesn't seem to be anything like that going on around here. I don't know what the supermarkets do with their "best before" stuff but it might just as well be going to our parents.'

'Oh that does sound like a good idea, 'arriet. It might be as well if you 'ave a word with 'im, too. 'ere 'arriet, write this down. It's 'is mobile phone number. Oh and if you need any 'elp with that I'd be only too pleased.'

'Well I need three trustees. Would you fancy being one? I'll need a treasurer, not that there'll be much book-keeping. This comes under "social enterprise" so as long as it passes the public benefit test, it should qualify.'

'Oh I don't see that as a problem. Definitely count me in.'

'Ah thanks Tricia.'

'And I expect you'll be recruiting our friend Joris?'

'No, not if I can help it. Anyway I told you he's going away on Saturday so he won't be around to get involved. Actually I can't wait to be shut of him and Mark. It will be good to get going on something useful again. Look I've already downloaded this form. Are you sure it's alright to put you down as a trustee of my charitable trust, then?'

'Ooh I'll look forward to that and who else will you be askin'?'

'Well I thought I would ask Mrs. Bustard Tricia. I'm going to phone her now. I think it would be good to get her views from the parents side of things.'

'Yes that is a very good idea. It'll make a big difference to your parents all that free food. Oh I'll 'ave to make sure fat-face-four-cheeks Bob doesn't find out or 'e'll be down there stuffin' 'is face.'

'Did you manage to sound out Clive Engells on where you'd stand if you wanted a divorce?'

'Yes I did and 'e was very 'elpful. 'e said 'e'd give me as much support as I needed without charge.'

'Gosh Tricia, that's good. He hasn't got his eye on you has he?'

'That would be tellin' 'arriet!'

Monday morning and Harriet breathed a sigh of relief. Mark had done his best to appear civil on his departure but she knew he was simply going through the motions. She felt the outside chance of it working between them had just been smashed what with him now knowing of Belinda Oxfordshire's lies together with the news of Melissa Scott's pregnancy. She knew he couldn't wait to get away from them both. Just a peck on the cheek and "it could be difficult keeping in touch Harriet as I may be moving on to the Galapagos Islands and I haven't got a clue when, or how available I'll be to phone. Don't worry about me though, I'll get a message to you one way or the other if there's problems." Clutching the cat she'd waved him off almost devoid of emotion. The last couple of months were taking their toll. All she wanted now was to get on with her charity work. She'd been pleased to gain Mrs. Bustard's full cooperation. She'd had to tell her to hold back on the praise though until it was up and running and even then she'd suggested it should be jointly shared. There was a fair bit of work ahead for the three of them.

'Right Pepper. I'm going to phone Clive Engells now. See if he's OK with this. See if he can't speed it up for me.'

'Good morning. Engells here.'

'Oh good morning Mr. Engells, it's Harriet Glover speaking. I'm sorry to disturb you but I was wondering if I could possibly have a word with you?'

'Certainly Harriet. Now do call me Clive. What can I do for you petal? I seem to be in great demand from that end of the country just now.'

'Oh yes, yes. I was wondering if you would be so kind as to allow me to use your name as my legal advisor. I'm hoping to set up a food distribution charity for our parents as soon as I possibly can. Do you have a scale of fees for this type of thing?'

'I'll treat you no differently from your friend, Harriet. You know I feel I owe both of you an apology for my atrocious behaviour that night on the camp site. You were both genuinely trying to alert me to what you thought would turn out to be a life threatening situation and I'm afraid my good manners went straight out of the window. I'm afraid it's only after hearing from Patricia how badly that Rapping Hammer boy has treated you both that it occurred to me I wasn't much better myself. I'm afraid Patricia tends to gabble on a bit and so there wasn't an appropriate pause in which to get this across in the manner in which I would have liked but I would be most grateful if you could extend my apologies to her as well.'

'Oh certainly Clive and thank you so very much. Really I just can't thank you enough for agreeing to provide your services without charge. Is it alright if I put your name on the form then? I want to get this underway as quickly as possible. A lot of our parents are struggling to survive at the moment.'

'Yes Harriet, you do that. I'm absolutely one hundred per cent with you on this. Now have you appointed a chairperson?'

'Well I thought *I'd* better do that.'

'No, no Harriet. I'll combine the roles. Put me down as your chair, you're going to be having enough to deal with organising the logistics of it all. Also as your chair I'll get this moving for you today. Fax me the form dear. I'll make a few phone calls. We should get this thing up and running by the end of next week at the latest.'

'Oh Mr. Engells, er Clive, I can't thank you enough. Mrs. Bustard has agreed to be the parent trustee and Tricia's going to be the secretary.'

'Well, well, an excellent choice if I may say so. I'm sure Joris will be happy to accommodate us when we have our meetings. I'll no doubt be staying there and he'll need to be kept informed. Excellent idea Harriet. Also it gives me an excuse to come up there. Such a lovely peninsula and so convenient for accessing the whole country. Oh yes there's quite a bit of sightseeing on the agenda for me, up there. Now you get that form faxed to me straight away and I'll see what I can do. Good day honey. Oh the fax number. Write this down.'

Harriet replaced the receiver to go cold. What had she done? No doubt she's find out soon enough.

'Oh I'm panicking for nothing. He's on his honeymoon Pepper, Clive Engells won't be wanting to disturb him to tell him about this. No Pepper it will all work out I know it will. It's worth doing if only for Mrs. Bustard. How can the children learn if they're hungry?'

She shot upstairs, the cat at her heels, completed the form, listened to the tinny, robotic sound of the fax machine as it sent the message through.

'All done now Pepper, all done. Cross your paws. We're really going to make a difference.'

Which she did. It wasn't long before Clive Engells phoned to give her the go ahead. She'd clung to the faxed permissions unable to believe this was her very own charity. Unable to believe she'd put herself in such a strong position to help her parents. A very disgruntled Mr. Brown reluctantly offered his assistance whilst the school cook had even agreed to the use of the fridges during the holidays but had said Harriet must make other arrangements for September. That was alright. At least she could accept the fridge food immediately. This was often the most expensive and least purchased by the parents. In any case once hearing of the situation Clive Engells assured her he'd take full responsibility for installing a new one, just for them, before the new term started.

'You're a good'n you,' Mrs. Bustard was frequently heard to say. There was a long way to go but at least the parents were smiling again. She'd requisitioned a small disused store room next to the kitchens right by the side door. Just a couple of tables and a stack of donated carrier bags, oh and a run of plastic crates for all the fruit and veg. She'd issued the parents with simple vouchers to ensure fair distribution and enjoyed seeing them swapping them around. Not even operating to full capacity yet but this was starting to make a difference.

'I'm managing to pay that nasty man back a bit more, thanks to you,' Mrs. Bustard had said. 'There's not one of us 'ere that doesn't think you're an angel.

We all say "never mind a damehood she should be made a saint, 'ere and now, for what she's doin' for us." ' Harriet had smiled. She knew a saint she was not but it made her feel just a little better knowing for once something had become more important to her than her feelings for Mr. Sanderson.

Pleased with herself, she pushed the cat in behind the door before banging it shut.

'School first,' she thought as she drew up at the lights at Starboard Marine North West. 'We'll have all five supermarkets delivering by the end of the day I'll be able to distribute the rest of the vouchers.'

She looked across to see Belinda Oxfordshire parking her car alongside Tricia's. 'I'll pop in there on the way back but I must get to school to make sure the extra tables have gone in the shop.'

She drove in, parked as far away from Mr. Brown's car as possible. Decided she must be as careful as possible with him. He'd been very touchy of late. She'd need his full cooperation if this thing was to keep on working.

'Ah good morning Mr. Bown. A nice sunny day. Did you manage to get the extra tables in place? We're taking in the last two supermarkets today.'

'Not so much as a please! You needn't think I'm working for you like this while he's away. Mr. Potts knows all about it, you putting all this extra work on me. One false move from you will 'ave 'im down 'ere before you can turn round.'

'Oh right, yes. Well I'm not intending to make any false moves Mr. Brown, infact I'd like to apologise for all the misfortune I've inadvertently heaped on you.'

'Well that's a false move for a start. Do you expect me to believe that? You're not trying to tell me you 'aven't got it in for me, are you?'

'Of course I haven't got it in for you Mr. Brown. I just have an unfortunate knack of misjudging things sometimes. Look I am really sorry. Can we put it all behind us and start afresh?'

'It's a plot. I can see it coming. You're tryin' to put me off my guard. I know you. You needn't think because 'e's given you a bit of power you can laud it over me.'

'Oh come on Mr. Brown, the last time I took charge I didn't. If I remember correctly we didn't have one cross word between us.'

'Aye that's only because you were so engrossed in chalking yourself up for that damehood. You weren't going to blot your copybook then, were you?'

'Look Mr. Brown I'm only doing this for the holidays and they've nearly finished. I'm sure Mr. Sanderson will be back in September.'

'Well that's not what I 'eard. I 'eard it would be Christmas at the earliest. He'll not be rushing back 'ere while 'e's on his honeymoon, now will 'e?'

'It's not what he told me Mr. Brown anyway I'd like you to advise me on something very important.'

'Advise you?' Mr. Brown's face registered suspicion.

'Yes, the supermarket vans are struggling to get parked. It might be better if we could allocate them specific parking places especially as we're expecting a couple more.'

'Spaces just for them? Come off it, you can see I 'ave enough trouble getting the school delivery wagons parked.'

'Well I'm afraid we're going to have do something about it Mr. Brown. Our parents have come to rely on these free groceries so they won't want them blocked off, now will they?'

'You and your free groceries, I never 'eard the like. Turned into a right little fairy godmother now, 'avn't we?'

'No Mr. Brown, I've set this thing up to help them. Some of them are really struggling you know.'

'Struggling my arse. They'd best be cutting out the fags 'anging from their mouths for a start.' He swirled the ball of his foot in the tarmac as if stubbing out a scatter of cigarette ends.

'Well that's easier said than done Mr. Brown. Smoking is a prop to keep them going. It's also very addictive. It's not something they can just stop doing when times get hard.'

'Alright, alright, I don't need the lecture. If I 'appen to be around I'll wave them in. It's not possible to allocate space to anything in advance round 'ere. Just look at it now. The place is packed. Some posh cars there. Half the kids don't even come to this school, I'm sure. I don't know why we 'ave to 'ave sports activities all week 'ere during the holidays. It makes my job a lot harder.'

Harriet bypassed his ill-informed assumptions.

'You're doing a very worthwhile job Mr. Brown. If it wasn't for you being here no one would be able to use the place. You are actually keeping the kids off the streets. Do you realise that?'

'Well no, I hadn't really looked at it that way.'

'Well you should Mr. Brown, because you are,' Harriet smiled. 'This place wouldn't work without you.'

She caught a hint of a smile as she went to pat his arm.

'Ouch that's my bloody sore toe you've just stamped on. Get away with you!'

Harriet hurried away wondering how she'd managed it. 'Stupid man. Should keep his feet to himself,' she thought as she made her way in.

Completely engrossed in her mission, she knew she'd never let Mr. Brown stand in her way. She still worried at the drawn faces of some of the parents and yes Mr. Brown was right, there seemed to be more of them smoking than ever. She worried about the children too, how they could ever learn anything, arriving tense, tired and hungry each morning. These were desperate times with all the signs of things getting worse, much worse. She was impatient for results. She needed to know what she was doing was going to work for the parents and children alike.

Chapter 42

Harriet delighted in the support she'd received from Clive Engells. She'd spilt out her worry for Mrs. Bustard and many of the parents who were well in the clutches of the pawnbroker round the corner from the school. Clive Engells had expressed serious concern and promised to look into it for her whilst warning her not to get involved herself. She was very grateful to him for giving so generously of his time. He was turning out to be a very good friend and she desperately wanted to make amends for misjudging him the way she had but wasn't quite sure how. It was something she'd work on. He was as good as his word, keeping in touch regularly. He'd researched industrial fridges, even ordered one and assured her it would be installed during the first week of September, before the start of term. In fact he was even intending to come up to supervise the installation.

With Mark still away it was good to be able to have someone like him to talk it all through; good to be able to iron out the small niggles that had beset it at the outset. Not that they were anything to do with the parents or any of the five supermarkets she was taking on board. No, it was the likes of Belinda Oxfordshire initially refusing to allow Starboard Marine North West to be an outlet for any produce. Of course she didn't give a toss for the convenience of the parents. Much to Harriet's relief Clive Engells soon won her round as with Enid Frost, who had initially sniffed at the whole idea. Yes, it was going well, brilliantly well thanks to him. It was almost the beginning of September and the thing was running like clockwork in time for the start of the autumn term. Clive Engells would be up tomorrow. Harriet couldn't wait to see him. Couldn't wait to get her very own fridge.

She was wondering just when Mr. Sanderson would return. How he'd take to her idea. Clive Engells had persuaded the education office to clear the plan in Mr. Sanderson's absence, there was no way he could tell her off for what she was doing. All she wanted now was to know exactly when he'd be back. Geared to taking charge of the school, she was just waiting for final confirmation. This she wanted to do. This she needed to do. She wanted free rein to make sure this new venture would be established to her liking and would prove sustainable during her forthcoming period of maternity leave. School had taken on a new dimension now. She couldn't wait to get back there!

Chapter 43

Harriet drove into school to see Danny in tears running towards her.

'What's the matter Danny? Where's your mum? What's happened to make you cry like this?'

'It's me mum she's brought me 'ere and now she's gone.'

'But she'll be back Danny. Not all parents stay every time. Gosh they wouldn't be able to get the washing done, or clean the house, if they did.'

'No,' Danny sobbed, 'I don't mean that.'

'Well what do you mean then Danny?'

'She's gone to see that bad man in that 'orrible shop and she's taken me silver trophy with 'er.'

'Why Danny, why would she do that?'

Then it dawned on her just as Danny started to explain.

'She said 'e'll give us money and only keep it for a few days until we can pay 'im back but she takes everythin' and she never brings them back.'

'Oh I see Danny. Now don't you worry. You go along to the gym and get changed. It's football this morning, isn't it?'

Danny shook his head, his dark hair falling forward to his eyes.

'Yes of course it is. Now you get changed and enjoy the game. Are you in a scoring position in this one?'

'Yes Miss it's my turn to play centre forward. I was goalie last time and I got two out!'

'Jolly good Danny. Now see if you can get two in for your team today while I go to the shop and get your trophy back for you.'

Harriet felt an instant burst of appreciation as two young arms promptly wrapped themselves round her thighs. She patted his head.

'Now your mum's only doing the best she can to put food on the table. She knows if our plan continues to work, things are going to be much easier for you all. She's very good your mum, she's helping me with all of this and in return I want you to help her. I want you to be a good boy for her Danny. You love her don't you?'

'Yes I do. Yes I do Miss.'

'Well show her by being as helpful as you can. Don't upset her by crying like that. Just remember everything she does is for you because she loves you.'

Danny wiped his nose with the cuff of his sleeve. Harriet hugged him before walking back to her car. Just at the moment this was the most important thing she had to do.

Chapter 44

Harriet could see no sign of Mrs. Bustard as she drew up outside the pawn shop. She placed her hand across her stomach in an attempt to settle the nerves needling too close to her baby, for her liking. This would be quick. She'd make it quick. Buy the silver trophy back for Danny and explain all to Mrs. Bustard later.

The bell rang loud and harsh as she pressed the handle down. The place appeared empty, the silent clutter of objects shouting loudly to be claimed. The atmosphere somehow sordid, sinister even. Harriet shuddered, couldn't wait to get out of the place.

'And what can we be doing for you now?'

Harriet froze as she turned back to face the counter.

'You in 'ere for something or are you just looking round?' The huge shaven-headed guy suddenly pulled at his pocket producing a dirty looking handkerchief, then proceeded to wipe the perspiration from his forhead.

'Er yes, as a matter of fact I am. I don't suppose you've got such a thing as a small silver trophy?' she asked, keeping her head down as far as it was possible.

'Funny you should say that. I 'ad one brought in 'ere only this morning. Let me see now where did it go?'

He bent down, Harriet looked away as his sage green polo shirt chose to pull away from the waist of his trousers.

'I've got it. Yes this is it. I'm supposed to be putting a seven day reserve on this but that fat-arsed woman never brings the cash. I only took it because it's hallmarked silver.'

'Right, yes, I see. That's just what I'm looking for.'

'Three hundred and seven pounds twenty pence and it's yours.'

'I beg your pardon?' gasped Harriet. 'Er that's a bit over the top isn't it? Last time I checked those online they were coming in at one hundred and eighty.'

'Means nothing,' he humped, 'how do you know what you're buying online? This is finest silver. See this hallmark 'ere?'

He twisted it around, catching it between his grubby, chipped finger nails.

'Genuine this. There's more weight 'ere in my hand than you'd think.'

'OK, OK I'll take it but not at that price. You'll never shift it at that price and you've just said that woman never brings the cash.'

Itching to get out of the door Harriet wondered just how she was managing it.

'Look I'll give you two hundred and no more.'

'Two hundred? I'll get more from the scrappy than that.'

'Two thirty then and that's my final offer!'

He tossed it about a bit then chose to polish it off with his sweat-laden handkerchief.

'Two fifty. Take it or leave it. Just a minute haven't I seen you somewhere before?'

'It will have to be a cheque I'm afraid. I don't carry that kind of cash.'

'I'm only taking cash at the minute. There's a machine outside the post office on the second corner.'

'Right I'll be back.'

Harriet jumped into her car, thankful to be out of the place. Tempted not to return she knew she could never let Danny down. She thought of him ringing her doorbell and of him making that scene in the takeaway. She wanted to lambast the huge man behind the counter that put her so much in mind of one of the PM's heavies but she couldn't do it. Not this time, anyway. Her nerves had taken over and it was going to take her all her time to go back inside to close the deal.

'Right. I think you'll find it's all there.' She waited while he counted. Then she looked up absolutely mortified. Hanging above his head the picture of her, pregnant, naked. She could feel the colour rushing to her cheeks. For the time it was taking this man to finger every note she thought she'd never get out.

'All correct.' She heard him saying. Thought. 'Just pass the flipping thing over, NOW, WILL YOU?'

'Just a tick there should be a box for it. Now where did I put that?'

He tapped his fingers on the counter top then turned round to look up at the picture. Harriet could take no more. She reached across to snatch it from his fingers then shot out leaving the door to slam behind her. Couldn't get the car started quickly enough. Screeched down the road. Without looking behind and only one place to go she landed in a heap at Starboard Marine North West.

'Oh Tricia, Tricia….' She couldn't speak for shortage of breath.

'Oh 'arriet whatever is the matter? What's 'appened 'arriet? What's 'appened?'

'Oh it's that place Tricia. That pawnbroker's place. That guy. That heavy. Oh Tricia he's just hung the picture Barry did of me on his shop wall.'

'Bloody 'ell 'arriet. What where you doin` in there?'

'OH NO Tricia. It's him now. Look he's driving in. He's wrapped a scarf round his face. Bloody hell Tricia. Get down, hide.'

The doorbell chimed as he pushed hard against it, for a split second silence. Then him bending, his face peering down at them from the side of the counter, full on, straight into theirs.

'Yeah it had to be you two. "Conny and Onny" I think Brad said. UP NOW and OUT. IN THE BACK OF THAT. NO MESSIN' THIS THING'S LOADED.'

Like a pair of white sheets Harriet and Tricia stood.

'Get your arms down you daft buggers. Get in the back of that. No messin` or I shoot.'

Instantly the office door shot open.

'What on earth is going on? Where are you taking them? Oh good heavens. Go away you nasty man. Tell those two to come back this minute. She's got work to do. Go away!'

'Fuck off prissy arse unless you wanna join them.'

Belinda Oxfordshire paled as she saw the van doors close then slumped to the floor in a faint.

Chapter 45

'Let us go this minute, you 'orrible bully. Just you let us go. You needn't think they won't be gettin' you for this. So where do you think you're takin' us anyway?'

Harriet petrified, marvelled at the fact Tricia had been able to find her voice. It was dark in there. From the little light afforded by the small cab window she was just able to make out they'd been dumped in with all the odds and sods and bits of furniture and anything else likely to be appearing in the shop. She looked around stretching her leg to catch a small torch rolling at her feet. She grabbed it quickly, flicked it on and off before putting it in her pocket. Knew if they were going to be trapped for hours in this, they would be needing it.

'STOP THIS THING AND LET US OUT NOW!!!' It was Tricia again but this time banging hard on the small cab window sitting behind the back of his head. 'YOU JUST WAIT UNTIL I TELL MY LAWYER FRIEND CLIVE ENGELLS ABOUT YOU. ONCE BELINDA OXFORDSHIRE'S PHONED THE POLICE HE'LL GET YOU PUT IN PRISON JUST LIKE THE OTHERS. YOU DO KNOW YOU WON'T GET AWAY WITH THIS DON'T YOU?'

Suddenly his podgy hand twisted behind him to slide the window across.

'Fucking shut it will you if you don't want this round your gob.' He waved the scarf he'd just pulled away from his face straight at her.

Harriet dug her elbow into Tricia. This was bad enough without the pair of them being gagged or tied up even. Her heart pounding she felt sick to the core. Wished she'd heeded the warnings about going near that place. Sorry but glad she'd inadvertently involved Tricia. She knew she'd be dead by now, just from shock, had she been on her own. She could see Tricia mouthing something at her. The van was slowing down and Harriet suddenly twigged, Tricia was going to make them both jump for it. Then his voice booming from the open glass as he pulled it back again.

'DON'T EVEN THINK OF IT. THEM DOORS ARE LOCKED!'

Harriet's life flashed before her as the van gathered speed. She thought of Mark and her girls on the threshold of life, just married. She thought of the tiny baby inside her, growing. *His* baby. Hated herself for never growing up. Hated herself for wrecking peoples' lives. Wished with all her heart she'd just got on with life the way it was. Venice, now this! They'd both been warned. Why oh why had she gone her own way to end up getting them both captured? A flash of sunlight through the tiny window. She looked at Tricia. Her face lit up, burning like a bonfire, emitting fury from any and every crease she could manage. She looked like she'd swing for him given half a chance. Harriet carefully pointed her two fingers like a gun and nodded her head vigorously. She needed to warn Tricia against doing the slightest thing to rile this big bully. She looked at her watch. Looked up at the window to see his mobile phone plugged to his ear. 'Where oh where are they taking us?' Her words panicking round her whole body until she could feel every hair on her head, every hair on her arms standing. She looked at her watch again. Five minutes. It felt like eternity and they were still on the move. Suddenly they stopped. Daylight flooded the van for a moment as the doors flew open then closed. 'You fuckin` well let us go will you?' Then silence. The words nicely trapped in the scarf just bundled and knotted round Tricia's mouth. Harriet nearly passed out. She could see the blindfold would be next from the handful of cloths at her side. She felt for the torch in her pocket. It would be no use now. It would be her turn next. Then another voice and the sound of a car door banging. Roughly grabbed and lifted into the fresh air they were now being pushed into the back seats of something. More voices. Doors slamming. The engine revving. They were bumping along somewhere at great speed. Then the sound of crude laughter.

'We'll milk this pair of conny-onny butties for all they're worth. He's got the bread. We'll bake him for a van load.'

The words floated around Harriet's brain, totally disembodied from their structure. Then piece by piece it slowly came together. They'd just been kidnapped for a ransom. Mr. Sanderson was going to have to clean himself out to get them released.

'Oh bloody hell he's sodding well on his honeymoon. Who knows where he's gone with her? Oh no, no, no! He mightn't appear until Christmas. He won't want to answer his phone. I know him. He'll evade everything if it suits him. And it will!' Harriet's mind was in a complete pelt. She thought of Barry. Would Barry somehow put two and two together and rescue them? 'What if we're separated Tricia and I? Oh no, no, no no.' She couldn't help the tortuous convolutions cutting at her mind. Now diverted. The door opening. The fresh air hitting her legs as she's being pulled from the car. Just briefly outside, a door closing behind them. Then both of them being shoved and pushed forward. Harriet winced. The scarf was caught. Her hair was tightening. The knot was loosening. It was dingy, very dingy. Tricia was still there. Relief, sweet relief! They were being pushed toward steps. Harriet looked down. A single flight, stone, all cracked and chipped. Then a door, an old wooden, heavy door, creaking as a hooded man pulled it open. Then it banged shut behind them to open again.

'Any messing about and lover-boy gets it!' He was speaking straight at Harriet. She heard the word "painting" and then mutterings followed by a bellow of laughter.

'Keep this zipped or he'll never fuck for another kid again!' The door closed on the laughter and Harriet felt the last remnants of energy fade away.

'At least they didn't tie our `ands,' Tricia trembled letting the scarf fall from her mouth to the floor. 'Still can't see a thing. It's pitch black in `ere, I wonder where we are?'

'Oh Tricia, thank goodness I grabbed this. She pulled the torch from her pocket. Flashed the beam around the dark, dank walls. Now where are we? I looked at my watch we haven't come far. We can't have done.'

'Get walkin` `arriet.'

'Walking Tricia? How far can we walk in here?'

'Shine it over there. I think I can just make it out. If I'm not wrong that's a sharp bend there. Quick get goin`. We don't know `ow long we've got before they come back. If I'm right we're in the other side of that tunnel. I smelt the sea. I'm sure that's where we are. Quick keep goin`. Just keep goin` `arriet. If we get caught we'll lose this one chance to escape.'

'Oh I hope you're right Tricia, but what if the door's locked?'

'We'll just `ave to take a chance `arriet. Come on we'll need to run. We should get through `ere in five minutes if we keep runnin`.'

Harriet puffed and panted, her ribs bursting. The torch shining eratic bursts of light at the walls in front of them. They daren't look back for fear of discovering they were being chased. It felt like they'd been running forever. Running forever to save their lives. Every minute convinced her this was their only chance. She was running and praying they were where they thought they were.

'Tricia, suppose this tunnel goes somewhere else?' Harriet panted. 'We don't know if there are others leading from the island. Oh bloody hell Tricia, I'm so sorry to get us into this mess.'

'Stop talkin` arriet and keep runnin`. We're runnin` for our lives `ere.'

Then flat across Harriet's foot, a picture. She kicked it away and fell behind Tricia as the tunnel narrowed to the walls lined with paintings.

'Oh that's a relief `arriet. Keep goin`, don't slow down now.'

Over Tricia's shoulder Harriet flashed the torch straight ahead to light up the door, the huge, heavy old door. They gasped.

'Keep your fingers crossed `arriet it's open.'

'I'm saying my prayers Tricia.'

Their panting bodies momentarily rested against it.

'Oh please, please, let it open, please.' Harriet panted hard as she watched Tricia turn the handle. Nothing!

'Oh no, oh no! Here Tricia let me try.'

With both hands Harriet turned and twisted the handle again, then it moved. They were on the other side, standing just where they'd stood with the children.

'Close it again `ard `arriet. As `ard as you can.'

The latch clicked into place. They turned to the Madonna and Child gleaming from the wall.

'There's no light on it `arriet. Look you're shinin` that straight ahead. `ow's it managin` to do that?'

'Golly you're right.' They stared in utter disbelief. 'We've got to go Tricia. Let's get out of here. We'll say our thanks once we're out. If we get out. Prayers do get answered. Well I hope they do. Keep going, we're not safe yet.'

Tripping and stumbling on the loose sandstone lining the walls, they panted their way up the tunnel never daring to look back.

'Please may this door be open,' Harriet's prayer articulating from her breathless chest, every word squeezing itself to be heard.

The last few yards. The door. The door into Mr. Sanderson's house. It wasn't even ajar. Closed. Closed tightly shut.

'We can't shout `arriet. If they're followin` us we don't want them to `ear us shoutin` for `elp first.'

Then Harriet's mind cleared.

'Tricia we haven't tried the handle. We haven't even tried the handle yet. Let me try the handle.'

She screwed her whole heaving body up against it and turned it until her hands hurt. Then, they both jumped. A voice from the other side.

'Mr. Swift I'm sure I've just seen that handle turn. Come back here. Look it's going again. Someone's trying to get in. Phone the police while we keep them in there.'

'HELP, HELP, OPEN IT PLEASE MRS. HARRIS! OPEN IT! *Please hurry they're after us.'*

No answer just a thump against the door and the sound of a body sliding, slumping to the ground.

'Oh no, what's going on?' panicked Harriet.

Then the turn of a key in the lock. Half supporting Mrs. Harris, Mr. Swift peered round the door.

'Oh Mr. Swift. Quick, quick, let's get out. Now lock it again!' Harriet panted. 'Sorry, *please*. **Please lock it again NOW**.'

'What in the name of goodness are you two doing in there? You've frightened the living daylights out of Mrs. Harris. Mind how you step over her, she's just fainted I think. Help me lift her up will you?'

'Lock the door first, PLEASE Mr. Swift.'

With great relief Harriet heard the key turn as she took Mrs. Harris by the shoulders allowing Tricia to grab her feet.

'She's not too heavy for you both is she? Can you manage to get her in here?'

Mr. Swift pushed the library door open ahead of them lifting an armchair to place it alongside the French windows.

'Sit her here. Just let me open this.'

'She's coming to, I think,' said Harriet. 'Here Mrs. Harris, just place your head between you knees while Tricia makes a nice cup of tea. Is that OK Tricia? We could all do with one.'

Tricia as white as a bowl of flour nodded as she found her way to the kitchen. Harriet still panting held Mrs. Harris's hand. Breaking through the fear came a sense of relief then a flash of belonging, of being in control, of being in command. Now, in this house, Harriet suddenly felt very comfortable. She felt at home. Knew this was where her baby belonged. The tears welled in her eyes. Rolled down her cheeks. She sobbed and panted and sobbed and panted. It could have been this way. She'd just left it a little bit too late to grow up.

'Now don't you cry Harriet. I'm alright. I'm alright now. I'm well enough for you to be able to tell us what this is all about. I know you wanted to take me through the tunnel dear but I wasn't expecting you to arrive quite this way.' Mrs. Harris smiled, trying to lighten the situation. 'Mr. Swift you'd better cancel that call to the police station now. I don't think we'll be needing them. These two are obviously not burglars.'

'I haven't even done it yet but there's something not right here. You were calling for help. Did I not hear you say there were people after you? It sounds like we'll be needing the police and pretty sharp.'

'No Mr. Swift please don't,' begged Harriet, remembering the threat to Mr. Sanderson if they opened their mouths. 'Well not at least until I've phoned Barry. He'll know what to do. Look do you mind if I make an urgent call.'

'No, of course we don't dear,' Mrs. Harris replied. 'Take it wherever you like.'

'I'll just use the kitchen. His numbers already in my mobile.'

She went to get her bag then realised they'd been left behind.

'Oh no, his number. I don't know his number. I need his number.'

'Now you just calm yourself down young woman. Is it so important we can't think our way round it over a cup of tea first?'

'Look here it comes. Ah the tea. What was your name again dear?' Mr. Swift asked.

'Tricia,' she panted. 'Now where are we `avin` it?'

'Let's go where it's comfortable, in the lounge. I think we're all needing a comfortable seat.'

'Oh we certainly do Mrs. `arris, but are you feelin` better now? We're sorry to `ave given you a such a bad fright like that, aren't we `arriet?'

'Now you catch your breath, don't be apologising to us.'

'But we are really sorry Mrs. Harris,' Harriet insisted. She turned to Tricia. 'Look I'm trembling. I bet you are too. But Tricia I need to phone Barry. He'll know what we should do. We haven't got our bags, they're down at Starboard Marine North West.'

'Then it's best I go and collect them.' Mr. Swift offered. 'When I've drunk this.'

'No, no Mr. Swift. You can't leave the house. You must lock all the doors. They'll know there's only one place we could be and that's here. If they've searched the tunnel and opened the door in the middle, this is the first place they'll come to. Quick lock all the doors and windows.'

Instantly Mr. Swift leapt to his feet, a grave realisation of the situation sweeping over his face.

'Oh my goodness Harriet, what on earth is going on?'

'We'll be alright Mrs. Harris. Tricia put that tray down and pass Mrs. Harris a cup of tea, please.'

'Oh yes, sorry. I'm tryin` not to drop it. It never crossed my mind to find somewhere to put it down. It's bad enough the mugs wobblin` without me `oldin` it when I don't `ave to.'

'Oh thank you Tricia. Oh that's better. Much better. Get yours, both of you.

I don't know what's happened but the two of you look in a terrible state.'

'I need Barry's number Tricia. What are we going to do?'

'Now would this be somebody Mr. Sanderson is in touch with?' asked Mr. Swift, anxious to help.

'Well he knows him. Yes, oh yes he might just have his number. I remember he wanted to thank him for the wedding present.'

'Er that would be for Lucrezia, if that's her name, would it?' Mrs. Harris enquired.

'Yes probably,' Harriet replied, sorry she'd just mentioned wedding presents.

'Or is it Lucinda? Oh there's so many of them I can never remember their names but then he never tells me anything very much. I'm always expecting him to come back married to one or other of them.'

'Mrs. Harris where does Mr. Sanderson keep his contacts book? Please, are you well enough to see if there's a phone number for Barry Giordano?'

'Oh you do it dear. It's sitting on his desk in the office. You know where that is.'

'Yes, right. Thank you Mrs. Harris.'

She shot through, rippling the still peaceful atmosphere with raw panic. Lifted one or two diaries then spotted a smaller, leather ring binder. Leafed her way through to "G". Found it! Drew the curtains closed. Shot back to tell Tricia to do the rest. Sat down, lifted the receiver, dialled the number.

'Oh come on, come on, come on Barry, *please.*'

'Barry Giordano speaking.'

'Barry, Barry, it's Harriet. We need your help, desperately.'

'What's happened Harriet?'

As fast as she could she gabbled it out.

'Hells bells Harriet. Don't move. Don't phone the police either. I'll get our boys on to it right away. Harriet you still there?'

'Yes, yes. We've locked the doors and closed the windows. Oh Barry we're terrified and now Mrs. Hall and Mr. Swift are involved. How do we know they won't try to kidnap them as well?'

'Right OK Harriet. Listen carefully to this. I'll get armed guards on the house right away. There'll be a chopper arriving in approximately twenty minutes to take you all to an undisclosed destination. Don't mess about. The four of you get in it. Wait in the library. As soon as you hear it wait for this sequence of knocks on the French doors. Write this down now. I'll contact you again once you've arrived. Oh and keep the experience to yourselves.'

Harriet changed from white to grey. She rushed back to the library to gabble the message.

'So grab your bag Mrs. Harris and anything you might need. We've probably only got about five minutes to go now.'

She rushed off, then the whirring of blades. It was landing already.

'Mrs. Harris it's here. Quick we've got to go. NOW!'

She came rushing in with her handbag swinging from her elbow and a packet of something in her hand.

'Oh listen for the knocks. It's got to be three quicks, one short, three quicks, one short and then two quicks. Here I've written it down.'

''ow will we 'ear it with that thing goin' round and round?'

'Oh I don't know Tricia. Come here glue your ear to the window.'

'It's slowing down. Don't panic, we'll hear it. I don't know wherever we're going to be ending up. Mrs. Swift will be wanting me back for tea.'

'Oh Harriet, you did speak to the right man, didn't you? We're not all walking into a trap are we, oh do say we're not.'

'No Mrs. Harris, definitely not. We could get killed if we stay here!'

'Shhh 'arriet. It's gone quiet. Oooh 'e's knockin', three, one, three, one, two. Open the door now Mr. Swift.'

Gingerly parting the curtains, Mr. Swift turned the key. Two guys in body armour rushed them across the lawn then piled them into the helicopter to slide the doors closed as it whirled and lifted vertically through the air. A stunned silence followed as they saw a larger second one coming into land.

'Oh I'm not sure I like any of this at all Mr. Swift,' said Mrs. Harris nervously clutching her pack of biscuits to her handbag.

'Well do you know I've always wanted a ride in one of these, just as long as I get back for Mrs. Swift's steak and ale pie.'

'Mr. Swift how could you think of your stomach at a time like this? How do you know we're all not being kidnapped?' Mrs. Harris was not convinced.

Tricia leant across to Harriet.

'She might be right. I don't want to end up in somewhere like South America.'

'Oh gosh no Tricia, I just want to go home.'

'You 'aven't any idea where we're goin' 'ave you?'

The dark, curly haired guy turned to the hand on his shoulder and grinned.

'I hope so pet, we don't spend our days going round in circles you know.' His grin broadened to a huge smile. Tricia brushed at her hair, just managing to cross her legs before reciprocating.

'Brize Norton,' that's as far as she goes.

'Ooh dearie me, that's in Oxfordshire,' Mr. Swift piped up. 'I'll be needing to water those tomatoes today.'

'And Molly and Percy are coming for supper tonight. I completely forgot. We're supposed to be playing bridge with Mr. Hanson.'

'Oh Pepper, she'll starve. Mark's away too. Oh gosh Tricia what about the cat?'

'What about the kids 'arriet? I'm not exactly expectin' Bob to turn up to feed them. Still my mum won't want to be leavin' them on their own there. She'll probably walk them back to 'ers. At least we're all alive.'

'So will these young men be flying us all home once they've caught them? I'm getting the gist of it now,' enquired Mr. Swift, hopefully.

The young man turned round again. 'Not us. Our remit finishes at Brize

Norton.'

'Oh dear, what on earth are they going to do with us then?' An uncomfortable urge to know escaping from Mrs. Harris.

'Don't worry Mrs. Harris we'll all know what's what when we get there. Barry promised to phone and he will,' said Harriet trying to console her.

They sat, looking down at the green world turned miniature, below. Harriet looked at her watch, almost lunchtime. Could scarcely believe all of this had happened in one morning.

'Er what's the e.t.a. young man?' Mr. Swift asked earnestly looking at his watch.

'Another hour and a half will do it,' came the reply from the front.

They sat back in silence, resigned to their fate, just grateful to be alive.

Chapter 46

They were met by a large Landover on arrival. All around straight roads, blocks of uniform rows of houses then open space. Then buildings, offices, sports and recreational buildings, then a monument towering over huge beds of neatly planted geraniums. They were being driven to somewhere in this uniform military town.

Still under armed guard they were escorted to a barracks. In through reception and then down a couple of corridors to the officers' mess. It was busy, bustling. They were invited to take a seat at a table for four in an alcove, then presented with a no frills menu.

'Oh lunch at last,' beamed Mr. Swift. 'My stomach thinks my throat's cut. Now what about you Mrs. Harris, you need to get something inside you, you know?'

'Which one of you is Harriet Glover?' A smart young man in uniform demanded.

Harriet looked across.

'Follow me, you're wanted on the phone.'

Harriet took a deep breath, pursed her lips, then stood.

'Right, yes that's me, thank you very much.' She turned to the others to show them her crossed fingers.

'Barry thank goodness you've phoned. What's happening? What on earth is happening? Poor Mrs. Harris and Mr. Swift, they're taking it very well but I think they'll want to get back today.'

'No Harriet, they'll be kept there for protection until the whole thing's over. We've contacted Joris Sanderson and he's to stay put, exactly where he is.'

'Not possible Barry if he's on a ship.' Harriet fished but to no avail.

'You and Tricia will be joining me tomorrow. You'll be taking the next scheduled flight to Ascension Island. I'll be meeting you there.'

'Gosh Barry why? Why all this when all they have to do is round them up?'

'There's a lot more to it than that Harriet and you two need to be well out of the way. I believe the e.t.a. for your flight to be approximately seven thirty in the morning. You'll be given all the details in due course.'

'But we haven't even got our handbags or our passports.'

'Special dispensation Harriet. You've got your lives. You want to keep them don't you?'

'Yes thank you Barry, we do. Oh and thanks, thanks so much for all of this.'

'It's a scoop Harriet, one hell of scoop as long as it's not bungled.'

'That's not why you want us out of the way is it Barry?'

'Of course it is. Is there anything you don't bungle?'

'Oh thanks a bunch Barry and there's me thinking you're our knight in shining armour.'

'That's exactly what I am. At least I'll get my painting back. Saved you from a great deal of exposure. You should be grateful!'

'You were the one who painted it Barry. As if I asked for it!'

'You ask for everything you get Harriet. You took no notice of my warning whatsoever.'

'Well, maybe you should be grateful to us for the scoop?'

'We were almost there, we'd have done it anyway without need for any of this. Meet you at the plane tomorrow morning.'

'Where are you now Barry? Are you still in Peru?'

'No, not. Now have a good flight.'

'But Ba...' It was no good, he was gone. She replaced the receiver just as the young man who'd escorted her through arrived to take her back again.

'Oh I don't believe it `arriet. I don't want to go to Ascension Island. `e's meetin` the flight in the mornin`, did you say? And then what?'

'We'll be flying straight out to Peru I imagine.'

'Oh bloody `ell `arriet this is goin` much too far. Didn't you tell `im we've only got what we stand up in, not even our `andbags.'

'He told us we had our lives and this was the best way to keep them. Don't forget Tricia what it felt like running through that tunnel.'

'Oh no, no I know `arriet. Let's `ope `e takes us to a nice `otel and we don't `ave to sleep in a barracks like them over there.' Tricia pointed to the window, across the road drab, grey building studded with small windows stuck to the wall like a perforated sheet of postage stamps.

'And what about us?' Mr. Swift enquired, 'Will we be going too?'

Mrs. Harris buried her head in her hands.

'No, no you won't. I'm sorry I should have told you first. No, it seems you'll both be staying here just for a couple of days until the whole affair is over with. It's for your own safety. Mr. Sanderson has also been instructed to stay put.'

'Oh I see, well as long as we're not being flown out of the country. I must say I wouldn't fancy being there at Mr. Sanderson's house all on my own tonight in any case.'

'Where's the phone Harriet? Do you think they'd mind if I gave Mrs. Swift a ring. I'd best be telling her to freeze the whole pie. No point in her leaving my half to go begging with all the gravy running out.'

'Oh here Mr. Swift, have a biscuit and I don't want to hear about that pie again!'

Chapter 47

Harriet looked at her watch, relieved it was eleven o'clock at last. A smart young officer arrived promptly to lead them out into the darkness, the three of them following the lights to the steps of the plane.

'Oh thank you ever so much for all your kindness while we've been `ere.'

Tricia was fast getting used to this uniformed, male dominated world and starting to like it.

'Oh you're not comin` up `ere as well are you? Oh I thought you were comin` with us for a moment then.'

'I am! I'm your escort until a certain Mr. Giordano meets you, I'm given to understand.'

'Yes, that's right,' said Harriet. 'I believe this gets in at around seven-thirty in the morning.'

'Always does.'

'Oh so this is a regular trip for you?'

'Certainly is. Well, twice a week. Best way to take it is fast asleep.'

'I think `arriet and I would find that a teeny weeny bit `ard to do just at the moment, wouldn't we? My brain's shootin` off all over the place. I feel like I've got fireworks goin` off in my `ead.'

'You'll be OK then seeing as we'll be landing in Wideawake Airfield.'

'You trying to be funny?' Tricia enquired.

'No honestly that's what it's called. There's not much there you know. They had to think of something to call it.'

'Oh I see. It will `ave a runway I `ope?'

'Just about. They'd hardly be chartering these if it had to land on grass.'

'Oh my `ead's too far gone for all this.'

'Oh me too, Tricia. We never could have imagined the day would have turned out this way.'

'No `arriet you're right. Now who's goin` to sit by the window and who's goin` to be in the middle?'

'I'm on the outside,' the young man stated. 'You please yourselves.'

'Oh you go by the window `arriet. I'll sit in the middle. I'm sure this young man will `ave plenty `e wants to talk about.'

'That's just where you're wrong. We're trained to say as little as possible.'

'Oh right. I'll sit by the window `arriet if you don't mind goin` in the middle. You can `ave the window when we fly on to Peru.'

'She'll be lucky. No flight to Peru from there.'

Before they could ask the uniformed officer exactly what he meant he'd dozed off, leaving Harriet and Tricia in a complete spin.

'Do you know Tricia, it's just struck me, I should have phoned Clive Engells to let him know what's happened. He's coming up today to oversee the installation of the new fridge. Gosh he probably won't be able to stay at Lower Tideside if the place is still under guard. Golly he's in for a shock.'

'Well they 'ave contacted our friend Joris, 'e does know about all this so 'e's bound to 'ave phoned Clive Engells.'

'Yes of course, you're right. My brain's completely gone. Perhaps we should take a leaf out of his book and crash out.'

The sentence barely finished and oblivious to take off, they both closed their eyes to fall fast asleep.

* * *

'We've arrived,' the young, uniformed officer yawned and stretched as he tapped Harriet on the shoulder.

'Where are we? What on a plane? What's happening?' Harriet awoke with a start.

'This is it, Georgetown. Come along now it's "Wideawake Airfield", time to get off,' the young man insisted.

She nudged Tricia's elbow, the full realisation of yesterday flooding in.

'Come on Tricia. We're here. Gosh it's just a field and a landing strip. I do hope Barry's arrived.'

The young man went ahead to escort them down the steps to the two men patiently waiting at the bottom, surrounded by suitcases.

'It's Barry and Andy 'arriet. Well fancy that. We're gettin' to see Andy again!'

'Hi girls. Quick, no dawdling, we've got a boat to catch,' rushed Barry.

They both reached to their inside jacket pocket, flashed some kind of card past the security officers then hurried them through and out to the waiting taxi.

'Clarence Bay Port,' said Barry shoving a few notes into the driver's hand. He smiled, nodded his head as he opened the rear door for them all to pile in.

'We meet again,' bounced Andy. 'Venice wasn't good enough for you two then?'

He grinned that cheeky grin pointing at Tricia. 'Especially you!'

'I didn't want to be comin' 'ere I can tell you. We didn't did we 'arriet? We've 'ad a terrible time and we're still runnin' for our lives.'

'We know,' smiled Barry, shifting his gaze from Harriet. 'That's why we've booked you a little cruise.'

'A little cruise Barry?' Harriet grabbed her hair and pulled it hard against her face.

'Where to?'

'You'll soon find out.'

'But we 'aven't got any clothes to be goin' cruisin' in Barry,' Tricia flapped.

'Cases, full of them.' He grinned at Andy. 'Hope you like our choice.'

'You do wear those long legged dark brown flannelette knickers we take it? Oh and we've got you both some nice crimplene trousers in pale green. Elastic waists of course and some very fetching high necked long sleeved green and brown striped tops.' Andy was laughing.

'Don't forget the matching sets in purple. Purple and orange stripes these,'

Barry reminded him.

'Oh no I do 'ope you 'aven't been buyin' stuff like that. We're not your grannies you know. Anyway who told you to buy them and who's supposed to be payin' for them? You needn't think we're payin' for a load of rubbish.'

'She doesn't change does she Barry? No wonder they got themselves into this mess with a mouth like that!'

''arriet did you 'ear that?'

Harriet didn't hear that at all. She was all but exhausted. Wondered if her baby would ever survive the trauma. She was desperate for more sleep. Looking out of the window, her tired mind puzzling at the variation in the landscape. From lush green fields to brown, barren scrub skirting the occasional volcanic crater. Palm trees in all their variety dotted against the stunning blue sky. They were nearly there. The sea a deep cobalt blue paling to turquoise at the shore. They drove down the hill to the small port. One small jetty that's all it was in Clarence Bay.

'She's still docked,' said Andy. 'We'll just make it if we're quick.'

With formalities disposed of they rushed through to hurry along the gangway of this old, long-serving, cargo ship.

'Oh I see,' Tricia began. 'This is the Royal Mail boat. Ooh we'll be sailin' with all the letters 'arriet. I do 'ope we don't get stamped.'

'So do we Tricia, you might find yourself being posted somewhere; now let's find out where our cabins are shall we?' said Barry banging the suitcases at his legs. 'We'll take these down and you two can sort yourselves out.'

Dazed, Harriet followed behind. This was nothing like "The Christiana", the cruise liner that had so luxuriously taken her on that mini cruise to Bruges. Much smaller for a start, though there was a pleasant, homely feel about it. Barry steered them to the purser's desk, a quick word, a couple of keys being passed over, swift instructions from the purser as to the whereabouts of their cabins and they were on their way again. Three flights of stairs to a deck high up just below the bridge. Barry opened their cabin door.

'There you are, this was all we could get at short notice. Not bad eh?'

'Oh just look at this 'arriet. Look it's like an apartment. Look there's three doors goin' off this lounge.'

'The Owner's Cabin, I think he said. At least you get a bedroom each. Not like us, I've got to share with *him*.' He pointed at Andy, laughing.

'Not the same bed I 'ope,' said Tricia in astonishment.

'Certainly not!' Andy exclaimed. He looked at Harriet. 'Though he would have had me sharing at the "Cielo Misterioso", he was that hell bent on getting back to Venice.'

'Not with you I wasn't.' Barry looked hard into Harriet's eyes. 'Up for swapping cabins with him?'

Harriet's pale face instantly flooded with colour.

'No thank you Barry. I'm trying to hang on to my life, don't forget.'

'You'll be as safe as you can be in my arms Harriet.'

'Well you needn't think I'm `avin` `im in the bedroom next to me,' declared Tricia, waving a finger at Andy.

The guys started laughing.

'Just joking,' said Barry, 'oh look, actually we're only next door. Meet you downstairs in the bar girls.'

They closed the door behind them, Harriet carefully putting the key in her pocket.

'Gosh Tricia this is nice. I wonder where it's going? Oh I do feel so much better for being with them, don't you?'

'Yes I do but it all feels like a dream. I'm findin` it very `ard to get my `ead round endin` up `ere on this.'

'I know exactly what you mean Tricia but it's certainly no dream, I just hope they've caught them all once and for all.'

'Yes, I wonder when we'll get some news `arriet? I think I'll feel as if I'm really `ere when we find out exactly what's goin` on.'

'Well we've got radio, television, a phone. I don't think it'll be too long before we get to know what's what.'

'Ooh we're movin` off. We're movin` away from the jetty. Just look at the colour of that water `arriet. Look at it lappin` at the white sand. Oh just look down there, it's so clear you can see tons of fish. Look at that luminous green stripe on the sides of them all and their tails. It's takin` my breath away. I `ad no idea `ow beautiful an island beach could be.'

'Yes, it's certainly something else. Oh thank goodness we've got a bed to lie on. Thank goodness we're not still stuck in that tunnel. Let's hope it takes more than a couple of days on this to get to where we're going. Oh look Tricia look at that shoal turning around. Wow all those green stripes and tails.'

'Talkin` of stripes I wonder what we've got in our suitcases? Come on `arriet, let's `ave a look.'

'Wow, it looks like we're going to be away a couple of weeks. Gosh pants, socks, jeans, bras. Oh how embarrassing. Oh no how did they know this is the exact size?'

Harriet flopped on the sofa, mortified.

'Well you're luckier than me `arriet. Look at this, it wouldn't go round a banana. Oh `ang on a minute there's some more `ere. No, these look as though they'll do. Yes, good guess these are perfect. They must have bought that one and `ad second thoughts.'

'36 DD,' Harriet said, then tossed it in the case. Checked to see the others were the same. Thought. 'There's only one person who knows my bra size other than Mark and that's Mr. Sanderson. Now where does he figure in all of this?'

'Don't worry about it `arriet. They've probably just been guessin` and got it right. At least we've got somethin` to change into. Wow these are pretty tops. Oh no there's a bikini in the bottom of `ere. `ave you got one `arriet?'

Harriet scrambled through to find one. Thought of the painting. Placed her hand across her stomach. She was over two months now, sometimes she felt it was starting to show. She wished Barry hadn't done that.

'Yes but I won't be wearing it.'

'No of course not. Sorry `arriet I forgot about your baby. It's not showin` yet though. If it get's very `ot on deck maybe you'll change your mind.'

'I might as long as Barry Giordano doesn't go near a sketchpad.'

'`e wouldn't dare `arriet. I'd `it `im with it if `e tried that one again.'

'No you're probably right Tricia. I'm just a bit over sensitive at the moment. I just need to flop on the bed and go to sleep.'

Chapter 48

Harriet woke to the sound of Tricia knocking on the door.

'You've 'ad a couple of hours now 'arriet. The boys 'ave been back to tell us they finish servin' lunch at one o'clock. We 'ave to meet them in the dining room as soon as we can.'

'Oh thanks Tricia. Gosh I just crashed. Did you do the same?'

'No I've been watchin' the telly seein' if there was any news.'

'And was there anything?'

'No, not a sausage. We'll see what we can get out of them over lunch.'

One deck below they came to the cosy dining room furnished in royal blue and gold. They hovered in the doorway until catching Barry's wave and moved across to the table for four in the corner by the window.

'It's a buffet lunch girls so lets all go and help ourselves. I say you're both looking good. Great choice eh Andy? That's not to say we didn't have a bit of trouble with the brassieres! How about the knickers? Do they fit?'

'We'd 'ave chosen them ourselves wouldn't we 'arriet? We don't know 'ow you guys did it.'

'Actually we didn't we engaged a shopper to do it on your behalves.'

'Well we can't thank you enough. I can't pay you yet, I haven't got my bag, never mind my purse,' worried Harriet.

'Oh there she goes again. She was like this in Venice wasn't she Andy? Flapping about paying all the time.'

'Well I don't like to owe money. I promise to sort it out when we get back.'

'Ah, that reminds me.' Barry fished in his pocket. Produced two folded wads of notes. Just check the currencies before you spend it. There's a shop on the deck below this. You'll be able to get yourselves the bits and pieces you need.'

'Barry thank you so very much but there's at least five hundred pounds here, apart from the foreign notes.' Harriet couldn't believe her eyes.

'Same 'ere. Gosh thank you ever so much, can I ask where it came from?'

'You can ask Tricia but I'm not saying, apart from the fact it has been provided without need to pay it back, it's to see you through until you get home.'

'Well please thank whoever for us, will you Barry? That's most kind and generous of them. We'll both feel better when we've got a handbag to call our own.'

'We certainly will 'arriet. Let's go down as soon as we've 'ad this.'

With plates in hand they joined the queue to take from the tempting array of cooked meats, salads and cheeses, fresh seafood, sauces, rice and pasta of all kinds, pies, pizzas and quiche.

'Wow this isn't far off the cruise ship,' Harriet thought. Totally spoiled for choice, she felt her appetite return.

'I hope this cruise will last a few days at least,' she said to Barry.

'Come on back to the table. We'll talk about it shall we?'

'What are you having to drink girls?' Andy said. 'Tea, coffee, soft drinks, wine? It looks like it's all here.'

'Wine,' chorused Harriet and Tricia.

'Wine it is. Shall we do both?'

He followed them back to the table with a bottle of red and white in one hand.

'You've been through a hell of a time. I don't like having to do this but if you could run it all past me again. First you Harriet, exactly what happened, then you Tricia. I want to make sure we pick up as much detail as possible.'

They ate and talked, Andy making only the occasional interjection. Barry stripping the experience down to the last blink of an eyelid.

'Right I get this now. You can rest assured we've got our people on to it.'

'But have they got them yet Barry?' Tricia asked, impatient for some answers.

'I'm not at liberty to tell you anything, unfortunately, apart from the itinerary, that is.'

Harriet watched Andy top up their glasses. She felt safe, very safe in their hands but they were giving little away. She needed to know just where this was all going and felt compelled to find out.

'You're both in Peru just now then?' She asked, trying to sound nonchalant.

'That's about right I guess,' returned Barry.

'You're not still tracking down the PM's heavies are you?'

'And the rest,' Barry replied, shifting on his seat.

'Is that where we're goin` then? Are you takin` us to Peru on this?' Tricia piped up.

'Do you know just where it is?' asked Andy, incredulity in his tone.

'Of course we do,' defended Harriet. The whole thing's bizarre. We could be going anywhere in anything right now. Actually we were hoping you'd throw some kind of light on it all.'

'OK, OK,' said Barry, 'now listen. Obviously we had to arrange something at speed keeping away from normal means of transport as far as possible. It was damned lucky you were able to pick up that flight from Brize Norton to join this Royal Mail cargo ship. As you can see there's very few passengers, we're away from the mainstream.'

'Yes we can see that Barry but where are we goin`?' Tricia couldn't contain herself.

'We're going to St. Helena first. It's a small island two days sail from here. She'll overnight there before continuing for another five days to Cape Town.'

'Cape Town?' queried Harriet. 'But that's in South Africa.'

'She knows her geography,' Andy laughed.

'Oooh I don't want to be goin` to South Africa Barry. I can't be expectin` my mum to keep the kids for that long.'

'No choice Tricia, except you won't get to see much. We'll be flying straight back to Peru from there.'

'Oh I don't believe I'm `earin` this. Do you `arriet?'

'Be thankful you are hearing this,' Barry declared, 'you could well have been hearing nothing, you could well have been dead.'

'Oh so we'll be on this for a week,' said Harriet, not too displeased.

'She can count, too.' Andy laughed again. 'What else can you do Harriet?'

'She can dig bloody great holes and drop everyone in.' Barry turned to face her.

'You're good at that aren't you Harriet?'

Chapter 49

Harriet woke the next morning to the sun shining through the cabin window from a clear, vivid blue sky. She lay still to absorb the motion, it was sequenced, almost like a waltz as it moved and pulled, moved and pulled its way across what felt like the top of the calm, sparkling sea. It was hot, very hot. Whoever had shopped for them had completely forgotten the nightdress. No dressing gown either. She let the top sheet fall to drape gently over her naked body as she slowly came to the full realisation of where she was. She wondered about Mrs. Harris and Mr. Swift. Hoped they'd be safely home by now. Wondered if it had reached the press, there was nothing on the BBC world news yesterday. Wondered if they'd managed to cover it up. Of course, she realised they would have tried, if the operation was to stand any chance of success. She wondered how Tricia was. There was no sound from her bedroom, then she remembered Tricia hadn't slept yesterday afternoon as she had. She'd certainly be needing to catch up on her sleep. Suddenly the musings stopped. Harriet sat up. She thought she could hear a couple of taps on the door. Then again, yes there was definitely somebody there.

She panicked. It might be urgent. There might be one of the gang after them, here, now on this ship. Why hadn't she thought to ask Barry about that possibility? Louder now, someone wanted to get in. She wrapped the sheet around her and tip-toed to the door, then waited. Three knocks, pause, one knock pause, three knocks, pause, one knock, pause, two knocks. It could only be Barry. Immediately she opened the door.

'Sorry to disturb you Harriet. It's urgent!' He shut the door quickly behind him then went over to the phone. 'Dead, this one's dead, too. There's something wrong here. Look it might be something or nothing but we can't risk another five days in isolated waters. I'm not at liberty to say any more but we need to get off this ship as soon as it docks in St. Helena.'

Harriet felt sick, started to tremble as she held the sheet firmly across her body.

'But what is it? What's going on Barry?'

'It's a trillion to one chance but it looks like we've walked straight into a fuckup.'

'Whatever that means Barry, I don't know, but it doesn't sound good.'

'It's not. You two must stay here at all costs. Keep this door locked and only answer to the code. Apart from grabbing a bite to eat for us all we'll be in here with you. I suggest you get dressed and wake Tricia. I'll be back to fill you in on where we go next.'

Harriet let him out and locked the door quickly.

'It was much too good to be true to be cruising on this,' she decided after turning her brain inside out in an attempt to determine what it was all about. She woke Tricia, wanting her to come to, before spreading the panic.

Showered and dressed Harriet filled the kettle. Switched it on expecting it not to be working. Relieved, she shook the sachet of coffee granules into the mug stirring in disbelief as she poured the boiling water from the spout. She sank into the sofa, placing her drink on the small table in front.

'Mornin` `arriet, I'm nearly ready now,' Tricia called from her bedroom. 'Oh it is `ot today I think I'll put these shorts on. `ave you got yours on `arriet?'

'No Tricia jeans. I feel far more secure wearing these today, I can tell you.'

'Why `arriet what's goin` on?'

'Sit down, let me just get you a coffee, you'll need it,' Harriet insisted.

'Ah thanks `arriet. What's goin` on?'

'I wish I knew. Barry did that coded knock to get in a few minutes ago. There's something going on. He tried our phone but it's dead. He said we've got to stay here until the ship docks in St. Helena and then we've got to get off. He said it might be something or nothing but there's a trillion to one chance we've walked int a .. Well I'm not saying the word. It ended in up.'

'Oh that'll be a fuckup I would think, whatever that means.'

'Yes, that was it Tricia and that's exactly what I said but he just isn't saying anything except they'd be joining us in here when they're not grabbing us a bite to eat.'

'I wonder if they think there's a heavy on `ere then? But they wouldn't know we would be on `ere. No it can't be that `arriet.'

'I don't know Tricia. It might be something to do with whatever mission they're on in Peru. Or it could be pirates are coming on board. Oh yes he did say something about not risking another five days in isolated waters. Honestly I haven't a clue. I was just thinking how good it would be to relax and try to get over the nightmare we've just had and now this. What is it about us Tricia?'

'Oooh I'm blowed if I know `arriet. I'm just `opin we're not `avin` to go underground in St. Helena. I don't think I can take any more of this.'

'Oh that's them now I think. Just listen for the knocks. Yes that's it, just let me open the door.'

They entered, each carrying a tray loaded with croissants, cooked meats and all the choices that constitute a generous continental breakfast.

'Kettle back on girls. Eat up, we don't know when we're likely to get any more.'

'Well that's a good start Barry. You've already frightened the life out of us. Surely you can tell us a bit more about what's goin` on?'

'Sorry Tricia, we can't. You don't have a clue how we work do you?'

'Well I wouldn't, no one would because you don't tell anyone, so `ow could I `ave a clue?'

'Yes, sorry Tricia. We couldn't do our job if any of us talked. Just trust us will you? Just now our mission is keeping you two safe and don't worry you'll both get home eventually.'

'Eventually? That sounds like a long time to me. Did you `ear that `arriet?'

Harriet nodded.

'Well I know we're both very grateful to have you two protecting us but I just don't get how you are factoring all this into your normal work. Have you just abandoned it to bail us out? Are you allowed to do that?'

'Too many questions Harriet. Just stop thinking and focus on keeping breathing,' instructed Barry eyeing up Tricia's shorts.

'They look great but you'd be better in jeans should we be forced to evacuate.'

'Just let me get changed. 'ang on a minute, I'll be back.'

Barry pushed the two armchairs towards the sofa inviting Andy to sit down.

'We need to talk. Great, she's back. I was just saying Tricia we need to talk, come and sit down and finish your breakfast whilst we give you the facts.'

Harriet put her coffee down to spread a little strawberry conserve over the split croissant now in her hand.

'She's trembling,' Andy pointed out. 'You're going to have to steel yourselves for what's ahead. Now all we can say is there's indications of an insider job on this and we've got to get off as quickly as we can. It could break any time.'

The jam sweet on Harriet's lips stayed just there. Just at this minute she was incapable of swallowing anything.

'Right the plan,' said Barry in his most efficient no-nonsense tone. We'll be stationed near the gangway. As soon as the ship docks we leave immediately. We'll be taken by road to a small airfield where we'll be picked up by helicopter to join HMS Sherlock, a fairly new stealth destroyer. It's a naval vessel heading for the Falklands. From there we'll fly to Chile and then on to Peru.'

'But why do we 'ave to go to Peru Barry? Why can't we just fly straight 'ome?'

'Because Tricia, at present we're operating from there. I need to wait until we get the all clear before I can fly you back. Besides which, as loathe as I am to say it, the pair of you have a distinct penchant for upsetting the applecart, to put it mildly. You can be detained elsewhere or stay with us. It's your choice.'

'No, never, we don't want to be detained. We're not as bad as all that are we? Oh 'arriet it looks like we're gettin' ourselves a bit of a reputation. I think we'll be more than 'appy to stay with you and Andy.'

'Good, now any sensible questions?' asked Barry.

'What will we do in Peru while you are both working?' Harriet wanted to know.

'Precisely what you are doing now,' replied Barry. 'One of us will be with you at all times in the hotel room.'

'You mean we won't even be able to go out?' Tricia howled.

'Look Barry, Mark's in the Antarctic right this minute. We'd be safe there. I'm sure if I asked him he'd be able to get permission for Tricia and I to join him. I know they fly there from the Falklands, I'm sure they do. We could go there and you and Andy could just get on with your work.'

'No chance Harriet. I wonder if you've heard a word I've been saying. This work is confidential, highly confidential. We don't embroil civilians ever, from choice.'

Barry stood, looked out of the window. Looked at his watch.

'Let's just hope we can make it through the rest of the day all the way to the morning.'

Chapter 50

It was early, very early. They were both up and dressed waiting for the code of taps on the door.

'Cases, right got everything? Follow us down to the main deck to the gangway. She's due to dock any minute now.'

Nervously they hurried their way down empty stair flights until finally reaching a small cubicle close to the purser's office. They pulled in listening to the crew shouting across to the berthing gang standing behind the bollards as they hurled the heavy twisting ropes towards them. The gangway down, a short walk across, then over a road to a waiting vehicle. It was fast, very fast. From the window could be seen lush green pasture dipping to valleys of huge exotic plants. Moving along now, a naval helicopter overhead. They watched it coming in to land. Harriet suddenly felt very sick.

With blades still whirring they rushed to board it. Hardly seated to feel it lifting, leaving the mighty bronze cliffs behind.

'Ooh we're not goin` to be tryin` to land on that are we?' queried Tricia, fifteen minutes later, pointing to HMS Sherlock; its pale grey structure just discernable in the morning mist rising from the sea.

'Only it looks like it's movin` to me.'

Harriet caught the guys exchange a grin but that was all. There was no conversation going on up there.

'Oh I'm closin` my eyes. That thing's never goin` to stop for us. Oh I `ope we don't drown, I'd rather be in a detention centre than drown.'

They'd caught it up. Harriet could see the large white circle marked on the deck and the two men with flags waving, guiding it in. A vertical drop and they'd landed.

'Oh thank goodness for that. I'll make sure I never go in another one of those things as long as I live, I'm tellin` you.' Tricia wasn't addressing anyone in particular. She caught a smile from a very good looking young man in uniform.

'Oh I wished I'd left my shorts on now,' she whispered to Harriet.

Their twin cabin was somewhat cramped for space as were the bathrooms and alleyways and various other places. Having been warned of the jail in the depths of the ship Tricia saw fit to say as little as possible for the next five or six days and they spent most of this time trying not to get under anyone's feet. Contact with Barry and Andy had, for some, reason been minimal. It felt quite strange walking alongside them again as they left the ship at the port.

'I don't know `ow people work on that. You'd `ave to be desperate to work on that. It feels like we've been on it for years, doesn't it `arriet?' Tricia exploded in a rush of confidence, knowing she was now completely safe from serving time in the ship's prison.

'We'd have no defence if they didn't,' Andy reminded her. Quickly she moved on.

'Where did you two get to anyway? We `ardly saw you did we `arriet?'

Harriet smiled, she too was glad to be off, it had felt like eternity. All she wanted to do now was to fly on to the South Pole to join Mark. Impossible! She sat on the thought.

'Right I think that's ours. Just a short hop to the airport. We'll be in Punta Arenas by lunch time. Then a quick bite before we join the flight to Lima.'

'Lima? Oh no you 'aven't changed the plans again 'ave you? I though we were goin` to Peru?'

'Lima in Peru Tricia. It's where the airport is.' Andy sounded impatient. 'Teach her some geography will you Harriet?'

For the next ten hours and no opportunity to see anything other than the insides of planes and airports, Barry and Andy finally steered Harriet and Tricia out of Lima Airport and into a waiting taxi to their hotel. It was huge, one rectangular glass and concrete block. At least its name was familiar. This was one of many in a chain scattered everywhere from the UK to the outer reaches of wherever and it was certainly feeling like 'wherever' to Harriet just now. One thing for sure, she knew she couldn't possibly move to anywhere so far south of the equator should Mark's job dictate it.

Barry checked them in. Harriet already knew the room layout. Internal ensuite to the left of the door. Two single beds centred from the wall behind it. The window, the dressing table and chair. The wardrobes. It could have been any of the hotel chains, or even a cruise ship's cabin for that matter. She flopped on the bed.

'Oh Tricia whenever is this nightmare going to end?'

'I only wish I knew 'arriet. I'm beginning to feel like a puppy on a lead. Now that was a good metathingy, I think. Do you know I'm gettin` so good at them I can now make them up for myself.' Tricia put the hairbrush down, then twisted in the chair for Harriet's approval. Too late. She was fast asleep.

* * *

'You missed your dinner last night 'arriet. Barry told me not to disturb you, I do 'ope you don't mind?'

'No of course not. Gosh I went flat out. Did you manage to sleep well?'

'Oh yes I did as a matter of fact. Now we're 'ere do you think we'll get to 'ave a look round? We must 'ave travelled 'undreds of miles and we 'aven't seen anythin` much, except airports and they all look the same. Well the little one's 'ave been more like garden centres really. The last one was even smaller than that.'

'We are supposed to be lying low, don't forget. That's why we had to get off the mail boat. I wonder what that was all about?' Harriet, still in yesterday's top and jeans, made for the ensuite.

'Oh they're not knockin` already, are they?'

'Check it's them,' Harriet called back. 'Listen for the sequence. That's OK Tricia, open it. It's them.'

Andy followed Barry through the doorway, cases in hands.

'Whatever `ave you brought those for? We're not on the move again are we?'

'Afraid so girls. It looks like we need to get somewhere more remote than this.'

'We couldn't have done better than the South Pole Barry,' Harriet returned.

'Too remote Harriet, now, good you're both dressed. No time for breakfast we'll get something on the plane. The taxi will be here in five minutes, we've just got enough time to check in for the flight to Guayaquil.'

'Now where the bloody `ell is that Barry? `arriet and I are gettin` just a bit fed up with all this? What's goin` on anyway? I think we `ave a right to know, don't you?'

'You don't have a right to know anything. Get packing. We done for if we don't catch that plane!'

Chapter 51

Standing a short distance from border security, Harriet and Tricia could see the uniformed officials giving Barry a hard time until eventually one of them reached for his mobile. Andy, tapping impatiently at his wristwatch, stood watching the seconds tick by. Just a few words then to Harriet's relief she watched the security guard put the phone away.

'That's it,' Andy declared, ushering them towards Barry 'Let's go!'

Relieved to find themselves in the departure lounge, Harriet and Tricia sank into the chairs, still keeping their heads down, wondering just where they would end up next.

''ow remote is this place we're flyin' to now? We don't want to end up in a small hut on top of a high mountain. We've flown over a few of those, I can tell you.'

'Guayaquil is just a staging post. It will only take two and a half hours at most. We'll connect with a flight to somewhere remote, after that.'

'Look Barry, we've come 'alf way round the world already. I know, our Adam's got one of those globe things. If you swirl it round you can see 'ow close America is to China. I 'ad no idea. I thought that big ocean went all the way up. Anyway I do 'ope we're not goin' to end up in outer Mongolia. I need to know we're goin' to somewhere we can get 'ome from.'

'No Tricia, we're not going to outer Mongolia. You've got to be joking! If they didn't lock you up the minute you opened your mouth they'd send you down the mines to keep you out of their way.'

'Now that's very cruel Barry. I'm tryin' very 'ard indeed not to think about tunnels. You 'aven't taken account of any post-traumatic stress we might be 'avin'.'

'That's just where you're wrong Tricia. Where we are going you'll both be checked out, somewhere where it's safe to do so.'

'What exactly do you mean Barry?' Harriet didn't like the sound of that.

'You'll go to the hospital, that's all. It'll just be an ordinary doctor checking you out. There's no need to panic.'

'And what if we refuse?'

'Refuse at the expense of losing all this protection.'

Harriet and Tricia went quiet. They spent the next hour in silence, as Andy and Barry went back and forth to the vending machines.

* * *

At last, touchdown in Guayaquil International Airport. It was huge and very smart. For some inexplicable reason Harriet felt a sense of relief. Just one more flight to where, though? She didn't know but she was hoping desperately it would be the last place of rest before returning home. She looked over to see Barry briefing the officials, obviously having better luck this time. They moved swiftly through security then he marched them straight to the bistro instantly alighting on a table for four in a corner by the window.

'A "sanduche" ' he declared, 'that's about all we've got time for in any case.'

He returned carrying a tray sporting four huge burger buns filled with chicken, spilling lettuce and tomato from the sides.

'I'll get the drinks, tea coffee?'

'Oh tea please,' Harriet answered.

'Four teas then?' Andy was away before Tricia had time to open her mouth.

He returned with four huges slices of "flan de coco", the plates struggling for space between the cups.

'Oh that's better,' said Tricia. 'That was very nice that was, thank you. Now `ow long `ave we got before we catch one of those.' She was pointing to the neatly parked row of white and blue tipped aircraft ready and waiting on the ground.

'By the time we've all been to the loo they'll be letting everyone through,' said Barry.

'And `ow long is this flight goin` to be?'

'No longer than three hours. It's scheduled to land at seventeen hundred hours.'

'What time's that then `arriet? I never did get this twentyfour hour clock thingy. Do you take two off or add it on?'

'Show her how to do sums as well Harriet. Have you got room for her in your class?' Andy laughed.

Tricia saw fit to belt his backside with her new handbag.

'Now I don't think that would please your benefactor,' Barry declared.

'And who might `e be then Barry?'

'How do I know? We only act on instructions.'

* * *

Somehow Harriet got pushed onto the plane first to end up sitting by the window. She watched the doors being closed and for a few seconds closed her eyes only to get a nudge from Barry alerting her to the stewardess about to run through the emergency procedure. All finished then the sound of the engines. They were moving, reversing away from the covered walk-way. Almost a full turn and then forward along the straight stretch of runway ahead to turn round. Gathering speed in the opposite direction now passing the parking bay they'd just left; the white runway markings rushing past along with the huge, blue hangars standing neatly alongside each other. Lifting now, the broad strip of grass paralleling the tarmac falling away. The high density of buildings, in all their variety, fast becoming the size of Monopoly property overcrowding a green-edged board. Mountains in the distance, coming closer. They were climbing and turning to huge purple mountains swathed in mist, clearing now below them dense white bundles of cloud all stacked beneath them like squeezed cotton wool balls piled into too small a bag. She looked up at the perfect blue sky. Its clarity and colour taking her mind to Mr. Sanderson. She could see his eyes sparkling, about to smile, then fired with anger. All his expressions flooded her mind. After Venice, what would he say about all of this? He was away. She was supposed to be taking charge of the school now. She returned to the window, the duvet of cloud behind them, just small dollops of white fluff floating past. In her mind's eye, the sky just waiting to be cut, stitched and gathered to make a pair of nursery curtains for her new baby. She looked down to the blue of the sea, wondering if they were going to an island again.

* * *

'Wake up 'arriet. Look, look down there. Just look at all those islands. Look 'ow blue the sea is. Just look at 'ow it changes to that gorgeous, gorgeous lighter blue then jade as it moves towards the land.'

Harriet awoke, smiled and looked down.

'This is it,' said Barry, 'we're coming into land at San Cristobal airport.'

'Oh that will be in the Carribean I expect. I 'ave seen them islands on our Adam's globe. Oh that's very good that is. I do know you can see our country from there. On the globe I mean. Well you might 'ave to flick it round a bit,' Tricia hastened to add.

'Give her some geography homework as well Harriet,' laughed Andy. 'We've been going in the opposite direction. Haven't you noticed we've been flying over the sea?'

'Well no actually, I 'aven't. 'ow could I when I've 'ad my eyes closed fast asleep?'

'We're going to know exactly where we are once we've landed Barry. You might just as well tell us now.'

'So how good is your geography Harriet? Can't you work it out for yourself?'

'No, no, it can't be?' said Harriet, stunned.

'Can't be what?' returned Barry.

'We're not coming into the Galapagos Islands are we?'

'Ten out of ten. Give her a star! Bang on Harriet.'

'Oh and where are they supposed to be then? You said we weren't goin' to outer Mongolia, Barry Giordano. I 'ope you 'aven't taken us to some deserted islands right next door.'

'Oh don't panic Tricia,' reassured Barry. 'You'll like it here. I didn't see a bikini in the bottom of that case did I? I'm hoping this'll turn out to be a bit of a break for us all.'

Chapter 52

'Angle Beach Hotel, please,' said Barry as Andy opened the rear doors of the bright yellow cab to allow them all to pile in.

'Sounds nice and looks nice,' Harriet decided, gazing out of the window to see them passing the terminal building they'd just left.

'Oh look, this road's following the runway. It's all grassland over there. Just `ow deserted is this place we're goin` to Barry?'

'Oh it's not too bad, it's a small fishing harbour but it seems to be expanding like these places do.'

'So what's there?' Tricia wanted to know more.

'A nice beach to share with the occasional rainbow coloured crab. They're huge Tricia. You'll have to mind you don't get eaten!'

'Oh I do `ope you're jokin` me Barry. What else is there?'

'Blue footed Boobies, they're great big birds with blue feet, oh and giant turtles. They don't do donkey rides here. You just get on a turtle for a very slow ride to the sea.'

'You are jokin` me. Now where's this place where `arriet and I are supposed to be going to get checked out?'

'Oh that would be the Angle Beach University Teaching Hospital and Research Centre. It's just on the hill behind the hotel.'

'Well, at least we don't `ave to go anywhere else `arriet.'

Harriet pricked her ears at the mention of "research centre". She wondered if that was where Mark's people would be going to link up climate change data. She wondered if by some stroke of good fortune Mark would be there. Wondered how she could find out. Then she dismissed it from her mind. The chances of that happening would be one big fat zero.

The road followed the coast, drawing a line under the astoundingly beautiful inky blue sea, the sunlight impacting, sprinkling its ripples with a shimmer of silver. As the land rose Harriet looked down to see every shade of blue, moving, twisting like long ribbons, then rising, running sideways to curl into a rolling wave, tossing the pure white foam away before flooding to a turquoise shallow over the beautiful white sand.

'Are you OK Harriet?'

'Yes thanks Barry. I'm fine. How about you and Andy? We've certainly given you the runaround, not that it's your fault either Tricia. This is all down to me and I want you all to know just how sorry I am.'

Barry smiled, reached forward to take her hand.

'It's all part and parcel of a day's work eh Andy? It hasn't exactly been unpleasant. Just that bit of a blip aboard the mail boat. Just as well we cleared off.'

'Why Barry what `appened? Ooh before you say,' she turned to Harriet. '`arriet I just want you to know we're both in this together. It's not of your makin`. Don't forget it started in Venice, well no, Switzerland really. I know `e was one of the 'eavies that big lump. I know I rubbed 'im up the wrong way then.'

Tricia, her enquiry lost in this uncomfortable flashback, refrained from further chatter to concentrate on the view from the window.

'Do we actually know what happened to the mail boat?' Harriet prompted.

'We do, you don't,' returned Barry. Evidently this was all he was prepared to say.

Following a steep climb the view of the sea began falling away as the cab followed the road to the right then back again to descend towards the harbour. High up and head on, the view caught Harriet's breath, she'd seen nothing like it in the whole world.

'Yes, it's something else, isn't it? With a bit of luck we'll get to see it all from our bedroom windows.' Andy smiled then rubbed his hands. 'This is the best part of the mission. We're now incommunicado.'

Harriet looked across to the modern glass sided building perched high on the hill wishing she wasn't incommunicado.

'Is that the hospital, Barry?'

'Yes that's right. See that line of words along the top?'

'Yes, I can't make them out though.'

'It says "Angle Beach University Teaching Hospital & Research Centre".'

She nodded wishing for all the world she didn't have to go there for a check-up. Then she allowed herself to draw comfort from the fact if this was the right place she might just bump into Mark. Even a very remote chance was worth clinging to. She was aching to pour this nightmare experience out to him; she needed him now more than she'd ever done in the whole of her life.

They took a sharp right turn to follow a narrower road winding along to the bottom of the hill on the other side of the harbour. A whitewashed building about the size of two large houses came into view. Sprays of colour tumbling from the row of flowerboxes hanging below the first floor windows; above the front door large gold lettering, "POSADA OCEANO ANGLE BEACH HOTEL."

Tricia gasped.

'Ooh now that does look very nice. Just look at those tables with all the sunshades by the pool. Oh I don't think I've ever seen such pretty colours altogether like that. Oh just look down there 'arriet. Look those steps go straight from the 'otel to the beach. I mean *h*otel. Oh it looks very posh. I'm going to *h*ave to make an effort to fit in.'

'I wouldn't bother Tricia. Minimal contact. We'll be keeping ourselves to ourselves.'

'Well I 'ope we'll be allowed to say "please" and "thank you". It would be very rude not to do that Andy.'

'Very funny Tricia, as far as I can tell you do at least manage to pronounce *those words* correctly. Start trying to be something you're not and you're bound to forget yourself. Next thing you'll be blabbing this whole thing to the world.'

'Oh no I won't Andy and it's none of your business if I want to start talking posh. I'll *have* you know I've made a new solicitor friend called Clive Engells and I might just want to speak a bit better for him.'

'There she goes, blabbing again!'

'Don't you be so rude Andy,' Tricia retorted.

'Why have you made yourself a new solicitor friend anyway?' Barry piped up. 'What do you need a solicitor for?'

'Well for one *he's* advisin` me over gettin` a divorce from that useless lump I married and for two *he's* going to *help* me get my "save Venice" tin back.'

'Why who's got it?' Andy asked.

'Flippin` Rappin` `ammer, that's who! Er sorry just let me say that again, Rapping *H*ammer has got it. Stolen it *he has* and *he's* trying to force us into doing all kinds of `orrible things before *he'*ll return it.'

'What kind of `orrible things? You missed one there Tricia!' asked Barry, suddenly alerted.

'Well not very nice things are they *H*arriet? I think the word's lewd, or somethin` like that. Not things *H*arriet and I would choose to engage in. Anyway I don't know why I'm blabbin` all this out. You're not much better yourself Barry Giordano paintin` a picture of my friend like that.'

'He's waiting for us to get out,' Harriet reminded them all. 'Look he's standing there with the suitcases.'

They waited and watched listening to Barry breaking into Spanish as he paid him. Just a few steps, a short walk past the patio and the swimming pool and they were inside. Harriet looked around. The reception area uncluttered, everywhere white, save the oak furniture and the regal red carpet caught with gold rods on every stair.

'Oh let's `ope we're `ere for a good few days `arriet,' said Tricia flopping on the bed. 'We've been `undreds of miles, I'm sure we `ave. We could do with `avin` a rest before we go `ome.'

'Let's hope so Tricia. I'd say we're pretty remote here. Just let's hope this time it's safe and we'll not be having to move on.'

Chapter 53

'That meal last night, was fantastic wasn't it? I've never tasted seafood so fresh but the prices Tricia! Golly you'd need to win the lottery big style to be able to afford to come to this hotel for a holiday.'

'Yes that's right Harriet. We need to make the most of this if we can get over the shock of it all, though I must say I didn't `ave a very good night for dreamin` about that tunnel.'

'Oh I am sorry Tricia. I suppose we can both expect to go through that from time to time.'

'Well I'm hopin` not. Now what was it I was goin` to say? Oh yes it would be good if we could treat it like a *holiday*. We didn't really get a break in Venice. We were too busy wonderin` what was goin` on.'

'Well I don't think we'll be meeting up with any heavies here or anyone else by the sound of it, although I have been wondering if we'll come across Mark.'

'Mark? But what would `e be doin` *here* Harriet? I thought *he* was goin` to the South Pole?'

'He said something about the possibility of linking up with the Galapagos Islands to compare climate change data but he didn't know if he'd be the one to get to do it. He didn't seem to know who would be going or when. No, I'm sure he won't be here. I don't even know if this is the right island. It's just when Barry read out the hospital name with "Research Centre" on the end. I wondered if that could be the place he was talking about.'

'Well it could be. It doesn't look to me as though there'd be too many of those kind of places round *here*. After all this is pretty much where the airport is.'

'No, well I really don't know. Oh I wish we didn't have to go to the hospital, either. It seems a bit late to me to be giving us chek-ups.'

'Yes you're right Harriet. Maybe they'll be tellin` us `ow to `andle post traumatic stress before it gets out of control. We `ave been through an awful lot you know.'

'Yes, it's just that I don't want to have to be telling any of them I'm pregnant. I don't want to be kept here by myself for eternity.'

'Oh don't say anythin` `arriet. Just don't mention it at all. I'm sure it will be nothin` more than a few questions and a blood pressure readin` for both of us.'

'Right girls, it's the beach or the beach this morning. I suggest both of you make the most of your chance to stretch out in those bikinis. Then it's a bite to eat here followed by a swift march up the hill to get yourselves checked out,' declared Barry as they left the breakfast table.

Harriet was hesitant, very hesitant about the bikini. In a few days time she would be three months pregnant. She sensed the swelling across her abdomen growing, though as yet she still fitted her clothes. She decided to pass. 'Sun top and shorts will do,' she thought hoping to be able to find something suitably light for such a hot morning.

'Oh I've got my bikini on under this Harriet. Oh it's startin` to work. Did you hear how easily I sounded all those aitches then?'

'You did Tricia but don't change too much will you? There's absolutely nothing wrong with an accent you know.'

'Oh but there is Harriet. There is when you're goin` to be hob-nobbin`with a lawyer. I wouldn't like to embarrass him in court.'

Harriet laughed as they walked through the foyer and down the steps to join Barry and Andy stretched out on the beach.

'Right girls, let's just rearrange these sun loungers. Oh this is the life. No bikini Harriet?'

She could feel herself blushing as Barry nodded towards the small group of women stretched out to their right.

'Look at them, they all look six months gone and at their age it's got nothing to do with being pregnant. None of them are bothered and why should they be? You certainly haven't got anything to worry about yet.'

She thought of the painting, wishing he hadn't just said that. Then his arm instantly around her. 'Sorry Harriet, that was highly insensitive of me. Forgiven?' He tossed his long dark hair away from his shoulders, raising his eyebrows whilst his deep brown eyes searched for an answer.

'Forgiven,' said Harriet suddenly feeling sorry for him. He was walking her away from the others towards the boulders sunk deep in the sand, skirting the edge of the cove. Splashing their feet in the pools of turquoise water they paddled, their legs sprayed by the sea until he finally sat her down, the water swilling at their toes while he spoke.

'And the painting Harriet? Am I forgiven? Honestly it was the only way I could think of to hold on to you, or at least to prevent you from marrying *him*.'

'It did that alright. He had his diary in his hand to sort out a date and then suddenly remembered your wedding present. He brought it in from the car, opened it and absolutely hit the roof. He wouldn't believe I hadn't sat for you posing like that.'

'Oh I am sorry. You do know that, don't you? With all my heart I'm sorry. I was jealous, desperate. I never ever felt that way for Maria and we were very much in love. It was and still is just like a bombshell's hit me Harriet. What I feel for you courses through my veins, I swear my very life blood has become totally intoxicated with this driving need for you.'

His head, down now, low between his knees. This intelligent, sensitive, artistic man scooped the seawater to his face then shook his head lying back against the rocks to let the sun dry to salt whatever tears had fallen from his eyes.

Harriet caught his hand.

'It's not your fault you got caught up in this affair Barry. It's flattering, very flattering to think how much you feel for me. I'm me, just me. I am the way I am and I don't know how I manage to wind people up like this. My life consists of digging one big hole after another. Look at all this now. However did I manage to get us all into this mess? The trouble is I can't leave well enough alone. I don't listen to anybody very much. I just seem to go my own way regardless of the consequences and drag everyone else along with me. I'm scared Barry. I'm three months pregnant and I'm scared. Mark was all for standing by me but he's now found out he's managed to get the girl he works with pregnant. Oh you wouldn't believe the coincidence. Each on a "one night stand" to use a better expression. We've been trying on and off for years to have another baby, Mark and I and not managed it. We change partners and hey presto! The odds against that happening must be phenomenal.'

'I would think so Harriet. So how is Mark dealing with all of this?'

'Not very well to be honest. He's with the research team in the Antarctic at the moment as you know, but he left home threatening to stay there. He just can't deal with commitment, I know he's feeling totally cornered at the moment. Anyway they're rationalising the travelling at their place. It could be they'll want him to relocate to this hemisphere. He was talking about us both going but honestly, after this exercise I know I don't want to be this far away from home.'

'So you'd rather stay put. Home is home with or without him? You don't feel that strongly towards him to be able to set up home together this far away?'

'It's gone too far now Barry. How can things be the same between us when I'm carrying someone else's baby? Everything's changed. We've got two grown-up newly married daughters, Rachael and Clare; they know the wedding fell through but they don't know anything of this.'

Harriet placed her hand on her stomach. 'Goodness knows what Mummy will say when she finds out. They don't know either. I'm just hoping it doesn't finish them off.'

'Oh our parents are a bit more resilient than that Harriet. They'll do what they always do for their children, pull out all the stops to help.'

'All Mummy can do is go on and on about making a new wedding date to marry Sir Joris. Goodness knows what she'll do when she finds out he's already married and on his honeymoon cruising the world.'

'Already married Harriet. Are you sure about that?'

'Oh perfectly sure. It's all over the school.'

'Doesn't mean to say it's true.'

'It's true alright Barry. Him and Lucinda Lawton, that's his deputy by the way, are both on leave. I'm supposed to be in charge of the school. Goodness knows what's happening down there.'

'It will be running as normal. Someone will have stepped in, none of us are indispensable Harriet.'

'No Barry I suppose you're right. Do you know I always hated being unmarried. I met Mark at university and the first thing he did was get me pregnant. Well I know it takes two. I think the sudden freedom and independence went straight to my head. But I was attracted to him, very attracted to him. It was the start of my very first year and he was in his final. He got a job and we set up home. It was always one day, some day. I didn't know

I'd fallen for a commitophobe. Of course we're both Glovers, you can see how that wouldn't help! Oh I just wish I'd sat on it and gone along with him. We wouldn't be in this mess today.'

'I believe these things are predestined Harriet. We think we make choices but we don't. It's already happened. We're one step behind all the way. We can't change anything. We shouldn't waste time and energy trying. All we can do is follow our hearts at the time. We're part of a universal plan of which we know nothing and maybe something if we can keep our heads clear. Clear enough to listen to what's calling us.'

'Thanks for that Barry. Thank you so much for that.' She leant over to kiss his cheek. He glanced down to glimpse the fullness of her breasts from the natural gape in her sun top.

'Harriet, I love you.' He touched at his cheek. 'May I do a little better than that?'

She smiled as he caught her in his arm. Then his lips set gently against hers. His finger following the line of her top from one shoulder to the other. She pulled away.

'Sorry Harriet, am I out of order again?'

'No, it's OK. Really it's OK. It had already happened,' she smiled. 'It wasn't in my control at all.'

Chapter 54

'Ooh I don't really know why we're `avin` to do this. By the time I get to the top of this *h*ill they'll be havin` me in intensive care,' groaned Tricia. 'As far as I know this is the last thing you should be doin` after lunch.'

'We're not climbing to the top of the hill Tricia. It might look it but it's only about half-way up and it's at least an hour since we finished eating,' replied Barry.

'I'm too puffed to answer and you two needn't think you're comin` in with us either. You can wait outside.'

'She's off on one again Barry. It's not taking her long to forget how she could have been left for dead in that tunnel.'

'Oh no I `aven't Andy. I'll *h*ave you know I had nightmares about it last night. I ended up tryin` not to go back to sleep because I was so scared.'

'There you are then. Sounds like a spot of therapy is just what you need.' Barry turned to Harriet. 'Are you alright there Harriet? Nearly there now, the road's just behind that hedge.'

'Oh it needs to be. This hill's steeper than it looks. Oh it's alright for you two, look, there's a bench seat outside. Lucky you, what a place to admire the view.'

'She could be right Barry,' laughed Andy. 'I don't consider there'll be any threat to them in there. Her maybe, if she opens her mouth again. Maybe a nice wide bandage?'

'That's not funny Andy seein` as `arriet and I both got gagged. Now you two sit `ere. Where is it we're supposed to be goin`?'

Barry fished in his pocket to pass them each a card. 'Just wave them at reception. You'll get pointed in the right direction.' He pulled the heavy glass door open holding it back for them both to pass through.

The dark haired receptionist smiled as she swung round to the computer to check off their names.

'Top floor, exit the lift or the stairs to the central corridor, turn left and left again. The health clinic reception faces the sea. Oh you will need these.' She returned the cards. Obviously not indigenous, with her English so perfect, Harriet wondered how she'd ended up here.

'Oh you're using the lift Tricia. I'll see you there. You'll not get me in one of those things just at the moment.'

'Well I'd walk up the stairs with you `arriet but I'm puffed out. Oh it's comin`. See you in a tick.'

Harriet climbed trying to remember which number floor she was supposed to be going to. ' "Top floor", she said. Yes it was definitely the top floor but how many flipping floors are there?' she thought, after counting three flights of stairs. Suddenly deserted of all logic she pushed her way through the double doors to the central corridor then proceded to turn left and then left again. Mesmerised by the deep blue sea she took a seat then waited and waited completely lost to the white foaming breakers rising and falling, rolling their way to the warm dry sand. She looked at her watch. Twenty seven minutes had passed. Then a door opened. A man in a white coat looked out.

'Ah no clinic today, but you pregnant? Come in, I'll see you.'

Harriet nearly died. Furious she decided Barry had no right whatsoever to pass that information along.

'No, no, sorry wrong place. Wrong floor. There must be another one.'

She shot off, turning left instead of right. Found herself heading towards a maze of wards. One glance sideways to mums and babies and cots. 'Gosh I'm in maternity!' She rushed off continuing in a straight line then had to make a choice, right or left? With left still on her mind she went for it, wishing she could read Spanish she followed the arrows along the walls to a single door, pushed hard then tried pulling. She was standing at the top of the fire exit, a little giddy she clung to the handrail pinned to the side of the building and gingerly made her way down trying to avoid looking through the gaps in the steps. Grateful for the alignment of the sea and feeling very silly she walked forward, turning the corner to find the three of them all sitting on the bench watching the waves.

'Ooh you 'ave spent a long time with 'im 'arriet. Oooh wasn't 'e gorgeous?'

'I wouldn't know Tricia. I've been sat outside maternity for nearly half an hour. I assume you didn't send me there Barry Giordano?'

'No of course not. You've just admitted to getting lost.'

'Well yes, but I didn't know it then, at the time I thought you had. After that I got really lost. I've just come back down the fire exit from round there. Golly all those steps trying not to look down the gaps. It was very scary that was.'

'You what?' laughed Barry, 'I don't believe it! Do you relalise you're now about forty-five minutes late for your appointment?'

'Oh 'e won't mind 'arriet. 'e's such a nice doctor. I could 'ave spent the rest of the day with 'im, and the night come to think of it.'

'You're going to have to check in again and explain what's happened. What exactly did happen by the way?' Barry asked.

'How many floors are there to this place? I couldn't remember. I obviously exited too soon,' Harriet replied.

'Teach her to count Barry,' Andy laughed, pointing to the windows. 'Ground floor, first floor, second floor, third floor, fourth floor. Just keep going until the stairs end.'

Harriet did just that. From the central corridor at the top of the stairs, two left turns saw her out of breath, sitting in a reception area identical to the one below. She gazed out to sea, the higher vantage extending the horizon. She took a very deep breath. In her heart she knew this was somewhere she wanted to be with Mr. Sanderson.

'Harriet Glover.' She jumped. Her name was being called. Gathering her bag she walked in. Startled! She couldn't believe her eyes. Her stomach instantly churning. Mr. Sanderson closed the door behind her. Blushing to her neck and beyond she sat down at his invitation.

'Now Miss Glover, believe you me you couldn't be more shocked than I was this morning to see your names on the patient list. As I understood it, it was the intention to fly both of you to Peru from Cape Town, according to the PM that is. I'm afraid when I put the question of "What happened?" to Mrs. Harrington she was quite unable to respond with any sense of coherence. Perhaps you'd like to explain.'

Harriet watched him recline in his chair, swivelling it slightly to the right to catch the view whilst waiting for her answer. Tanned, his thick blonde hair bleached even fairer by the sun and now almost touching his shoulder. His expression intent, his eyes narrowing slightly before relaxing as he scrutinized her every movement. His stethoscope resting on his white coat, 'obviously a tradition still maintained in this part of the world,' she thought whilst desperately trying to steel against the nerves spreading through her whole body, sickening her to the core, blurring her senses to confusion, wondering just what he was doing there. 'He's supposed to be cruising with her, his bride. What on earth is going on? Oh yes, that's it they've come here to get married and he's been called in to help. It's an emergency and they're very short of staff. It's a small island, they'd know a doctor had arrived.' Flummoxed by her thoughts she clasped her hands to her lap in silence beginning now to doubt the stability of her mental state.

'Perhaps an answer to my question later then, Miss Glover? Let's get you checked out, shall we?'

'Look Mr. Sanderson I'm not sure if this isn't all a dream. With respect please could you tell my what you are doing here, of all places?'

'Sure, it's a perfectly reasonable question. Let's just call it a working holiday shall we?'

'Oh right, sorry Mr. Sanderson I didn't mean that to sound intrusive. But you were going away with Lucinda Lawton Mr. Sanderson, that's why you asked me to take charge of the school?'

'Yes indeed Miss Glover and it's not turning out to be the case, is it? Did you not recall my warning to keep clear of that damned pawnbroker?'

Harriet looked at her feet.

'I wanted to help Danny Mr. Sanderson. I couldn't bear to see him so upset. That silver trophy Ross Farquerhart presented to him was his pride and joy. He was heartbroken when his mum took it to the pawn shop. I had to get it back. It was just when I saw that painting of me hanging up behind him, I flew out of the shop. Oh it's been the biggest nightmare of our lives.'

'And where is it now?'

'That depends on what's happened to the place and whether or not they've been caught. It was in the shop last time I saw it.'

'Yes, I made a very big mistake in giving it back to you. I should have had Swift throw it on the next garden bonfire.'

'Somehow they got hold of it. Did you know it was one of a whole line of paintings sat along the walls of your tunnel the other side of the door? You know, the door in the middle of the tunnel where we took the children to see the Madonna and Child?'

Mr. Sanderson looked intent, simply murmured, 'Hmm, hmm.'

'Well Tricia accidently discovered the door was open. We looked in and that's when we saw it.'

'And you saw fit not to mention any of this to me Miss Glover?'

'We didn't like to Mr. Sanderson. It wasn't our concern.'

'So you imagined I had a change of heart and stole my way into your house to remove it in order that I might add it to my gallery?'

Harriet didn't dare meet his eyes.

'Really Miss Glover, I ask you? It would have been far wiser to look a little closer to home.'

'What do you mean Mr. Sanderson?'

'I've been speaking to Mark.'

'You've been speaking to Mark? What you phoned him? He phoned you? Why? What's this all about?'

'You know where you are Miss Glover? Well let me remind you anyway. You are now seated in "The Angle Beach University Teaching Hospital & Research Centre". He spent all of last week here. Did you not know that?'

'No, he's obviously not been able to contact me the way things have been.'

'Quite, quite. I'm afraid I took the opportunity to have a very serious talk with him Miss Glover. I wouldn't like to try to second guess his feelings for you since he discovered the painting that morning. Not the best way to start the working day, I'm afraid. Apparently he was looking for his shoes and found it under the bed. He put it straight in his car wondering what to do with the damned thing. Oh he tried to put it to the back of his mind but not surprisingly, I'm afraid he couldn't deal with it. He returned from work the same morning to place it by the bin and since it was no longer around, he assumed it had been suitably collected.'

'Oh no what a stupid place to leave it. So he knew all along. No wonder he wasn't bothered about going away.'

'Quite Miss Glover and I wouldn't have been either in his shoes. You see Miss Glover you carry on regardless of others' feelings but there are consequences arising from the kind of behaviour you and indeed Mrs. Harrington choose to indulge in that never seem to cross your mind. It's a very dangerous game toying with people's feelings. If you continue in this way you will find yourself excluded from the lives of all those who care for you.'

Harriet looked down at the tiny red dots on her white cotton skirt. Could see them starting to magnify and jump around as the tears filled her eyes. Making a determined effort, she swallowed hard in an attempt to pull them back.

'So how would the painting get into their hands?' she asked.

'Think about it! If the fraudster didn't get there first to take it then his shop would be the first place the refuse collectors would take it in the hope of making a few quid.'

'Yes, yes of course. Oh gosh Mark's seen it. I didn't even get chance to explain I never even posed like that.'

'Does it matter now?' Mr. Sanderson rose from his chair. Strode round the room.

'What do you mean does it matter now? Of course it matters!' Harriet returned, catching the wet from a falling tear on the back of her hand.

'Is he not aware of your pending engagement to this so called artist, Barry Giordano?'

'Pending engagement? No Mr. Sanderson I'm not getting engaged to him.'

'The truth Miss Glover. I witnessed your telephone conversation in my very own lounge if you do recall? And though loathe to inform you I'm afraid Ross Farquerhart saw you cavorting with the very man down on the beach this morning. Don't try to deny it Miss Glover. If Belinda Oxfordshire's correct it would seem you were behaving in exactly the same manner as you did with him on the cliff top at the campsite.'

'No Belinda Oxfordshire was wrong and Ross Farquerhart's wrong. It was no more than a kiss. Anyway what's Ross Farquerhart doing here? I just don't get any of this at all.'

'He's gaining first hand experience of Darwin's visit, attempting to collect data to support his PhD thesis. Evolution Miss Glover! Galapagos Islands! Get the connection?'

'Oh I see. I see now. You are all here getting first hand knowledge for the school project and sort of combining it with a holiday.' At last Harriet understood.

'Amongst other things, Miss Glover. Amongst other things. Now shall we proceed with this health check?'

'Yes and I know what they are,' she thought, swallowing hard again.

'Your right arm, if I may?'

Harriet felt his white coat brushing against her as he wrapped the black band tightly around her arm, thinking her head would burst as he pumped away.

'Mmm a bit on the high side. Not good you know all this self-induced stress. Goodness knows what you're doing to everyone else's blood pressure Miss Glover. Don't you think it's high time you calmed down and grew up?'

'No that's unfair Mr. Sanderson. That's most unfair. None of this would have happened if Mark hadn't been such a commitophobe.'

He sat behind his desk again.

'Any physical or psychological adverse reaction to this unfortunate experience?'

'Yes, as the receptionist would have explained, I'm afraid I kept you waiting because I wouldn't go in the lift. I never did like them but it wouldn't surprise me if I don't end up with complete claustrophobia after being in that tunnel.'

'Yes understandable, perfectly understandable. And are you getting any flashbacks at all?'

'I try not to think about it but yes, every now and then the whole experience crashes into my thoughts.'

'Again a perfectly natural thing to happen. Miss Glover I received a call from the PM shortly before you were called in. I think it would help you to know they've been caught. As far as they can tell they've rounded the lot up. It would seem this pawnbroker guy was in fact linked to the gang you got involved with in Venice. It would appear he's been dealing in stolen and fake paintings and the insolent swine, as you know, has been trespassing, using the far side of the tunnel for storage. Of course the island access is remote, who knows how long they've been getting away with it? Unfortunately it would seem Swift has failed in his duties in not ensuring the door was locked.'

'But it might have been Mr. Sanderson. Look at that wiry thing you gave me so I could open the filing cabinet the morning of the wedding, er, that didn't happen thanks to Mark! Anyway they could just have easily had something similar.'

For a brief moment she caught the hint of a smile. Encouraged she continued.

'But you already knew what had happened so why did you ask me?'

'Yes indeed, but I wanted your side of the story Miss Glover. Anyhow it would seem you will be returning home very shortly. How do you feel about resuming your duties at school?'

'Fine actually. I think it will be so good to get home knowing there's no threat. I know you and Lucinda will be away for a long time and I've got such plans to get on with.'

She looked at him realising she'd gone ahead without a mention of it to him. Could feel herself blushing.

'Yes indeed Miss Glover, Clive Engells has told me all about it. It would appear to have given him a new lease of life. In fact he's been made a school governor in your absence. Hetty Armitage retired and Clive stepped in nicely. Of course there wasn't going to be anyone against it, not after the time and effort he's put in to making this project of yours work. Still I do wish to congratulate you Miss Glover on such a splendid idea and I'm delighted you can't wait to get back to it.'

'Oh thank you Mr. Sanderson. I wondered what you'd think but with you going away I didn't want to bother you with it.'

'Perfectly in order. I placed you in charge and with it goes such responsibility. You ran it past the Office and evidently Mr. Whittle saw fit to approve it.'

Suddenly Harriet felt so much better. She caught his full smile now as she was about to leave.

'No I can't wait to get back to it all,' she said, 'just as long as I don't find the cat dead on the doorstep.'

'Highly unlikely Miss Glover. Nine lives! A bit like yourself! Take my advice, take stock now before you find yourself running out of them.'

'I certainly will Mr. Sanderson, may I go now?'

'Just a quick examination if I may. If you'd like to strip to your bra and pants just the other side of that curtain and lay on the bed in there, it won't take a minute.'

It took all her willpower not to leave the room. She thought he'd finished then remembered Tricia. This must have been what it was all about for her. Oh gosh in the next few seconds he'd be seeing the reason she'd decided against wearing the bikini.

'Hmm, right Miss Glover just turn to this side. I'm not sure if I'm hearing a heart murmur or not. Over to this side now. Right and back again, right over if you will? I think we'll need to slip this off. Just sit straight, ah that's better, now lean to your left as far as you can. Just a hint of something but only when you're in that position, oddly enough. Perhaps an ECG when you get back? Just to be on the safe side. Now lie flat again. What are we now, three months?'

'No, no, not at all Mr. Sanderson. I told you I'm not pregnant.'

'Now why is Mark telling me you are?'

'Mark told you that? I don't believe it!'

'He saw the painting Miss Glover, it must have been enough to convince him.'

'Precicely Mr. Sanderson! Information based on a lie and I never even got chance to explain it.'

'Look Miss Glover, if you're unsure about this I can conduct an internal examination now. It won't take a minute. It's really something I should know having been given responsibility for clearing you, in the light of what's happened. You know you are making my job extremely difficult.'

'Sorry Mr. Sanderson I'm afraid not. It's just something you're going to have to take my word for.'

He walked away closing the curtain behind him. Harriet quickly dressed. Furious with Mark she picked up her bag, thanked him and hurried away.

'Ooh you `ave been a long time in there `arriet. Are you alright?'

'Yes thanks Tricia, I'm fine. I wish you'd have warned me though, I'd have cried off.'

'Oh no you wouldn't,' Barry insisted. 'Who was it anyway?'

'You mean you haven't told them Tricia?'

'No, it's got nothin` to do with them. Don't you tell them either `arriet.'

'It wasn't Sanderson was it?' Barry said in disbelief.

The girls kept quiet.

'How the heck did he get here?'

'He called it a working holiday "Amongst other things, Miss Glover." Other things being getting married at some point and finishing it all off with a cruise,' Harriet informed them.

'So that's him out of the way then?' Barry replied.

'Oh no I wouldn't count on it Barry. *He* certainly didn't give me the impression `e was just about to get married.' Tricia couldn't hold it in.

'Charmed the socks off you did he?' Barry asked.

'The pants more like,' laughed Andy. 'Come on let's get back to the beach.

Don't forget it goes dark at six o'clock here.'

'Yes let's tell them the good news,' said Barry leading them back all the way down the hill to the steps onto the beach.

Chapter 55

'Oh I am sorry to be goin` `ome. No, not `ome, *home*. I must remember to sound my aitches for Clive seein` as *he*'ll be fightin` my corner. *He h*ad our friend Mr. Sanderson pass a message on to me. As soon as we get back he wants to take me out to dinner to go over it all. He wanted me to have something nice to help me get over this trauma. Do you know I think it must have sparked a teeny weeny bit of jealousy in Mr. Sanderson, he was so lovely with me. Oh `arriet I don't think I could be any happier.'

Harriet disturbed from her thoughts looked down from the window. She could see land clearly now. It wouldn't be long before they'd be landing at Manchester.

'I'm really pleased for you Tricia. It's nice to have something special to look forward to, especially after all we've been through.'

'Oh now I want you to `ave somethin` nice to look forward to as well `arriet.'

'She has, she's got me,' Barry cut in.

'I thought you were asleep Barry Giordano. You made me jump then!'

'I never sleep with two eyes closed Harriet which makes me well qualified to handle you.'

'Enough said,' Andy laughed. 'Only flaw in that, we're never around long enough to handle anyone. We're off to Somalia tomorrow.'

'You won't be wantin` to handle anyone there either. "Look don't touch", that's what you said in Venice. I reckon they've got the perfect jobs then, don't you `arriet?'

'I reckon we've got the perfect friends Tricia. Goodness knows where we would have been by now if they hadn't stepped in. It just doesn't bear thinking about.'

'Yes friends for life seein` as I don't expect we'll be changin` our ways any time soon,' decided Tricia.

'Harriet will, at least they'll be changed for you. This'll stop your gallop,' said Barry patting her tummy.

'Oh you won't let that stop you will you `arriet? I might even have one myself so we can push prams together and when we get fed up of that we'll dump them on Mrs. Harris. Now I'll just have to see how I make out with Clive.'

'I thought he was spoken for,' said Harriet. 'What about Lucrezia?'

'Oh I haven't `ad chance to tell you yet, Mr. Sanderson told me that relationship was finished. She never got over us knockin` on `er campervan while they were, er, well, like that. She accused poor Clive of havin` another woman, she didn't know there was two of us `arriet. Anyway she dumped him and he's decided he's moving up here.'

'Gosh Mr. Sanderson certainly opened up. He hardly told me anything.'

'Except about Mark confirming I'm pregnant,' she thought, feeling the fury rise yet again.

'Haven't you just heard the announcement? Seatbelts on you two, we're coming in to land. We'd have seen you home but we've got some sorting to do for tomorrow and there just wouldn't be time.'

'No Barry, please don't worry. That's absolutely fine. Tricia and I will get a taxi home.'

'Right, well we'll see you through border control, then shoot. I'll be in touch Harriet.'

'Just you two take care. There aren't words enough to thank you both for all you've done for us but I'll work on finding a way.'

'Don't worry about it Harriet,' Barry said. 'As it happened we were inadvertently linked to other things. We could well have missed out if we hadn't joined that mail boat.'

'And that's why you're going to Somalia now?'

'Questions shall never be answered Harriet. You should know better than that by now.'

'Sorry Barry, both of you take very good care and thank you again.' Harriet kissed them both on the cheek, followed by Tricia. They watched them dart away.

'I feel quite sad at leavin` them `arriet. I'm glad they're our friends.'

'Yes me too Tricia. Both of them are friends well worth keeping. Now let's get one of those taxis, we need to be getting home.'

'Oh look `arriet isn't that a beige Bentley parked over there? Oh guess who's gettin` out. Wouldn't you know, it's our friend Clive Engells. Look `e's wavin` at us. I think `e's been under the sunlamp `arriet or `e's sprayed it on. Oh I don't think I'd be wantin` to `ave `is baby after all `arriet. I'd forgotten `ow flashy `e looks. Still it's very nice of `im to give us a lift home.'

'Ah girls, so good to see you both safe and well. What an appalling time the two of you have had. You can rest assured I'm here for each of you, both in a legal capacity and as a friend. You need have no fears now they've all been caught. All done and dusted as they say. Now Joris has asked me to collect you on account of your handbags, keys, etc. needing to be returned to enable you to access your homes. Come, do come along, pass me those cases, the sooner we get you back the better.'

Feeling like royalty they sank into the back seat rummaging through their handbags while Clive Engells chattered enthusiastically about his plans to move up.

'Of course at the moment I'm staying at Joris's house, between us I think Mrs. Harris and Mr. Swift are glad of the company since that traumatic time. Do you know the place was under guard for a whole week. They certainly made sure they were going to haul in the lot of them and apparently they did so with great success. A most unfortunate occurrence during Joris's absence. Still I've been able to hold the fort as it were. Now did you know I've been co-opted onto the Board of Governors at the school Harriet? I must say I'm thoroughly enjoying it. Of course a little legal expertise to hand has got to be a bonus for them. I must say I was able to iron out one or two snags arising with regard to the food distribution but apart from that it's gone swimmingly. Well done you, dear, for making such a difference to these people's lives.'

'Thank you so much, with all this going on it would haven fall flat without you. I'll always be in your debt.'

'Not at all, not at all, it's certainly given me a new lease of life since Lucrezia and I split. You know I'm so much enjoying being on the school's governing body.'

'Yes Mr. Sanderson did mention that, I'm delighted and please do accept my congratulations, the success of it is all down to you. I've got to say it again, the whole thing would have floundered, never to be resurrected again, had it not been for you. You can't mess these big companies about. I really don't know how to thank you.'

'You just have, now say no more about it. It's all my pleasure Harriet, my petal, and if you hadn't approached me I can't think what my life would be like now so it's me that needs to be thanking you.'

Harriet smiled taking genuine delight in her new friend.

'Now you're back both of you, I'll be able to focus more clearly on sorting this problem out with Wayne Hammer. I've sent two letters without any response. This lad's in danger of getting prosecuted if he doesn't get his act together. We'll work on getting that tin back Patricia. We'll have a little chat over dinner. Don't worry, I won't let you down.'

'Oh I do know that Clive, I'm just so grateful you are willin` to `el, er *h*elp.'

With ease the Bentley swallowed the forty miles or so motorway from the airport to home. Harriet was grateful to be dropped off first. Clive Engells saw her in then scurried down the drive to Tricia still sitting in the back of the car. Overwhelmed to be home she waved quickly to them both, glad to be closing the front door behind her. No sign of the cat, she had a quick look round, the green light flashing messages catching her eye through the banister as she rushed upstairs. Still no sign of the cat, she came down to put the kettle on. Then wham! The cat flap opened, she turned to see Pepper dashing in for dear life, scratching and clambering at her legs. She lifted it to her face, burying her head in its fur, helpless to stop the tears from streaming.

'Oh Pepper, I thought I'd never see you again. I thought I was going to die Pepper and then I thought you were going to die. Who's looked after you? You can't have gone all this time without food.'

She looked at her watch. Four o'clock. Heard the key in the door. Jumped! Panicked! They were coming for her again. Her heart pounding she peered round the kitchen door into the empty hall wondering just who it could be.

'Oh you're there Harriet. Thank the dear Lord you're back. I'm sorry to give you a fright like that. I can't bear to think what you've been through. I'm sure it's killing Daddy. He's outside, he always waits while I feed her. Just let me wave him in.'

'Oh Mummy am I glad to see you?'

For the first time since she was a little girl she flung her arms round her mother, sobbing like a child into her soft lilac cardigan.

'There now Harriet, love, don't cry, now don't you cry. You've never really grown up you know and I blame myself. You were the baby and I suppose I wanted to keep you that way. That's why your life's got into such a tangle. You're still my little girl, just like that photograph in there. I brought it back Harriet, something inside me made me think it would bring you home.' She turned as her husband hurried through. 'George we've got our Harriet back. Thank the dear Lord she's safe.'

'By gum you've given us a load of worry young lady. What have you been getting up to now?' He flung his arms around her, his wife shifting her own tears away with her finger as she watched his eyes filling up.

'It's been a complete nightmare Daddy but they've all been caught now. It's over Daddy, it's all over.'

'Now don't even think about it Harriet my love. You'll tell us all about it in your own good time, just when you're ready. Give it some food Frances. The poor thing's getting squashed to death here.'

'How did you find out about it?' Harriet asked, letting the cat go.

'Oh we first heard about it from James. Of course Joris is away but he was in touch with James most of the time. James was amazed at the lengths Joris and the Prime Minister were prepared to go to ensure your safety. Of course, we were only given the outline of what had happened, I don't think Joris knew exactly himself. Apparently it was the PM keeping Joris updated. From what we could make out it seems like you led them straight into making a scoop that had eluded them for years. So some good came out of it all Harriet, you must look at it that way. We all must, it will do none of us any good to dwell on what could have happened to you or that girl. I think it's been the worst time of our lives, hasn't it George? Even worse than your wedding day Harriet when that good-for-nothing let you down at the church. And where was he when you needed him most? Swanning around the Antarctic again! It breaks my heart Harriet how he's ruined your life. He only needed to marry you to give you and those granddaughters of ours the stability and status due to you. No, you've done nothing to deserve this at all. You're a good, kind-hearted girl and I want you to know how proud Daddy and I are of you for getting that damehood. It's been in the local papers Harriet. They're all singing your praises for getting that food distribution thing set up. We're very proud of you aren't we Daddy?'

'Too right we are love. It's not sweeties they're giving out when they dish up these honours you know.'

Chapter 56

Harriet drove to school the next morning anxious to relieve Enid Frost of her headship duties. She'd prepared a short assembly based on the strength of love. She'd never felt as close to her parents as she had yesterday afternoon. They'd wanted her to return home with them but buoyed by their love she'd slept well. In any case it would have been a retrograde step now she'd made a conscious decision to grow up. She needed to grow up and fast for her new baby. She'd need to tell them but only too aware of just how much she'd put them through, she knew just now wasn't the right time but for when it would be, they'd taken the fear away. It was a weight lifted from her shoulders. Yes she must tell the children this morning that love makes us all feel better. She'd hardly needed to write it down. She thought of the Galapagos Islands, of Barry's words to her while splashing their toes on the beach. This morning's assembly had already been written.

'Glad to see you back Miss Glover.' It was Mr. Brown, Harriet could hardly believe her ears.

She popped into her classroom, had a word with the supply teacher Susan Curtiss then bumped into Danny hurtling down the corridor towards her.

'Danny don't run, you'll fall over.' He wasn't listening. He hurled himself at her throwing his thin arms round her skirt, his hands clasped tightly around her back.

'Miss, Miss, I told my mum you'd come back and give me my trophy. I knew you would. I knew you would.'

'That's right Danny,' Harriet smiled. 'Come with me to the office. It's in my bag.'

Danny skipped alongside her, following her into Mr. Sanderson's room.

'Now let me see, there, there it is Danny. I'm sorry I couldn't get it to you any quicker.'

'That's alright Miss. That nasty man's gone now and my mum's going to get `er money back and because you've opened a food shop that you don't have to pay in we're not feelin` hungry any more. My mum says you're a good'n you and we'll be able to go to Butlins next year. Are you comin` back to teach us Miss, we don't like Miss Curtiss as much as you?'

'Hopefully Danny. Just as soon as Mr. Sanderson gets back I'll be with you all again.'

'I got them goals for you. I got two Miss. I've been waitin` ages to tell you.'

'Gosh, well done Danny. Very well done indeed.' Harriet smiled as he skipped about.

'Danny where `ave you gone to now? Oh sorry Miss Glover. Is it alright if I come in `ere?'

'Of course it is Mrs. Bustard. How are you and Mr. Bustard anyway? Danny's telling me things are looking a bit brighter.'

'They certainly are Miss Glover. We can't thank you enough for what you and Mr. Engells have done for us all. But we've been very worried about you. We all 'ave since that shop closed down and you 'aven't been 'ere. There was something about some arrests being made in this week's paper but no mention of you. There's been all sorts of rumours flyin' round like you've been captured and taken to that tunnel in Mr. Sanderson's house, but then that's the children, they always do let their imaginations get the better of them. Still all we need to know is you're back safe and well. You see our Danny knew you were goin' to that place to get his trophy back and you didn't return. He kept sayin' "Miss must have been taken. Miss would have brought it back because that's what she said she was going to do." We 'ave all been very worried Miss Glover. We've all been sayin' a little prayer for you down there.' She shook her head towards the kitchens. Harriet turned away. She didn't want Mrs. Bustard to see her eyes filling, yet again, with tears.

Chapter 57

At last the weekend. It had been a good week. She'd been very grateful to Clive Engells for his support. With the headship responsibilities crashing in she'd had little time to visit the school shop, at least while the parents had been there. Of course it had suited her. The response to her return had been completely unexpected. She felt there wasn't one parent in the school who hadn't gone out of their way to express delight at seeing her again. Friday night and glad to be home. She placed her briefcase at the bottom of the stairs while the cat brushed its black furry tail against her legs. She looked at the answer machine. Just one message flashing green. She wondered if it was Mark's. Of all the goodwill messages left, there had been nothing from him. She pressed play.

'Oh `ellow `arriet, it's only me. I'm sorry I `aven't `ad chance to phone you, I'm just leavin` this one quick. First of all I `ope you're alright. I've `ad a terrible time with my mum, she's sayin` she's `ad enough of bein` dumped with the kids and if I go off again like that she's puttin` them into social services. As if it's our fault `arriet, we don't ask for it do we? I `aven't `eard anythin` from Bob, it looks like `e's just buggered off. Belinda Oxfordshire's not givin` the game away either. Snooty cow. `e's got to be with `er, there's nowhere else `e'd go. She's doin` nothin` but moan about `ow she fainted and if Tarquin Bridgewater `adn't come in she'd `ave just died. Pity she adn't `arriet. Well I don't really mean that but she doesn't want to know `ow we could `ave so very easily lost our lives. It would `ave done `er good to `ave been in our shoes. Anyway I must go `arriet, I'm goin` out to dinner with Clive Engells tonight. *H*opefully `e'll be able to get me my "save Venice" tin back. I'll let you know `ow we get on. Oh by the way `arriet I lit the fire last night, just so I could burn that diary. He's gorgeous `arriet. I never thought I'd see the day when I was just lyin` there for `im in my bra and knickers.'

Harriet smiled, cancelled out the message then went to feed the cat.

'Ah the phone Pepper. Go on eat it! Leave me alone.'

'Oh Mark, this *is* a surprise, I haven't spoken to you for weeks.'

'No sorry Harriet, you've been difficult to get hold of. I've been worried sick though. I heard you got back alright I'm relieved to say. It sounds like you walked yourselves straight into this one.'

'Well not really, well I suppose so, in a way. It's been a nightmare, I'd rather not go into it.'

'You OK now?'

'Yes, I think so, thanks. Everyone's been fantastic, really kind, including Mummy.'

'That's good Harriet, that's good.'

'How are you getting on down there? Do you know I missed seeing you by days?' Harriet asked.

'What do you mean Harriet?'

'The Galapagos Islands. We detoured there. You knew we were with Barry and Andy didn't you?'

'Yes Joris Sanderson told me that much. It seems there's been a lot of subterfuge going on to keep you both protected. You're damned lucky to get bailed out like that.'

'Yes I do know that Mark. I believe you've had a chat to Mr. Sanderson. Thanks for telling him I'm pregnant.'

'You what Harriet? The guy already knew for goodness sake. That's the way he was talking.'

'Well not from me he didn't. I've been stalling him and still am so if you're in touch with him again please don't say any more.'

'There's more important things to think about now, well for me at least. I've got some news for you Harriet.'

'Oh very nice and I don't think. What kind of news anyway?'

'I'm being promoted to become director of the main Basingstoke Research Centre.'

'You're joking Mark! Well done! Congratulations! I thought they were cutting back and you were going to get offered a post somewhere way down the southern hemisphere. I didn't realise this was on the cards.'

'I told you it was all up in the air. You haven't been bothered to realise very much of late Harriet. Anyway to be fair it took me by surprise. It just goes to show you can't be sure of anything.'

'When will you be taking it up then?'

'January 2012, I believe. At least I won't be having to do any more of this sort of thing.'

'No, that's great. So we'll be moving to Basingstoke then?'

'Look Harriet, I've got something I want to say.'

'Oh no Mark, I think I know what's coming. It's the painting, isn't it? You found it and put it by the bin. You couldn't have wrapped it again once you'd seen it, either since it ended up in that pawn shop. You don't want me any more because of that bloody painting and I didn't even pose for it.'

'I know you didn't Harriet. Joris Sanderson told me that much. No Harriet we've had too much together and still got too much, not to stay close but I know I can't, well don't actually want to deal with this baby. I'm sorry Harriet, I've thought long and hard and I just don't want to do it. Basingstoke isn't the end of the world, not like here. We'll still see each other, it's not as if we've ever been married so we can't get a divorce. We'll stay something more than good friends but I want to get on with my life away from all that and this promotion is a heaven sent opportunity.'

'Oh I see Mark and what about the house?'

'I'll get it transferred to your name in January, you can sort out what you like then with Joris Sanderson. I won't have any trouble buying something on the salary I'll be earning.'

Harriet swallowed hard on the lump in her throat.

'And what about Melissa Scott, she's not going to be very happy you being so far away being the father of that baby?'

'I'm not the father Harriet. Don't let this go any further, Joris Sanderson broke a patient confidentiality to help me and I admire him for it.'

'Yes Mark I had noticed you'd stopped calling him "lard ball". What did he tell you?'

'It's Geoffrey's baby she's carrying.'

'You what? Did she get back with him or something while she was seeing you?'

'No Harriet apparently the first thing they did when they got married was to store Geoffrey's sperm with a legal agreement she could use it in any circumstances whatsoever.'

'Golly, so that's what she was doing consulting with Mr. Sanderson. Gosh he must have done the insemination bit and it worked. Gosh Mark you must be relieved about that. I'm so pleased for you I really am. I wonder why though? Do you think she was trying to keep you on board or what?'

'Well it was a coincidence Harriet that she should have got pregnant around the same time as you. It was only after I'd told her about you expecting she came back with all that. She never wanted me to go back to you and it must have been the only way she could think of to keep me; in which case she must be off her rocker, especially if the child turns out to look like Geoffrey! Tell me I'm better looking than that!'

'Of course you are Mark. I'm pleased for you but I'm sad it hasn't made it any easier for you to cope with this one. I do love you Mark, I don't want to loose you. I really wanted to start afresh.'

'Well I still love you, too Harriet. You know that but we can't turn the clock back. We can't change what's already done. Actually he's a decent bloke Joris Sanderson. He's the father of the child. I'm not going to try, nor do I even want to take over his role, now. We have to stand by the choices we've made Harriet but we'll never lose touch, I promise.'

'Got to go now Mark,' Harriet could barely speak for the lump choking in her throat. Her hand wet from the tears streaming down her cheeks. 'You will come here as soon as you get back? All your things are here Mark. I will see you again?'

'Of course you will Harriet. Now don't cry. I'll phone you the minute I know just when I'm going to be on my way.'

'Take care Mark, do love you. Sorry, I'm just so sorry for it all.'

'You too Harriet. Phone the girls won't you? They'll need to be knowing what's going on. Must go.'

Harriet replaced the receiver, all the joy of the week gone, like bubbles blown to the wind. The cat meowing at her feet, she picked it up, its fur now wet sticking to the side of her face. Suddenly she didn't feel very grown up at all. She looked at the photograph of the little girl on the mantelpiece. Felt just as naïve and vulnerable now as she did then. Crying, she sat on the sofa, allowing the cat to settle in her lap.

'We've come full circle Pepper, it's just you, me and the baby again. We'll manage Pepper, we'll have to.'

Distraught, she squashed the cat to her face, sobbing her streaming tears into its fur.

'He's married now Pepper. He's married. I had my last chance and I threw it all away. For all I know he'll be leaving the school, standing for parliament too.'

'Wrong on all counts Harriet.' She jumped, looked up. Hadn't heard the silver Mercedes pulling to a halt. Hadn't heard the car door slam. Hadn't heard the key in the door.

'Mr. Sanderson but, but I thought you'd lost the key.'

'I'd taken it off the ring ready to give back. It was under my diaries. Mrs. Harris must have inadvertently shifted them during the course of dusting. Yes, sorry Harriet it slipped my mind. You must have wondered why I didn't get round to changing the locks.' With her chest shaking violently, she barely heard.

'But I thought you were still away. I thought you were...' She sniffed, grabbing at the tissues by her side.

'Marrying Lucinda Lawton then going on a honeymoon cruising the world.' Her eyes flooded again, cascading tears she was helpless to stop.

He smiled, lifted the cat away then sat down beside her, hugging her close to his chest.

'What do you take me for Harriet? I was never going to let you come home to face all this on your own.'

'You knew what Mark was going to say then?'

'Yes I knew Harriet. You have to let him be now. He's not going to lose touch you know but he'll be doing what he wants to do. Probably doing what he does best. That's a massive promotion he's been given. Be pleased for him and proud. I think this is just the achievement he needs right now.'

His arm around her she rested her head against his chest, her ribs still shaking in a sideways sob, just as they did on the morning of the 26th June. His hand on her forehead now, smoothing back her hair.

'But Mr. Sanderson it's all over the school, everyone knows you are marrying her, even Mr. Brown.'

'Rumours Harriet, all rumours. I think there's been a mix up all along resulting from the day you were let down.'

'But what were you both doing there together?'

'Oh we were all involved in community projects. It's a place I've always wanted to visit and to be honest it was some time ago I learned of Ross Farquerhart's intention to join the research project as a volunteer. Of course there's nothing like having access to the place in his situation. He's another four weeks there then he'll be returning to school to begin his work experience.'

'Oh I see and what is Lucinda Lawton doing there?'

'She's working in the school's special needs unit basically as a volunteer. It's struggling for helpers. Of course she was snapped up. She's also another four weeks to go but if she can pick up bar work or the like she'll stay. She's very keen to stay on you know. She's aiming for a permanent post in the unit.'

'Oh I see,' said Harriet, feeling the cat back on her lap, 'but what about school?'

'She's left, she didn't want a fuss. The post has been advertised and the appointment will be made by the end of the month.'

'Oh,' she said, dabbing the clutch of tissues at her nose. 'Will you be wanting me to stand in to take her place now that you're back?'

'Naturally Harriet. In fact without a shadow of a doubt I can categorically say the post is yours should you want it. Of course you'll need to do the interview bit but this time I promise it's a mere formality. Mr. Whittle and the governors have already sanctioned the appointment should you agree.'

Harriet pushed the cat off her lap. Her knees hurting from the constant stretching and retraction of her claws.

'But I'm pregnant Mr. Sanderson. Can I still have the job?'

Feeling safe in his arms now, she buried her face in his aran sweater realising just what she'd said. He lifted her chin, looked straight into her eyes. 'Ah! "**Tandem**!" that means "*at last*", Harriet. **At last**!! "Amo te nunc et semper".'

'And what does that mean Mr. Sanderson?'

'Oh I think that one's better left untranslated for the moment. Now Harriet I'm having no nonsense. I insist on you sleeping over at Lower Tideside, at least for the next few nights.'

She looked up, opened her mouth to speak.

'And yes you can bring the cat. We've rather got used to having one around now.'

'Well only if I can have the front bedroom where the picture is please?'

'Indeed you may, Mrs. Harris showed you that, did she?' He looked across to the photograph on the mantelpiece, ran his fingers through his hair. 'Almost identical. There's a story to be told, one day,' he said, taking a deep breath. 'Now is it to be a baby girl or boy, I wonder? Had a first scan yet Harriet?'

'No, I want it to be a surprise.'

'No, no, the purpose of that one is simply to check normal development of the foetus. Have you not seen Dr. Holden at all?'

'No, no I don't do doctors very well Mr. Sanderson. I'm alright, apart from a little morning sickness on occasions I've been fine.'

'You know Harriet you're going to have to learn to do as you are told. This is one doctor you're not going to evade.'

'But I just wanted to stay on amber Mr. Sanderson.'

'Indeed? Well we'll see about that. Oh that reminds me…' He stood to fish in the side pocket of his jeans. 'Just a little something for you to open when I've gone.' He looked at his watch. 'Get a few things together, I'll be back shortly. Just need to get sorted out, oh and I'll tell Mrs. Harris it will be dinner for two.'

'Oh thank you Mr. Sanderson,' she looked at the box, 'for this and everything. I mean everything, including this.' She patted her tummy. He smiled, turned to the photograph again.

'Conceived on the sand in the light of an amber sunset Harriet. If it's a little girl, we'll call her Amber shall we?'

'We shall!' Harriet agreed. He took her hand, 'I'll be back in a tick.'

She walked with him to the gate, watched him get into his silver Mercedes. This gorgeous, gorgeous hunk of a man smiling, running the steering wheel through his hands to reverse, then forward. One sharp wave and he was away.

'Come on Pepper we're going for a little holiday. You'll like it there. Overlooking the sea with lots of garden to play in. You can make friends with Molly's cat if you like.'

She closed the front door, went to find the cat basket, then realised she was still holding the small square box. She broke the seal to let the brown patterned paper fall to the kitchen table. Opened it to see her two pressed buttercups carefully wound into the white satin lining of the lid. She pulled gently on the small tab at the top. Found a tiny piece of paper folded in two. Words: "Amo te nunc et semper", below, "I love you now and forever".

'Oh Pepper, so that's what he just said. He's just said that now, to *me* Pepper. And look, it's the ring, it's the amber ring, it's the buttercup ring I showed Tricia in the jewellers. Oh look it's got an inscription, just like before. Oh let me get that other ring Pepper and the gold bracelet he gave me.'

She rushed upstairs to her dressing table to find them somewhere at the back of the top drawer underneath her bras and pants and socks. She eased the bracelet onto her right wrist and placed the plain gold band onto the engagement finger of her left hand.

'Now what does it say Pepper, what does it say on this one?'

As if curious to see, the cat, still wet from her tears, clung fully stretched to her legs.

'It says " *amor caucus est*" ' she read, twisting it round to read the inscription on the opposite side. 'Ah, that's what it means, "love is blind".'

Smiling she slipped it on top of the other, gazing at the two rings on her finger in disbelief, before lifting the cat to her cheek.

'So, "love is blind" is it? We'll see about that Pepper. We'll see about that!'

Margaret Henderson Smith

"Love, like words, intangible, yet substantial and forever"

www.ingramcontent.com/pod-product-compliance
Lightning Source LLC
Chambersburg PA
CBHW051539260626
47170CB00003B/1009